The Boys of Ballycroy

Whilst Erin fights for its
Whilst the crown ignores our cry,
Our spirit is indeed lifted,
By The Boys of Ballycroy.

They beat the Erris Elys,
And the bailiff who did try,
To stop them feeding their folk,
Those Boys of Ballycroy.

As long as salmon swim and
As long as pheasants fly,
Defiance will live forever,
In The Boys of Ballycroy.

So shed a tear for Erin, but
Don't wipe it from your eye,
As they'll rid us of kings' vermin,
Those Boys from Ballycroy.

Written by the Bard of Burrishoole prior to the 1910 court appearance.

'The Boys of Ballycroy' © by Kieran Ginty

Published March 2013

Visit 'The Boys of Ballycroy' on Facebook

ALL RIGHTS RESERVED including the right of reproduction in whole or in part in any form

ISBN 978-0-9575516

This 2nd edition printed and bound in the Republic of Ireland by:

Lettertec (Irl) Ltd, Springhill House, Carrigtwohill, Co. Cork, Republic of Ireland

www.selfpublishbooks.ie

No part of this publication may be reproduced or transmitted by any device, without the prior written permission of the copyright holder.

In memory of those brave Mayo people who left behind their families, their farms, their friends and their futures to fight for freedom.

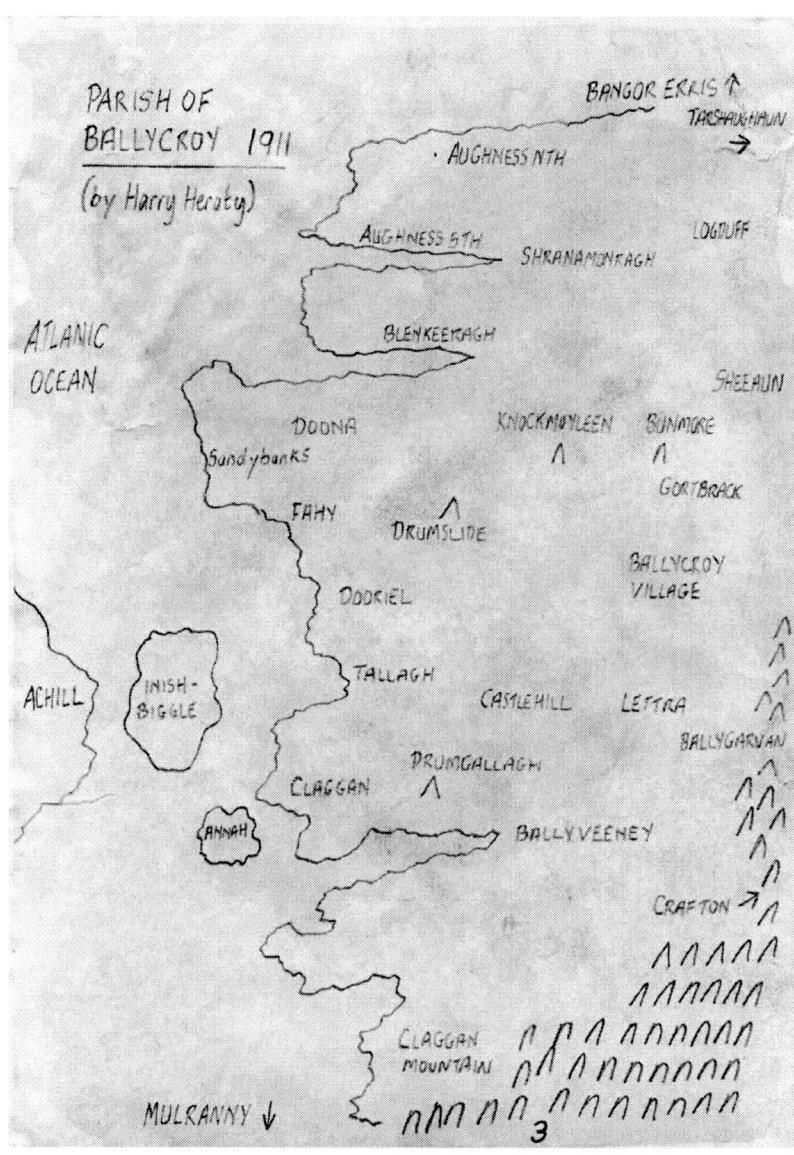

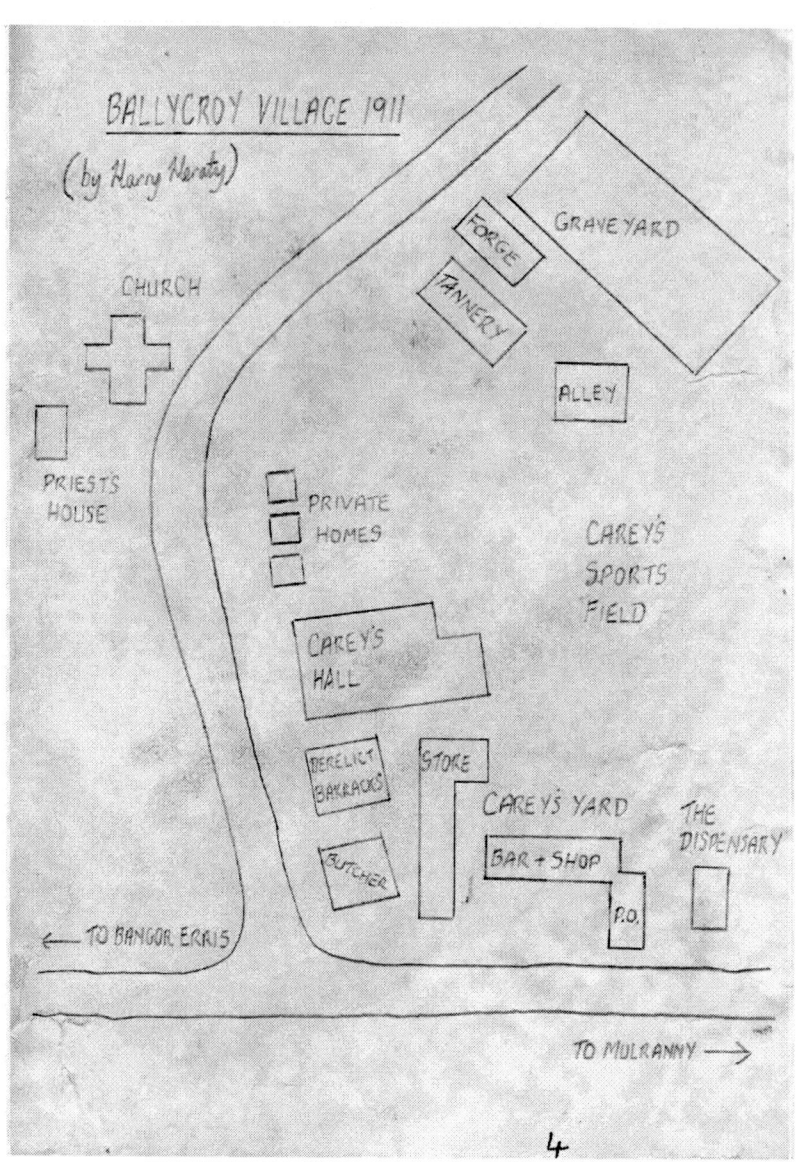

AUTHOR'S INTRODUCTORY NOTE 7
CHAPTER 1: SENTENCED 10
CHAPTER 2: THE STORY TELLER 13
CHAPTER 3: POACHERS 22
CHAPTER 4: THE WHITE COW INCIDENT 26
CHAPTER 5: THE ERRIS ELYS 34
CHAPTER 6: THE LEGEND GROWS 43
CHAPTER 7: BALLYCROY 1911 46
CHAPTER 8: A UNION 50
CHAPTER 9: A REUNION 55
CHAPTER 10: PARTINGS 61
CHAPTER 11: MORE DEPARTURES 71
CHAPTER 12: THE WILD SPORTSMEN OF THE WEST 81
CHAPTER 13: REVENGE? 89
CHAPTER 14: MORE REVENGE? 96
CHAPTER 15: HEADING FOR THE FRONT 104
CHAPTER 16: THE WAR YEARS 110
CHAPTER 17: THE LONG WAIT 115
CHAPTER 18: LAND OF OPPORTUNITY 122
CHAPTER 19: TALES FROM ABROAD 128
CHAPTER 20: LOVE AND HATE 136
CHAPTER 21: ONE WAR ENDS, ANOTHER BEGINS 146
CHAPTER 22: NOVEMBER 1919 153
CHAPTER 23: ENTERING THE TWENTIES 163
CHAPTER 24: BALLYCROY F.C. 167
CHAPTER 25: PROVOCATION AND PREPARATION 172
CHAPTER 26: TROUBLE IN PARADISE 181
CHAPTER 27: REUNION ISLAND 191
CHAPTER 28: MOUNTAIN MUTINY 198
CHAPTER 29: TAKING STOCK 207
CHAPTER 30: A DIVIDED PARISH 216
CHAPTER 31: LIFE ON THE RUN 225
CHAPTER 32: THE BUTCHER 231
CHAPTER 33: LOST FOR WORDS 238
CHAPTER 34: BUTCHERS IN ARMS 245
CHAPTER 35: SEARCHING 254
CHAPTER 36: A HARSH WINTER 263
CHAPTER 37: HUMILIATION 273
CHAPTER 38: TOWARDS THE END OF THE LONGEST YEAR 279
CHAPTER 39: THE WAR GOES ON 287
CHAPTER 40: OPERATION STATION 292
CHAPTER 41: REVELATIONS, ROMANCE AND RETRIBUTION 300
CHAPTER 42: EN ROUTE TO A SHOOT 311

CHAPTER 43: ANOTHER IRISH SPLIT 317
CHAPTER 44: FROM THE MOUNTAIN TO THE SEA 323
CHAPTER 45: LIFE DURING THE CIVIL WAR 330
CHAPTER 46: THE ANVIL 339
CHAPTER 47: HOME IS THE HERO 350
CHAPTER 48: A MEMORIAL... 359
CHAPTER 49: BROTHERS 365
CHAPTER 50: MISTER TOTALLY UNNECESSARY 372
CHAPTER 51: BOB 377
ACKNOWLEDGEMENTS... 389

AUTHOR'S INTRODUCTORY NOTE

I spent only one third of my forty two years in the wonderful parish that sits between Mulranny and Bangor Erris in County Mayo – just inland from Achill Island. But I will always be a Ballycroy man. And proud to be one.

Like most people who are raised there, I've had to leave to make a living. But the rugged town-land is home. And what a place it is. Báile Cruaich – translated from Irish as 'the town of the peaks'. The magnificent Nephin Mountain peaks.

No book could do justice to its natural beauty. The sea, the rivers, and the lakes. The hills and the mountains. The bog and its wildlife. The trees and the rhododendrons. The old buildings. The well-kept houses and farms. The animals. The sand dunes. The ruins and the graveyards. The place is steeped in history. For those who have yet to visit this oasis in North West Mayo, I hope this book prompts a pilgrimage to there. Then you may understand my inadequacy in describing it.

Similarly, it is difficult to accurately portray the people of Ballycroy. They are innately kind. They are good, solid men and women with a strong faith. This faith has helped them survive the many challenges the parish has faced down through the decades and centuries. They are hard-working. They are tough. They are reserved. They are honest. For the most part, they don't seek attention or acclaim. They are not boastful. They simply want to get on with their work without fuss, and pass the parish onto the next generation in a better condition than they inherited it. And if they see a neighbour struggling, they drop everything to lend a helping hand.

The people of Ballycroy actually don't want to be portrayed. The vast majority are not into reading about themselves or promoting themselves. They leave that to others. They just want to get on with life – real life – and not dwell on fantasy. The curse of emigration and economic neglect has rendered 'survival' as the name of the game. A harsh climate and soft soil add to the challenges. But the people also know how to enjoy themselves at times of celebration. No better boys or girls!

My biggest fears in writing this tale about my parish are that I am deemed to intrude or to insult. To avoid this I have tried not to use the names of current families of the parish (with only a couple of exceptions). The names and the characters are fictional – but I hope that the spirit of the people is captured. The names and the characters are fictional – but the places are real.

It is my firm belief that the world needs to know what a magnificent place Ballycroy is, and how its incredible inhabitants have batted away the threats of famine and conflict that have presented themselves at its door. The world needs to know that there has always been and that there will always be a fighting, indomitable spirit in this section of Ireland. Ballycroy can inspire.

At a time in which Ireland is looking around for heroes, it should look at Ballycroy. And at a time when we approach the centenary of the Great War and the Easter Rising, we should remember and admire how our parish forefathers and foremothers dealt with what was thrown at them during those difficult days. I hope this book brings some of the parish's possible history to life.

This book is based on the fifteen year period 1909 to 1924. It is based on how seven imaginary male characters from the parish lived at that time, and how they coped with the arrival of World War I (1914-1918), the Irish War of Independence (1919-1921) and the Irish Civil War (1922-1923).

Although the seven characters are fictional, those conflicts were very real. One has just to visit the marvellous marble memorial by Castlebar Cemetery to read the names of the Ballycroy men who were lost to both World Wars. We should see traits of our ancestors in the seven characters. Traits of which traces still survive. And we should take some time to appreciate what obstacles they had to overcome in an era that had no modern transport; only primitive infrastructure; no proper education system; no electricity; no telecommunications; and very limited medical facilities.

You will hopefully see that the parish itself is a character in the story. And in order that we focus on the happenings within the county of Mayo, you will see (with only a couple of exceptions) that we rarely venture beyond county borders – and rely on others to feed back on what has been happening in the wider world.

In keeping with the simplistic attitude to life that continues to this day in Ballycroy, I have tried to keep the story simple. So if you are looking for flowery language and fancy phrases, you won't find them here. Just a basic narrative – with some conversations thrown in. In advance I apologise for some of the coarser quotes that I use in trying to portray the more unscrupulous characters and the situations they found themselves in.

I hope you enjoy the story of the 'Boys of Ballycroy'. Fictional characters born out of a real people; and shaped by real wars in a real setting - that is simply out of this world.

Kieran Ginty
2013

CHAPTER 1: SENTENCED

"Order in the court! I say order in the court!" shouted Judge Patterson. In front of his raised bench there was commotion. Wailing, shouting, cries of despair mixed with cries of relief.

Three of the seven men who had been brought before him had just received sentences of two years each. The other four were free to go home. But the infamous 'Boys of Ballycroy' were split – for two years at least. This was big news. Amongst the journalists scribbling their notes was the tall and lanky figure of Gerard 'Toothy' Lucey, who had known the seven since they were born. He had known all of their families. But he could not get caught up in the emotion on display in Castlebar courtroom – he had an article to write and a deadline to meet.

After several minutes, with the help of the ushers and policemen present, order was restored in the courtroom, although sobbing could still be heard from where Judge Patterson was perched. The four freed men by now had joined the public gallery, and the three new prisoners stood to learn further details of their fate.

First up was the stocky figure of the eldest son of the Cooney clan. His white head of hair bowed as he stood to attention. Tears streamed down his face, but he stared at the floor as an eerie silence came over the congregation.

"Michael Cooney, I hereby commit you to two years of hard labour, for which your base will be Castlebar Jail" said the judge. His mother again cried out and buried her head into the chest of her husband.
"You'll be fine son" shouted the father quickly followed by "I love you Mikey" from his youngest sister, 6 year old Kathleen.

The clear sweet voice of his baby sister broke Michaeleen, and he cried uncontrollably at the sight of her waving up to him with her right hand, clasping her favourite doll in her left hand, as she stood beside her embracing parents. It was almost a relief for him to be guided through the exit door away to start his sentence. For the journalists, it was hard to believe that such an innocent looking young lad had been just found guilty of assaulting two Royal Irish Constabulary Officers and a Fisheries Bailiff.

As Michaeleen's white head disappeared, the second of those guilty was asked to stand. The man known as 'Roger' stood calmly, taking deep breaths in through his flaring nostrils, looking straight ahead and studying the beams of sunlight that were lighting up the aisles of the courtroom.

"Roland O'Grady, I hereby commit you to two years of hard labour at Galway Jail. Take him away" was the order from the judge. Roger winked at his brother Liam, who smiled ruefully at the sight of his younger but larger brother head for his prison carriage. Unlike the others, who had ample support on the day, Liam was the only person Roger had there. A neighbourly hand patted Liam on the shoulder as his brother was led away.

The third member up was Terence McDonnell, and the courtroom erupted again as he took the stand as he had a large entourage of support. Judge Patterson had to call for order to be restored again as the curly haired hero stood to await his fate. He knew already he was in for two years hard labour, but when the judge declared that it would be in Sligo Jail he smirked and realised now that the authorities were ensuring that the trio were to be kept apart so that their prisons would not become a sowing ground for more plots against the establishment.

As his parents shouted out messages of encouragement, his brother Sylvester raised a clinched fist as he tried to keep the tears from emerging. Terence looked down and swelled with pride as he saw his huge body of supporters. His heart beat faster than it ever did and as he was being guided by his prison guard to the door he turned back towards Judge Patterson and shouted "The rivers of Ireland belong to the people of Ireland and not the fucking Brits" ...as the court was stunned into silence, "...and two years in Sligo will not change that, you Saxon bastard!" as yells of encouragement came from the Ballycroy contingent.

Boosted by the reaction of his highly charged audience, Terence continued

"Ye starved us during the fucking famine but ye won't fucking starve us while I'm alive and…" and before he could finish his sentence we was wrestled to the ground by his guard with the help of two more who had jumped up onto the dock.

"Get the vagabond out of here!" shouted Judge Patterson over the cries of "Good man Terence!" and "You tell them boyo!" that threatened to drown out the judicial order. "Leave him alone!" said Sylvester McDonnell as he jumped onto the dock to help his brother who was by now being punched by the three guards as he lay out of sight beyond the wooden barrier. "No, Sylvester" cried the McDonnell father, realising that he could well have two sons instead of one on their way to prison if his eldest son was arrested. After all, Sylvester had just been one of the four men to escape a prison sentence.

Fintan McDonnell succeeded in dragging Sylvester away from the dock and amidst the disarray he managed to catch a glimpse of Terence's black curly locks as he was forced through the exit door.

The journalists were in shock. They didn't know whether to keep writing notes or just sit and observe, as they didn't want to miss anything. The red faced judge gathered his notes and made for his exit, to a hail of abuse from the fellow parishioners of the new trio of prisoners. Two of those who had just escaped sentence, the Kerrigan brothers, were cousins of the McDonnell brothers, and they stood pale-faced and silent at the rear of the court. It had just struck them how lucky they were to be heading home. The fourth man to escape prison, Batty Bourke, was already heading away with his parents and solicitor across the bright green lawn that lay out in front of the grey walled courthouse. He too knew he was lucky.

Inside the near empty courtroom, Toothy Lucey glanced up at the calendar on the wall of the sunlit room. "October 10th, 1910" he said to a colleague, "Ten, Ten, Ten – a dark day for Ballycroy". He had his headline!

CHAPTER 2: THE STORY TELLER

Roger settled himself into his prison carriage as he tried to absorb the bumps in the road. His left wrist was shackled to a metal bar, and opposite him sat another Mayo prisoner on his way to Galway. Towards the back of the carriage, facing each other were the two prison guards. Roger could hear the driver yelling at the horses and giving them the odd lash of the whip. In between the bodies of the guards he saw the town of Castlebar disappear as the party made their way south to Galway. He silently wondered when he would see the town again.

There was a lot more on his mind as well. The sad image of his brother Liam in the courtroom. The last image he had that morning of his silent father heading to tend his flock of sheep. The image of his girl Rosa, with tears in her enchanting eyes as they had bade a secret farewell the night before. The image of his mother's headstone which he had visited on his way from leaving Rosa. He wondered what lay ahead of him in Galway. What would the hard labour entail? Would he be fit for it? Would anyone come to visit? Would he get out of there earlier if he behaved?

His thoughts were broken by the first words he had heard from his fellow prisoner. "Ballycroy, where's that?"
"It's between Achill and Bangor Erris" replied Roger.
"I see. I never heard of it until this 'Boys of Ballycroy' lark – so you're one of those, yea?"
"I'm supposed to be!" replied Roger.
The guards decided to join in.
"No more 'Boys of Ballycroy' now" said the one sitting alongside Roger, "Magistrate Patterson has put an end to that for ye. Three separate prisons".
Roger refused to rise to the taunt.
"What's your name again?" he asked of his fellow prisoner
"Mongey" was the reply.
"You got done for stealing, yea?" said Roger.
"Yea, just like yourself!"
"Poaching is not stealing!" retorted Roger, "And anyway it was the assault of the Brits who tried to stop us that has got me here".

"There were no Brits there, just Irishmen!" said the second guard in his Dublin accent.
Again, Roger decided to ignore the guards.

Their rocky journey continued on past the towns of Balla and Claremorris as they headed for Galway. Silence amongst the four continued for about 20 minutes until Mongey again broke it.
"That small fella in yer gang, the one with the pure white hair, what happened to him?" he asked.
"It's a long story", replied Roger.
"Well, it's a long journey" said Mongey, "Why not pass the time?"
"*Tempus fugit.* We'll have plenty time to tell stories in jail" said Roger as the two guards burst out laughing.
"That's what you think!" said one. "Come on, tell us. Tell us how he got his grandfather's head of hair!"
"Did they not say you are a bit of a storyteller?" piped up the second guard.
"And what about these 'Erris Elys' that they mention in the poem about you, who were they?" added the Dublin accent.
"I'm not talking about that shower" said Roger, "Anyway, ye two yeomen are probably connected to them!"
"Careful!" said the guard beside him, "You can't afford to be smart now; and you with only one hand free".
Come on", said Mongey, "At least tell us about the white haired buck".

Roger decided that his tale might make the journey shorter, and indeed it did as his captive audience listened to him talk of what he termed 'The White Cow Incident'. But before that, he would have to have a build up to that event, and that was "The Poaching Incident" that had seen him and two of his friends jailed. As he cleared his throat to begin his tales, word was reaching Ballycroy of the sentences handed to three of their people. At Ballyveeney Barracks, the newly arrived Constable Scully was being briefed by his superior, Sergeant Clive, on the seven 'Boys of Ballycroy'.

"They all know each other mainly through the football – the local Gaelic Athletic Association, and through serving together as altar boys at mass" said the sergeant, "And they are all in the 18 to 22 age range".

"I see" said Scully, "Have they a leader?"
"I suppose Roger is the leader, the brightest of them" replied Clive. "He certainly is the largest of them!"
"And I suppose they are all related in some way?" asked Scully.
"Indeed. Two sets of brothers – and three others. That's the easiest way to think of them. The two McDonnell brothers are cousins of the two Kerrigan brothers. Then you have Roger, Batty and Michaeleen. Bring the tea over here and I'll go through them with you one by one, Constable".
Later that week, the fascinated Constable Scully consulted the notes he took from his briefing and wrote the following into his own private dossier on the seven men he expected to cause him problems.

Roger
Roland O'Grady has been known as 'Roger' since his schooldays. He is well over 6 feet tall, and weighs about 18 stone. He is a massive presence, with his combed back brown hair and rotund face. He has a small perky nose but a set of smiling eyes which won the heart of Rosa Carey, daughter of the local businessman Roy Carey. Old Carey does not approve of the relationship, as he expects a better prospect than Roger to arrive for his girl.

Roger is from local farming stock, although he hates the farm work. He leaves that element to his older brother Liam and his father William O'Grady. The family farm is in Bunmore. The name 'Roland' comes from his mother's side of the family. She was Dorothy Roland, one of the descendents of the French Colonel Lionel Roland who came to Killala in North Mayo with General Humbert for the Rising of 1798. Roger is proud of his French roots. He rarely speaks of his late mother, as he never got to meet her. She died hours after giving birth to him in 1890. He has an uneasy relationship with his father, who disapproves of the activities of the 'Boys of Ballycroy' gang which has spread well beyond the parish. William is a quiet, introverted religious man only seen at funerals or fairs. Liam is much like his father, and eagerly works the farm. Liam and Roger's maternal grandparents, who died in 1907, were the last of the Ballycroy Rolands.

The people of Ballycroy like Roger for his huge presence and cheery demeanour. They love his smile, the way he always has a word for the elderly, the way he quotes the great English writers like Shakespeare and Dickens. In an era when the English are hated, it is refreshing to have in their midst a young lad not afraid to point out some of the finer merits of Ireland's closest neighbour.

He is often on the receiving end of comments about his large girth. But Roger is witty and well able to deal with that. He is known as an excellent organiser, and arranges many ceili dances and raffles, as well as storytelling events in various houses which help to pass the long hours of winter. He is a source of great entertainment, and well able to charm an audience with songs, poems or stories. He regularly talks of his dream of going to America. Many consider him a 'day-dreamer'.

He worked as an Office Clerk in the Whaling Station off Blacksod. This involved staying on Inishkea Islands during the week and travelling to Ballycroy at weekends. But the jailing costs him his job. Despite his popularity, only his brother is there to support him in the court room when he is sentenced. There was no sign of his father or his girlfriend.

Michaeleen
Michael Cooney Junior is another who often talks of America. He has an uncle in Cleveland Ohio who has made many offers to send him his fare. His intention is to make money, and return to Knockmoyleen to take over the family farm and make it bigger and better. But his two year sentence has delayed that.

His father Michael Senior is known as 'The Coon', to help differentiate from the other Cooney families in Ballycroy. Married to Victoria, The Coon is short and stocky like his eldest son. But he has a flattened nose from all his boozy encounters, and is known as an able fighter. The Coon is proud of his brood, especially Michaeleen, despite his new head of shocking white hair. When queried about it Victoria puts it down to the stress of being picked upon unfairly by the forces of the crown.

Michaeleen is the eldest of seven Cooney children, the youngest of whom is young Kathleen who is the apple of his eye. He is seldom seen without the family dog, Sailor, or indeed without the blonde tresses of the blue-eyed Kathleen.

In his early teens Michaeleen struggled to meet the expectations of his father, but that all changed when at a sheep fair in Newport, he came to the rescue of The Coon who found himself outnumbered outside a pub in which he had insulted the locals. As the local RIC man stood idly by when The Coon was kicked on the ground, Michaeleen came upon the crowd and realising what was happening, jumped into the fray to fight off his father's attackers. He won many admirers for his brave actions. Since that, The Coon saw his son in a new light and life was more blissful as they farmed their land together.

Michaeleen has inherited many of the wild traits of his father, and gets easily intoxicated. Nonetheless he is considered a loveable character, who would do anything for his family. This may seem at odds with his desire to go to America, but it is always his intention to return and take over the homestead. He just wants his farm to have the best machinery and therefore the best produce.

Batty
Bartholomew Bourke from Aughness South is known to all as Batty. Born in 1890, he is a fisherman, and well known in the region as a fine runner. He has accumulated many medals for his sporting endeavours. He is the son of the very religious couple of Patrick and Agnes Bourke. He has a younger brother Andrew, and a younger sister Martha who is confined to an invalid-chair following complications just after her birth. The Bourke family are very close, and his parents despair of his involvement in 'The Boys of Ballycroy'. But he has been friends with Roger and Michaeleen since their schooldays in St. Kieran's in Shranamonragh.

Batty is 5ft 9 in, but stands as proud as if he were a foot taller. He is strong and athletic, and not very talkative. He is very shy with girls. His hair is light brown, and tends to go blonde after exposure to prolonged sunlight. He has a deep interest in history, and reads whatever books he can get on the subject. He has resisted the urges from his mother to join the priesthood, who wanted him to follow in the footsteps of her brother, Fr. Rea, who is based in Enniscrone, Co. Sligo.

It was to Fr. Rea in Enniscrone that Batty was immediately dispatched following the 10/10/10 court case in Castlebar, where he escapes prison for his part in the Poaching Incident. His parents credit his 'escape' to the fact that they had hired a 'better' solicitor than the others. Anxious for him to distance himself from further trouble with the gang, the 20 year old becomes a gardener for the parochial house in Enniscrone, under the watchful eye of his uncle.

John Peter
There is a consensus in Ballycroy in 1910 that the second-born of the Kerrigan clan of Doona is one of the finest men the parish has ever produced. Tall and dark, John Peter Kerrigan is considered as very handsome and is coveted by many of the young women in the area. However, he shows little interest. The only woman he has been known to have been involved with is Rebecca Carey, and of course her father Roy moved to prevent that relationship from flowering! He is shy and rarely speaks, but when he does speak he does so clearly and instantly commands respectful attention.

This respect is shown in the way that everyone proudly calls him his full name and not 'Johnny' or 'JP'. He is his mother's pride. The people of the parish know that John Peter is her favourite. He reminds her of her husband John when she met him over 30 years ago. Her eldest, Josey, has not inherited his father's looks and has become too fond of the poitin. He is known as 'a bit of an eejit'. The third son, Willie, is not as handsome as John Peter and lives in his shadow. They get on well though, and are rarely seen apart. They work together at the stone quarry in nearby Bangor Erris. John Peter has won many trophies for weight-throwing events and is well known on the sports circuit. His square jaw is the main attraction at many sports events. He resisted a call from the Achill Tug-o-War team to join them. Their coach reckoned such a move could lead to a place on the Irish Olympic team.

Born in 1891, he drinks very little, having seen the damage it has inflicted on his older brother. His ambition is to save enough money to start his own stonemasonry business.

Willie
Just as Mrs Kerrigan can't hide her favouritism for John Peter, Willie can never hide his love for his mother. He adores her, and is ridiculed for sitting beside her at mass when the rest of his peers are gathered at the back of Ballycroy church. She is the only woman he shows any interest in!

Willie Kerrigan is 5ft 10in and just a year younger than John Peter. He is more talkative than his brother, and also has a bit of a wilder streak. He is more hot-headed and tempestuous. He is good at handball and a decent footballer, but is not held in the same esteem as his brother. However, he is accepting of this and is not envious, and simply joins in the legions that look up to John Peter!

He cycles daily the twenty mile round trip to work in Bangor Erris with his brother. This, and the laborious nature of their stone-breaking work, keeps them both extremely fit, and they each have a set of admired broad shoulders. Whilst most of his friends have intentions to emigrate and explore opportunities abroad, Willie is just content to stay in the locality. His mother, Mrs Bridie Kerrigan is a sister of the bould Fintan McDonnell from the village of Claggan, and is disappointed that his sons are not as cultured as her boys! She blames her nephews for adversely influencing John Peter and Willie.

Sylvester
The eldest son of the local blacksmith, Sylvester McDonnell has an older sister Beatrice and a younger brother Terence. They hail from Claggan, where Fintan has his main forge, although he has a smaller version in Ballycroy Village which he rents from the businessman Roy Carey. Born in 1887, he has a long narrow face, a long nose and a head of black curly locks. He has piercing blue eyes. He has a dark complexion and jokes that he is descended

from the Spanish! He works in the forges with his father, but is only half-hearted in his interest in the blacksmith trade.

He is known as the most talented footballer on the Ballycroy GAA football team, but his love of ale regularly affects his performances. He is close to his brother, and fiercely proud of his grandfather who was a well known Fenian activist in Mayo. He is distraught that his brother is jailed and can't contemplate the fact that they will be apart for two years. Though not as loud or as confrontational as his younger brother, he has a violent temper.

Terence
This man had definitely inherited his father's wildness! Better looking than his brother, he also has the longish McDonnell facial features but with a devilish glint in his eyes. He has cast his spell over the girl considered to be the most beautiful in Ballycroy, Antoinette McArthur from Bunmore, daughter of the Head Mistress in St. Kieran's. Like Roy Carey, Charles McArthur disapproves of a daughter becoming involved with one of the 'Boys of Ballycroy', and she was kept from the court case which saw Terence imprisoned for his central role in the Poaching Incident.

Before his sentence, Terence McDonnell had been gainfully employed at the same whaling station as Roger. However, his work was manual and much more dangerous. Spending so much time with Roger – they shared lodgings on Inishkea Island together – planted a seed of exploring America and Terence now speaks openly of his intention to emigrate and create a better life for himself there. He is a larger than life character, always full of chat and energy, always ready with an insult or put-down. But he has a foul mouth on him. His flirting with women meets with disdain from many men, especially if the women involved are wives, girlfriends, daughters or even mothers!

One person who has a particular dislike for Terence McDonnell is the son and heir to Roy Carey's business 'empire', Royston Carey. And the feeling is mutual! Royston is about five years older than the Boys of Ballycroy and is not at all liked. Terence confided to Roger that one of the reasons he would not work at his father's forge in Ballycroy Village was the fact that Royston works in close proximity, and Terence does not wish to end up hanging for his murder!

Despite his flirtatious ways, Terence is very much in love with Antoinette. But she too is flirty, and their relationship is by no means certain to end in marriage. She knows, of course, of his desire to emigrate but this prospect does not appeal to her. Terence almost got his sentence increased by the way he lashed out at Judge Patterson on 10/10/10. As he headed for Sligo Jail, it strengthened his determination to escape the shackles of the hated British Empire, and sail to America.

*****

Young Constable Scully was happy with his dossier. He felt as if he already knew the men. The prisoner Mongey felt the same. He could not wait to find out more about the 'Boys of Ballycroy'. Roger prepared to update him on the two main incidents that had landed them in front of the magistrate.

CHAPTER 3: POACHERS

The seven friends had been regular salmon poachers on the Owenduff River which passed through the north of their parish, from the Nephin Mountains to the Atlantic Ocean at Shranamonragh Bay. The straight stretch of river in front of the lawns of Lyall Lodge in Logduff was the best place for catching salmon. However, it was the most difficult section of the river to poach as it was overlooked by a footbridge which was regularly patrolled by bailiffs from the Fisheries Board. The risk was accentuated by its closeness to Lyall Lodge and the staff and guests there had a path worn by the river's most productive stretch.

The seven, therefore, had usually confined their activity to other pools on the river but chanced their luck on a Saturday in late August 1910 as there was a full moon and they were aware that one of the bailiffs was getting married in Crossmolina. It was likely that his colleagues would be at that wedding. They thought the river might be less guarded.

That Saturday night, a splendidly mild evening, under a clear moonlit sky, the seven had walked through the bogs to get to the front of Lyall Lodge. As well as having to avoid being spotted by any of those staying in the lodge, they had to minimise the chances of being spotted by any of the surrounding homesteads, as they could not trust who would 'shop' them to the local RIC barracks.

Roger was the main organiser and acted as the main lookout, at the gate which led to the lodge. Directly across from the gate stood the footbridge. At the other end of the stretch, the lookout duties were carried out by Batty. The Kerrigan brothers held separate lookout posts further upstream in the other access areas to the river, and had their whistles primed to announce any unwelcome arrivals. So, with four on lookout duties, the actual act of poaching was left to the McDonnell brothers and Michaeleen Cooney.

Everything appeared to be going to plan as the net was dragged by Terence from the south side of the river, where Sylvester stood neck high in water to anchor it, to where Michaeleen grabbed hold of it and secured it on the north side. It wasn't long before the net was bulging with salmon, and the silence was broken by the rustling of Terence who got a sack ready to bag his catch.

An increasingly confident Roger moved from his lookout post to the middle of the footbridge, and admired the beautiful scene that was the moonlit stretch of river below him. He could barely hear the whispering of his hard working trio of colleagues in the water just yards downstream from him. His thoughts moved to how happy his father and brother would be to have a feed of salmon for their Sunday lunch, how tasty it would be with spuds and melting butter.

But Roger's thoughts were interrupted by a crushing blow to the back of his neck by a hurley stick which made him yell out in agony. As he fell to the floor of the footbridge he received another blow to the back, and as he tried to cope with what was happening to him he felt his wrists being grabbed and chained to the metal bars on the footbridge. All he could do was cry out in pain, and then he began to drift off as the stinging became unbearable.

The scene developing below Roger was a frantic one. Hearing the lookout's yell, the three in the river obviously knew something was wrong. Terence tried to run off along the riverbank with his sack of salmon but he was tripped to the ground by a burly figure. In the distance the shrill of whistles could be heard but Terence, Sylvester and Michaeleen could not be sure whether the whistles came from friend or foe.

An RIC man managed to pin Terence to the ground just a couple of yards from the river, whilst a second RIC man and two bailiffs entered the river trying to apprehend the other two poachers – plus of course trying to acquire the net.

The poachers were in shock. Where had this body of men come from? Why hadn't the lookouts spotted them? Sylvester was now out of the river and guided by the moonlight, went to the aid of his struggling brother. "Run with the bag!" was the order that came from Terence, and his brother did just that, running in the direction of the Bangor Erris Road.

"Run everyone, run!" shouted Michaeleen as he was dragged up from the river by two of their apprehenders. At this stage, both he and Terence had two men each to deal with. Where was their help? Where were the Kerrigans? Where was Batty?

"You're under arrest Cooney!" said one of the RIC men as two of them struggled to tie his hands with a rope.
"Keep fucking fighting!" yelled Terence from a few feet away as he tried to get out from beneath the two trying to tie him. It was clearer to see things now as the lights of the lodge had appeared to have lit up – no doubt everyone inside was wondering what the disturbance by the river was all about.

As the two separate struggles continued, two tall figures emerged at the scene and as Michaeleen looked up he wondered if they were two more enemies. They weren't! The two Kerrigan brothers were on hand and they lashed into the two RIC men and the two Bailiffs. They were merciless! They kicked and punched incessantly. They were so strong. It was four versus four now! The patrollers had never encountered this degree of force before.

With ropes hanging off each of their right hands, Michaeleen and Terence took revenge on their assailants and within a minute they had their men rolled down into the river! And Terence was not satisfied with that, he jumped into the water on top of the RIC man from Belmullet that he had recognised, and continued to punch him in the face.

"Run, lads, run!" he shouted out to his three fellow fighters on the bank as he grabbed the wet hair of a second man in the water. He now recognised the pudgy face of the man whose hair he held with his left hand. He was Benny Hughton. A Ballycroy man. An ex Fisheries Bailiff who had obviously come out of retirement for the special night!
"Take that Hughton you fucker!" said Terence as he thumped him with his right fist, submerging him into the water.

Terence climbed up onto the banks and thought about which way to run. He could see the shapes of some people running through the lawn of the lodge towards the footbridge. He could hear the men in the river trying to get back to the bank. Then –another sound pierced the air. It was a loud shout from an awakening Roger. Terence ran towards the footbridge. The sight he saw under the moon's glow was one that would remain imprinted in his memory forever. There, hanging by his right arm from the metal bars of the footbridge was the considerable silhouette of Roger, his feet dangling beneath him.

"Help me, help me!" he shouted. Terence didn't know whether to laugh or cry. He ran up onto the foot bridge. He went towards Roger.
"The arm is pulling off me" yelled his friend. "Jaysus Christ almighty!" Terence checked the base of the metal post. His friend's wrist was shackled. If it had been a rope he would have tried to free him, but there was nothing he could do.

Behind him he heard footsteps on the foot bridge coming from the south side. He had to run. He did. Towards the north side. Quickly. And off through the bushes he ran, up onto the bog. He hated leaving his friend behind, but damn him; he was supposed to have been a lookout!

CHAPTER 4: THE WHITE COW INCIDENT

The seven had pre-arranged to meet at 2pm at The Sandybanks the next day, Sunday. There, they had their own hideout which they called 'The Carthouse', as it had been made up from timber beams from two old horse carts. They had used these beams to act as a roof joining two grass covered sand dunes, and this had created a man made cave for them.

The day was much cloudier, but sunnier, and the Kerrigan brothers were first to arrive. Next to arrive, with the family dog 'Sailor', was Michaeleen, and the three of them excitedly compared scratches and bruises from the previous night's encounter.

Batty Bourke and the McDonnell brothers were next on the scene, so they were just one down.
"Where the hell is Roger?" asked Batty.
"Where the hell were YOU?" asked Terence, "Some fucking lookout you are!"
"They must have been camped in the bushes waiting for us", said Michaeleen.
Batty was anxious to defend his honour.
"I saw no-one, I heard someone shout 'run' and I did" he said.
"You're good at that, aren't you?" shouted Terence

Accusations began to fly and without their 'leader' Roger it threatened to descend into a civil war. There was accusation and counter-accusation and even Sailor started barking as the excitement levels grew. Sylvester succeeded in altering the mood and calming everyone down.
"I've the bag of salmon, nine!" he said and they all laughed.
"And I've two bottles of whiskey here" said Batty as his peace offering.
The six of them took a mouthful each from the first bottle, and so began a boozy afternoon by The Sandybanks. In between the mouthfuls they recounted what had happened and what must have had happened to Roger. Batty tried to regain ground by suggesting that perhaps Terence should have not left Roger behind alone but he was shouted down.

"We were the talk of mass again", said Willie Kerrigan, "They reckon we will all be arrested today".
"Well they arrested me last night but I'm still here!" said Terence, as he told them how he recognised Benny Hughton and the RIC man from Belmullet.
"I think his name is Comerford", he added.

The six were well on the way to intoxication when Sailor's barking announced the arrival of Roger. They shouted out a welcome in unison as their limping friend drew closer to The Carthouse.
"Here comes 'the lookout' that could not look!" said Terence.
"Let me have a swig of that first" panted Roger as he took his place under the beams. "I'm half dead".
"Are you hurt?" he was asked as he drank, sweat pouring from his forehead.

"I'm not good. My wrist and axter are ruined and I've a terrible pain from where I was clobbered at the start. I'm sorry lads – they must have been sitting in the bushes in wait for us. Is everyone alright?" he asked. He went on to tell them that he had been released from his shackle to the foot-bridge just after Terence had left. They all drunkenly laughed as he painted the picture of his unchaining and 'plopping' into the river below! He described how he had been brought into a room in the lodge by the captors, and given 'a few belts'.

"It could have been much worse" he said, as he went on to tell the six others that the women in the lodge had given him warm clothes to replace his wet ones, and had given him a fine breakfast in the morning. This changed the mood of Terence!
"Typical fucking Roger!", he said, "I have to beat up a few peelers and then make my way through bog and stony fucking roads in my bare feet and soaking fish-smelling clothes, and this yoke gets warmed up in front of a warm fucking fire with hot milk from lovely maidens all the while. Fucking typical. You probably got the ride there as well from one of them – or maybe two of them? Are you going back to them again tonight?"

They all laughed at Terence's latest outburst, as the whiskey was joined by a bottle of brandy that Roger had previously hidden in one of the hundreds of rabbit holes that surrounded them. They discussed how to split up the salmon before Roger turned the conversation serious.

"I was arrested. The old fella's not happy" said Roger. They brought me back to the house. They said to tell ye to report to the barracks tomorrow or else they will track us down during the week. And before you say anything, they got nothing out of me. And guess who was there – bloody Ben Hughton!"

"We know" said Terence, "Sure didn't I try and drown the bastard!"

"And they reckon we took one of their pistols" said Roger to a deafening silence. "They searched the bank for it and reckon we have it, and if we don't hand ourselves in we're all done for".

The quiet John Peter Kerrigan spoke up. "We better do that. We will draw them back here if we don't, and we don't want them knowing about this place. We'll go tomorrow. Let's have a drink today and we'll go tomorrow. They can't imprison us all".

"But I'm on a warning", said Michaeleen, "I'm for prison now".

"So am I", said Roger, "But they have us, I'm telling you. Let our solicitors take it from here but there's no point having them come back here as John Peter says".

"Sure they have nothing on me," interjected Batty. "But I'll go to the barracks".

"I know you will, good man", said Roger. "All for one and one for all".

As Sailor lay on the grass, the seven drank into the evening and soon Michaeleen was showing signs of being worse for the effects of the alcohol.

"Blast that Benny Hughton anyway, the traitor, himself and his prize cows" he said. "If I caught him I'd..."

"You had your fucking chance last night!" roared Terence, as aggressive as ever.

"I didn't know it was HIM", replied Michaeleen, "But I'll get him..." Michaeleen stopped suddenly, as if inspired, gazing down towards the other range of sand dunes to his left, on the Blenkeeragh side.

"Why didn't I think of it?!" he said, his eyes glazed "Sure Benny Hughton leases the land down there from one of the Gilroys for some of his cattle. Come on lads, let's let them out into the sea, let's get him back, the bastard!" And off he went running towards the far sand dunes, Sailor running alongside him barking excitedly.

The others looked at each other. They had barely noticed that dark clouds had gathered overhead and their sun was disappearing. One of those August downpours was brewing. The six of them ran after Michaeleen who was running like a child in the distance. Of course, being the heaviest and least mobile, Roger was the most reluctant to go but he trailed after the drunken group.

It had started to rain by the time they all caught up on Michaeleen, who had just finished undoing the gate and was entering the field with Sailor. Most of the seven had picked up a stick or a branch on the way, and Michaeleen led the gang as he started to round up the four cows in the field and with the help of his barking Sailor, put them running for the gate beyond which lay the beach, and beyond that again lay dangerous inlet Atlantic water between Doona and Blenkeeragh.

"Have you ever seen a cow as white as that?" asked Batty, as the unfortunate animal and her three companions reacted excitedly to having their peace disturbed in this little heavenly piece of North West Mayo.
"Impeccable. As white as snow" said Roger. "Not a speck on her. Look, even her hooves, she's pure white. Not even a splash of shite on her".
The others joined in the admiration as the cow passed the gate running, glancing at the onlookers as she did.
"Most of those white cows are not really white at all, but cream, but this one is lily white" said Roger before being interrupted by Terence.
"Will you stop talking bollox, you're drunk!" he said. "Come on, white or not, this cow is going for a swim".

Michaeleen led the seven lads across the beach as the rain came down heavily and the sky grew darker. He and Sailor ran closely behind the four animals, marching them to the waterline. He whacked them with his branch and Sailor snapped at their heels, and the six caught up quickly as the looing cows entered the water.

Roger was last as always, and decided to stop and urge a cessation to the action. The Kerrigan brothers stopped too and Roger shouted at them.
"It's not right, leave them!" he urged. "They're loose on Hughton, damage done, that's enough!" The brothers nodded in agreement but their two cousins, Batty and Michaeleen were now in the water trying to force the four cows further out into the channel. Sailor was barking loudly and the rain was lashing down, and the first clap of thunder shuddered the skies.

The three on the shore shouted at the four lads in the water to stop but they didn't. Through the rain dripping down from his hair Roger could see that the white cow was trying to turn back, and the three others were being swept away. A shouting Michaeleen and Batty were hitting the white cow, forcing her towards the deeper water and away from the shore again. The McDonnell brothers had stood back a bit, up to their midriffs in seawater and they had also started urging Michaeleen and Batty to stop, sensing that this incident had gone too far. They could see the bobbing heads of three of the cows being carried away down the channel. The looing had stopped.

The white cow, now floating, and with her eyes rolling wildly, made another attempt to swim past her attackers but Michaeleen was having none of it, and kept lashing her, and shouting loudly and excitedly.

"Ah leave it!" pleaded Roger hoarsely from the distance, "This is not right. Leave the animal!"

Then came the moment that marked their lives forever. Just as a second clap of thunder came and a flash of lightening streaked through the darkening sky, a sound echoed all around, coming from deep within the body of the beautiful animal about to be swept to her death.

"God, God, May none of these eight lay beneath Irish sod" was heard from the cow. Like a roar from the dungeons of hell.

The rain suddenly stopped. The shouting stopped. The barking stopped. The cow rolled her eyes once more just before she went beneath the water. The seven men reeled in shock. Stupefied. They had just witnessed something supernatural. Michaeleen stumbled under the water and had to be helped up by Batty, and all seven of the friends then gathered at the waters edge.

"Did you see that?!"
"Did that really happen?!"
"The cow spoke. The fucking cow spoke! We are cursed!"
"A plague on all our houses!" quoted Roger.
"I've heard of things like this – we'll burn in hell"
"It was the devil himself!"
"Shut up. Shut up, all of ye!" said John Peter Kerrigan. "We are the animals, NOT the poor creatures. May God forgive us".
They all looked out at the channel under the charcoal skies and there was no sign of the animals.

There was silence as they all turned to head for The Carthouse. Each of them still in shock, their heads spinning from what they had just seen and heard. They could not blame the whiskey – this had happened for real. And it sobered them up instantly.

At the Carthouse, the strange silence continued as they tried to come to terms with what they had witnessed. John Peter cried. Michaeleen stood up and left to spend time alone, crying too, running towards an adjacent dune. It was growing darker and darker. They repeated what they had heard come from the mouth of the beast. "She said eight – there were only seven of us", said Batty.
"Sailor is eight!" snapped Willie Kerrigan.

31

"Michaeleen's fault," said Terence, "We are all damned. If this gets out we will be shunned forever. Nothing but farmers and fishermen in this parish".

"Be quiet", said Roger, "Michaeleen's coming back, don't blame him, we ALL ran down there. We should have stopped but..."

His sentence was interrupted by the sight of Michaeleen appearing in front of his friends again. They froze with shock. They were rendered speechless. Again. His brown head of hair had turned white!

Michaeleen had not realised this, and wondered what they were all gazing at.
"What is it?" he asked. "Lads I'm sorry, it's my fault. We'll go to confessions, get a mass said, buy new cattle for Hughton, nobody will ever find out".

But find out people did. And as if there was some chance that they would somehow forget the incident, the sight of Michaeleen's white head would be a permanent reminder to all who participated in the drowning of the innocent animals.
All seven reported to the Ballyveeney Barracks that evening, and everyone bar Roger were arrested.
"What happened to your hair, Cooney?" asked Sergeant Clive, "Eat too many salmon?!"
No one spoke. The white cow had spoken. That was enough. Even though the prison sentences loomed, the dreaded barracks was a comforting place to be that awful evening.

"So that's how Micheleen got his white hair", said Mongey.
"It is" replied Roger. "Many don't believe the story, but it's as true as I'm sitting here in Galway Prison".
"I believe you" answered his cell mate. "Sure I've seen the fairies myself. And they are not to be messed with, I tell you".

*****

On the last day of 1910, each of the seven silently recalled the events of the past year and wondered what 1911 would bring. For three of them, they hoped it would be freedom from their prison cells. The other four tried to get on with life as best as they could. But all seven of them hoped that they would never have to experience again anything like 'The White Cow Incident'. It would haunt them for the rest of their days.

As the dark clouds of political strife loomed over Ireland and Europe, millions of people faced into 1911 with apprehension. But to have been present in Carey's Bar on New Year's Eve, no one would have thought that! There was great merriment and celebration as a proud Royston Carey announced his engagement – to one Antoinette McArthur.

The news reached Terence the following day in his freezing Sligo cell. What an awful way to start his new year!

CHAPTER 5: THE ERRIS ELYS

As Terence digested news of the engagement, Michaeleen Cooney was thrilled to receive a visit from some family members in Castlebar Jail. His eyes lit up as he met his parents and young Kathleen. They brought him some Christmas cards, and he gave an overjoyed Kathleen a belated Christmas gift of a wooden doll he made in the prison's workshop.
"Oh I miss you, Mikey" she says as she is allowed sit on his knee.
"And I miss you too", said the white haired lad.
"Do you miss Sailor?" she asked.
"Of course I do, why didn't he come?"
"Daddy said he is not allowed up here and anyway Brendan needs him for looking after the sheep today".
After some more playful interaction with his young sister, Michaeleen became serious with his parents.
"Please, ask them to send the fare over for me, Da. I'm sorry, but I have to leave this God forsaken country. I hate it here. I can't wait to get out of this hole of a jail and escape these shores".
"Can I come too?" asked Kathleen.
"No Loveen, you're too small. You have to stay behind and look after Daddy and Mammy for me, yea?" smiled Michaeleen.
"Alright so!" she whispered, but her eyes lit up again as he told her that he would send her a porcelain doll all the way from America for her 8th birthday.

In Galway Jail, no one was visiting Roger or his Castlebar pal Mongey. They shared a lonely cell that looked out over foggy Galway Bay. Mongey reminded his cellmate that he had yet to tell the tale of the Erris Elys, and that now was as good a time as any to pass the time!

The Elys were a family of Protestant landowners of British descent. It was said that they were distantly related to the British Royal Family. The family were based in Doohoma in Erris, just across the inlet from Aughness North in Ballycroy. Their palatial home was surrounded by the trees there, but they owned tracts of land all over the Doohoma, Geesala and Mountjubilee region and collected rent from the natives. They were known as being cruel and heartless. The Ely family was led by Sir Frederick Ely, and he had four sons and four daughters. Their name was hated by the Catholic population of the barony of Erris, which extended from Bangor Erris to Blacksod. The Elys were prominent hunters and fishermen. In 1909 they set about creating a lobster farm of the inlet between Aughness North in Ballycroy, and Doohoma to the north. Of course they did this without any consultation with the local population.

It wasn't long before a minor 'war' broke out between the Elys and native fishermen from both sides of the inlet. The Elys accused the fishermen of destroying their lobster pots, and threatened to sink boats if they continued fishing on the waters of the inlet. One evening they carried out their threat and sank the boat of a Doohoma man. They followed up this by firing warning shots over a boat being rowed by Batty Bourke and his brother.

When news got out of this event, the seven 'Boys of Ballycroy' discussed possible revenge. Roger had to counsel against physical attacks as he knew the Elys had connections in all garrisons and barracks and could summon manpower and weapons at any stage.
"The pen is mightier than the sword" he quoted to the amusement of his friends.

During his weeknights on Inishkea Island, Roger composed a poem that alleged the Elys indulged in incest and bestiality. Using paper from his office at the whaling station, he made about a hundred copies and on his way home one weekend, he and Terence posted the poems on walls around Belmullet, Geesala and Bangor Erris. He knew this would infuriate the land owners.

The following weekend, when he returned to the mainland he found indeed that there was a bounty on his head, but this did not deter Roger. In Heneghan's Pub in Belmullet the locals realised that the poet was in their midst and several pints of stout were sent his way. Before long, the intoxicated Roger took to the Speakers Corner in the square of Belmullet and had the locals laughing hysterically as – with the encouragement of his new found admirers – he publicly read the poem. And being as talented as he was, he added a few more damning verses that he had just made up!

Of course the drink had loosened his tongue and dimmed his senses, and he should have realised that it would not be long before the RIC men who observed his display would have gotten word back to Elysville. Roger and Terence made it safely to Ballycroy that night, but as they did Sir Frederick was hosting a conference on the matter. The Elys got word that Roger had arranged a 'ceili' at MacGinty's house in Aughness North, just across the estuary from Doohoma. It was to be held on Saturday night.

MacGinty had got word from Doohoma that something was afoot and he tried to have the ceili cancelled, but the persuasive Roger talked him out of it. He wasn't afraid of the Elys! A raffle had been organised as well and the tickets were sold and so there would be widespread annoyance and anger had the event been cancelled.

It was late September and the Ballycroy people started to gather at MacGinty's at 9pm when it was getting dark. No one noticed the flotilla of four small boats coming towards them from Doohoma.

Aged 70, MacGinty was one of Roger's favourite people and he loved watching the reaction on the old man's face when he warmed up the audience with tales of 'The Great El Ginto'. This was a running yarn, based on the time of the Spanish Armada, in which Roger told the story of this Spaniard who had been part of General Leiva's body of seafaring soldiers who had been shipwrecked off The Sandybanks of Doona.

The joke was that MacGinty was a descendant of this man, who having survived the shipwreck and lived in Ballycroy for a few months, eventually made it back to Spain. There, he yearned for a return to Ballycroy and eventually did some years later, operating as a pirate off the Mayo coast and terrorising British merchant ships. The adventures of 'The Great El Ginto' always enthralled those who came, and both Roger and MacGinty loved the attention it brought them. El Ginto was not only a pirate but a lover and a fighter, and tales of his heroic and sometimes hysterical exploits were always a great start to any evening event organised by Roger.

As the music was about to start, Terence, standing by the door noticed a bright light and looked outside. There, just yards away from MacGinty's house, the haystack of his neighbour was ablaze. "A fire, a fire!" Terence shouted to those inside and the bodhrans bounced off the stone floor as everyone headed towards the exit. The McDonnell and Kerrigan brothers headed to the rear of the house to get water from an outside barrel. They heard screaming and shouting from the women, and one male voice which cried "It's the Elys, it's the Elys that are in it!"

Terence immediately knew that this was revenge time for what had happened the evening before in Belmullet. He grabbed the three lads that were with him.
"Never mind the buckets, just get hold of Roger and get him out of here. The fire's a fucking trap!"
"Why Roger?" asked Sylvester, not knowing what had happened the previous evening.
"Just do as I fucking say and get Roger away down", shouted Terence, "Or they'll fucking lynch him".
MacGinty opened the back door and the light from the room shone on Terence.
"Terence, I told him not to have the ceili, I warned him!" said the old man.
"I know", said Terence as the commotion from the other side of the house grew louder and the shouting and screams increased, "But we have to fight them, get back inside, good man".
"Ely castrated a man before for mocking him" said MacGinty, "May God spare us".

The sight that met Terence when he came from the back of the house was frightening. In the light of the blazing haystack, he could see the Elys using whips and sticks to hit out at the Ballycroy people, men and women. He approached the scene with a bucket in his hand and whacked it over the head of a man who was grappling with his brother. He went on to kick another man who had just stamped on one of the women on the ground. Trying to take in the mayhem in front of him, he heard the sound of glass breaking and turned around to see two hooded men smashing in the windows of MacGinty's house. He reckoned that there were at least twenty invaders. As he turned towards the fighting and the fire he received a fist in the face. But it didn't knock a stir out of him, and he punched his assailant to the clay.

The mother of all battles raged in the space between the two houses that night but the Elys and their friends had underestimated how many people had come to see Roger do his storytelling. The Elys found themselves being attacked by men and women, and all sorts of weapons were used – shoes, sticks, candlestick holders, stones, pitchforks, scythes, stable brushes, bodhrans, tin whistles, chains. One of the Ely sons, realising the beating they were taking, shouted out his orders to "Retreat to the boats on the shore, retreat to the boats!"

He had not realised that the descendent of The Great El Ginto had beaten them to the boats and was boring holes in them! As the battle raged by the inferno, the old man MacGinty had shown his cunning.

Most of the Ely gang ran towards the boats on the shoreline, but at least two of them were unable to get off the soil at the site of the battle, and they lay moaning as the Ballycroy women kicked at their curled up bodies. The invaders were in shock! There was no sign of Roger as he had been spirited down the road to safety by two women, on the orders of Terence. The Kerrigan brothers had accounted for about five of the Ely gang, and the McDonnells had done something similar. Most impressive of all was Michaeleen Cooney who leathered into men much taller than him, one of whom Terence recognised as the RIC man Comerford. Confirming the presence of RIC men amongst their numbers, Batty Bourke had managed to get hold of a baton which he had been hit on the head with, and which had caused blood to pour down his face from the wound sustained.

Batty was ignoring the pain and instead using the baton to batter some of the retreating Elys, and he sought out one of them he had

observed punching Lilly McCarthy. That guy screamed in pain on the ground as Batty rained down blows onto his back and neck. "Take that you English bastard!" he roared.
Terence again surveyed the scene. Now there were about five people prostrate on the ground, all of them 'visitors'. As he ran the few yards to the shore he heard the wails of those trying to escape who realised that they were sinking. The Kerrigan brothers had managed to entangle two Elys in MacGinty's old fishing net, and Terence laughed as Batty came along with his baton to belt them as they rolled along the ground in the net.

When morning came around, the remnants of the burning stack were still smoking. Dr Skelton was there and was treating the two most severely injured, who were under the guard of the Kerrigan and McDonnell brothers in MacGinty's bedroom. The house owner examined his broken windows, having earlier rowed with his neighbours who demanded compensation for their burned hay.

Fr. Wallace arrived on the scene and was aghast at the damage done. He would have a small turnout at mass later that morning as too many parishioners were showing the scars of battle! The burly priest came into the room where the doctor was treating the two 'prisoners'. He said nothing and just scowled as he looked up at John Peter who was sporting a black eye. Beside him stood Willie, looking towards the ground trying to hide the bruises on his face. Batty had a bandage on his head, and two black eyes! More importantly, the baton was still gripped by his right hand! The two McDonnell brothers looked like they had run through a forest of briars all night, they were all scraped. Michaeleen's nose now looked as flat as his father's!

The priest finally spoke, but it was to the 'prisoners'. They were both badly beaten, and barely able to speak. One of them, who identified himself as one of Elys' staff, said that they had come to abduct Roger. He confirmed that they had underestimated the volume and ferocity of those attending MacGinty's. They meant no harm to anyone, just Roger. Batty was furious, and felt like using his new weapon again!

By the time mass arrived, everyone in Ballycroy had heard what had happened. There was an almighty buzz outside the parish church as stories were exchanged of the heroics of the McDonnells, the Kerrigans, Batty and Michaeleen. The Coon was the proudest man in the chapel. But the frothing Fr. Wallace was having none of it, as he stormed towards the altar and commenced his mass. During his sermon, he denounced those who had fought and said that he was ashamed to be the Parish Priest. This made everyone feel uneasy, but only one man – with adrenaline rushing through his veins – was prepared to publicly counter the insult.

"Go back to where you came from so!" shouted The Coon, as the congregation gasped. Fr. Wallace was livid.
"Leave the House of God! NOW!" he roared from the pulpit.
"How dare you!"
"Me and my people were here well before you and we will be here well after you" shouted The Coon, his face scarlet. "We built this church – you did not. Get back to where you came from, you landlord lover!" Fr. Wallace's face was boiling with rage, and he ran from the altar into the sacristy. His curate Fr. Green took over, and nervously finished the mass, afraid to look down at The Coon who stared defiantly at the pulpit. As far as he was concerned, the men of Ballycroy had defended themselves and fought as any man would fight. Even the women had done themselves proud.

An entire book could have been written about the incident of the Erris Elys, and the legend of 'The Boys of Ballycroy' was created when a photograph circulated of the seven friends posing by one of the Ely boats that MacGinty had scuttled. Of course, the only one in the photo unmarked was the target of the invasion, Roger! His friends made sure to remind him of this at every opportunity.

The fallout from the incident was huge. Rightly or wrongly, the seven 'Boys of Ballycroy' became feted as heroes, and their subsequent appearance at court – where there was not enough evidence to jail them – heightened their popularity and they became known all over Mayo. Toothy Lucey contributed by regularly mentioning them in his weekly piece in 'The Mayoman' newspaper.

The anti-RIC sentiment grew as the court case publicised that at least two of their members partook in the attack on 'the poet'. Their credibility as witnesses was shot to pieces. Nevertheless, Judge Patterson warned the seven about their future behaviour, and said that he would not hesitate sending them to prison if they appeared in front of him again for assault.

Fr. Wallace never said mass in Ballycroy again and was sent to another diocese. MacGinty's neighbours successfully sued the Ely estate for their loss as it was admitted during the court that the haystack was set alight by one of the Ely sons. However, within months, the Ely family had sold up and left for Kildare. The embarrassment of being humiliated by a 'gang of bog-peasants' was too much. They were openly mocked on the streets of Belmullet, and their tenants took heart from what the Ballycroy people had inflicted upon them, and decided en masse to withhold their rents. The Land Commission took over their estate and apportioned it fairly. The famous Bard of Burrishoole wrote a song about their demise. It was rumoured that one of the Ely sons would never walk again; he was beaten so badly in the failed attempt to abduct Roger.

*****

The prisoner Mongey was delighted. The tale had filled his cold heart with warmth and enthusiasm. He had a new found respect for his cellmate, although he had never raised a hand during the incident.

"Maybe the pen IS mightier than the sword!" laughed Mongey.
"And what became of MacGinty, is he still alive?"
"No, poor MacGinty died that Christmas, but he died with a smile on his face" replied Roger.
"I bet he did. I would have loved to meet the old soul" said Mongey.
"And to end the story", said Roger, "Guess who got his place?"
"Never!" said Mongey, "YOU got it?"

"Indeed and I did. But there wasn't much left over after we found out how many debts he had. He was the last of the MacGintys in Ballycroy. My brother bought the cattle off me and I got a few quid for the land and the house. So I paid off a loan my father had and the rest is set aside for me and Rosa to go to America and get set up there".

"God rest him" said Mongey.

"God rest him is right", replied Roger. "I promise you, someday, believe you me; I will make him and El Ginto very proud".

"You already have", said Mongey, "You already have...."

CHAPTER 6: THE LEGEND GROWS

The fateful court case of 10/10/10 had originally been scheduled to be held two weeks earlier, but was postponed as Judge Patterson had become ill that morning. The seven, all in their best attire, had turned up in Castlebar for the case and posed happily for one of the photographers from 'The Mayoman'. Within days, every newspaper reader in Mayo had the seven proud Ballycroy men smiling at them from the front page. In an era where the downtrodden Irish nation was clasping for heroes, they fitted the bill. The photograph undoubtedly helped nourish the legend of the 'Boys of Ballycroy', and poem of that name composed by the Bard of Burrishoole – which that issue of the paper also printed – gave them iconic status.

They all became recognisable wherever they travelled in the county, especially John Peter with his striking good looks, and the bear-like figure of Roger. John Peter was a regular winner at weight-throwing events throughout Mayo each weekend, and Batty also became well known for his running prowess at races.

A number of stories enhanced their reputation, although many of them were not true. None of the seven or their growing band of fans did anything to dim the hype. They were credited for banishing the Elys from Erris, and for exiling the despised Fr. Wallace from Ballycroy. The seven received further praise for coming to the rescue of two children who had become trapped under a collapsed sand dune near The Carthouse. It was said that they had also come to the rescue of a drowning member of the gentry in the fishing pool beside Shranamonragh Lodge, but in reality this had been a solo effort by Batty.

It was said that they had come to the aid of a family threatened with eviction in the neighbouring parish of Mulranny, but there was never any proof of this. Rumours abounded that young Kathleen Cooney had received a slap from her teacher in St. Kieran's, and that the 'Boys of Ballycroy' had visited the teacher's house that night to ensure the action was never repeated. Of more substance, was a story that a hotel chambermaid named Nuala O'Brien from Ballycroy Village had been sexually abused by

43

her employer in a Mayo town, and that he was beaten and robbed by the seven, with the proceeds going to Nuala.

Some things grew out of all proportion. Sylvester was supposed to have scored six goals for his local club in a football match! The story of Michaeleen coming to the rescue of his father at the Newport Fair was resurrected, but this time he was supposed to have left a dozen men injured in his wake!

It is only natural that such legendary exploits cause resentment amongst some, and the man who struggled most to contain such resentment was Royston Carey. Being the only son to the wealthy Roy and therefore the heir to the Carey business, Royston considered himself to be the most desirable man in the parish. He did not take too well to seeing what he called "people of a lesser class" win the adoration that he could only dream of, but which he thought HE deserved.

Royston had never mixed well with the other men of the parish. This was partly down to the fact that he had spent most of his youth in boarding school in Claremorris, and partly down to his own delusions of grandeur. He was groomed to be a businessman, and it riled him that as part of his apprenticeship he would have to lower himself to such tasks as serving alcohol in his father's public house, which forced him to mix with the natives. Another task he abhorred was preparing corpses for coffins. He could not wait for the day that he would be in a position to sub-contract that work!

It also riled Royston that his two sisters had been romantically linked to two of the 'Boys of Ballycroy', and he joined his widowed father in discouraging Rebecca and Rosa to have anything to do with John Peter and Roger respectively. He hated the seven lads and everything they stood for.

Royston gained a large measure of revenge when he quickly took advantage of Terence's imprisonment to court the beautiful Antoinette McArthur. She was widely considered as 'the best catch' of the up and coming generation. He set about charming the coveted beauty and convinced her that a wealthier and happier future would be found with him – and not 'the convict'. He capitalised on the fact that Terence was set on a move to America, to coax Antoinette into accepting the option of a privileged life in the parish she loved. He deluged her with expensive gifts, and the McArthur family were immensely proud when the wedding was announced for August 1911.

It was set to be the social event of the year.

CHAPTER 7: BALLYCROY 1911

Everyone in the parish knew that no expense would be spared for the Carey-McArthur wedding. Over 90% of the population of 800 were considered poor, and knew nothing but the never-ending struggle to put food on the table. It didn't take much to boost spirits, but the parishioners had been demoralised by the jailing of three of their finest.

Word of the engagement also reached Michaeleen in Castlebar Jail and Roger in Galway Jail. They felt for their comrade Terence in Sligo Jail, and knew the announcement would cut deep. They also knew that the devilish Royston 'would be in his element' and proudly parading his beautiful bride-to-be for all to see. Rosa had written a letter to Roger, and said she wished that he was free to see her appear as a bridesmaid in August. Roger chuckled as he read the letter, knowing well that Roy and Royston Carey would never countenance his appearance at the wedding.

Roger's cellmate Mongey asked what he was laughing about and he was told all about the Careys. How most of the family considered themselves 'a step above everyone else'. He said that Rebecca and Rosa though, were much more 'down to earth' and not nearly as snobbish as the menfolk. He described how the family always wore the finest clothes, always sat at the top of the church, and all had been sent to private schools.

"So Royston has notions about himself", said Mongey.
"That's one way of putting it!" was the reply, "Sure with a name like that he has no choice really, has he?" he added laughing.
"I hate the bollox already!" stated Mongey.
"They run most of the businesses in the parish", said Roger, "And whatever other businessmen that exist have their premises leased, so they get a cut of everything".
"Old money?" asked Mongey.
"Old AND new – ALL of it", was the reply.
"In fairness I have to say that Roy Senior is much more humble – he has had to be in order to keep his customers on his side – but he can be as two faced as they come. For example, he never seemed to mind whenever he saw me with Rosa, but behind the

46

scenes he gave her a terrible time about me, the poor girl. He can mask his emotions, but Royston can't, his face always betrays him. And Mongey I'm telling you it is an evil face he has, he has this cunning smile that irritates me beyond belief".

"It must irritate your friend Terence too", laughed Mongey, before asking Roger to tell him more about the parish of Ballycroy and its people. Roger was only too happy to oblige!

"It's a townland really, 20 miles long stretching from Mulranny to Bangor Erris. Ten miles down is Ballycroy Village, right in the middle I suppose. We are nestled between the Atlantic coast and the Nephin mountains. Once you leave the picturesque village of Mulranny and head north, you avoid the turnoff for Achill to your left and keep heading straight on. When you pass under the railway bridge, the bay will come into view just below your left. To your right, you see the start of the impressive Claggan Mountain which is very steep. You feel like an ant beside a loaf of bread as you head for the windy road that snakes for three miles. Just picture it – to your left the bay and the sight of Achill's hills reflecting down on the water; in front of you a narrow winding road on the edge of the water; with a steep incline immediately up to your right. You wonder how the rocks on the incline don't roll down; and the sheep appear to defy gravity by grazing on the slopes. After those three miles you hit the first sight of the flat blanket bog and at the five mile mark you are at Ballyveeney Bridge, with its tree-sheltered barracks by the Veeney River just as it enters the bay.

Then further ahead, about three miles with nothing to see but bog and mountains to your right, and bog and Achill to your left – with some houses speckled in the distance. The two miles before Ballycroy Village, it starts to become a little greener, but it is still mostly brown and trees. More dwellings come into view at this stage though.

I'll pass Ballycroy Village for the moment and come back to it later – but as you head further north you see Bunmore Hill to the right, and I live on the northern side of that. At this stage, out to your left the Atlantic comes into view again before being obscured by Knockmoyleen Hill. Two miles further down the road the village of Shranamonragh with its neat row of houses comes into view to your right. Beyond that is Logduff, Aughness South and Aughness North, and then further on Bangor Erris.

The top of Bunmore hill gives a glorious view, and if you look out to the west from its summit you can see all of the parish, Achill and Erris in the distance. It gives a great view of Innishbiggle Island sitting between us and Achill. Out into the horizon, on a good day, you can see the island of Black Rock rising as a pyramid from the Atlantic. You can barely make out the Inishkea Islands where I used to work. And where Ballycroy hits the sea you can see The Sandybanks and the ruins of Fahy Castle. I swear, on a beautiful day there is no more splendid a sight. You can actually see the curve of the globe in front of your eyes as God tries to fit so much beauty into one view.

Going back to Ballycroy Village, the focal point is Carey's Bar and the adjoining Carey's Grocery Shop, which are both situated on the ground floor of a large two-storey building. The Carey family live in the plush rooms on the upper storey. There is no other pub in the parish! When you come out of the door of Carey's Shop, to the left is the Post Office and then the Doctor's Surgery, known to all as 'The Dispensary'. Of course the Careys lease that building. In front of you lies a cobblestone area which is usually full of tethered horses and carts or market stalls. Many's the pint of beer and pint of blood that has been spilt on those cobbles! On the far side of the road lies nothing but bog which spreads out like a massive brown carpet in front of you. So, all of the buildings in Ballycroy Village – bar the church and the priest's residence – are placed on the one side of the road, the eastern side.

Coming out of Carey's Shop, the door of the bar is immediately to the right and beside that is a yard owned – of course – by the Careys. Just beside that is Paul the Butcher's which is on the corner as the road branches up an incline to the right. Just up from there is a derelict police station. Beside that is Carey's Hall, in which dances are held but it doubles as a funeral home! Roy Carey himself is the only undertaker in the area, and when he is seen shining his coffin carriage it's always bad news for somebody! There are several houses between the hall and the sports-field, which includes a handball alley. Directly across from the sports-field, surrounded by more bog, is the leafy entrance to Ballycroy Church, which is hidden by magnificent ash trees, which in turn are protected by immaculate stone walls. Back on the east side, The Tannery is leased by the Careys and is where goods of leather, wood and wool are made by the O'Brien family. The last premises on the line is McDonnell's Forge, where Sylvester works. Then, appropriately enough at the end of the village, is the end place for us – well not for me as per The White Cow – the new graveyard! It lies on a slope, and it too is walled. From it you have a grand view of the imposing Bunmore hill. I suppose it's hard for a townie like you to believe a place exists with only one public house. And I suppose it's hard to imagine a village with all the buildings on one side and nothing but wasteland on the other side.

I've suggested that the place should be instead called 'Ballycarey' you know!" laughed Roger, but there was no reply. Mongey had fallen asleep!
"I know our place can be boring, but little did I think it could be THAT boring. Perhaps there's a fortune for me to be made with a cure for insomnia!" smiled Roger, as he too became drowsy, thinking of his family and friends back in the place he loved. He was so proud to be one of the 'Boys of Ballycroy'.

CHAPTER 8: A UNION

The first eighth months of 1911 were good to the hard workers of the parish and they thanked God that the pleasant weather ensured that the turf and the hay were saved without much trouble. They were now all set for the harvest wedding and indeed the Carey and McArthur families ensured that when the long-awaited day came, the onlookers who stood outside the church were not disappointed.

Antoinette was a vision in her white gown as she stepped from the hired marble-coloured carriage on the arm of her proud father. The sun again shone, and those who had come to see the couple showered prayers and good-wishes on her as she entered the church to the sound of the ringing bells. At the top of the aisle waited a dashing looking Royston, who beamed at the sight of the beauty who was about to become his bride.

About an hour or so later, after the new Parish Priest Fr. Kinsella had completed the ceremony, the church bells again rang out as the glamorous couple appeared at the front door of the church and smilingly accepted the cheers and confetti of the locals gathered outside. They posed happily as Toothy Lucey arranged a photograph. It was a joyous day for the whole parish as the wedding party made the short journey across the road to Carey's Hall where a feast was laid on, provided by caterers brought in from the hotels of Achill. Roy Carey had seen to it that the uninvited guests would be treated to some whiskey, lemonade and pastries that were laid out on a table at the entrance to the hall.

The music and dancing went well on until the early hours of the following morning and the air of happiness that filled the parish was infectious and put everyone in good humour. Royston spirited his bride away as soon as he could to Westport where their honeymoon would begin.

One man who was not in attendance in Carey's Hall that day was John Peter Kerrigan. Days earlier Rebecca Carey had confirmed that she would shortly be leaving for Dublin to commence her training to become a teacher. The couple decided to end their relationship – if it even could have been termed a relationship. John Peter did not show any outward signs of disappointment, and on the day of the wedding when the Carey sisters led the dancing for all of the guests, he and his brother Willie simply worked an extra shift at the Bangor Erris Quarry.

In Galway Jail, Roger tried to imagine how the wedding was going and how lovely 'his' Rosa was looking. He had posted her letters but to his disappointment she had not replied, and he had suspected that either her brother or father had intercepted them. One letter that was delivered successfully was one he sent to his Bunmore neighbour and good friend Antoinette, and he wished her well on her big day.

That very day, a visitor was announced for Roger and as he made his way to the prison's meeting room he tried to fathom out who it could be. The only one who had visited him so far was Liam and he had indicated that he would probably not make the journey again. He dared to hope it was his father. He knew it would not be Rosa on the wedding day. Mongey had just been released a week previously and it was highly unlikely he would return to the place of his incarceration again so soon!

As the short burly figure entered the meeting room, Roger recognised the face and the baldy sweaty head of the well dressed man but could not immediately remember how he knew him. As the prison guard announced that they had five minutes to meet, he struggled but could not put a name on the gentleman, but as soon as the man said his name it all came back to Roger.
"Foy, Timothy Foy, hello Mister O'Grady", said the visitor.
"Oh yes, you're Batty's solicitor", replied the prisoner, still trying to figure out what was going on.
"You are here to see ME, definitely ME?" asked Roger.
"Definitely you", was the reply, "Sorry if I have startled you. Am I keeping you from something?" the solicitor asked half sarcastically?
"Loads, I'm a busy man!" laughed Roger in response. "I'm heading out for a whiskey shortly!"

Mr. Foy made the most of their five minutes and got straight to the point, telling Roger that he had been hired by William O'Grady to try and get the sentence reduced. The early release of Terence and Michaeleen were also included in his remit. An appeal date was set for the week before Christmas and the solicitor said that he was hopeful of getting them out at that stage. He was using the issue of the press coverage as a factor, and would be asking the appeal judge to reduce the sentence on the basis that the photographs, poems etc influenced the decision to hand out a two year sentence.

When the five minutes were up, the two men shook hands firmly and Mr. Foy said that he hoped they would both meet as free men before the end of the year. The three prisoners would not have to attend the court sitting, and would have to sit through an agonising wait for news of the verdict to be despatched. Mr. Foy expressed confidence that he would succeed, and said that if he had been hired to represent all of the men – and not just Batty – at the outset, they would never have set foot in prison.

Back in his empty cell, Roger tried to retain his composure but broke down, crying at the thought of what his father had just done. It hit him hard, and he felt a physical pain in his heart and stomach as he wailed away to himself. The father who had always been distant, who had hardly ever spoken a positive word to him, had just done the best turn for Roger that anyone had ever had. "Blood IS thicker than water", the Bunmore man whispered to himself.

That evening Roger excitedly scribbled more letters to his two fellow prisoners from Ballycroy. Within days Michaeleen Cooney had been visited by his excited parents and young blonde Kathleen, who were delighted that an early release looked possible. Michaeleen was struck though by Kathleen's lack of enthusiasm, he thought she would have shown more delight at the prospect.

"What's wrong, Kathleen, do you not want me home?" asked Michaeleen.

"I do surely", she said with her head bowed, "I'm just not feeling well after the journey, my eyes are sore".
"We'll get you sweetcake soon and you'll be fine for the way back", said The Coon to his youngest daughter, and she started to perk up a little.
"When you come out, Mikey, will you bring me to the apple tree again? Please! Please!" she begged.
"Of course I will, it's the first thing we'll do", answered Michaeleen, "And we'll bring Sailor to act as a lookout in case the people in the lodge find us robbing their orchard! If he barks, we dive into the long grass like the last time, right?"
Castlebar jail was not used to such happy scenes.

Things were less happy that week in Sligo jail, where Sylvester McDonnell had cycled the arduous 80 miles to see his imprisoned brother. Despite the big wedding, he had hoped to find Terence's spirits buoyed by the news of a possible Christmas release. He was to be disappointed!
"You can tell that eejit in Galway not to be writing stupid fucking letters to me!" roared Terence to his brother, who was allowed sit in the cell for the duration of the visit.
"Look at these – one letter about a fucking appeal and another telling me not to be heartbroken and that all is fucking fair in fucking love and in fucking war!"
Sylvester and the other cell occupant looked at each other and smiled, as the stampeding Terence continued his tirade, cheeks scarlet and eyes bulging, his sweaty curls matted to his forehead.

"I thought he was soft in the head BEFORE he went to jail but he's fucking softer NOW, is that fat article. What are they doing to him in bloody Galway? He's turning into a big fucking sissy! What do I want with a letter about fucking love and quotes from fucking Shankspeare and them other English fuckers??!" he continued furiously. The laughing from the other two men made Terence even angrier.
"I can have ANY fucking woman I want, ANY woman!" he roared.
"Royston is welcome to her – he is welcome to my fucking leftovers anytime he fucking likes, and he can fucking have her as I'm fucking well finished with her. I feel sorry for the man having to spend the rest of his fucking life with that sulky cow!"

His companions laughed and eventually persuaded him to sit and calm down. Sylvester chuckled all the way back to Ballycroy on his bike and he and his father kept breaking into laughter in the forge the next day as he recounted the foul-mouthed outburst. But on a more serious note, Sylvester told his father that it was clear to him that Terence was becoming increasingly influenced by his cellmate, Colm Tierney from Ballina.

"Them Tierneys were ALL rebels", said McDonnell Senior, "Great men. Irish to the core. Terence could learn a thing or two from a Tierney. It will do him no harm, no harm at all".

Another man being subtly influenced was Batty, still 'exiled' in Enniscrone. Fr. Rea made sure that books about Robert Emmet and Wolfe Tone were conveniently available in the young man's room. He certainly was not pushing the bible on him! Articles by Arthur Griffith and other Sinn Fein literature were also placed discretely around the parochial house, and Fr. Rea took immense pride in introducing his nephew as "one of the famous 'Boys of Ballycroy' from Co. Mayo – a future rebel leader of the Irish!" The printed words of the Bard of Burrishoole took pride of place in a wooden frame in the hallway.

Trouble was stirring. The union between Britain and Ireland was under threat. And blood was about to be spilled.

CHAPTER 9: A REUNION

Timothy Foy delivered on his promise and two days before Christmas Roger, Michaeleen and Terence walked free. There would be one hell of a session in Carey's!

Upon meeting Terence in Bangor Erris, Sylvester made the mistake of asking his brother if he had any problem with 'the reunion' being held in Carey's.
"Why the fuck would I have a problem? What the hell are you on about? Sure if I had to avoid every fucking man whose woman I fucking rode I would never drink in company again for the rest of my fucking life!" exclaimed Terence. Sylvester got the message, and kept quiet for the rest of the cycle back home!

At 3pm on the grey-skied Christmas Eve, Roger arrived in Bunmore hoping for a warm embrace from his father. Although he gladly received one from an emotional Liam, he just received a hard handshake and a muttered "welcome back" from the stern William O'Grady.
"Thank you Dad", said Roger, but the only response he got was a shrug as his father headed out the door to head for the stable. The two brothers looked at each other and locked each others eyes. At least there were two of them in it who could share between them the experience of having a cold and distant father.

Liam grew more upset as Roger told him that he had already booked his ticket for America for January 15th, just three weeks away. He had given up on Rosa who would not hear talk of the prospect of emigration, and was heading over with the other two lads just released. Mr. Foy had arranged the tickets.
"It's best we keep out of trouble or the authorities will have the three of us behind bars for the slightest bit of aggravation", said Roger to his tearful older brother.
"I know", said Liam, "Sure they will torment the three of you. Sure you are sitting ducks for the constabulary. You're right to go. I only wish I could go with you".
"You need to look after himself out there" said Roger.
"I know" sobbed Liam. "But I will be lost without you. It will be so hard".

In the Cooney homestead, Michaeleen's homecoming was spoiled by how weak he found his youngest sister. She looked pale and her blue eyes which normally lit up the room were dim and looked sad. Despite the hugs, tears and kisses, the atmosphere plunged further when the white haired son and brother announced that he too was America bound in three weeks. This did not go down well.

Michaeleen kept his emotions together but when he got to his bedroom he burst into tears as he read the school-made 'welcome home' card that Kathleen had left there for him. It upset him to have to upset his family, and as Kathleen entered the room to find out his reaction to the card, he had to quickly hide the gifts he had brought her for Christmas. They were woollen sheep puppets – a white one and a black one – that the dinner lady in the jail had knitted for him to give to the sister he had talked so much about during his 14 months there.

The drinking session began in Carey's at around six and the mood was euphoric. Each of the three released men was carried shoulder-high into the bar by the overjoyed men of the parish, whilst RIC men Clive and Scully kept a discrete distant watch from beside Paul the Butcher's. Inside, the beer flowed and the Carey profits increased, despite Roy standing a round for the house! It wasn't long before the seven 'Boys of Ballycroy' were united amongst a gang of rowdy onlookers and the rebel songs commenced at that stage. Roger managed to catch a glimpse of Rosa behind the bar and received a quick smile in return. There was a moment of tension when Terence and Royston first met at the bar but the occasion swept them along and a firm handshake was exchanged from either side of the bar, and mutual congratulations expressed through gritted teeth.

As the children of Ballycroy went to bed in anticipation of their Christmas gifts, nearly every male adult in the parish was squeezed into the bar. The spirits were high and the craic was mighty. This was going to be an evening to live in the memory – even though many would not have any memory of the event on

Christmas Day! The RIC men had done the right thing by sneaking away to let the crowd enjoy themselves.

One of the party who left for home early was Michaeleen. He was ill at ease over how much Kathleen had deteriorated. His parents had said that she had been unwell but they didn't think any more of it and were not overly concerned. They had brought Dr Skelton to her and he had just told her to rest and not read too much during the school holidays, as it might strain her eyesight. She appeared to have some sort of fever. He would organise an eye test in the New Year.

When he got home, Michaeleen spent some time playing with his other brothers and sisters before going to kiss Kathleen good night. He was surprised to find that she was not in her bed when he went to check her. He panicked and asked the others where she was, and was told that she was in HIS bed! She had slept there every night since he left!

Back in the bar, the crowd grew drunker and giddier as the music, singing and drinking continued. Roger and Terence got intoxicated quickly not having had alcohol in over a year. They spotted Toothy Lucey entering the bar and the unfortunate man quickly became a target!

"Would you look who it is", shouted Terence, "It's the fucking ugliest man in Ballycroy" and the pub erupted in laughter. Toothy was used to this kind of slagging and barely blinked as he ordered his tumbler of ale, his protruding gums and teeth masking – as ever – whether he was smiling or scowling.
"The man with the constant grin – will you have a gin?" said Roger to further howls.

"Yer out!", said Toothy, wiping the sweat from his long forehead.
"And so are you!" replied Roger, hitting form.
"What do you mean?" was the hesitant response, knowing that he was in all likelihood setting himself up to be a victim of Roger's wit.

"You're out – your teeth are sticking out!" was the reply as the dimly lit pub descended into roars of hearty uncontrolled laughter at poor Toothy's expense.

"Ah come here", said Roger, feeling bad for his victim and pulling him to his sweaty self, embracing him, spilling half of Toothy's drink in the process. But he wasn't finished his verbal assault on the journalist yet! Turning to his captive audience, Roger shouted "Do you know what the best thing about being in jail for 14 months was?"
Everyone waited in participation, especially poor Toothy who had half an idea what the dreaded punchline would be...
"It was not having to lay eyes on this creature!" laughed Roger, and the pub rocked with another outburst from the cheering crowd.

Toothy was mortified and tried to take some measure of control, which was difficult as Roger had his right arm clasped around him and the surrounding crowd were pushing ever closer, anxious to see Roger toy with the unfortunate man.

"Have ye any stories for the paper for me from inside" Toothy asked, trying to stop the rest of his ale from being spilled onto the sawdust.
"I have a story for you Toothy!" exclaimed Terence, and the crowd grew quiet.
"Do you know Toothy, that in Sligo jail every Sunday night they brought in a whore who fucking looked after all of us, one by one, did you know that?"
Toothy nodded embarrassingly, hating being the centre of attention on this occasion.
"Really?" asked the profusely sweating journalist, "I'll write about that in next week's edition".
"You do that", said Terence, "You do that!" But he wasn't finished...
"And do you know what the whore said to me last Sunday, Toothy, do you know what she fucking said?" teased the intoxicated Terence.
"What?" smiled Toothy, knowing again that more laughter was about to erupt at his expense...

"She said I'll let myself be shagged by any fucking man in Ireland, except one Toothy Fucking Lucey because he is so fucking ugly!" and the screams of laughter almost deafened the poor journalist as he wriggled away, jostling for the bar again hoping someone else would be targeted next.

Taking advantage of his audience, Roger hushed the crowd and said that he wanted to make a speech. Silence descended and Royston reluctantly rang the bell at the bar to enforce the message, whilst his sister Rosa finished pulling a pint to concentrate on what was about to be said. Roger was on a winner here and knew his every word would be cheered.

"Gentlemen – and lady" he said as the crowd all turned to Rosa

"On behalf of the three ex-prisoners, I want to thank you all for your warm welcome tonight, but above all, for your great support you and your families gave to us since October twelve months. It was an honour to serve time for you." Cheers rang out.

"But I want to stress. This fight is not about the three of us. It's not about the seven 'Boys of Ballycroy'. It's about us ALL! And even though some of us will have to follow our brothers and sisters to foreign shores to escape the tyranny of our captors, we will continue the fight there and make sure it is funded with dollars!" Again, more cheers rang out for their huge hero.

"To each and every one of you again – thanks for your support and may God bless you all this Christmas. Erin go bráth!" And with that, another rally of shouts rang out and the rebel songs re-started. Roger looked behind the bar where Rosa winked at him, which he took as a promise of some amorous action later! Toothy retreated with his new drink towards the door to stay out of the limelight.

He was the first to notice a smiling Sergeant Clive enter the bar, followed closely by a stern looking Constable Scully. Within seconds the singing stopped, and the crowds parted to make way for the RIC men. Everything went quiet, and all that could be heard was the sound of the steel capped boots pacing the sawdust covered stone floor.

"Mister Carey, you were supposed to stop serving at ten" said Clive.
"Sorry Sergeant" was the meek reply.
"You are all aware that Father Kinsella asked us to cease at ten. He wants no drunkenness at midnight mass" and a few chuckles were heard. Clive then looked towards Roger, who all of sudden felt as if everyone was cowering behind him. As the sergeant was about to speak again one of the drunken revellers, hiding behind John Peter at the rear, shouted "Off home you British Bastard" before he was hushed by all present. Scully's look grew sterner. Clive continued as if he hadn't heard. He looked towards Roger.
"Welcome back, Mister O'Grady" he said, as the crowd laughed nervously, as it was rare they heard Roger addressed as that.
"Thank you, Sergeant" replied Roger confidently.
"Any cows talk to you lately?" asked Clive with a smirk.
"Just you!" was the rapid reply as yet another outbreak of laughter erupted – this round the noisiest of the entire night! This was too easy for Roger – even when he was drunk! Clive's smirk did not last long!

Clive glanced at his uniformed colleague who was staring at the floor, scarcely believing his superior had walked straight into that retort. It took a few minutes for the noise to die down as the sergeant poised to speak to Roger again.
"Now lads, I want no more trouble in these parts, having the spotlight upon us from high above is no good for any of us, do you hear?" He was met with stooped heads and silence.
"Ballycroy must be kept out of the courts and out of the papers. I want 1912 to be a quiet one." After a pause, Clive looked around and surveyed the bar before focusing again on the barman.
"Royston – let them all finish whatever they are drinking – and quietly off to mass then." His final sentence surprised them all.
"Merry Christmas to you all and your families". With that, he headed for the exit. Everyone was stunned that he had just wished them that.

Fr. Kinsella would do well to get such silence at midnight mass!

60

CHAPTER 10: PARTINGS

It didn't augur well for the coming year that most of the population ended up attending a burial in the graveyard on the 1st day of January, 1912. It was the day Toothy Lucey's father was buried. The only son cut a lonely figure as he looked down at the grave being filled in with orange gravel by his friends and neighbours. He was all by himself now. His cousin Myles Lucey, even taller and thinner, was in attendance but they were not close. The only time the man known as 'Myles Long' was contacted was to cover Toothy's job as the local postman whenever some journalist duties had to be attended to during his postal hours i.e. court cases.

Toothy was not blessed with the best of features. He had a very long and narrow face, with a long flat nose that ended just above his protruding gums and teeth with wide nostrils. His eyeballs bulged out of his head. His hairline started at the centre top of his skull, making his forehead look massive, and from his hairline back long wisps of gray and black scraggly hair reached down to well below his collar. As he watched his father's coffin being covered, he sobbed loudly and snot dripped from his nostrils.

All seven of the 'Boys of Ballycroy' he had often written about were there, and some of them took turns at the shovel. As they watched him cry, they all felt pangs of guilt for the way they had treated him down through the years. When the grave was filled, Roger made his way over to the grieving postman and journalist.

"I'm so sorry Gerard, I did not know your Dad had been ill, I really didn't", he said.
"That's alright" replied Toothy, "He hadn't been too bad, was able to get up and about, but just took a bad turn Christmas Day".
"I'm sorry for giving you a hard time in Carey's the other night", said Roger.
"That's alright, sure it was only the craic!" said Toothy as he wiped more tears away.
"We went too far", said Roger guiltily, "There is a big difference between wit and shit. And it was unfair to pick on you, and I'm heartily sorry".

"That's alright" smiled Toothy.
"You know we all really love you and would crucify anyone who dared lay a finger on you, you know that, don't you?" said Roger as he put his arms around Toothy pulling his sobbing head into his chest, not caring about the mess that would be made on his jacket.
"You know", said Toothy pulling back, "Dad spotted you the other day when you arrived at Carey's and said "Roger must be the only man ever to come back from a year of hard labour even heavier than he was before!"
Roger burst out laughing, with his hand still on Toothy's shoulder.
"Why didn't you tell that one the other night in Carey's – you would have gotten a round of applause for that!" exclaimed Roger.

Roger had to move on as a queue of sympathisers was gathering behind him at the graveside and he went to visit his mother's grave and nearby the grave of her parents – his grandparents – the Rolands. He always felt lonelier at their grave as he had known them and had loved them dearly. As he prayed, he sensed a presence behind him and after blessing himself turned to see the solicitor Timothy Foy and a moustachioed man wearing a tweed coat and hat. The crowd had been so big that Roger had not spotted them before now.

"Great to see you Mr. Foy" said Roger grabbing his hand, "And thanks again for all you've done for me".
"Don't mention it, it was a pleasure" replied Foy. "Roger, I'd like you to meet my friend here, Harry Heraty from Westport".
"I've heard a lot about you, hello Roger" said Harry.
"Welcome to Ballycroy. I suppose you both know the Luceys?"
"We do", said Foy "But we'd like to have a chat with you while we're down here. Would that be possible?"
"It sure would", said Roger, "Will meet you in Carey's in ten minutes. Can I ask what it is about? Has my old man not paid the bill?" he laughed.
"Nothing like that at all I assure you", smiled Heraty. "I'm in Sinn Fein and I was hoping you would think about joining us?"

"Mister Foy", said Roger, "Did you not tell him that I'm off to America, sure I'll be no good to Sinn Fein there!" laughed Roger. "On the contrary", said Heraty, "We need a man like you over there. Let's talk more outside Carey's, is that alright?"

*****

After a few pints and their dinners, the seven pals met at The Carthouse in The Sandybanks at 3pm, as they had previously planned. It was their first time together there since the White Cow incident. The lads who had not been jailed had done some improvement work and the hideout was now reinforced with better beams of wood, which had been painted green, and they had even made a green door! Camouflage!

They spent the afternoon conversing and catching up as Sailor ran around after rabbits. The long grass blew in the breeze and the air was dominated by the crashing sounds from the waves at the rear of the dunes. Roger didn't get to talk about the Sinn Fein offer to sign up. Talk was dominated by an upset Michaeleen describing how quickly downhill Kathleen was going. He talked about her love for the two puppets, who she had named Snowy and Sooty, and how he might have to back out of the American trip. It was a depressing couple of hours. They had hoped for a cheerier first day back at HQ.

The Sunday before the sailing, the seven met for what Roger termed 'The Last Supper' at The Carthouse. Again, the mood was downbeat, as Michaeleen was even more upset this time. Terence and Sylvester tried to cheer everyone up by telling them that they had "loads of sex" with two women from "up the country somewhere" who were staying at Sheeaun Lodge. Their mother worked there so it was a credible story. Batty told the lads that he had joined Sinn Fein. Roger didn't mention his meeting with Harry Heraty. The Kerrigan brothers were as quiet as ever and spent most of the time fooling around with Sailor. It was a strange atmosphere. The sky was very dark and it reminded them of the day that they did not dare mention, the day that the beast cursed them. Roger thought about bringing up the subject but knew he would be shouted down. Michaeleen was depressed enough in any case.

They made arrangements for 'The American Wake' in Carey's that would take place the night before they took the train from Westport to head for Queenstown in Cork where Roger, Michaeleen and Terence would board The Olympic. There was no ceremony as they headed home in the January rain and left The Carthouse behind, but for Roger and his standard attempt at a Shakespeare quote.
"Parting is such sweet sorrow" he said as he cast a final glimpse at their base.
"Stop talking shite!", said Terence. "Three weeks on a boat with you – you'll bloody drive me mad!"

On the day of the wake Roger was finishing packing his suitcase when young Brendan Cooney galloped up to the O'Grady front door on his brown stallion.
"Michaeleen won't make America, Roger", he said from his mount. "Kathleen is dying, the doctor said she won't make February".
Liam had joined Roger by the horse at this stage. For a change, the poet was stuck for words.
"God love ye, God love the little creature" said Liam. Roger was biting his lip. He felt such a pang of sadness for his friend. He knew how much he adored Kathleen. He knew that this would bring indescribable pain to the family. He was gutted. The little girl who they had all come to love was dying. He had never thought her illness was THIS serious.
"Can't the doctors or nurses do anything?" asked Liam, but Brendan just bowed his head.
"I'd better get back, lads", he said, "Will ye let Terence know?" The O'Grady lads nodded in unison.
"Michaeleen won't be in Carey's tonight but he might be with ye as far as Westport in the morning as he will have to get his ticket changed" added Brendan.
Roger cleared his throat and managed to speak, but his voice was breaking.
"We will call back to ye before we go, Brendan, God Bless for now..."

Liam cycled to break the news to Terence, who was finding it an emotional day even before that. He could barely look Sylvester in the eye. He knew his brother was taking his departure hard. His mother was almost in constant tears, and his sister had come over from her husband's house for the day.

Terence was relieved to get away from the atmosphere for a couple of hours and he met Roger at Bunmore crossroads where they cycled to Cooneys. It was like entering a wake house. There were neighbours there and a lot of sobbing, mostly from the siblings that came between Michaeleen the eldest and Kathleen the youngest. The Coon himself gave the duo a strong embrace. He was reeking of whiskey. They met Michaeleen at the door and he hugged both of his friends. The sight of Mrs Cooney sitting down holding the hand of the sick little girl was the saddest they had ever seen.

They could see the sweat on her forehead. She was pale and had gone so gaunt since they last saw her. She was murmuring something to her mother, who got up from her chair to let Terence sit beside her. Roger stood, tears flowing unashamedly down his chubby cheeks. Kathleen's eyes opened, and after a few minutes tried to sit up and focus her sight on her two visitors. It was clear her eyes were hurting her.

"Do you remember me?" asked Terence gently.
"Of course I do, Terence". "You always say the bad words!" Everyone laughed.
"How is Sailor?" he asked.
"He's fine thank you", she whispered, "He's a good little dog".
"Are these your little puppets?" asked Roger smiling down through his tears.
"Yes Roger"
"What are their names?"
"Snowy and Sooty"
"They're great names", he said quietly, "Is Sooty the white one?"
"No silly Roger", she perked up "Snowy is white because he is like snow".

Everyone laughed again and just as he was about to stop sobbing Roger noticed that the sitting Terence had tears in his eyes and that started him off again.
"Why are you crying Roger" asked the little blonde girl, her head slipping down her pillow again.
"I'm crying because no one brought me any nice presents for Christmas".
"Mikey always buys me presents; he is the best brother ever. Don't you have a brother?" she asked, yawning.

Before he answered her mother came to the bedside again and said that it might be best to let her have more rest as the doctor had asked not to tire her out. The two lads agreed and stepped back and even by then Kathleen had turned her head in towards the wall and was falling off to sleep.

It was a heartbreaking departure as they left the room. They both hoped against hope that a miracle would happen and the tiny bundle of beauty would be up and about again, dancing and playing. But deep down they knew they would never ever see the little girl again. And after tearful words with all members of the Cooney family there, they cycled away, both of them upset. How could they possibly enjoy their night in Carey's after that?

Roger had more farewells to get through and Liam joined him as darkness grew in the graveyard. They had prayed at the Roland headstone and were now at their mother's grave. For the first time he ever could remember, Roger shed tears at it.

"I don't think Dad ever forgave me for losing her" sobbed Roger.
"He did. He's quiet. It's just his way" his brother replied. "And don't be expecting anything much from him in the morning".
"Has he spoken about me going?" asked Roger.
"Not really, no."
"Do you think he is alright with me going?"
"It's hard to tell. Sure is he ever alright with anything?" replied the elder brother.
"I tell you this, Liam, I'm going to make it good for myself over there but don't be expecting much contact from me. I'll send you an odd note, but that's it".

"Why?" asked Liam.
"I'm cutting all ties with this place, I have to. I can't have people holding me back; I've had enough of that" replied Roger.
"What do you mean?" asked Liam. "Sure you'll have Terence with you".
"Not for long, I tell you that, I'm not going all the way to America to spend my time in jail! I'll shake him off, don't worry" asserted Roger.

They stared at the headstone for a few silent moments.

"Do you remember much of her?" asked Roger.
"No. Just the warmth of being held close to her", replied Liam.

There was more silence, as the grey snow clouds gathered above the cemetery.

"Liam, you're a good brother. I'll send over what I can. But look after yourself. Get yourself married. You'll do me proud" said Roger in a cracking voice.

On hearing that Liam broke down and they both hugged each other and cried. After a few minutes, they headed for nearby Carey's Bar.

The planned night of merriment was a subdued affair. It could not have been anything else as all of the patrons were feeling sorry for the Cooneys. Poor Kathleen. The unfortunate little girleen. The McDonnell brothers cheered up when they were beckoned outside by one of the servants from Sheeaun Lodge who was taking them back there for the night to meet their fancy women! Roger had a few hours of pleasure with Rosa in The Dispensary, as Dr Skelton was away and the keys were in her care!

"I'll write to you Rosa" promised Roger.
"You told me the other night you were cutting all ties! Make up that mind of yours!" she responded.
"YOU are different. I wish you could have sailed with me" he stated.

"You KNOW that was never going to happen. Now, off you go, you've only a couple hours before the train leaves", whispered Rosa, placing her hands on his shoulders and gazing up at him as they both stood.
"I love you Rosa" he said in a serious voice.
"No you don't! If you did you would be marrying me and not heading thousands of miles away from me, you big softie. Now, go and make your fortune!" she replied.
"I will love you ALWAYS!" he said, squeezing her body close to his.
"Stop that! You will meet plenty of nice girls over there and Rosa will soon be forgotten!" she whispered.
"Look after yourself, won't you?" he said.
"I suppose I will have to!" she replied. "Now off with you. And you look after yourself too. Do you hear me?"

They had their final kiss and embrace and Roger headed home in the cold for a few hours sleep. When he awoke the carriage was already outside waiting for him, with Michaeleen on it, and a thin blanket of snow covered the ground. It didn't take him too long to get ready. Again, he embraced Liam a final time as their father stood with his back to the fire he had just lit.

"Bye Dad" choked Roger.
"Bye son" said the old man, tears visible in his eyes. The sound of Liam's crying grew louder. Roger walked towards the fireplace to shake his father's hand, and received a firm handshake but no eye contact.
"We need to leave now!" voiced the driver from the porch door. Roger had one last look over at Liam, headed for the door, and stopped. He then turned around and faced his father again.
"I'm sorry for everything, Dad. I didn't mean to lose you your wife. I hope I've repaid SOME of the debt" he said firmly. Liam was stunned. William O'Grady was staring at the stone floor, his lower lip trembling.
"Have you anything else to say to me?" said Roger to his father. There was a silence before an answer came.
"God bless you son. God bless you". He stepped forward a couple of paces and splashed holy water from a bottle in the direction of his second-born.

Roger blessed himself, looked over at Liam again and headed out through the cold porch for the carriage.
As he was about to board, he heard his father's voice from the door.
"One more thing son" he said, walking towards him. He looked down at Roger's stomach and reached out and gently pushed it. "Lose that gut – or it will kill you. You're carrying too much weight!" he said.
Roger was again shocked into silence. He looked at Liam by the door, stared at his father one more time, and joined Michaeleen in the carriage. He threw his case onto the floor. He was in a temper. At that moment he did not care if he never got to see Bunmore again. Off they trotted to pick up Terence at Ballyveeney Bridge.

As they carted through the snow many parishioners came out to catch a glance of the emigrating lads and wave them off. They were confused to see Michaeleen in the carriage as word had gotten around that he was postponing, so they were not expecting to see him.

"Some fucking night I had" said Terence after boarding, "She was mad for it". It didn't take him long to overcome the tearful farewell he had with his beloved brother and the rest of his family.
"She has me worn out" he added, "I'll never meet one that good in America".
"I'm sure you will", said Michaeleen, glad to have his mind taken off his troubles.
"Lose that gut!" repeated a dismayed Roger over and over again. "That's all he had to say to me – lose that gut". His companions laughed.

Terence and Roger boarded the train at Westport after a sad goodbye to their white haired friend. No words could comfort any of the three. Not even Michaeleen's proclamation that he would see them in New York City on the fourth of July.

The 'Boys of Ballycroy' were boys no more. They were men. Men who were having to get used of shedding a tear or two. As Roger stared at the top of snowy Croagh Patrick which was gradually disappearing from his view, he swore he could see a vision of Kathleen Cooney waving at him, like a white angel wishing him on his way. He daren't mention this to Terence. It gave him a bit of comfort as he began his long journey.

After all, it wasn't the first apparition that had happened in Mayo!

CHAPTER 11: MORE DEPARTURES

As Dr Skelton was away, he had arranged for a doctor from Castlebar to check on young Kathleen Cooney. This doctor had assigned a nurse to care for the child. Her illness mystified them, but it was obviously a version of scarlet fever that she had acquired and the little girl seemed unable to fight it off. She was deteriorating by the day, and a daily mass for her recovery was attended by every household.

On the morning of January 25th the nurse told the rest of the Cooney family to 'prepare for the worst'. Victoria Cooney kept her composure and was the strongest of the family, she had to as her husband and eldest son were not able to deal with the trauma. The Coon was drinking more and more whiskey as a crutch, and Michaeleen, who should have been halfway across the Atlantic, was in a constant daze. He blamed himself for what was happening to his baby sister. He blamed the drowning of the animal and the accompanying curse. He had brought bad luck to his family.

At 5pm that dark evening the family squeezed into Michaeleen's bedroom where the little patient was. An air of desperate sadness filled the air. They commenced saying the rosary and amidst the humming the panting of the young Kathleen could be heard. The nurse advised them what to do, and The Coon positioned himself so that he was sitting with his back up against the headboard, with his legs spread out on the bed in front of him, and young Kathleen resting face up between his legs, with her head back on his stomach. He rubbed her blonde tresses as his wife held the little girl's hands and kept rubbing an icy cold handkerchief on the little perspiring forehead.

"That's my girl" said The Coon, "You're safe now with Daddy; Daddy has got a grip on you and Daddy is not going to let you go".
"Water" whispered Kathleen and Victoria put a cup to her lips and it was sipped.
Her panting grew harder and faster, and then slowed. The Coon kept stroking her and talking to his dying seven year old.

"Mikey" she whispered and he knelt in beside her, the rest of the siblings gathering behind him.

"What Loveen?" he whispered tearfully.

"Mikey, will you bring me to the apple tree tomorrow?" she asked, barely audible.

"I will of course. We'll get lovely juicy apples, won't we?" he replied.

"Can I bring Snowy and Sooty?" she asked, her voice failing even further.

"Of course Loveen, we'll get apples for them too".

"Mikey, will you bring me to the apple tree?" she said with her eyes closed.

"I will" he said, as the sobbing in the room grew louder

"Mikey, Mikey..." she continued, her eyes still closed and her head swaying.

"Don't leave me Kathleen" shouted Victoria, kneeling in closer to the bed and grabbing Kathleen's cheeks, "Don't leave me! Kathleen – don't leave me!"

"Mamma...mamma...oh mamma" panted the child. And then her lips stopped moving.

Kathleen's little head flopped downwards and her father behind her tried to prop it up, but it was now lifeless. Victoria threw herself on top of Kathleen with her arms clasped around her. The heads of the parents and their youngest born were now all touching each other. Michaeleen could see the limp little arm flop down from the side of the bed and the nurse managed to get herself to it and check the pulse. The Cooney children all cried openly at the sight of their parents clasped together on the bed with the baby of the family lying in between them, with just her left arm and some strands of blonde hair visible.

The kind-faced nurse broke down crying and Michaeleen and Brendan grabbed each other and then turned to hug and kiss their younger brothers and sisters. The sound of their mournful wailing filled the room, and the neighbours and relatives outside prayed their rosary even louder.

"She's gone, she's gone poor thing. She's a little angel now" said the nurse. Michaeleen made his way to the bed and tried to pull his mother off but she would not let go. He stared at the curly hair of his father who was cradling his dead daughter in his arms. The nurse helped Michaeleen to pull Victoria away and the rest of the siblings piled in to kiss and hug Kathleen. Only then did Michaeleen realise that the wooden doll he had given her in jail was gripped tightly in the right hand of the dead girl. As he let loose his grief he felt a tug from behind and turned to see it was Fr. Kinsella. He had just arrived, and his eyes were glazed too as he got his first glimpse of the lifeless girl.

No words can adequately describe the grief of the tight knit family as they tried to come to terms with the loss of their pride and joy. Even Sailor whined and the many mourners who visited the wake remarked on the sorrowful look of the animal, who just lay outside the house, with no sign of his usual playfulness.

The evening after her death, the little white coffin was carried all the way from Knockmoyleen to the church in Ballycroy Village, about three miles. Relatives and neighbours took turns, and for the final half mile to the church The Coon insisted that he and his three sons carry it. It was a tragic sight to see. Kathleen was buried the following day in a wet and miserable graveyard. With her in her tiny coffin were her favourite wooden doll and her two woollen puppets. The dinner lady who had made them cycled all the way from Castlebar to attend the burial of the little girl she had never got to meet, but about whom she had heard so much. John Peter and Willie Kerrigan, Sylvester McDonnell and Batty Bourke were a constant presence for their friend over the couple of days. A palpable air of loss hung over the parish of Ballycroy. It was so hard to understand why someone so young, vivacious, beautiful and innocent had been taken without reason.

In the following weeks The Coon took to the bottle and it wasn't long before he was lashing out at people – his neighbours, his relatives, his sons, his wife. He could be seen kneeling at the grave and wailing aloud. There were rumours that the Banshee was heard but it was probably her father, who could not come to terms with the loss of his treasured little daughter.

Michaeleen had considered giving up on his American dream but deep down he knew he had to go. When he got a whack in the jaw from his drunken father which floored him, that helped make up his mind. The Coon could not even remember the incident the next day. Mrs Victoria Cooney put on a brave face; she had to for the sake of the rest of the family, as it was obvious her husband had broken. She did not try to persuade Michaeleen to stay. She knew that he still had the ticket money, and that the experiences of his imprisonment and Kathleen's loss needed to be overcome. The lad needed to get away. Goodness knows, she would have sailed herself if she could have gotten away from it all.

A sympathy card and letter arrived from Roger who said he would meet Michaeleen in New York on July fourth. The white haired lad re-booked his trip. The Coon raged against this move but after an outburst he just headed to Carey's Bar again. Brendan Cooney knew he would have to fill the role of the head man in the house.

On April 5th Michaeleen again boarded a carriage but this time he was not coming back that evening. He was heading for America. His uncle over there had a job lined up for him in Cleveland. The four remaining 'Boys of Ballycroy' had shared a farewell drink with him the evening beforehand in Carey's. It was a sombre affair. Everyone knew the move was tearing poor Michaeleen apart.

The Cooney household was a desperately lonely place as Michaeleen bade farewell.
"Five years, mother", he said "I'll just give it five years and I'll be back".
Neither parent could bring themselves to say much. They were inconsolable. It was left to Brendan to spray some holy water on the departing son.

Michaeleen asked the carriage driver to stop at the graveyard and his lonesome cries could be heard at Carey's as he laid some spring flowers on his baby sister's grave. Michaeleen was heartbroken.

Twelve days later, Sylvester McDonnell was working in the space just in front of The Forge at Ballycroy Village, when two men on horseback rode up. He stopped his hammering and looked up, recognising one of them.

"Colm?" he asked tentatively.
"It is indeed. Colm Tierney!" was the reply. "How are you Sylvie?"
"I'm grand" was the reply "What brings you all the way here from Ballina?"
"Is Terence around?" was the question from the dismounting man
"Nah, he's gone to America three months now" said Sylvester, who was now joined by his father Fintan who had come outside.
"Ah no", said Colm, "I knew he was talking of going but I didn't think he would go that soon".

Sylvester introduced his father to Colm and the second man, who was his brother Ignatius Tierney. The elder McDonnell was chuffed to meet some of the 'Rebel Tierneys' and started talking about the exploits of their father and grandfather. The horsemen were treated to tea and currant bread inside.

Colm said that he had been hoping to get Terence involved in "some volunteering activity" as there was aggravation afoot, and he wanted a good contact in the Ballycroy area. Sylvester offered his services. Colm wasn't as enthusiastic, but said that he would be back again. He said that there was a lot of "mobilisation" in progress in Ulster and the rest of the country should begin preparing. He asked where the Kerrigan brothers could be contacted and was glad to hear that he could call in to see them in Bangor Erris Quarry on his way home. As he was getting back up on his horse, Colm broke news that was to send reverberations through the parish.

"Did ye hear about the Titanic?" he asked.
"The ship", said Fintan, "What about it?"
"It fecking went down last week, thousands dead. Struck a damned iceberg. Some of them Irish. Some of them Mayo I believe" replied Colm.
Sylvester felt faint. That was Michaeleen's ship.

As the Tierneys galloped off, the McDonnells wondered what to do, and decided to cycle to Knockmoyleen to check in on the Cooneys to see if they had heard anything. Victoria Cooney was hanging out her washing and seemed surprised to see them. Her husband was asleep inside with a hangover so she thought they were after an unpaid bill for their cart, but as they drew nearer she sensed something was wrong.

"What is it Mister McDonnell?" she said to Fintan nervously.
"Well...well...I'm not...I'm not sure", he stuttered, "There might be nothing in this but..." he could not finish his sentence and he looked away.
"What is it Sylvester, is it Michaeleen?" she asked in despair.
"Mrs Cooney, just calm down a moment. Can I ask you what ship was Michaeleen supposed to take. Was it the Titanic?" asked Sylvester, hoping the answer would be anything other than the affirmative.
"It was. Why?" she asked.
"Well, as my father said there may be nothing in this story, but a man who just came from Ballina told us that it has sunk" he said.
"Oh my God, oh my God, no, no, no – this can't be true" she said, panicking.
By now Fintan had gotten control of his breathing again and grabbed Victoria as she began to buckle in front of them.
"Victoria, there may be survivors, we don't know, but we will have to find out more about it. We need to find out more" said Fintan.
"Oh no, oh no, not again. Not again God!" she panted, now on her knees.
"Michaeleen!" she roared out as she threw her eyes to the heaven from her kneeling position, her basket of freshly washed children's clothes scattering out onto the muddy ground.
"Michaeleen, my Michaeleen, oh my Michaeleen!" she cried mournfully.

The commotion roused The Coon and the wailing increased as Mrs Cooney banged her hands against the chest of her sick looking husband.

"It can't be true, it can't be true! Those ships just don't sink!" she cried.

"She's right" said The Coon to the lads, by now pulling his crying wife into his chest.

"The Titanic would not go down. Who brought ye that news? It's madness!"

"We need to find out more", said Sylvester. "We need to get a newspaper".

"Indeed and you do!" roared The Coon, his face scarlet, "You should check out the facts before fecking cycling down here upsetting my wife. Do you not think she has been through enough all year, ha? Feck off the both of ye!"

Of course, the newspapers confirmed their worst fears, as news of the momentous sea-faring tragedy slowly spread. Less than three months after losing their youngest daughter, their eldest son was missing, presumed drowned. The sadness of the family plunged new depths. The agonising slow wait for news. Having no body was hell for them. In one of his rare sober moments, The Coon tried to make sense of it all with Fr. Kinsella.

"As bad as it was with young Kathleen, we held her in our arms and we let her go knowing that she was surrounded by her loved ones and all the comfort we could give her. We know where she lies, and we can visit her and talk to her. My poor boy died in the icy cold waters of the largest ocean. Unlike Kathleen, he knew he was going to die. We weren't there to hold his hand, to keep him warm. He must have had a sorrowful end. Father, I cannot stop thinking of how lonely and frightening it must have been for my poor boy".

Ballycroy was stunned by the loss of Michaeleen Cooney, their young hero, in a tragedy that captivated the world. His body was never recovered. The outpouring of sympathy for the twice-bereaved Cooney family was immense. Mass upon mass was said for him and a special memorial service was held in the cemetery at Kathleen's grave on his 22nd birthday. Batty, Sylvester, John Peter and Willie each did a reading. His white head, his love for Kathleen, his bravery, his tenacity, his liveliness and his devilment were all recalled. 1912 was a bleak year not only for the Cooneys, but for the entire parish.

An audience of over one thousand people were amazed by the bravery and calmness of young Brendan Cooney as he stepped forward to read a note their family had received in the post.

"Dear Mother, Father, Brendan, David, Nora, Sarah and Anthony. I am writing from Cork. We sail in a few hours. I love you all and will be thinking of you. You will all be proud of the headstone I will earn for Kathleen. She remains with all of us forever. I must go now – time is drawing near.
Michaeleen"

As the Cooneys and the entire community grieved, another message from beyond the grave arrived in August. A letter was delivered to the post office and Brendan was the reader again, but this time in front of his family only.

"To The Cooney Family in Ireland.

My sincerest condolences to you good people on your sad loss.

My daughter Catherine and I survived the tragedy of the Titanic thanks to your gentleman son. The boy we came to know as 'Whitey' ensured that we were given priority and he also arranged our inclusion in a lifeboat. That brave man even physically apprehended a so-called 'gentleman' who tried to take the place of Catherine.

When our blessed lifeboat was being lowered, he called out to us both that his proper name was Michael Cooney and that he came from Ballycroy in Ireland. He asked me to pass a message to his beloved family. I imprudently wasted precious moments by saying I would struggle to remember the name of his home town, but he shouted to think of his belly and cry! All with a smile.

Now that I have finally managed to ascertain his identity, and therefore your location, I have taken steps to ensure that your gallant son is accordingly remembered. Catherine and I have been in contact with the Irish authorities and you shall hear from them soon. We have allocated the authorities the sum of three thousand dollars and have commissioned a suitable memorial to dear Michael.

Please find enclosed an additional money order for three thousand dollars for your family. I have no doubt that had your son made it safely to his destination, that he would have posted a similar sum to you by now.

It is our intention to visit his memorial someday. Of course we would like to meet you in person then. We would like to thank you personally for your honourable son. We trust that you will understand however that it is not our will to sail again for the foreseeable future.

Catherine and I have spent hours making sure that our account of his message is correct so that it is relayed accurately to you. This is our effort – we trust it means something to you:

"Tell them I am happy, as I will be picking apples with Kathleen in the orchard".

Yours with eternal gratitude,

Mrs Thelma Monroe-Schwartz and Miss Catherine Schwartz,
Charlottesville,
River Street,
Annapolis,
Maryland, USA"

'The Mayoman' was permitted to print segments of the letter and the editor confirmed that he had never witnessed such an overwhelming response from the public. Michaeleen Cooney was now a hero in his own right.

Being a hero was of little consolation to the Cooney family. Nevertheless, they were all immensely proud as in early December 1912 a large crowd gathered again to honour the young

Ballycroy man. A bronze anchor standing over 6ft tall was unveiled just inside the gates of the cemetery. This of course, had been funded by the American survivors. The inscription beneath the anchor read:

"Michael Cooney Jnr, Born June 12th 1890 – Died April 12th 1912 aboard HMS Titanic. A worshipped son, brother, friend and hero. Forever remembered by everyone fortunate enough to have met him. May he Rest in Peace"

The dollars helped Victoria Cooney in some small way, although she had to use a lot of energy to ensure they were not all drank away in Carey's or the pubs of Mulranny and Bangor Erris. Kathleen received the marble headstone they wanted for her. Brendan was able to buy the best of modern machinery so that he and his brother could efficiently farm the land. The rest of the children had their university education funded.

On the rainy New Year's Eve it was the wish of every person in Ballycroy that the Cooneys would have a brighter 1913. But their wish did not last for long.

As daylight broke on the morning of 1/1/13, the rain-saturated corpse of The Coon was found huddled around the basement of the anchor memorial.

CHAPTER 12: THE WILD SPORTSMEN OF THE WEST

The four remaining 'Boys of Ballycroy' spent most of St. Patrick's Day 1913 together drinking in Carey's Bar. It was rare enough that they got to meet these days. They had outgrown The Carthouse and no doubt it had fallen into younger hands. Batty was very active with his Sinn Fein activities and spent much of his time cycling the sandy stony roads of North and West Mayo putting up posters and organising recruitment meetings. Sylvester was spending most of his time working in The Forge, save for the odd game of football for the parish team and the weeknight training sessions. John Peter and Willie Kerrigan were still gainfully employed at Bangor Erris Quarry, but like most men of their age they had an eye on the future. They were secretly smuggling out explosives for their quartermasters in Ballina, the Tierney brothers.

The Tierneys were insisting that Ballycroy lay in North Mayo, whereas Harry Heraty in Westport lay claim to the parish saying it sat in West Mayo. Both of these republican leaders were in the early stages of organising a volunteer movement to counter the Ulster Volunteer one up in the north of Ireland. The Ulster Volunteers were opposed to what looked like the imminent granting of Home Rule to Ireland, and anyone with a keen eye on the political world knew that a conflict was afoot. Having the 'Boys of Ballycroy' in their team would be an asset and a great source of pride to the Tierneys or Heraty.

The four friends getting drunk in Carey's that day weren't aware how coveted they were, but they were aware that both in Europe and Ireland there was a real prospect of war, and the issue dominated their conversation.
"Would you fight for the English against the Kaiser?" asked Batty of Willie.
"If we got independence in return, of course I would" was the reply.
"But they are not guaranteeing independence, are they?" said Batty. "Redmond and Ireland could sacrifice thousands of men and at the end of the war we would still be without a parliament".

"What about you, Batty?" asked John Peter, "If Willie joined the English would you fight with the Germans against him?"

"I'd probably stay here and prepare to strike them while they are occupied on foreign fields" said Batty seriously, but his friends laughed.

"If there was a written commitment that we would get our own parliament as a reward for helping the king, I'd consider it", added Batty, "But if that's not forthcoming then I'm not lifting a finger to help them".

"Conscription would leave us with no choice" joined Sylvester, "They are supposed to be drafting the laws in Westminster as we speak".

"If I fight it will be under an Irish flag" said John Peter, and the four of them toasted their country before talking about men who had been on their thoughts all day.

"You know, Roger was right", said Willie

"What do you mean?" asked Batty.

"He said that anytime Ireland is about to achieve anything from the British, the Irish split amongst themselves and end up achieving nothing".

"Divide and conquer" piped up John Peter, "It's a policy, not an accident".

"Well, just look at how the Ulster boys are now gearing up to scuttle the chance of an Irish parliament, there is another split as Roger had said", stated Willie.

"Roger read a lot of shite!" said Batty, "And spoke twice as much shite".

"Well sure he had all the time in the world to do it" said John Peter.

"You're right!" replied Batty. "Sure while we were quarrying and fishing and farming and footballing that fecker was lazing around like a pregnant duck reading books!" and they all laughed.

"Sure Terence often told me that while everyone else was slaving down at the whaling station Roger had his feet up in the office reading or composing!" said Sylvester.

"You'd miss him all the same" said Willie. "Ceili nights and raffle nights are not the same any more. No one can get the crowd worked up like Roger did with his jokes and stories".

"You're right I suppose" said Batty. "He was good at that lark alright".

"Strange he has not been in contact" said John Peter.

"I know" said Batty. "I was talking to Liam the other day and he just got a Christmas card with hardly anything on it. Not like him at all".

"He must be doing REAL work at last!" laughed John Peter and they all joined in.

"Who would have thought that Terence ended up writing more than Roger did?" said Sylvester, adding that the McDonnells had just that week received a letter from New York.

"How is he doing?" asked John Peter of Sylvester

"He says he's enjoying it, working on the docks, making a few dollars".

"Did he send any over?" asked Batty.

"How do you think I'm here?" replied Sylvester smiling, "Sure what we make in The Forge wouldn't keep me in porter!"

"Strange that they split up" said John Peter, "Did Terence ever tell you what happened?"

"Not really", said Sylvester, "All he said is that they parted ways and Roger headed for Pennsylvania and Terence stayed in New York".

"Well, he did say he would not stick Roger on the boat for three weeks" said Batty as he rose to buy more drinks.

"Brendan Cooney told me that Roger sent them a mass card from California – sure isn't that the other side from Pennsylvania altogether?" said Batty.

"He must be getting around" said Willie, "But wasn't it great that Terence was in New York to check the Titanic lists and get the papers sent over to the Cooneys?"

"He was a mighty help to the Cooneys alright" said John Peter before raising a toast to Terence.

The foursome was surrounded by plenty of merry makers that St. Patrick's Day and the craic was mighty. A drunken Mossy Cox made his way over to their table.

"Well how are the mighty 'Boys of Ballycroy'"? he spluttered, "They say that when ye cut onions, it's the onions that cry!" They all laughed and Mossy then started a bar of a song in their honour. Of course they knew it was ale he was looking for, and he had heard that some newly-arrived dollars were in the pub. Sylvester obliged with a drink for the match maker, and the four were rewarded with a joke, which brought more laughter from the five on what was a thoroughly enjoyable St. Patrick's Day – which helped to take their mind off of other things.

*****

Sport had been an important part of life in Ballycroy and indeed a book had been published some forty years previously by a Scottish writer named Maxwell who had stayed in the fishing lodges of the parish. His 'Wild Sports of the West' gave an account of his experiences as an outsider coming to Ballycroy, and he had provided an insight into the sporting and hunting activities of the time. He had also referred to some local myths and stories, one of which, 'The Legend of Knockathample' was often recited by Roger at gatherings. That story was of particular interest to Roger as it related to a medieval murder that had occurred in his village – now known as Bunmore.

By 1913, the sports were a little different to Maxwell's version and of course the GAA had become a central part of Irish life. As important as the Ballycroy football team was to local morale, the two most awaited events were the two annual sports days that took place in the parish. One was the first Sunday of June, and the second was the first Sunday of August. As ever with the Irish, two separate events had resulted from 'a split'.

Traditionally, the sports in June had always been held in what was known as 'The Master's Field' which was near St. Kieran's School, by the river at Shranamonragh. The event there always included running, weight-throwing, horse-racing etc, and Roy Carey had always set up a mobile shop to cater for the participants and spectators at the event.

However, one year he was annoyed when another shopkeeper from Erris was allowed to set up there, and he had since boycotted the event. Not only that, he established a second sports event that became known as 'Roy's Races'. In fairness to the man, he invested a lot of money in reclaiming and draining a field he owned that sat right across from the church at Ballycroy Village. It was an impressive park, and the proximity to his shop and pub always enticed the crowds on that first Sunday in August. He had also been innovative in inviting competitors from outside the parish to attend, and he always provided free transport for those attractions. However, what he did not have was a river, so the 'Master's Field Sports' also continued yearly with swimming as a popular event.

The first Sunday in June was sunny and there wasn't a cloud to be seen. The setting along the flowing Owenduff River was beautiful, and a steady stream of people began turning up at the entrance gate at 2pm, after having had their post-mass dinner. Excitement was building. But the nerveless Batty Bourke was calmly observing his potential rivals, as he aimed to retain his 'One Mile' title, the centrepiece event, which entailed running six laps of the large flat field. Batty was known far beyond the parish boundaries as an excellent runner, but his Sinn Fein duties had affected his training regime. For all of those attending, it was a foregone conclusion that Batty would win the 'One Mile' and the swimming sprint. In regard to John Peter Kerrigan, it was similarly inconceivable that someone would dispose him of his crowns in both the 'Half Hundredweight' and 'Tossing the Sheaf' events.

Youngsters and adults alike were awe-stricken when Batty easily won the swimming contest. John Peter was also impressive in throwing the half hundredweight block of iron furthest for his fifth year in a row. Some of the young maidens in the crowd shoved each other to gain the position of being closest to the striking looking Doona man when he took his throws. Bridie Kerrigan was so proud as he collected his 1913 trophy.

John Peter's next event involved using a pitchfork to lift and toss a heavy sheath of tightly-packed straw over a cross bar set at ten feet high. He had also been peerless in this event. However, not many had noticed the late entrance of the St. Kieran's new young schoolteacher Bosco Darby into the sports-field, and those who did sniggered as the wiry man put his name forward to toss the sheath. They were not laughing for long though, as the Leitrim man matched John Peter toss for toss. The gathered crowd were in shock! Darby looked a fit man, and although he was tall he was scrawny with thin arms and it seemed to defy logic that he could so easily toss the heavy bundle of straw over the bar that was taller than himself.

The judges had to start adding extra straw to the sheath in an effort to settle the contest for the trophy. John Peter did not seem perturbed, but he too was secretly amazed at the strength of the teacher, who he had assumed had returned to his native county for the school holidays. For the first time in years, the crowd saw John Peter sweating as he fought hard to hold onto his title. But hold onto it he did, as the teacher failed with his last attempt. John Peter graciously shook Darby's hand as the crowd applauded, and told his new rival to reconsider the type of footwear he wore as Darby had seemed to lose his footing slightly with his final effort. John Peter had a newfound respect for the man he had only spotted from a distance at mass. He would have to practice more for 'Roy's Races' in two month's time!

John Peter decided not to partake in the final event, the one mile. He knew there was no way he would beat Batty, and so he decided to sit and observe. Along with everyone else, he was surprised to see Bosco Darby strip for the race – even removing his socks and shoes to run barefoot! The school children of the parish were excited to see one of their teachers take part, and looked forward to slagging him after the holidays for being beaten by Batty.

Eight men lined up for the race, and when the starting flag was waved Batty sprinted into an early lead closely followed by Thady Finnegan from Innishbiggle and Sylvester McDonnell in third. An excited Toothy Lucey took notes for his newspaper report as the evening sun shone on the competitors and their gleeful crowd. Young Martha Bourke shouted encouragement to her brother Batty from her invalid-chair. At the halfway stage he looked comfortable, several strides ahead of the gamely islander Finnegan.

Then on the penultimate lap, Bosco Darby upped his pace and was on Batty's shoulder. Batty quickly glimpsed to try and see whose air was breathing down his back but then stepped up the pace and had a quick look at his watch. John Peter was sitting by the invalid-chair and commented to Martha that Batty was panting more than usual. Martha dismissed the observation as she could never remember seeing he brother lose, but as the bell rang for the final lap the crowd gasped as the wiry teacher from Manorhamilton sprinted to the front. Not only did he do that, but he shot further ahead and all of a sudden the mighty Batty was in trouble. He tried his best to immediately draw his man back but Darby seemed to lengthen his long stride and within seconds there was twenty yards between the men. The locals, even scholars of Darby who liked their young teacher, could not bring themselves to shout for him. The main reason was probably that they were in shock. Not only at the speed of the bare-footed leader, but at the sight of Batty struggling in his wake.

Other than Mr. Darby's fiancé shouting "Bosco, Bosco – come on Bosco!" there was almost complete silence as he crossed the winning line. He received an embrace and kiss from his girl, Peggy Maher from Mulranny, as young Thady Finnegan sprinted past a stunned Batty to take the runners-up prize, much to the delight of the islanders present. What an end to the day! There was a new order. The 'Boys of Ballycroy' were no longer going to have it all their own way!

To make up for the silence at his moment of victory, the sporting Ballycroy natives gave Mr. Darby the warmest applause of the day when he collected his winner's trophy. Both the pleasant-looking teacher and his bride to be were beaming widely, and he humbly bowed to the reception he received. Nobody had seen this coming. Other than some playing around with the children during lunch hour or at the annual school sports, he had given no indication of his athletic prowess. As a spirited and happy community of parishioners filed past the gate on their way home on the early summer's evening, Batty Bourke grabbed the hand of Bosco and congratulated him again on "a mighty, mighty run", and promised him a drink in Carey's. A great night was had by all. Everyone agreed that Roy's Races in two months time could not come quickly enough!

CHAPTER 13: REVENGE?

John Peter and Batty promised themselves that they would be stronger and fitter for the first Sunday in August. They had plenty of time to prepare. However, as with most plans, they ended up being distracted. The main source of this distraction was the increasing demands of the Tierneys and Harry Heraty. The former had Batty working 20 hours a day throughout all of North Mayo. It was good exercise, but he wasn't getting much sleep! Of course by now he was no longer working at the parochial house in Enniscrone, although he did visit his uncle there whenever he was within a few miles. On the other hand, Harry Heraty had identified Sheeaun Lodge as an ideal training location for his volunteers, and he had roped Sylvester into doing some of the groundwork there.

The owner of Sheeaun Lodge was Admiral Gay from London, retired from the British navy. Approaching his seventies, the old man had mellowed in later years and spending so much time fishing and getting to know the locals, he had educated himself of the history of this enclave of western Ireland which was now his home. He had become sympathetic to the Irish cause, and had concluded that the cruel colonialism that had been imposed on the peasant Irish had been too heavy handed. He loved the Irish love of the land and love of sport. He loved the humour. He loved the fighting spirit of the Ballycroy people. Although he always considered himself British and a loyal subject of the empire, he advocated fair-play. He always thought both Ireland and Britain could co-exist peacefully and rely on each other in times of trouble. He had become particularly close to the McDonnell family. Mrs Claire McDonnell had worked for years as his cook and housekeeper at the lodge, and Fintan had always ensured that Admiral Gay was always given priority whenever there was some ironmongery or blacksmith work required for the many gentry who visited Sheeaun Lodge.

Sylvester McDonnell was now capitalising on the good will of Admiral Gay, and had assured him that any Irish Volunteer training was for defence purposes only. After all, it was the Ulster Volunteers who had set up such a movement first. And he knew

Admiral Gay was no lover of Ulstermen. And there lied an irony. It was during the plantation of Ulster over 200 years earlier that dozens of catholic families from there were thrown off their lands and sent to Connaught. Many of them to Mayo. Plenty of them to Ballycroy! About 70% of the Ballycroy population were descended from the poor people who had been banished from their rightful lands. That was why so many northern names were still to be found in the parish – the McDonnells, the Cooneys, the McRorys, the O'Neills, the McMahons, the Coxes, the Deeneys, the McGanns, the McArthurs and the Glennons.

But there was only one surname troubling John Peter and Batty as first Sunday in July arrived, and that was Darby. Bosco Darby! He was back from Leitrim and Roy Carey had the excitement at fever pitch with his posters for the big event. "Will Bosco Better Batty? Will Ballycroy hold the Achill men?" This referred to the Achill Tug-o-War team who were being brought by Carey to the event for the first time. This all conquering collection of fishermen had won county and provincial titles, were undefeated, and were down on Carey's poster as the main attraction of the day, in the final event. However, in the minds of most Ballycroy folk, the main event would be the 'one-mile' race. They would gladly pay Roy Carey the one shilling entry fee for that!

The first Sunday in August was also a sunny day and a large crowd gathered in anticipation. Batty and John Peter received great welcomes as they arrived, as did the perennially late Bosco Darby and his wife-to-be. This time they had friends and relations from Manorhamilton and Mulrasny in tow. Roy Carey's fine sports-field had been freshly cut and the smell of the nearby drying hay filled the senses. There was plenty of music, dancing and children's games in progress as the proud businessman tried to show that his event was the best sports event of the year. The only thing that threatened to spoil the day was the plentiful wasps buzzing around. His daughters Rebecca and Rosa were present to manage the drink and food stalls. Royston and his wife Antoinette had their baby twins proudly on display.

John Peter easily won the throwing of the half-hundredweight and curiously Darby did not enter. But when the two carriages carrying the Achill Tug-o-War team later arrived John Peter counted his blessings as each of the eight men in their red outfits looked like they could have easily beaten him! Roy Carey proudly announced the arrival of the Achill men who received a generous round of applause for their exploits. They were accompanied by about a dozen supporters from Achill, all wearing red. Considering the sometimes fractious nature of the history between both parishes, it was safer to travel in numbers!

The Achill contingent watched as the sheaf tossing competition began. They were under instructions from their coach not to partake. This was the same coach who had previously tried to recruit John Peter onto his Tug-o-War team. Before long it was down to the final two, as expected, John Peter and Bosco Darby. They had the undivided attention of the crowd as the final throw-off began, under instructions from the judge – who else but Roy Carey! His instructions were simple. The weight of the sheaf would remain the same, and the height of the bar would remain the same. The first man to fail would be the runner-up.

John Peter won the toss to go first and each of his four efforts was matched by the wiry teacher. Even the Achill visitors were stunned at Darby's capacity to toss what seemed to be twice his body weight. However, it was clear to all that John Peter seemed to be tossing it effortlessly, whereas Bosco seemed to be fading gradually. When John Peter went to toss his up over the bar for a fifth time, an almighty crack could be heard and his pitchfork broke with the weight and snapped in two, the sheath falling dangerously onto his shoulder from where he had hoisted it above his head. The weight of the sheaf knocked him. As he rose off the ground he asked his brother Willie for a replacement pitchfork. However, there was annoyance when to everyone's surprise; Roy Carey blew his whistle to announce the competition was over, and that the winner was Bosco Darby!

"What do you mean?!" shouted Willie Kerrigan.
"We had agreed – the first to fail is runner-up, and John Peter just failed!" said the red-faced judge.

Mayhem broke out and even Bosco Darby said that John Peter deserved another go, but the stubborn Roy Carey was having none of it. He was anxious to get the remaining events underway. "Rules are rules!" he stated amidst the abuse "The judge's decision is final and I'm the judge!"

By now even Roy Carey's esteemed guests from Achill were calling for fair play. John Peter refused to complain and quietly walked away to change into his gear for the Tug-o-War. Roy Carey was booed loudly and even Royston tried to talk his father out of his controversial decision. Shouts of "Shame, Roy" and "You've ruined the day" were not what the sponsor had been expecting, and he sternly announced the participants for the one mile race to prepare.

Of course, one of these participants was Bosco Darby and he won many admirers when he refused to accept the winner's trophy for tossing the sheaf. The Achill people joined the applause for his stance.

Bosco had another trophy on his mind and to the amazement of the crowd he easily won the race, leaving Batty well behind in second place. This time he gleefully accepted the trophy from a growling Roy Carey, and he had more support than he had at the Master's Field. Batty sportingly joined in the salute for the new one-mile king. Thady Finnegan, who had finished 3rd, silently wondered what he would have to do to defeat the bare-footed sensation.

Now, there was just one final event left and the eight Ballycroy men lined up to try their best against the might of the Achill champion pullers. Lining up in green jerseys for their parish were anchorman John Peter Kerrigan, Willie Kerrigan, Batty Bourke, Sylvester McDonnell, Bosco Darby, John Brophy, Royston Carey and Brendan Cooney. The Achill men could have complained that the referee, Roy Carey, was the father of one of the Ballycroy team but they were confident that the outcome would not be in doubt.

How wrong they were! In front of a frenzied crowd, nothing could separate the two teams and the Achill Islanders were clearly rattled by the strength and skill of their neighbours. There were three 'blow-outs' where a draw had to be called as neither side could pull the other past the target marker. With 'The Carey Cup' in view, neither team could claim it and three more 'blow-outs' were declared. Roy Carey called in both coaches and it was agreed that a drastic move would be made to decide the outcome. The two anchormen would pull each other and the winning one would take the cup! Step forward John Peter Kerrigan and the big balding square-shouldered Achill man known as 'Shark'.

The red evening sunset looked down on the crowd of enthralled spectators as both men tugged at the rope and neither showed any sign of giving in. Each man leant back on the rope and dug his heels in, but any few inches gained were lost whenever the other man drew breath. The Achill supporters gathered at one end to roar on 'Shark' whereas the vast majority were shouting for John Peter as he manfully pulled against the provincial champion captain at the other end.
"Excuse the pun" wrote Toothy Lucey in his notepad, "But this was gripping!"

Roy Carey could not separate the two men after three blow outs. This was an epic contest. Sweat poured down the massive Achill man as his daughter knelt in to speak to her giant of a father, now going purple in the face from his exertions against one of the 'Boys from Ballycroy'.
"Stop Daddy, you won't make the wedding" said the girl who looked in her early 20s. "Please stop. Please someone, get him to stop!" she shouted as Shark ignored her pleas, gazing at his opponent at the end of the rope as if he was a shark at the end of his line! At the opposite end, roars of "Come on John Peter" and "You have him! You have him!" roared out as his hands began to bleed. His every muscle ached and his mouth was dry as he continued his almighty effort.
"Kill the shark!" was shouted out by an excited Mossy Cox but he was hushed by the Ballycroy people as the Achill supporters glared up towards him.

The Achill lady continued her pleas to her father. She was desperate for the competition to end, as she could see what strain he was under. She genuinely feared that he would suffer a heart-attack.

All of a sudden, Shark fell backwards onto his backside with the rope still clutched between his blood-drained white fingers. At the other end, after about an hour of one-on-one pulling, John Peter had given up and let go of the rope. Everyone was in shock. There was silence. John Peter's footsteps could be heard by all as trudged to the other end of the rope towards the man he had just ceded defeat to.

The Achill crowd did not celebrate and the Ballycroy crowd did not shout in despair. Continuing to walk erectly, John Peter approached Shark and offered his hand to the purple faced man who was still on the ground, but unable to get up from it, panting heavily. John Peter knelt beside him and grabbed his shoulders. "Well done Shark!" he said, but Shark was not able to speak and just stared up at John Peter, his broad chest heaving heavily. "Thank you, thank you for letting go" said the Shark's daughter and the Achill and Ballycroy people joined to applaud both men. Despite being exerted, John Peter stood up and dragged Shark up into a standing position. The Achill man's knees buckled but he was supported by his daughter and several team mates as he struggled to regain his breathing and speech. John Peter acknowledged the applause and gave the cup to the grateful Achill girl.
"Here you go", he smiled "Maybe next year I can win it!"
"Thank you sir, thank you again!" she said almost breathlessly.
"I'm getting married in three weeks and I thought he would die on that rope. Thank you so much".
Her fiancé grabbed John Peter's hand.

"Thanks for saving my wedding" he said to John Peter "But I fear she will want to marry YOU now instead of me!" and everyone laughed.
Shark was coming around by now and he warmly embraced John Peter in a bear hug, towering over the Ballycroy man.
"You're some man!" panted Shark and again onlookers clapped as Bridie Kerrigan pulled her son away to see if he was alright.
"I'm fine Ma" he said.

"Why did you let go at the end?" asked Toothy Lucey.
"Well, I didn't want to be responsible for killing a man for a start" said John Peter after a pause.
"And if this is about being the better man, then it clearly is him" he added.
"What do you mean?" asked the journalist.
"Well Toothy, it's like this. He's fifty if he's day, and look at him. He's twice my age. Imagine what he must have been like at my age!"
Toothy struggled with this logic, as did a few others, but he was the only one being vocal.
"You're by far a better man than he is" said Toothy, "You would have won if you had held on a few more minutes. He was about to croak".
"Listen" said John Peter getting annoyed. Pointing towards the graveyard he said "There are plenty fine men there too, but they're not here to enjoy sport today. Today is about sport, not about who's the best man. Sport is to be enjoyed. And as soon as I stopped enjoying the pull, I let go".
Toothy was still bemused, and the normally quiet spoken John Peter could see that.
"Would you have preferred a priest to be here now giving a man his last rites, Toothy, would you?" asked the Doona man.

As everyone headed for Carey's Bar, John Peter and Batty had a quiet word.
"John Peter", said Batty, "I was beaten today but you weren't. My man deserves his trophy but your man doesn't".
John Peter did not reply and just smiled at his great friend.
"My God" said Batty, "Whatever side YOU are choosing in the war, that's the side I will be on for sure!" and they both laughed as they headed for a well earned pint.

CHAPTER 14: MORE REVENGE?

The following Tuesday the Kerrigan brothers cycled to work in Bangor Erris as usual. John Peter was still in some pain although he wasn't admitting it. It was not his cut hands or his aching muscles from the strenuous Tug-o-War effort that was causing this pain, but the sheaf had come down quite heavily on his shoulder after the pitchfork had snapped and it seemed to have caused more damage than he had realised.

Just before their morning tea break Willie was approached by the quarry 'go-for' from Bangor Erris, a young lad named Mark McGee. Mark idolised the Kerrigans and had cycled to Carey's Field to watch them in action.
"How is your brother?" he asked Willie.
"Fine" said a startled Willie. "Sure isn't he over there by the hut Mark?!"
"Not John Peter!" said Mark, "I mean your other brother, Josey".
"He's fine" said Willie even more startled, "Why do you ask?"
"Did you not hear he was beaten up last night?" asked Mark.
"What?!" replied Willie crossly.
"Yea, one of the lads told me that he was beaten in Carey's" said Mark.

By now Willie was quite agitated and he grabbed Mark's shoulders and demanded that he tell him all that he knew. Mark said that John Brophy had made a few comments in the pub about John Peter, saying that he had let the parish down against the Achill men and had cost him a few bob in bets. Apparently, Josey Kerrigan, almost a constant fixture in Carey's nowadays, had responded to Brophy and was punched to the floor. Brophy had then humiliated the eldest Kerrigan brother, taking off his own leather belt and lashing the cowering Josey in front of the Monday night regulars. Willie was furious. He simmered with rage.

"Whatever you say, Mark, keep this news from John Peter. Or else I'll have a murderer as a brother, do you hear?!" and Mark responded in the positive.

As usual that evening, as the Kerrigans cycled home, there was barely a word exchanged after a hard day's work. On this particular evening, Willie was fuming as he contemplated what to do about John Brophy. His cycling companion was anxious to get to bed to rest his shoulder, but his pain was being eased as he remembered how Rebecca Carey had pleasured him that Sunday night by the handball alley. If only Roy Carey had known what his daughter had been up to with the man he had deprived of a trophy!

At the Teacher's Cottage just up from St. Kieran's on the red skied August evening, Willie told John Peter that he was continuing straight on to Ballycroy Village instead of turning right with his brother to head home.
"Tell Ma to keep my dinner warm – I've just a bit of business to do with Sylvester".
"Alright so" said John Peter as he turned for the home strait.

On the way up to Ballycroy Village, a livid Willie was thinking about the Brophys. They had only come to the parish a couple of years earlier from the East Mayo area, having been bequeathed a small cottage and holding near Shranamonragh Lodge by an uncle of Brophy's. John Brophy had intermingled somewhat with the Ballycroy people but was not a likeable character. He had a constant grin and wide slanted eyes. He had a thick head of tight curly hair. He was stocky, but not massively tall, and he fancied himself as a strongman. He had made the final eight for the Tug-o-War team but his efforts in the weight-throwing competitions were nowhere near John Peter's standard. That galled Willie, the thought of that gobshite insulting a man whose boots he was not fit to lace. What really infuriated Willie as he pedalled like a demon was the thought of a poor Josey being lashed by the belt of the grinning blow-in. That almost brought tears to Willie's eyes. He thought more about Brophy, and the fact that he had a few children in their teens but neither they nor his wife were ever seen around the parish, even at mass.

"It's true," said Sylvester as the friends sat down in The Forge, "The fecker was supposed to have whipped Josey badly. Only for

Rebecca Carey coming from behind the bar and throwing herself down on the poor fella, it would have been a lot worse".

"I'll destroy him" said Willie, clenching his fists as he got up to leave.

"He's been in Carey's all day", said Sylvester.

"Not for much longer" said Willie storming out the door. "And he can count himself lucky that it's not John Peter coming for him!"

"Wait, I'll come with you!" said Sylvester locking the forge door. He ran to catch up with the fast pacing Willie.

"You stay behind" said Willie, "I have to do this by myself. I won't have it be said that I rounded up a gang to get him. He would love that".

"Alright. If you say so" said Sylvester. "Have you that knuckle duster I made you last year?"

"I have it always, but I won't use it" shouted back Willie as Sylvester wished his friend well:

"He's a stout stumpy fecker – be careful Willie".

Silence struck the bar as a fast-ventilating and serious-looking Willie entered.

"No trouble now Willie!" shouted Rosa Carey from behind the bar.

Willie took a few paces towards where John Brophy was supping his beer.

"Mister Brophy. I dare you to take your belt to ME!" he declared in front of an aghast group of drinkers. "Come outside and let's see if you have the guts to try on ME what you tried on my brother".

"Ah look at who it is!" said Brophy. "Willie has come to fight Josey's battle. Well, go on outside while I take off my belt. I'll make you squeal just as loud as your queer of a brother, you gobshite Kerrigan".

Willie took up his position on the cobblestones and the drinkers spilled out of the door. Brophy had his shirt off and the sound of Rosa Carey ringing the bell for help was symbolic as the fighters squared up to each other. Gripping the buckle, Brophy lashed his belt out at Willie who ducked. He tried his same trick again but Willie grabbed the belt and pulled it off Brophy, and then flung it to the ground.

"Come on now, you black bollix" he said to Brophy who like a bull responded and charged head first at Willie's stomach, knocking him to the ground as the shouts erupted from the onlookers, including a worried Sylvester. He need not have worried though, as Willie wasn't long rolling Brophy onto his back. Pinning Brophy's neck with his left hand, a kneeling Willie blasted several punches into his face with his right fist. Brophy groaned in agony. Willie stood up. But he wasn't finished. Far from it. He dipped his hand into his pocket and pulled out his knuckle duster. He quickly put it onto his right hand before jumping knees first onto the sprawled Brophy's stomach, causing his head and chest to reflex upwards. Willie promptly banged the black head back against the cobbles. This was much easier than he thought! Some 'strong man' Brophy was! Then after raising up his right hand into the air, the kneeling Willie brought it crashing down into the mouth of Brophy. Rosa Carey screamed as Brophy's smashed teeth went flying onto cobbles after being struck by the metal fist of Willie. Brophy let out a painful cry and the watching Mossy Cox gleefully shouted that "Brophy has shit himself, Brophy has shit himself" and sure enough his soiled pants were soon on display.

Willie rose and took the applause of the crowd, but he still wasn't finished. The sight of blood gushing from Brophy's mouth wasn't enough. He put his knuckle duster back into his pocket and grabbed Brophy's long leather belt from the cobbles. He again knelt as the mumbling Brophy tried to rise from the ground. Within a flash Willie was standing again but this time he had the belt around Brophy's neck, and he yanked it hard so that it looked like he was a dog-trainer yanking a young sheepdog on a leash. Brophy cried out again and so did Rosa Carey again, urging Willie to stop, as he had done enough.

Sylvester was astounded at the sight of Willie dragging Brophy along the cobbles with the belt. The man on the ground couldn't do anything, and began to sound as if he was choking.   Sylvester decided to intervene in case Willie broke his neck, and he pulled his friend away.

"That's enough, Willie, good man, leave him now, he's learned his lesson" said Sylvester.
Willie still had a grip of the belt, the other end of which was still wrapped around his victim's neck. He had one last yank and shouted to the half choked Brophy.
"You dare lay your finger on one of my family again and you'll get worse than this, you black bastard. And if you ever stray onto our paths again, you better step back out of the way, do you hear me?! Do you hear me?!"

Of course Brophy did not hear as he had lost consciousness and the Carey sisters splashed him with water to try and awaken him. They could not stick the stench from him though. And as a proud Willie Kerrigan cycled home for his dinner after getting his job completed, a warm feeling of satisfaction filled him. He had restored the family honour! A seething Royston Carey was left with the messy job of picking Brophy up from the gutter. Left behind though were his belt, several teeth, and his pride.

The following morning the Kerrigan brothers again cycled towards Bangor Erris. At this stage John Peter was totally ignorant of what had happened the previous two nights in Carey's Bar. His thoughts were still focused on the lovemaking of the Sunday night! As he approached Shranamonragh Bridge several yards ahead of his brother he got a nasty surprise. He had not seen the twine rope that had been tied from the east wall of the bridge to the west wall of the bridge by the hiding sons of John Brophy. His thoughts of Rebecca Carey went crashing to the ground as his head hit the solid. He was propelled from the bike by the twine trap and he yelled out in pain as his shoulder also hit the road. His brother also hit the twine which by now had broken and slackened, so he just threw his bike to one side and went to the aid of his fallen brother, kneeling beside the bleeding man.

Before they realised what was happening, the duo were being attacked by Bobby and Billy Brophy who rained blows down on the cyclists with their thick blackthorn sticks. Aged only 16 and 17 respectively, the brothers were out to avenge what had happened to their father the night before. Of course, Willie came to realise this pretty quickly but a stunned John Peter did know what the hell was happening. And it felt like hell, as blow after blow of the heavy stick came down on his head, shoulders and back as the vicious ambush continued. Eventually, John Peter was able to reach out and grab the boots of his assailant, tumbling him to the ground. Despite the agonising pain, he managed to jump on top of the Brophy son and proceeded to hit him an almighty left handed punch into the face.

As blood poured down from his head over his eyes, an almost blinded John Peter glanced across to see Willie beating the other Brophy brother on the other side of the bridge. He then re-focused on the grounded Bobby and kicked him several times. "What the fuck was that for?!" he roared in temper as he kicked out. Willie was surprised to see his brother using the foot, and he realised that by the way he was holding his arm that John Peter had damaged it in the bicycle fall. Willie put on his knuckle duster again and aimed it at the mouth of the lying Billy. For the second time in twelve hours, Brophy teeth were smashed by Willie's weapon. He proudly marched over to the crouched Bobby and repeated the trick, the youth almost choking as he swallowed several of his own teeth. But the on-form Willie was not finished. As the bloodied John Peter kneeled in the middle of the road trying to figure out what had happened, Willie went to either side of the bridge and after knocking one more roar out of each brother by stamping on an ankle and smashing it, he lifted each one and in turn tossed them over the wall into the river below!

"Take that ye little bastards!" he shouted, before attending to the injured John Peter. He then left John Peter's buckled bicycle behind the wall of the nearby school, with the intention of getting Sylvester to repair it later.

As he turned around to decide what to do next he was met by the sight of his jogging brother, soaked in blood, holding his right arm to his chest, but smiling!
"Where the hell are you going?!" Willie shouted.
"Where do you think?" replied John Peter running "I am not going to let those amadáns cost me an hour's wages".
"You're fecking mad in the fecking head – it's to hospital you should be going! They've damaged your head!" shouted Willie.

Willie cycled alongside his running brother as they headed for the quarry, and tried to convince his brother to go to the doctor as he was losing so much blood. But to no avail. Giving up, Willie then updated him on what had happened the previous nights, and enlightened the dazed but unfazed John Peter.

That night Sergeant Clive and Constable Scully visited the Kerrigan house. They were met by the sight of three wounded brothers and two worried looking parents. Everyone was now up to date on the events surrounding the Brophys. Josey Kerrigan still had marks on his face from his beating by John Brophy. Willie had a few facial cuts from the blackthorn blows. John Peter had his broken arm in a sling and had five separate sets of stitches on his head and face – Mark McGee having called the Bangor Erris doctor to the quarry's dinner hut to attend to his wounded hero.

"Have the cowards made a case against us?" asked Willie.
"No" said Clive. But we have three Brophys confined to bed with serious injuries, especially the father who is near paralysed".
"I suppose you would rather it was the Kerrigans who were near paralysed" asked Bridie in tears.
"I'm just here to warn you" said Clive. "You cannot just go around breaking bones and teeth like this".
The three brothers held their counsel but the normally quiet John Kerrigan Senior decided it was time to speak out and put the RIC men in their rightful place.
"Now listen here, you Royalists. No son of MINE goes around seeking trouble. But they have been taught to defend themselves from attack, and to defend our good name. Your enquiries will no doubt have yielded the truth, and the truth is that the Brophys attacked MY sons. Perhaps you ought to consider darkening THEIR doorway instead of mine, good sirs. Now, I would be obliged if you could leave us alone and walk".

'Walk' is not something that John, Bobby or Billy Brophy could do for some time. The father had injuries to his spine that caused him to look sideways for the rest of his days. The trio were a sad sight for Mrs Mary Brophy as she looked at each of them sitting around her table trying to eat pork while none of them had any front teeth left. By the end of 1913 the shamed family had sold up and were back somewhere in East Mayo again. The family had paid a heavy price for crossing the Kerrigans. The father had been extremely foolish. The sons had grossly underestimated the task of taking on the Kerrigan brothers, but in some quarters were admired for their youthful but naïve bravery.

Willie Kerrigan had just experienced his finest hour and he hoped that his parents would now show him the same attention and respect that they showed to what he perceived to be the 'favoured' John Peter. However, the legend surrounding John Peter grew as word spread to the corners of Mayo how he had overcome the ambush despite suffering a broken arm in the bicycle crash, with the other arm already injured from the sheaf, and how he ran eight miles to quarry rock afterwards! It was no wonder that republican leaders like Harry Heraty and Colm Tierney were fighting for his services. And it was no wonder that Rebecca Carey wanted to marry her handsome hero!

CHAPTER 15: HEADING FOR THE FRONT

The final days of December and the early days of January always seemed to bring a couple of funerals, and it was no exception as Ballycroy waved goodbye to 1913 and looked forward to what 1914 would bring. It was if people who had been ill in the months coming up to Christmas, somehow found the will to make it to the big day; and once St. Stephen's Day had passed they suddenly realised that the road ahead was too long and now not worth the effort. There was no Christmas to look forward to.

Penelope McDonnell, known to all as 'Nappie' was buried on January 1st in the freezing cold cemetery. Mother to Fintan McDonnell and to Bridie Kerrigan, she was of course a grandmother to four of the seven Boys of Ballycroy – Sylvester, Terence, John Peter and Willie. Terence was in New York unaware of her passing, but the other three were there and had struggled hard on New Year's Eve to dig a grave through the heavy frost.

Nappie was buried beside her husband who had passed away some 20 years previously. She had reached the age of eighty-eight. As a child, she had lived on salmon, seaweed and shellfish to survive the awful famine that had ravaged the country. In later life she had survived and worked hard to rear her children as her husband had spent time in jail for his Fenian activities. She enjoyed her final years in the care of her niece and she was proud of all her grandchildren. She had warned though, that as hard as times had been in the past, a great war was looming and she could see nothing but bloodshed and agony coming from it.

She was in the thoughts of Sylvester, John Peter and Willie as they signed their 'joining up' papers a few months after. They had little option. The Irish Home Rule Party under Redmond had convinced 90% of the recruited Irish Volunteers that they should join the National Volunteers along with their Ulster peers, and fight against the imperial enemy from Eastern Europe. Their loyalty would be rewarded once the war was won.

Many of course, such as Batty, were more reluctant to join but did so. Harry Heraty's campaign to halt Irishmen joining the forces to fight the German Kaiser failed miserably. The Tierneys from Ballina both signed up. John Peter tried to explain his reasons to his heartbroken mother Bridie.
"This is bigger than Ireland. We have a duty to defend all independent democratic nations. We cannot sit at home and mouth about the British and expect us to gain our own independence by sitting on our arses. This is a war that HAS to be fought".

Batty took a similar line with his mother, saying that "Now is the time for us Irishmen to stand up and show the rest of the world what we are about, that we can stand shoulder to shoulder with other nations and show them that we are every bit as good as they are, and not slaves to the British".

Admiral Gay did his bit for the empire by visiting the homes of the men and encouraging them to cast the Irish question aside for the time being, and fight for the greater good. He was driven to their homes in the first motor-car that Ballycroy had seen. An awesome sight. Of course, not to be outdone, Roy Carey soon followed with his own purchase.

It was Roy Carey's car that brought the Bourke family to Westport train station where the uniformed Private Bartholomew Pius Bourke posed proudly in his Irish Regiment uniform, just weeks after war had been declared. He kissed his mother and invalid-chair bound sister goodbye, and shook hands firmly with his father and brother. He received a final hug from Fr. Rea, who made a sign of the cross on his forehead with holy water on him as he boarded the carriage. As the train pulled off he waved from the window at his lonesome family. As they disappeared from view, Batty wondered if he would ever get to see them again. But he soon focused on the job at hand, and started studying the map of Europe that his father had given him as a going away present. From time to time as the train neared Dublin, he felt the holy scapula on his chest which his mother had given him. Batty felt good. He felt strong. He knew he was doing the right thing. He knew he would be a supreme soldier. His time to shine had come.

He would do his family and his parish proud. Ireland would be the better because of Batty Bourke.

A week later the Kerrigan brothers bade a sad goodbye to their parents and brother outside of their Doona home, as Roy Carey waited to bring the soldiers to the station. Both men cut fine figures in their Connaught Ranger uniforms. Bridie was inconsolable as John Peter whispered a goodbye into her ear and kissed her on the cheek. He also kissed his father on the cheek. Willie repeated the farewell gesture to his parents. All five were in tears, but John Peter was the most composed. It broke their parents' hearts to see John Peter and Willie leave the family home.

Fr. Kinsella waved down the car as it passed by the church and blessed the two soldiers. Admiral Gay was at Ballyveeney Bridge with their uncle Fintan to wave them off, and dozens more were dotted along the route to the railway station to say good bye to two of the 'Boys of Ballycroy'. There was no sign of Sylvester as he had come down with a fever.

An air of gloom descended on the parish. This bit hard. There had long been talk of war but now it was actually happening. Now the young boys they had watched growing up were heading for the very real danger of the war trenches. The cradle of the fields and the bogs was being left behind, to face the muck and blood of trench warfare.

But one returned sooner than expected! After one night in Dublin, Willie Kerrigan informed his brother that he was heading back to Ballycroy!
"You can't do it, Willie, you will be mocked!" pleaded John Peter but Willie had made his mind up.
"Did you see the state of Ma? And didn't you see the state of Josey? He's withered from the drink John Peter. He won't be able to look after them. I will."
"Please" begged John Peter, "Do NOT do this! You will be called a coward for the rest of your days".

"They can call me what they like. But they'll starve on the farm without one of us and I know you want to be a soldier" asserted Willie, "But I do not".

John Peter's pleading failed and Willie was home after two days! Although delighted to see him, Bridie was annoyed that John Peter was now 'alone'. As predicted, Willie's action caused much ridicule, especially when he had his first drink back in Carey's.
"Afraid of those nasty Germans, are you?" asked Pat the Thatch.
"No - he heard they won't accept knuckle dusters in the army" laughed Mossy Cox.
"The strings to Bridie's apron were just too strong!" roared Mickey Deeney.
"He was just stuck for clothes and wanted the free uniform!" piped up Royston from behind the bar.
"Why aren't YOU joining up, Carey?" asked a red-faced Willie of Royston.
"And who would feed ye beer and butter here?" came the reply.
"No" added Royston, "The wife wouldn't let me go as she needs sex every night and knows that I'm the only man good enough to give her what she wants!" he boasted to drunken applause and yahoos.
Pat the Thatch continued the theme:
"Sure now with most of the good men out of the way at war, there's a chance Willie will get himself an odd ride at last!" and the drinkers roared as Willie stormed off to his bicycle.
"Mammy's Boy!" shouted someone from inside the bar as a chastened Willie headed home again. Life would not be easy without his big brother around.

In Dun Laoghaire, John Peter prepared to board the huge army liner which would take him to France. He was still so annoyed with his brother. Hundreds of soldiers were gathered by the dockside, most of them with several of their friends or family in tow. Only one person was there with him. Rebecca Carey had taken the afternoon off from her teaching studies to see her sometimes lover off to war. She thought it might be romantic, but it wasn't.

"You look beautiful Rebecca" he said looking down. "You'll make some lucky man a beautiful bride someday".
"Maybe it will be you" she said with a suggestive smile.
"I wish it could Rebecca, but it won't. I know I won't be back" he said, looking out at Dublin Bay.
"Don't say that!" she replied, "You can't be going on like that".
"I know it!" he said, "And I can feel it. I shall NEVER see Ballycroy again. I shan't be returning".
Rebecca tried her best to keep strong for him, and she managed to prevent herself from crying. She gave him a long kiss as they wrapped their arms around each other for a final time.
"Think of the handball alley. Think of me in the handball alley John Peter" she said as he walked backwards away from her carrying his bag, looking splendid in his uniform.
"I shall!" he said smiling, and then he turned and faced the ship, mingling into the crowd by the quays, to board the giant ship.

It was a lonely journey for Rebecca back to her college, but she dwelled on the good time that they had together over the years. Wouldn't it have been much worse if he had left her with a flock of children to mind by herself? She tried not to love the man, but it was hard not to. She looked forward to the day he would arrive back victorious with his wonderful smile.

A month later, it was the turn of Sylvester to say goodbye to Ballycroy, and the well thought of man had many well wishers. Harry Heraty joined the McDonnell family and Admiral Gay at Westport station to wish him good luck, and he paid a personal tribute to Sylvester for all of the work he had done to arrange training for the volunteers in Sheeaun Lodge.
"You make sure you come back to me – I will have plenty of work for you after the war is over" said Harry.
"I will be back, don't worry!" asserted Sylvester. "Remember – we are the 'Boys from Ballycroy'!"
Sylvester reccived a gripping embrace from his father Fintan, who said that the forges would be a lonely place without him. He turned to tenderly kiss his mother and sister and tears flowed down his cheeks as he waved to them all from the train when it pulled slowly away from the station towards Dublin. He silently wished his brother Terence was with him, and wondered what he

was up to in America. He also wondered what had become of Roger, whom nobody had hard from in over a year, not even a Christmas card. Was he alive at all?

The outbreak of the war and its affects dominated life in Ballycroy in 1914. As poor as it was beforehand, the parish was even poorer now. At midnight mass on Christmas Eve, Fr. Kinsella prayed for the safe return of the young men of the parish who had gone to the battlefields. A drunken Mickey Deeney shouted out from the rear of the church "Sure hasn't Willie come home already father!" before being ordered to leave the church as a mixture of giggles and gasps ensued. As the congregation settled after the unwelcome intervention, a scarlet Willie Kerrigan sat by his mother and father in the middle of the church, furious and embarrassed. As Latin prayers were chanted all around him in the packed church, he wondered if he had made the biggest mistake of his life. How would he redeem himself from this?

That night, the people of Ballycroy wondered what was happening to the three 'Boys of Ballycroy' on the war front. Were they hurt? Were they afraid? Were they cold? Were they hungry? Were they thinking of home? Would they be back in the church for midnight mass the following year? Would they EVER get to return home again?

CHAPTER 16: THE WAR YEARS

Like any mother, Mrs Agnes Bourke hated her son being away at war. She prayed for Batty several times each day. She took great comfort from reading an article about 'The Angel of Mons' who was reputed to have appeared to assist the English in defeating the Germans at The Battle of Mons. Batty was stationed in that area. By January 1915 he had sent two letters home informing him that he was well, and giving some details of what he was doing. Mrs Bourke prayed to the Angel of Mons to ask that her son be brought home safely. And soon.

Mrs Bridie Kerrigan also prayed, for her beloved John Peter. He sent home two letters from his base at Ypres. Like Batty, he too was actually fighting in the small country of Belgium. He assured his mother that he was in good company. He confessed to having had a lonely Christmas Day, his first away from home. He enquired after everyone. Besides his family, the thing he missed most about Ballycroy was the smell of burning turf!

In January, Mrs Claire McDonnell received a late Christmas card from Sylvester. He reported that he had not been close to the fighting as of yet as once his blacksmith skills were discovered, he had been assigned to the stables to help look after the thousands of horses used by the British cavalry. He was delighted at this. He asked about everybody and if any word had come from Terence in America. He reckoned the war would be over within months and that everyone would be home safely by Christmas.

It was an agonising time for the mothers. They did not know whether to welcome or dread the sight of Toothy Lucey approaching with his postbag. They knew he could be the bearer of a welcome letter or the bearer of the worst news possible. They tried to remain focused by getting on with their daily lives as usual. Indeed, all of the women of Ballycroy had a crucial role to play during the war, as they did any other time. They worked hard to save the turf, to plant the spuds, to save the hay, to pick the spuds, to harvest the oats, to gut the fish and to feed the livestock. They knitted clothes to dress their children. They fed their children. They helped educate their children. They fed their men and did the farmwork when the men went to the fairs. When their men went to the pubs, they minded the house and put the children to bed. When their men drank and gambled they tried to stash away enough money to ensure the family did not go hungry or barefoot. When the children needed a story it was usually the mothers who read, often whilst darning or knitting. When prayers were to be said, the women usually led the way and were not afraid to pray loudly for the safe return of Irish sons from the fields of France, Belgium and Holland.

All throughout the war years there were rations in place on food and clothes. The people of Ballycroy were as resourceful as ever. Just as during the famine when the potato crop failed and they turned to fish, animals, mushrooms and berries for food, they had to produce new ways of survival. Bartering came back into fashion with farmers and fishermen exchanging goods. The same applied to the butcher and the baker. To the tanner and the cooper. To the carpenter and the blacksmith.

Donkeys became popular again as horses became too few and too expensive. Poitin became popular again as porter became too dear. Enterprising locals such as Maria Deeney and Annie O'Neill began a hair cutting service for the men and women who could no longer afford to travel to the larger towns and pay for a barber. Pat the Thatch reduced his normal charge so long as he was fed for the day in the house he was working upon. Willie Kerrigan invested in a new scythe and was happy enough to receive a meal at whichever farm he was working at, as it eased the burden on his mother Bridie. The new wife of Liam O'Grady started growing flowers in Bunmore which were much more affordable that ones Roy Carey 'provided' for funerals, holy communions and weddings. Bottles were recycled. The poultry population exploded as eggs became a key part of the diet. Neighbours began to share bicycles. It was even known that some families opted to bury their dead without a coffin as they could not afford that outlay. Indeed there were rumours in many parts that a night time activity was the retrieval of coffins from graves. Word was, that anything buried within the past five years was considered fit enough to serve a second tenant!

Of course, while war raged on foreign fields there was plenty of trouble in Ireland as well. Most of it was confined to Dublin and other larger towns, but that would not continue forever. Existing on the periphery, not many political activists bothered with Ballycroy – especially now that the 'Boys of Ballycroy' were scattered.

On the 15th of May 1915, Toothy Lucey shivered as he approached Kerrigan's Doona house in the torrential rain. The dog jumped up on him as usual and pawed his oilskins but Toothy kept on aiming for the door, he was not in the form for petting the mutt today. He tried to keep a solemn face as Bridie answered his knock. He tried to reciprocate her worried smile but his sad bulging eyes sold him out. All he can remember is handing her the brown envelope which had the military seal. The rest of that hour of 15/5/15 is a haze to him.

Unfortunately, that date remained forever cruelly etched in to the heart of the Kerrigan family. It remained forever a black day for the good people of Ballycroy.

That was the date that after opening a letter with her trembling work-worn fingers, poor Bridie Kerrigan fell onto her knees in the kitchen with her heart broken. That was the date that she found out that her beautiful son John Peter was dead. That was the date that she learned that the person she carried in her womb for nine months and reared from a bouncing smiley baby boy into a fine handsome soldier lay lifeless under continental soil. As she banged the floor with her fist in agony she let out a mournful roar that brought her husband and two sons in from the shelter of their shed. Immediately they knew that bad news had been received, and the sight of the crouched crying postman confirmed that.

The four Kerrigans embraced each other on the floor of the kitchen that had seen thousands of days of a happy family of five. Each of them felt the physical pangs of pain of their loss. The tall dark man they all worshipped would never be coming in through that door. The dog would never see the Kerrigan who spoiled him most walk through the yard again. They would never again hear his deep voice. They would never see him marry. They would never see him bounce a child on his knee. They would never see him buy something nice for himself with his hard-earned money. They would have to prepare to live the rest of their lives with a huge hole. John Peter was never coming home.

Within minutes neighbours and friends were gathering but it was of no immediate comfort to Bridie Kerrigan. She prayed aloud to her mother for help but cursed God for taking John Peter from her. No one could suppress her wailing. Her husband sat in the stable and cried his heart out. Josey tackled a bottle of whiskey and hoped it would ease his pain. Willie stumbled from wall to wall in a daze. He had just about coped without his best friend and brother until then, but what had kept him going was the thought that they would someday be reunited. The thought that someday they would lounge about at The Carthouse again or drill into the rockface at the quarry. The thought that someday they would cycle the roads together again.

Willie also felt guilt. Guilt that he had abandoned his brother in Dublin. Guilt that he had not been beside him when he fell in the battlefield of Ypres. Guilt that he was not there to help ease his pain. This was the emptiest of days.

With no corpse to bury, the gate of Kerrigans farm became a shrine as the people of Ballycroy left wreaths, masscards and messages for the fallen soldier. Every person in the parish felt the loss of John Peter. Old men and old women, young boys and young girls all cried unashamedly. He had been a hero in life, and was now an immortal hero in death. They recalled his weight-throwing. They recalled his sheaf-tossing. They recalled his running. They recalled his Tug-o-War heroics. They recalled his court appearance. They recalled the men he had fought and beaten. Now German bullets or gas had ensured that these would all be memories. They ensured that they would never again get to enjoy seeing him raise a trophy over his head and smile. The words 'Germany' and 'German' replaced 'England' and 'English' as the most cursed words in Ballycroy.

Within days a heartbroken Rebecca Carey was in Doona with a gift for the lady who might have been her mother-in-law had a war not come along. It was an enlarged photograph of John Peter in his uniform taken by the waterfront in Dun Laoghaire an hour before he last touched Irish soil. In it he was smiling and he was proud. Bridie Kerrigan could not have been more thankful to Rebecca
"Doesn't he look so happy?" said Bridie.
"He does indeed" said Rebecca. "Happy because he was doing what he felt was right. He so wanted you all to be proud of him."
"How could you not be proud of that man" said his mother looking at his photo.
"You know, he told me that he would not be coming back. It's as if he knew his fate", said Rebecca.

A lot more things happened in Ballycroy in 1915, but the date of 15/5/15 cast a tall sinister shadow over them all. Christmas midnight mass of that year saw Fr. Kinsella read out messages from the front to the people of the parish from soldiers Batty Bourke and Sylvester McDonnell. The mourning Willie Kerrigan could not bring himself to attend the mass. The O'Grady family received a Christmas card and one hundred dollars from Roger. 'From Baltimore to Bunmore' was the message! Terence McDonnell wrote of his sadness at hearing about John Peter's passing and said he hoped to be back in Ballycroy for Christmas 1916.

By the end of 1915 two of the Boys of Ballycroy were dead.

But life went on. It had to.

CHAPTER 17: THE LONG WAIT

The year of 1916 became a watershed in Irish history because of the Easter Rising rebellion of that year, but at the time it was not such a seismic event. As virtually all of the fighting was confined to Dublin, the effects were not immediately felt in Mayo. When the captured rebels were being led through the street by the British soldiers, many of the residents of Dublin verbally abused them and fired rotten fruit at them. They were considered fools. Many of those who had sons away fighting in Flanders were disgusted by the actions of Pearse, Connolly and their comrades. It was only in later months and years that they became beatified.

The Sinn Fein leader for West Mayo, Harry Heraty, was more in tune with events and was preparing for a war with the British occupiers on Irish soil. Despite losing so many potential warriors to the world war, he scouted the best men he could. It was a sign of the times that Willie Kerrigan was chosen by Heraty to be his man in Ballycroy. Willie would have probably been his fifth choice if all of the 'Boys of Ballycroy' were still around.

Willie was though an enthusiastic and willing soldier. He welcomed the distraction. It was doing him no good to hang around Doona and see his brother Josey get drunk everyday and watch both of his parents cry. The tasks Heraty set him helped to take his thoughts off John Peter. It would help counter an accusation that he was a coward for deserting his brother in Dublin. He was set a target to acquire 20 guns by the end of 1916. He was to achieve this by either fund raising or robbing.

"You have three fishing lodges, lad" said Heraty. "No doubt each of those keeps several rifles for hunting. Gay in Sheeaun, Lyall in Logduff, Fitzwilton in Shranamonragh – they should be your targets. The barracks at Ballyveeney too. And do not tell me that the Careys have no weapon. Once you have a plan, lad, contact me and I'll get help for you. But get hold of a local lad too and break him in, you need a deputy".
"Yes Harry" said Willie.
"You don't call me Harry – you call me Captain Heraty –alright?!"
"Yes Captain Heraty"

"Good. Good lad. I will be back in December for the guns" and off went Heraty.

That March evening, Willie stopped at the graveyard and looked over the gate. He had heard that Thady Finnegan from the island, fast gaining a reputation as a talented stonemason and craftsman, had laid a tribute to John Peter across from where the anchor memorial was for Michaeleen Cooney. Thady's was a class piece of work. A beautiful polished flagstone, with the chiselled inscription of 'JPK 1890-1915 Freedom Fighter' on it. As he leant over the gate, Willie said to himself:
"Two of the lads dead, and neither of them buried here. That white cow was right. God knows what fate awaits me".

"There he goes, talking to himself, he's definitely gone mad!" interrupted a voice. Willie turned around. It was Royston Carey bringing his twin children for a walk.
"How are you Royston?" asked Willie
"I'm better than you are, I'd say!" he said. "Understandable. You've been through a lot Willie."
"Yes, but sure we have to try and move on, for the sake of these" he said looking at the boy and girl.
"And what is your name?" Willie asked bending down to the little girl.
"My name is Charlotte"
"And what age are you?"
"I'm four".
"Wow, you're a big girl now. And what is your brother's name?"
"His name is Louis. He is four too!"
"Really" laughed Willie, "But he's very shy, isn't he?"
"He is sometimes. Daddy said your brother is dead and that you are sad".
Willie looked up and smiled at a slightly embarrassed Royston.
"Your Daddy is right. But I will be happy again soon" replied Willie gently.
"Daddy said the bold men shot your brother. Will they shoot me too?" Charlotte asked innocently.
"Of course not. Your Daddy and I will look after you and Louis" smiled Willie.

"Come on now kids, we have leaves to collect" said Royston, and off they rambled towards Gortbrack.

Within a week the two men met at the graveyard again when Willie buried his father. John Kerrigan Senior had gone rapidly downhill since his son was killed and died within an hour of being stricken by a chest pain on a cold March evening. The Kerrigans admitted that it was almost a relief to see the man leave this world, as the life had gone out of him for ten months previously.

"Do you know, Fintan" said Bridie Kerrigan to her brother, "The only time I saw him smile since May was with his last breath. A look of peace and happiness came over him then. I know that John Peter was there to welcome his father. If only I could join them now".

Present at the graveyard was Agnes Bourke, who took Fintan McDonnell aside for a quick chat.
"Any word from Sylvester?" she asked.
"We got a letter yesterday. He's getting on alright. He said that he expects to be in the thick of the fighting soon though as the horses are no good out there. It's all machines now" was the reply.
"Not a word from our Bartholomew" she said, "Nothing since the Christmas. I'm so worried Fintan".
"Ah you will hear from him soon. There's bound to be delays" said Fintan trying to raise her mood.
"I don't know how that poor woman is standing" she said looking over at Bridie. "First her son and now her husband. I don't know how she does it".
"Neither do I" said Fintan, "But she is ageing rapidly. I'm afraid for her. And Josey needs to cop himself on and not be a burden to her".

By the end of May there was still no sign of a letter from Batty. The wait was excruciating for his poor mother. For all of lent she set herself a penance of wheeling her daughter Martha all the way to mass and back every day. For the four miles there and the four miles back the two of them prayed aloud. Hail, rain or shine they carried out their pilgrimage. Their hearts raced any time they spotted Toothy Lucey. It was as if their fate was in his hands.

For a week or so they had been passed on the road by what looked like a military vehicle. One of the days they noticed Sergeant Clive from the RIC on it. The truck was also noticed by her husband Patrick and her son Andrew as they worked on the bog saving the turf. It passed by their land several times, driving very slowly and purposefully. On another night, Andrew was sure that he heard someone moving about in their hayshed, but he couldn't find anything when he went to investigate.

Then one evening as Andrew was leaving the bog by himself the truck drew up beside him. Sergeant Clive got out of it and spoke.
"Good evening, Mister Bourke, do you mind if we have a word?" asked Clive.
"No bother. What is it about?" asked Andrew
"Would you mind if we talked in the house?" was the reply.
"I suppose not. Come on so. It must be serious" said Andrew.
"Hop on" said Clive, and he did.

At the house Patrick and Agnes got a shock to see Andrew lead three uniformed men into the kitchen. The dinner was ready and they had not been expecting visitors.
"God no, not Bartholomew!" cried Agnes. "Oh please God no...".
"Please Madam, calm down!" said Clive. "We need to speak...".
"Oh please God, please, please I beg you no!" she repeated.
"Sit down please!" said Clive sternly.
"God blast you, no one tells us what to do in OUR house!" shouted a worried Patrick.
"Please sir, we are trying to help!" interjected the tallest of the uniformed men, and he convinced the Bourkes to sit down on one side of the table. He sat alone on the other side, as the steam rose from the bowl of boiled potatoes, and the smell of salmon filled the room. Clive and the third man stayed standing. Agnes and Martha were weeping.

"I am Corporal Rock from the Army Liaison Office. My colleague here is Sergeant Kennedy. You will already know Sergeant Clive from the RIC. We are here with no definite news, but on a mission to trace your son".

"What do you mean, trace our son?!" asked Patrick, "Is he not with yer crowd?"

"He was. But as of now he is unaccounted for" said Rock and the two women grabbed a hold of one another.

"Unaccounted for?! What do you mean?" asked an incredulous Patrick.

"Unaccounted for. Exactly that!" said the stone faced corporal.

"My Bartholomew, my Bartholomew, what have you done with him?!" groaned Agnes as Andrew gasped speechless trying to absorb developments.

"This is this story so far" said Rock. "Private Bourke was one of a party of four despatched behind enemy lines on a mission into Germany".

"Despatched?! Please explain?" demanded Patrick over the sobbing of his wife and daughter.

"They landed on the German coast, Sir" said Rock. "Three months ago. By night. In a boat. None of the four have been seen since. Our intelligence is that they were captured. However, we have no proof of this. They do not appear on prisoner of war lists".

"So YOU are here to tell US that our son is probably DEAD?" asked Patrick.

"I can not categorically state that," replied Rock. "Nevertheless we must be realistic. Some of my officers suspect that all four were immediately executed. But again, we have no proof".

"Has anyone come back safely from behind enemy lines so far" asked Andrew, finally managing to find the wherewithal ask a question.

"To my knowledge, not in this war" was the response.

The Bourkes were in total shock. Sergeant Clive decided it was time for his synopsis:

"What Corporal Rock is saying is that there is a strong possibility that your son has been got by the Germans. He may still be alive but the chances are quite low. We had to check out if he deserted as this has happened on occasion, so you may have noticed our recent activity in case he was back here".

"We noticed ye alright! And now ye don't even know where yer soldiers are! WHAT kind of army are ye?" shouted Patrick getting up from the table.
"This is a merciless war, Sir" said Rock. "The Germans hold few prisoners. It is standard procedure to examine the possibility of desertion in such circumstances".
"My son would NEVER desert!" shouted Patrick.
"I regret not having positive news", said Rock rising from the table. "I would ask that you contact Sergeant Clive directly if you hear any word".
"We'll hardly hear from him if he's fucking dead" shouted Patrick, swearing for the first time his children could ever recall.
"I understand your frustration and anger" replied Rock, "But you will excuse me if I choose not to commiserate with you because I believe that hope still exists. As far as we are concerned, Private Bourke is categorised as 'missing in action'. Now, I bid you good evening".
"Good evening?! Good fucking evening?!" roared the normally mild mannered Patrick in disbelief. "You walk into my house at mealtime and tell my wife that her son is lost and you bid me good evening?! Get the hell out of my house, get out!!"
"I'm sorry Sir, I'm sorry Madam" said Rock heading for the door, with his companions immediately following.

The four Bourkes cried together. They were destroyed. Just over a year after the Kerrigans lost a son and brother, they had too. Poor Agnes was disconsolate. She could not accept that God would have allowed this. Martha could not speak. She clutched her rosary beads. She could not bare the thought of never seeing her beloved brother again. Andrew held his father and they wept together.

News soon spread and the Bourkes had to deal with an influx of visitors and sympathisers. Bridie Kerrigan was one of the first to arrive, and it was a heart-breaking sight to see the mothers embrace. Fr. Rea came in from Enniscrone to say a mass. He refused to believe that Batty was dead. From the altar he spoke words of hope and encouragement:
"The shepherd will not rest until he has found the last of his flock. I ask my beloved Agnes and Patrick to be like that shepherd. For

my part, I will be like Saint Thomas who refused to believe Jesus was resurrected until he saw the wounds on our Lord's hands. I refuse to believe Bartholomew is dead until I see HIS wounds. This mass is to pray for his soul, but NOT to pray for his departed soul, as I do NOT believe he has departed us".

Just as 1915 became known as the year of John Peter, 1916 became known as the year of Batty. Willie Kerrigan visited the graveyard again. He again remembered the curse of the white cow.
"Three down, four to go!"

CHAPTER 18: LAND OF OPPORTUNITY

Almost five years since he left Ballycroy, it seemed that Roger had put in his best effort to date at writing Christmas cards. The festive season of 1916 saw delicately decorated ornate cards arrive at the O'Grady and Carey households. Again one hundred dollars lay in the Bunmore card. A beautiful masscard was received by the Bourkes, accompanied by a heartfelt note about Batty. Whatever word had reached America, Roger had it that Batty was dead, and not just missing.

Terence McDonnell did not make it to Ballycroy as planned for that Christmas. His Christmas card indicated that he could not get leave from his job on the railway until summer. His brother Sylvester sent a brief message from his station in Amiens, France. He said that he had been promised leave and hoped to get back to Ireland for a week in June 1917.

The fourth surviving member of the 'Boys of Ballycroy', Willie Kerrigan, was keeping himself busy on his new project. He had recruited young Marty Finnegan from Innishbiggle to help him. Marty was a brother of the runner and stonemason Thady, but was not as lively. When Willie signalled that he was ready, Harry Heraty supplied extra help from Achill, Mulranny and Newport for what Willie termed 'Lodge Night' as a plan was set to relieve the three lodges of their armoury. Willie had already partaken in raids in Achill on the gentry there, so he was owed a favour or two.

At 11pm on a miserable wet April night, Admiral Gay, his wife and his three staff were surprised by the intruders. All five were tied up and eight hunting rifles were taken. No one was harmed. Willie did not enter the Sheeaun Lodge and instead acted as lookout. He could not run the risk of being identified. After all, the mother of Sylvester and Terence was one of those tied up! Although Gay was a republican sympathiser, Heraty was determined to get his hands on as many guns as he could.
The operation at Sheeaun Lodge could not have gone smoother.

As one of the Achill men left the parish with the arms, the raiding party travelled across the bog for three miles in the dark and lashing rain to strike Lyall Lodge in Logduff at 1am. They met some resistance there from one of the Lyall sons but he was overpowered and was forced to show the intruders where his weapons and ammunition lay. A shotgun and eight more rifles were taken, and a large stock of ammunition. Within 30 minutes two more of Heraty's men were leaving Ballycroy with the takings. This was going to make Willie look very good!

Shranamonragh Lodge at the mouth of the river was their next target and the remaining six men set out to follow the river to there. Upon reaching it, they sat for a while in the darkness under Shranamonragh Bridge to recover their breath and to go over the plan. It was a weird experience for Willie Kerrigan as he recalled the morning he threw the two Brophys into the water there as his bleeding brother lay nearby. He silently wished he had been in Ypres to help his bleeding brother there.

To finish the task at hand, Willie kept watch on the bridge side of the lodge whilst young Marty kept watch on its sea side. The rain had eased off, and as there were no lights coming from the lodge at that hour it was very dark. The four raiders who went inside caused a commotion and there was lots of shouting. The lights were turned on and they lit up the river directly in front. Willie could see the outline of Marty standing by the river about 50 yards away from him. As the noise died down inside Willie knew the men were getting down to serious business. Suddenly, from Marty's direction, he heard a plop into the water. Something had fallen in! He peered over but the light was dazzling him. He saw someone move and for an instant thought he saw a man with a stick. He shouted out for Marty but there was no reply. He heard some more noise in the water. He froze. He could not decide whether to leave his post or to check if Marty was in the water or if he should go into the lodge and alert the men inside. Before he knew it, his accomplices from inside were heading towards him telling him to run. He did as he was told. The party headed as planned for the Teacher's Cottage a half a mile on towards Carey's.

In the darkness, Willie tried to do a headcount. Marty was missing! Out of breath, he did a quick review with his men in the hedged field behind the Teacher's Cottage.
"What the hell happened?!" he asked.
"We got our guns, it's all fine!" said one of them.
"What about Marty, where is he?" asked Willie.
"What about Marty YOU!" was the reply. "He's YOUR man. Not OURS. YE were on post. YOU lost him, YOU find him. We have our guns for Heraty and so we're off!"

A bewildered and panicked Willie headed back to Shranamonragh Bridge. He did not know what to do. He decided to head back to the spot where Marty stood. He was shaking. He could hear voices from the lodge. He kept looking around in case the man with the stick came back. He wondered if he was imagining things. He went home but could not sleep that night. He wondered if the poor lad was drowned. Heraty would kill him. The islanders would kill him.

After a restless night of tossing and turning, Willie went to the kitchen at first light and got the shock of his life to see Marty standing at the window, grinning in! Willie raced outside.
"Where the feck were you – are you alright?!" he said grabbing the young lad.
"You fecking left me Willie, you fecking left me!" said Marty.
"What happened? Did someone hit you?" asked Willie.
"Well. Someone TRIED to hit me. I heard someone coming up on me so I tackled him and fecked him into the river".
"So that was YOU with the stick?" asked Willie.
"Yea, he had a stick. I took it off him!" was the reply.
"Who on earth was it?!" asked Willie anxiously
"I don't know! Probably one of the lodge crowd!" said Marty.
"Did he get out of the river?" asked Willie.
"How do I know? I ran! I ran in case there were more of them" said Marty. "And YOU ran too, you fecker. Some comrade YOU are!"

Willie was just glad to have Marty back, but that was their last assignment together. Marty headed for America as soon as Heraty came up with his fare. The morning after 'Lodge Night' word spread that Pat the Thatch had been found drowned in Aughness. Sergeant Clive said that it seemed that the unfortunate man had fallen against some rocks whilst poaching and had lost consciousness and drowned. No connection was made between the robberies and 'the accident'. It looked like poor Pat had mistaken Marty for a bailiff and had attacked him. His family had lost their main provider. The RIC were just glad to have one poacher less to deal with. Willie had a lucky break at last. He was now a major player for Harry Heraty.

Another major player to emerge in 1917 was an old friend of Willie's. As the McDonnell brothers didn't get their wish to return to the parish that summer, they kept in touch with their family by mail. The Claggan-based family were amazed to get two pieces of paper to accompany Terence's letter received in September. The first one was a cut-out from the New York Times of a recent theatrical event attended by figures from the acting and political world. At first glance it was difficult to recognise the large man that stood at the right of a photograph of four well dressed people. The caption read: "Pictured at the opening performance of King Lear at the Metropolitan Theatre are Congressman Oliver J. Bryant, Actress Mabel Goodwin, Actress Lydia Tomlinson and Producer Jean Pierre Roland". Only when closer scrutinised, could one make out that the man on the right was none other than…Roger!

Fintan McDonnell could not believe it! He put his spectacles on to check. The tall, stout man in the suit with brushed back hair and moustache smiling out at him from the page was the man from Bunmore! He could not believe it! The second piece of paper was a poster for a performance of 'The Great El Ginto' at the Winter Garden Theatre in New York; written, produced and directed by Jean Pierre Roland. This was amazing! It was the best laugh the McDonnells had in ages. Fintan could not wait to bring the envelope to Bunmore to show William and Liam O'Grady.

Terence's letter provided more details. He had actually gone to the Winter Garden Theatre and met up with the man who he had sailed to America with. They had a fantastic night together catching up. It was true. Roger was now heavily involved in the American theatre scene and was very successful. He was now also becoming successful in the production of movies. He already had two profitable movies to his name, 'The Curse on La Spezia' and 'Wrong Side of the Tracks'. According to Terence's letter, he had even heard of Jean Pierre Roland in passing but of course had not realised that it was NOT a Frenchman who had been talked about, but a Ballycroy man!

The O'Gradys got a great kick out of Fintan's visit. It was a strange feeling for William to see his son again and for Liam to see his brother again for the first time in five years – even though it was only on paper. Liam's young son was very excited to see the photograph of his uncle.

Of course, word of Roger's success spread like wildfire. After bad news from the war and the threat of conscription hanging over the population, this was a welcome good news story that boosted the morale of the parishioners. By all accounts, it was looking like one of their own was making a name for himself – even though it wasn't his own name!

The biggest winner of all was Toothy Lucey, who convinced his bosses at 'The Mayoman' newspaper that Roger's success story as Jean Pierre Roland warranted a trip to America for an interview! It was back over to Myles Long to look after the delivery of mail!

So, on Christmas Day 1917 Roger treated Toothy and Terence to a feast at his 'retreat' at Croton Falls in upstate New York. The journalist could not wait to report back. The parishioners were eager to find out all they could about this Jean Pierre Roland fella and how rich he actually was!

As two of the 'Boys of Ballycroy' shared tales and tears across the ocean, a third prepared another plan to cause havoc for the British authorities in Ireland. Inspired by news of the revolt by the peasants in Russia, a revolution was taking shape in Ireland. Willie Kerrigan was the spearhead in his parish.

A fourth 'Boy of Ballycroy' was on his way back to his native parish, with a painful but non-lethal piece of shrapnel in his leg. Sylvester McDonnell reached his Claggan home on New Years Eve. His delighted mother, father and sister welcomed their wounded hero home. It was bittersweet for Bridie Kerrigan and Agnes Bourke to see Claire McDonnell proudly parade her discharged soldier son outside of the church on New Years Day.

As 1918 commenced Sylvester McDonnell was happy that his part in France had come to an end. But through the smiles, through the shrapnel pain and through the shell shock bouts he suffered – he knew deep down that the war he had just left would live with him forever - and that it would not be his final war.

CHAPTER 19: TALES FROM ABROAD

The returned soldier Sylvester noticed a lot of change in the parish he had left some four years earlier – and it wasn't all for the best. He could sense the desperation in the air. The natives were restless. They wanted an end to their poverty. They could take no more suppression. The people were weak. They were hungry. They had hit rock-bottom. But there was a sense that they would take no more. That they would fight back. Hatred towards the British had escalated and those activists who spoke out against them found fervent support in their audiences.

A new generation was rising, a generation which was not afraid to ask questions and openly defy what they considered as foreign occupiers. Agents of the crown such as the police, the tax collectors and the judiciary were subjected to venomous abuse. There was a feeling that the sacrifices made by Ireland in the Great War were not being reciprocated and that the Irish people were not getting the rewards they were due. Sylvester noticed that the people looked thinner. They were paler. Their teeth looked more yellow. Their clothes were tattered. More people seemed to be barefoot than before the war. After the initial smiles of welcome for a man who had returned safely from an as yet unfinished war, people seemed very bitter and hurt.

The roads looked worse – even though there were more cars to be seen throughout the county. Houses looked dilapidated. He noticed that many of them were in bad need of re-thatching or re-tiling. Even the cows in the fields appeared thinner and all of the sheep seemed to have their wool hanging off them. Was this what he had fought for? Is this what young Ballycroy men had died for? It wasn't long before Sylvester too became bitter and was linking with his cousin Willie to offer his services to Harry Heraty.

But despite the depression, the returned hero did not have to pay for a drink as the regulars in Carey's Bar fought to show their gratitude to him. In return for their purchase, they were usually treated to a few stories about what it was actually like to fight in the war. Although he was no Roger when it came to telling stories, Sylvester nonetheless had his listeners spellbound as he told of the cries of dying soldiers, of the smell of the hospital camps, of the muck of the rat infested trenches, of the sickly stench of the mustard gas. He told of rotting corpses in no-man's land. Of men hugging and crying just before they climbed out of their trenches to face the German machine guns and certain death. He told of soldiers fighting over food. He told of deserters being shot at dawn. He also told of forests being reduced to stumps of dead wood and of the swamps that formed from the combination of incessant rain and bomb craters. He told of the magnificent monster-like metal artillery tanks.

Young boys began coming to Carey's Bar each evening as word spread of Sylvester's stories. Many of these were repeated for fresh ears. Royston Carey would stop serving drink so that he too could concentrate and listen to the unbelievable accounts from someone who had been actually there. They pictured the scene as Sylvester described the observation balloons that hovered high over the trenches. They gulped from their tumblers when he told his stories about French prostitutes. They were gripped by his descriptions of the German uniforms and pointed helmets. They loved his mimickery of the French, German, British and Australian accents.

Within months, Sylvester had become just a bit too used to his free drink. He was becoming reliant on it. The taste of the porter combined with the attention he received helped numb the pain from his shrapnel wound. It also helped him sleep. But that sleep was often interrupted by the hellish nightmares of death cries and gunfire sounds that sprung him from his pillow sweating and screaming.

The only rival in those months to Sylvester as a story-teller was Toothy Lucey. He also entertained the locals with his tales from his American expedition. The whole experience seemed to rejuvenate Toothy. His eyes seemed livelier. He was more confident. He was happier. It was as if he had been injected with hope for the future. It was clear that he had been inspired that a man from the small peripheral 'backward' town-land of Ballycroy could make it to the big-time in the best country in the world. Toothy's feel-good mood was infectious and his stories cheered up those who heard them – but unlike Sylvester he received little free drink!

Many's the day that people did not receive their post because Toothy got delayed in some house telling a story! It was understandable why people who had been through so much suffering would cling to stories of positivity and enjoy seeing their smiling animated postman and reporter tell his tales. He brought their homes to life when he told of Roger's luxurious apartment on Broadway. Of his mansion on Long Island. Of his lakeside retreat in upstate New York. Of the colour of the theatrical performances. Of the beautiful attire and jewellery of the audiences. Of the negro shoeshine boys. Of the wonders of electricity. Of the magical streets and avenues of the city. Of the tall buildings. Toothy hummed the music. He tried to sing the songs. He tried to imitate the accents.

He told of how well Roger was looking, and of the warm welcome he gave to him. He told of Roger's perfectly tailored clothes. Of his fabulous furniture. Of his expensive ornaments and trophies. Of his domestic staff. Of the fine food. Of the parties. Of his two magnificent cars. Of his many friends. Of the beautiful women who all seemed to love him. Of the standing ovation his play received. He laughed at the way Roger would switch from his Mayo accent to his French accent depending on who he was speaking to!

Of course the most attentive audience Toothy had was the O'Grady family in Bunmore. Old William O'Grady sat and smiled contently by the fireside as he heard of his son's lifestyle across the sea. Liam O'Grady was so proud to hear of how well his younger brother was doing, as his wife and son talked of hopefully being able to go over there someday.

Toothy had won many admirers for what he had written in 'The Mayoman' about the loss of two Ballycroy soldiers on foreign fields. Now, his readers were delighted to see a new side to him as he relayed his tales from America to them. They were intrigued by the success story. In one article, Toothy gave a detailed account of 'The Great El Ginto' play, which was clearly inspired by Roger's experiences in Ballycroy. The play was about a Spanish pirate washed up onto a strand in Scotland, and whose adventures in sword-fighting and damsel-rescuing make him a hero. It was so good to read of a success story. The people of Mayo needed hope, and a dose of it was being given by one of the 'Boys of Ballycroy'.

And another one of that band of seven men returned in October of 1918. There was great joy in Claggan as Fintan and Claire McDonnell welcomed back their second son Terence. Cheers rang out in Carey's Bar as Sylvester brought his brother back. The tide was turning. The sight of these two fine men was a boost to the downtrodden folk of Ballycroy. They had survived their adventures and were home. One was in his soldier's uniform and boots, and one was wearing fine clothes and shiny shoes. Terence looked healthy. He looked more handsome than before. This did not go un-noticed by his former girlfriend Antoinette as she helped her husband Royston behind the bar. It was the first time they had spotted each other since he was sent to jail eight years previously. They exchanged a brief smile.

Terence was looking as mischievous as usual to the locals but it was noticeable that he was more refined. He had definitely lost some of his wildness. He was much smoother. He was more purposeful in the way he spoke. His cursing had eased – for the time being anyway! Sylvester joked that it was now the Americans who were using swearwords as Terence had contaminated them!

Terence had tales to tell as well. He also told of Roger's opulent lifestyle. Of the beautiful women who Roger counted as friends. He spoke of his own work on the railroads and how he was in charge of a gang of thirty men. He told of challenges they faced and how they were overcome. Of the deaths in work accidents. Of the large sums money that could be earned. Of the many opportunities that existed in America. Of the effect of The Great War. But it was also clear that like his brother, he was in tune with what was happening in Ireland. He knew that something big was about to really start in the country's push for independence. He revered the men who had fought in The Easter Rising of 1916 and not only could he list every name of those executed, but where they came from and what they had been doing before that fateful weekend. Terence had a focus. He was home to help the fight. But for the moment, he would enjoy a few drinks with his long lost brother and cousin as they took a table to themselves.

"Three of the 'Boys of Ballycroy' dead and three of us here!" said Sylvester.
"Roger is the odd one out as usual" said Terence, "That chancer has it so good, he really has".
"Sounds that way", said Willie, "He must be dripping with dollars".
"Dripping with women more like it" said Terence. "You would NOT believe the outfits. The gowns. The hats. The shoes. The stockings! They flock around him like flies to shit pies. But he doesn't seem to take advantage".
"Any sign of him getting married to any of them?" asked Sylvester.
"It's hard to know. There's one alright that he seems particularly close to. You should hear him with his fucking French accent though, you would not fucking believe it. They fall to their knees when he gets going – women AND men!" laughed Terence.
"And what about you Terence?" asked Willie, "Did you have a chance to marry over there?"
"Every weekend!" was the reply and they all laughed.
"Will you tell us, how come you and Roger ended up going in separate directions?" asked Willie.
"If you had seen us in The Olympic then you would not have been surprised. He just seemed to change. It was like he was trying to make an impression with the higher classes and cast me off. I could not believe it. And of course we argued every night. Then, when we got over there, on the first day – the first fucking day – he said he was heading for Philadelphia. We had another row. He said something about having to do his fucking journey alone and all that shite – you know what's he's like. So I told him to fucking fuck off for himself and that I hoped I would never fucking see him again".
"I see", said Willie, "Sure it was probably for the best – for both of ye – in the end".

"Best for him anyway" said Terence. "Sure I wouldn't even get a look in as one of his staff now".
"Is he gone too good for the rest of us now so?" asked Sylvester.
"No, I have to say, in fairness to him, when you're alone with him he's the same as ever", said Terence, "And he's never shy in digging into the pocket. He wouldn't let us pay for a thing. But it's all a big act. He has to put on a fucking act all of the time. It's impressing them dunces all the time".
"I suppose he has to, that's his game now" said Willie.
"True", said Terence, adding "And in fairness the fat fucker is making lots of money and is always sending some home. He also told me he sends dollars to Harry Heraty".
"Really?" asked a surprised Willie.
"That's what he told me anyway. He even gave me a package for him and I got it dropped off in Newport. I hope he sent plenty of money as we will need it" said Terence.
"By the way," he continued, changing the subject, "What's the story with Antoinette and bollix behind the bar – any children at them?"
"Oh yeah, your old flame!" laughed Sylvester before Willie gave an update.
"Three. A boy and a girl twin. And a couple of month's back she had another boy".
"I tell you one thing", said Terence, "I am going to ride that one again, and plenty more when I get going. I am going to do more fucking tunnelling here than I ever did on those fucking railroads!" and they all laughed and called for another drink. Despite friends being absent, it was good to be together again.

As the three men drank, they did not notice a car pass by. Roy Carey's taxi was *en route* to the house of one of them – Kerrigans. It arrived in their yard just as darkness was falling and Bridie and Josey were finishing their dinner. The dog barked as two figures emerged from the car, one a tall male and one a petit female. Bridie Kerrigan had the door opened as she heard an English accent asking the driver to return in an hour. The two people came into view from the light from her tilly lamp as she heard the car pulling away.

"I bid you good evening" said a sweet female voice in an English accent.

"Er, good evening!" said Bridie, "Are you sure you have the right house. The Kerrigans?"

"I am sure of it, Madam" came the reply from the English woman as she reached the door and Bridie cast eyes on her pretty face. The young lady had beautiful but sad looking eyes, and a warm smile. The tall man who towered over her shoulder looked less pleased to be there. He was darker in complexion and looked younger than the lady, but crosser.

"I am sorry to intrude on you like this Mrs Kerrigan" she said to Bridie who was still curious as to who her visitors were.

"Josey we have visitors!" she shouted inside as she welcomed the two English people into her kitchen, and asked them to sit alongside them by the fire.

"We have only an hour, and shall be on our way then Mrs Kerrigan" said the lady, as Josey Kerrigan surveyed his petite pretty guest. Her companion glared at him with disapproval. The two sat on the chairs provided as Bridie encouraged them to move closer to the glowing fire.

"My name is Alice Huckerby and this is my step-brother Patrick Huckerby. We are from Surrey in England" she said gently as her uncomfortable hosts listened in anticipation. Patrick stared into the fire, glaring, his arms folded as if he wanted to be anywhere else other than there.

"Get up and get them tea!" said Bridie to her son.

"A good Irish name you have there" she said to her male guest who just shrugged.

"I am a nurse and I am here because I got to know your son Johnnie when I was stationed on the front" said Alice as Bridie gulped and Josey came to a standstill by the cups.

"Johnnie told me all about you and I feel as if I know you already Mrs Kerrigan" Alice continued.

"Please call me Bridie" said her hostess, trying to hold back the tears. "My God, John Peter has sent you here!"

"Johnnie and I got to know each other in 1915 near Ypres as he called nightly to visit his comrade Alan who had been badly wounded" said Alice to her captive listeners.

"He was so nice and so gentle and always spoke so fondly of you all. He promised that if we both survived the war he would come to Surrey and take me to Ballycroy to meet you all!" said the smiling nurse. Bridie's eyes filled with tears.
"My God" she said, "Only today I asked John Peter to send me a sign that he didn't die alone or in agony, and he has sent me you!"
"You pray for that EVERY day, Mam" said Josey as he prepared the tea. Patrick kept staring into the fire with his arms still folded.

"My 18 year old step-brother here gladly agreed to accompany me on this journey that I just HAD to make" said Alice, reaching out to touch the sobbing Bridie. "Johnnie loved you so much and I knew that he was heartbroken to leave you. As a man, he had to fight his fight though". The two women stood and hugged as the tears flowed. Josey handed a cup of tea to a bored-looking Patrick.

"We are staying in the tavern in Mulranny and shall be back tomorrow early in the day if that is alright with you Bridie" said Alice as she cradled her cup of tea with both hands.
"Please do come back" said Bridie, "I have so many things to ask you Alice. Please do. And you as well Patrick. You might get to see our scenery in the daylight. You might enjoy it better tomorrow after your long journey".
"I very much doubt it" was the curt reply and Alice apologised for her tired companion.

Roy Carey was back in an hour to collect the two and Bridie insisted on paying their fare back and for the following day's fare. That night, for the first time in over three years, she slept soundly and with a smile on her face. God had answered her agonising prayers. Her beloved John Peter had sent her down an angel.

CHAPTER 20: LOVE AND HATE

The following day, Harry Heraty came to McDonnell's forge in Ballycroy Village to meet Sylvester, Terence and Willie. He was delighted to have the brothers back and immediately got them working on two plans. The first was an attack on the RIC barracks at Ballyveeney. The second was a scheme to establish a training base at Sheeaun. He had visited Admiral Gay on his way and apologised for the arms seizure. He had also paid a large sum to the Englishman to help settle a few debts, and so peace was restored. In a move that shocked Willie, he thanked him for his work to date and appointed Sylvester as Ballycroy Commander for the Irish Republican Army. He said that his army experience was the reason behind this move.

After the meeting concluded a disappointed Willie cycled to his home in Doona. Terence cycled alongside him as Sylvester hopped on Heraty's Sinn Fein car and went in the opposite direction. Terence tried to console his cousin and said that it was understandable that Heraty made such a change. As they both drew nearer to Kerrigan's house, they were looking forward to getting a good look at this pretty little English woman that Bridie had mentioned.

Sure enough, both of them fell in love with Alice as soon as they laid eyes on her. Her step-brother was a bit friendlier this time, and even managed an odd smile. Bridie Kerrigan had a fine feed laid on for her Surrey guests. The day was clear and provided a wonderful view of the Atlantic coast and nearby Slievemore on Achill Island. The mood was more relaxed. Alice explained how she and John Peter had become friendly when she was treating the injured Private Alan Dunne from Louth. The Ballycroy man had visited his wounded colleague each night in the medical tent. Terence and Willie were not surprised to hear this! What a pleasant experience it must have been for John Peter to lay his eyes on her shapely figure and beautiful eyes each night after a day in the trenches. Terence whispered to Willie that John Peter must have been hoping that Dunne had a slow recovery!

Alice caught him whispering and gave him a cheeky looking smile. A proud Terence responded with a wink. Willie observed this and realised that he would never stand a chance with her or indeed any woman once Terence was around. There was no point in even dreaming – Terence was already getting the looks from her that Willie could only dream of. Terence studied her fine clothes as she continued her story.

"Then one awful night," she said to an enchanted Bridie, "Johnnie did not show up. Private Dunne was asking for him. We knew it had been a particularly brutal day on the front but Johnnie was such a strong soldier we could not contemplate him getting injured. Then the next night, no sign of him again. I described him to my colleagues but there was no sign of him. Private Dunne was distraught. After a third night I feared the worst".

Bridie was crying again. Alice kept looking at the large photograph on the wall of the uniformed John Peter.
"I must get a print of that. Would you help me to do that?" she asked.
"We can arrange that I'm sure", said Bridie. "Please. Go on. Tell us what happened next".
"Well", Alice continued, "After a week or so Private Dunne was able to get out and about on his crutches and he asked a few questions. Because of the amount of casualties, I was unable to get to check the other tents. Then Private Dunne found out that a corpse had been spotted submerged in a water-filled crater. A soldier who was crossing over on a nearby duckboard spotted it. The corpse was pulled - boots first - out of the hole by a crew of soldiers and it seemed as if it was there for some time. There were shrapnel wounds all down the back of his head, neck and back. The identification on him showed it was Johnnie. He must have been struck as he headed back to base at the rear of a group, and fallen into the crater from the duckboard. No one must have seen it happen, or perhaps those who did died as well. Private Dunne said that if his body had not been spotted that day it would have probably been submerged totally in a day or two".
"Sure what difference did it make?" said Willie, upset at hearing more details of his brother's demise. It felt as if Alice was opening up an old wound. "Sure wasn't he buried anyway?!"

"God forgive you William!" said Bridie crossly. "May God cleanse your soul! At least he was given a Christian burial, the poor boy".
"Private Dunne never made it home either" said Alice. He was very upset at losing Johnnie. On top of this, he could not cope with the pain from his injuries" and she pointed to the groin area. "He put a bullet through his own head days later".

Patrick Huckerby had heard his fill of the story and he rose from his chair.
"Any chance of getting some ale in this country?" he asked. Within minutes he was cycling to Carey's Bar alongside Terence, who had also had enough of the depressing tale. He could have watched Alice all night though, but thought it was best to leave the Kerrigan family alone with their visitor. He would bring Patrick for a couple of drinks and then back to Doona before it got too dark.

The stranger did not get a good reception in Carey's. He was taller than everyone there, and much darker in complexion. His fixed heavy eyebrows made him look cross and intimidating as he looked all around him. The locals knew they had a stranger in their midst, and were a bit uncomfortable. When they heard his accent as he spoke to Royston, the tension heightened. There were six locals drinking in the bar, and none of them were happy to hear the English tones. Myles Lucey, known as Myles Long, stepped forward. As tall as he was, Huckerby stood taller. Thirstily drinking back his ale.
"Mister Terence" said a drunken Myles. "Your brother may have fought for the English, but that should not extend to bringing them back home with him!" Everyone laughed except Terence and Huckerby.
"This gentleman is here as a guest and should be treated as such" said Terence. "He has manfully accompanied his step-sister here to visit my aunt. She is a nurse from England who was at the front with John Peter".

Terence's attempt to satisfy the natives did not appear to work. Jimmy Cox, son of Mossy Cox the match-maker, stepped forward to join Myles. Royston spoke from behind the bar:
"I want no trouble!"

"You will get none as long as the man is left to drink in peace!" said Terence, staring at the two men in front of him, as Huckerby continued drinking.
"And what if he doesn't?" asked Myles.
"Doesn't fucking what?!" replied Terence crossly.
"Doesn't fucking finish his drink in peace!" said Myles.
"Then you will have ME to deal with" piped up the Englishman, rolling up his sleeves. "Step aside Terry, I fight my OWN battles".

Terence put out his arm out to stop Huckerby approaching from behind him. Mossy and Jimmy started posturing for a fight. Then Royston came out from behind the bar and placed his body in between the two sets of men.
"Gentlemen, just drink yer beer and stop this messing!" he said. Both sets of men backed off. It looked like Royston had been the peacemaker, but the rush of adrenaline prompted him to have a dig at his love-rival Terence, now that the opportunity had arisen. As he moved back behind the counter he re-ignited the situation.

"We have the brother of a war hero here and one of the famed 'Boys of Ballycroy'" he said with his mischievous smile. "I suppose that gives him the right to bring his boyfriends in here seeing that he does not have a woman!" His comment received a laugh from Myles and his crew but not from Terence. It was Terence's time to smile mischievously now.
"You can have MY leftovers any day Royston" he stated to the barman. "You can have MY crumbs. But I bet you cannot make that wife of yours groan like I did!"

In a shot an enraged Royston had leapt over the bar and tried to jump on Terence, but Huckerby apprehended him and pushed him backwards. As he staggered backwards, Jimmy reached out to stop him from falling.
"Come on then, come on!" said Terence taunting Royston, "Let's see what a strong man Antoinette has got herself".
Royston lunged forward again but Huckerby again intervened and grabbed him before he managed to reach Terence.
"Get back!" said the Englishman, "We are taking our leave of this cesspit. The ale here is like piss, and now I can see why!"

Without warning, Myles Long rushed forward from behind Royston and aimed a right handed punch upward at Huckerby's face. The Englishman ducked his head and as Myles stumbled forward losing his balance, Huckerby dug a right-handed punch into his ribs. Myles let out a single roar in pain as the drinkers all heard the crack of his ribs. He collapsed in a heap at the feet of Terence. There wasn't another sound from him. Everyone looked down at him and the posturing stopped. All of a sudden Rosa Carey appeared and asked what had happened. She was surprised to see her shaken looking brother on the outside of the bar counter, pure pale. There was total silence.

Terence and Royston stared at each other. Gone were the hateful, sneering facial expressions. Now they both looked as white as ghosts. They both looked seriously concerned. Rosa came and kneeled down beside Myles Long.
"What have you done? Who did this?!" she shouted, checking his pulse. The silence continued.
"You have killed him!" she exclaimed.
"I couldn't have!" replied Huckerby. "It was just ONE punch".
"Ya have driven his rib into his heart, ya bastard" said Jimmy.
"Ya have killed him stone dead".
"Then he should have let me drink in peace!" said Huckerby looking unconcerned, and swallowing the rest of his beverage.
"Come on Terry, time to leave mate. Time to leave this hell-hole!"

Terence was still stunned. Huckerby grabbed him by the arm. Terence looked down at the motionless Myles and kneeling Rosa. He looked over at Royston, who was also in shock, as were the other drinkers. Royston finally managed to regain his voice.

"You will pay dearly for this McDonnell!" he said to Terence as he was dragged out the door towards the bicycles by Huckerby.
"I will make sure every man, woman and child in the parish knows that one of their heroes had a Ballycroy man killed by a fecking Brit. Here are my witnesses. They will be writing no more fecking songs about the great Terence!"

His words echoed in Terence's head as the men cycled furiously towards Kerrigans, in the dark. When they reached the house,

Terence called on Willie to come outside. Instinctively Alice asked what had happened to her step-brother. He appeared at the door and assured her he was alright, that the three of them just needed to have a chat about something. Terence pulled Willie towards the yard.

"What's wrong?" asked Willie.
"We need a safe house Willie" said a breathless Terence, "And quickly!"
"What the feck happened? asked the bewildered Willie.
"Young Patrick here has just killed Myles Long!" exclaimed Terence.
"Myles Long is his name – you are joking me Terry!" said an incredulous Huckerby.
"Jesus Christ" said Willie. "Myles fecking Long. How the hell..."
"We need to get away from here, we have only minutes, they'll fucking come to lynch him" shouted Terence.
"I'll get the bike" said Willie, "And we will head for Bangor".
"How far is that?" asked Huckerby.
"Ten miles" replied Terence.
"Ten bloody miles – you are joking me mate!" blurted Huckerby. The response was not what Terence wanted to hear and he rushed at the tall English youth and pushed him up against the exterior stable wall, pinning his shoulders with his outstretched arms.
"Listen here you Swine! Do not ever fucking 'mate' me again, do you hear?! We are putting our fucking lives on the line here and me just back one day. Now, you fucking listen to EVERYTHING I fucking say and do what you are fucking told! And no more fucking cheek from you, do you hear?!"
"I hear!" said a startled Huckerby.

On hearing the commotion outside the figure of Alice appeared at the Kerrigan door, looking out into the darkness as the sound of Willie's rattling bicycle chain came around the corner.
"Are you sure everything is alright?" she shouted, "Are you alright Patrick".
"I'm alright Alice!" he shouted back, "Don't worry about me".
"We are taking your step-brother for a spot of poaching!" said Terence, "I'm just breaking him in for the bailiffs". With that, Alice disappeared back inside, and the three men put on their

bicycle lights for their cycle to Bangor Erris. Terence prayed that they would not meet a vengeful lynch mob on the way there. They didn't.

By the time the RIC men came to Kerrigans an hour later looking for the murder suspect, the three men were at the house of Mark McGee along the bank of the river, two miles beyond Bangor Erris on the Crossmolina Road. Mark had worked with the Kerrigans since he was a young fellow and now was newly married in a new house just yards away from his parents. Willie asked Mark and his wife to take Huckerby in for the night. They were reluctant, but Mark was a good friend of Willie's and could see that he was desperate. Terence told Huckerby to stay indoors and keep out of sight, and that they would be back in a day or two when things calmed down. He threw a few dollars at the visibly pregnant Mrs McGee and said that he hoped that would be enough to take care of him. Then the two cousins set off on their bikes back to Ballycroy.

They decided to cycle all the way to the Ballyveeney Barracks and tell their side of the story. It was pointless to wait until they were tracked down. They would tell the RIC men that Huckerby had absconded. Alice was already at the barracks having been taken there by Clive and his officers. She was very upset. Terence took pleasure in comforting her and telling her the same story as he told Sergeant Clive.

"Long started a fight. We did not respond. Long then went for Patrick. Patrick struck him one blow in self defence. Long collapsed. We panicked and ran. Patrick panicked more and God knows where he is now!" was his story. As he spoke he surveyed the room, thinking to himself that it would be in flames within weeks!

The following day, Willie cycled to Bangor Erris alone. He was wary that the RIC might be following him. He was mad at Terence. Not just because he had landed him in this mess, but because he had seen Terence and Alice in a passionate embrace by Ballyveeney Bridge after the interrogation at the barracks. He muttered to himself:

"I do the right thing and I get demoted by Heraty, that fecker gets a man killed and ends up with a beauty. Some fecking luck I have!"

He was right. And his luck was about to get worse. As he approached Mark's house he was met by an angry gang of several men who ran towards him. Willie dismounted his bicycle and wondered what was going on. A large man was heading for him with a stick and within seconds Willie and his bicycle were flattened on the road. As he wiped blood from his mouth he tried to make out was happening and what was being said. The roars of 'Ballycroy Bastard' and 'rapist' were standing out. 'Brit lover' another shouted.

The dazed Willie managed to get to his feet and the crowd of men gathered around him moved to part, revealing a battered and bruised Mark, tearfully staring at Willie.

"Mark, what the hell happened?" asked Willie, nearing tears at the sight of his beaten friend.
"Where did you root up that evil bastard?!" asked Mark in tears.
"Huckerby, Huckerby – what did he do?" asked Willie as the verbal abuse from the crowd continued.
"WHAT did he do? WHAT did he do? You brought a killer to my house and ask WHAT did he do? How could you do this to me?! Willie, how could you do this to me?!" cried Mark.
"Oh no Mark, God no!" said Willie, "Please tell me what he did, please, I don't even know the man".
"But you knew he was a killer, didn't you?!" asked Mark.
"It was an accident" said Willie. "Myles Long was an accident!"
"Well, beating me up, robbing me and trying to mount my wife was NO accident!" cried Mark.
"And she might lose the baby!" shouted Mark's father, having to be restrained by a neighbour.
"You bastards! You bastards! Why didn't you just leave us alone" cried Mark.
"We were having a lovely night to ourselves and Winnie was knitting baby clothes when you brought that demon into our home. OUR home".

A sod of clay hit Willie on the face. He looked at his distraught friend and he fell to his knees, crying.
"On my brother's grave I SWEAR I did not know he was a criminal" he exclaimed.
"John Peter would never have done such a thing to me!" said Mark, as he walked towards his kneeling ex colleague.
"I know, I know!" sobbed Willie. "You poor man. Your poor wife. Your poor babba".

Mark reached down and rubbed Willie's head, now feeling sorry for his inconsolable friend. He knew Willie was genuine. But Mark's friends and neighbours uttered their dismay.
"Nothing good ever came out of that parish!" said one.
"They're only bogmen! And they have them down as heroes" said another.
"Quiet!" shouted Mark. "Go home. All of you. Leave us be!"
He pulled the crying Willie to his feet.
"I'm so sorry" sobbed the Ballycroy man, "Your poor wife".
"He tried to kill me" said Mark. "He fecking tried to kill me and he tried to rape Winnie. But it looks like she lost the child with the fright. She's bleeding a lot. The doctor is with her now".
"I'm so sorry Mark. I will never forgive myself" said Willie.
"Go home, good man" said a calming Mark. Willie picked up his bicycle and faced it towards Bangor Erris town.
"Do you know where the bastard is now?" asked Willie.
"I don't know where and I never want to see the demon again" replied Mark. "I hope he rots in hell".
"I'm sorry Mark" said Willie one last time as he headed off, tears streaming down his face. The tears continued to fall throughout all of his cycle back home.

That night Willie vented his frustration on Terence. His cousin was upset, but it didn't last long. He had other things on his mind. Within weeks he was back drinking in Carey's having faced down the taunts and punching a few of those who made them. He and his brother had taken Royston around the back of the public house and put a gun to his head. They warned him that another smart comment would see him lose his life. The frightened heir agreed to co-operate. He withdrew co-operation with the authorities into Myles Long's death. He now had to respect the

IRA Commander and his brothers. The alternative was a bullet. The remaining 'Boys of Ballycroy' were not to be messed with. Royston had received his official warning.

Just over three weeks later Royston served the men as they celebrated the announcement of the World War armistice. Three weeks later on he served them again as Terence announced his engagement to Miss Alice Huckerby. As he toasted his bride-to-be and announced a Christmas wedding, he winked at his former love Antoinette who was working in the bar. That night, as Alice settled into John Peter's bedroom in the Kerrigan house and admired her engagement ring as it glowed in the candle-light, Terence was up to his old tricks. And up on an old flame. As Alice blew out the candle and smiled in anticipation of a wonderful wedding and fabulous future in Ballycroy, her husband-to-be was making passionate love to Mrs Royston Carey in Dr Skelton's unoccupied dispensary.

The world can be cruel.

CHAPTER 21: ONE WAR ENDS, ANOTHER BEGINS

On Christmas Eve of 1918 there were only a handful of witnesses present as Fr. Kinsella performed the marriage ceremony for Terence and Alice. The bride was the only one of her family present. Fintan McDonnell hosted a small party in his house for the couple. By the end of the week Terence and Alice had moved into an old cottage in Claggan, just yards away from the McDonnell home and forge, which had once belonged to Fintan's late uncle. Terence, his brother Sylvester and his cousin Willie enjoyed that festive season, as Fintan had stocked up the alcohol. The fourth surviving member of the 'Boys of Ballycroy' sent a card and one hundred dollars to the newly weds from New York.

Mrs Claire McDonnell really celebrated this Christmas as at last she had her boys home. The Great War was now over, and many mothers across the world were in a similar position. Bridie Kerrigan and Agnes Bourke though had not even the graves of their sons to visit. Victoria Cooney made the lonely pilgrimage to the anchor memorial to pray for her beloved son who did not even live long enough to see the war.

In Ireland, despite the armistice in Europe, the people were expecting an outbreak. There was much annoyance at the way the British were dithering on the issue of Home Rule. The Ulster Loyalists who sought retention of the Union were hated by most people in the south. Inspired by their great results in the 1918 election, Sinn Fein and their military wing, the Irish republic Army, entered 1919 with a determination that that year would mark an overthrow of British rule in Ireland. In January an independent republic was declared and the Dáil parliament sat its first session in the Mansion House in Dublin. On that very day, what became known as the 'Irish War of Independence' started in Tipperary when two RIC Officers were shot dead by members of the IRA.

The Tierney brothers were back safely from the war but found that Heraty had taken over command of Ballycroy which was coming under his West Mayo area. The Tierneys had to be content with a border drawn between Bangor Erris and Ballycroy.

The McDonnell brothers were entrusted with running army drills in the fields by the riverside in Sheeaun, situated in the grounds of Admiral Gay's estate. Participants had two main ways of accessing the area. One was by walking through the mountains and bog for miles on end. And one was by sneaking past Ballyveeney Bridge in the darkness. The strategically placed barracks so close to the main entry point to the parish was a problem that had to be overcome.

The plan to burn it was activated on May Day of 1919. Heraty stuck to the method of getting outsiders to do the main damage in order to safeguard local activists from being recognised. He was present that night as he saw the trees at the rear and sides of the two-storey building catch fire and send black smoke spiralling into the salty sea air. The panic caused by the burning trees forced the five RIC Officers to evacuate. When they went to get water from the nearby Veeney River to fight the flames they were confronted by several hooded men with rifles, and forced to lie face down in the grass. As they lay, each of them had their hands tied behind their back and they were marched in a line to Ballyveeney Bridge a short distance away. There, they were ordered to sit on a riverbank beneath the bridge so that their tied hands remained visible to the gunmen. They were told they would all be shot if one tried to escape. As they sat on the riverbank, their feet dangled into the water flowing past. They were forced to sit and watch as the barracks blazed on the glorious May evening.

Speaking from beneath a scarf wrapped around his mouth, Harry Heraty told an upset Sergeant Clive that any retribution from the RIC would be met with death.
"You better not dare causing upset amongst these good people of Ballycroy" he said jabbing his pistol into Clive's temple. "These are only farmers and fishermen. They will do you no harm as long as you leave them be. But if you harm them in the name of the British Empire – which we are at war with – then Clive you will die!"

Tears rolled from the eyes of Sergeant Clive as he saw his home and workplace go up in flames. He knew he had not deserved this. He had always been respectful and fair, unlike many of his counterparts in other regions. Now was the realisation that a war was raging between the Irish and the British – and with anything remotely associated with the British. He recognised the limp of Sylvester McDonnell and the cocky walk of his brother. Disguises also failed to stop him recognising Willie Kerrigan who was one of those standing behind him with a rifle. People began to gather from around the parish to see the inferno. The arrival of onlookers had not been expected, and Heraty hastily ordered that the five captives be taken to a quieter place in through some forestry. There each RIC man was tethered to a tree and had a strip of a blanket tied around their mouths to stop them from shouting. The IRA men then ensured their getaway, knowing that the five would be discovered before long and released. As Harry Heraty had a last look at the flames he praised his Ballycroy Commander for a good night's work. The barracks was destroyed. All of the RIC records and files were destroyed. Not a single bullet had to be fired. No one was hurt. And he had ten new guns for his arsenal.

Word came from other areas of Ireland that anti-establishment violence was prevailing. Magistrates had been shot and barracks had been burned. Irish members of the RIC and their families were being boycotted and intimidated. Many resigned their pensionable jobs due to pressure. Many RIC men were being killed, especially in the Limerick and Tipperary areas where two phrases which were to remain forever associated with the war were first heard. The first one was the 'IRA Flying Columns'. This was a small band of well-drilled and lightly-armed volunteers who would ambush the enemy, particular military convoys. They were swift mobile units designed to demoralise the British with their guerrilla tactics. The second phrase was one that came to haunt the nation – 'The Black and Tans'. These were officially known as 'British Auxiliary Forces' who were dispatched from Britain to protect its resources and personnel. It was assigned in particular to protect army barracks from the type of attack that razed the Ballyveeney one to the ground.

The Black and Tans received their name partly due to the colour of their uniforms. The other reputed reason was that it was a term that some Munster greyhound trainers had applied to their animals there. It was also alleged that many of the thousands who joined were criminals who had been released from British jails. Many of them were also veterans of the Great War, and regarded Ireland as a minor problem that would soon be eradicated by the same brutality that ended Germany's march. They were also disillusioned at the state they found their country in upon returning. Many of them also believed that they had not received the treatment they deserved for winning the war. They came back to find their families hungry and their jobs gone. They resented the fact that their country was neglecting thousands of physically and psychologically damaged soldiers, making many of them homeless.

All of this was not a recipe for a noble outcome. The majority of those sent to Ireland were coming to enjoy themselves and let loose their frustrations on an old enemy. They were relieved to be getting well paid jobs. Many had found it difficult to settle back to civilian life, and this was an opportunity to fraternise with like-minded comrades again. A lot of them did not really know much about Irish history. They believed they did not need to. This was just another job.

It was November 1919 when they were first unleashed on Ballycroy. Their truck, known as a 'Crossley Tender', made its way down from their Newport Barracks along the pot-holed windy road from Mulranny. The rattling of the engine and the sound of their shouting could be heard for miles as a dozen Black and Tans made their way to Ballycroy Village. Residents along their route peered out from behind their net curtains, fearful that they would become targets for shooting practice. The lawless reputation of the supposed law-keepers went before them.

In the middle of the afternoon the Crossley Tender pulled up in front of Carey's Bar. The uniformed men came down from the back of the vehicle and surveyed the buildings on one side and the bog on the other. The sight of them in their berets and carrying bayonet rifles was frightening for all who witnessed them. They split up into groups of two in what was obviously a pre-arranged move. Royston nervously looked out from behind his bar. Within seconds of two of them entering the Post Office he could hear the female staff screaming there. Then he could hear his sister Rosa screaming as two more jumped across the counter of the shop and started helping themselves to the money and food there. The two who entered the bar brushed past Royston and helped themselves to whiskey as the locals ran towards the outside toilets at the rear.

The roaring of the boisterous Englishmen continued as they went on a rampage of smashing windows and doors of the businesses all the way up from Paul the Butcher's to McDonnell's forge. Fintan McDonnell hid behind the boundary wall of the adjoining graveyard as he heard them drag away some crow-bars and his best anvil. They laughed as they terrorised the village. As all of this was happening, the tall officer who had sat in the front of the vehicle with the driver stood on the cobblestones outside of Carey's Bar. When he was handed a bottle of whiskey by one of the two soldiers who had raided the pub, he took one swig from it and then aimed it at an upstairs window shattering it as the screams of the frightened Carey twins rang out. As a bloodied Royston Carey stumbled out of the door of his pub, the tall officer blew his whistle and within minutes his party had reconvened by the truck, and were loading it with goods they had taken. The anvil and the crow bars were joined by a side of bacon, some chairs, and a barrel of ale. Loaves of bread were tossed onto it too, as well as two bicycles that had been parked outside.

The man with the whistle blew it again and the Black and Tans jumped onto the back of the vehicle. The driver took his place at the wheel. Yet again he shrilled his whistle until there was total silence. He stood in the middle of the courtyard with his arms down by his side; and holding his whistle in his right hand and his pistol in his left hand. His English accent broke the silence as he spoke loudly as if addressing a large captive audience.

"Listen up you shower of peasants! And listen good! I am Corporal Gilberthorpe from the Royal Kentish Fusiliers. I am in charge of you now! I am the sheriff around these parts now! You do as I say. I dare any of you 'Boys of Ballycroy' or whatever the hell you are called to torch my new barracks. You just try it! And all of you fuckers will regret the fucking day you were all fucking spawned. You got your way with the RIC, but NOT with my boys. You are IN a fucking war now that you will NOT fucking win! We crushed the Huns and we will crush you too! We will be back again soon. Thank you for your food and wine!"

The Crossley Tender reversed and headed in the direction of Mulranny, the soldiers cheering and firing shots into the air as they drove away. The shaken villagers converged at the shop. They checked each other and were relieved that no-one other than Royston Carey had been hurt. But everyone was terrified. Even Fintan McDonnell. He could not decide whether he was disappointed or relieved that his sons had not been around.

Just two miles up the road Gilberthorpe and his men stopped to check out their new home. It was near completion. What was to become known as the Castlehill Barracks was a renovated large two storey building that stood beside the ruins of the protestant church. It had once been a rectory, then home to a reclusive novelist from the north who had left some years previously. It now belonged to the Black and Tans. It stood tall in an area of mostly flat bog.

Sylvester, Terence and Willie were raging to hear of the incident. They had all been at a meeting with Harry Heraty in Westport. But they decided to keep their gunpowder dry. As Roger used to say "revenge is a dish best served cold". The main thing was that no one was hurt.

The following night, after another torrid sexual encounter with Antoinette as her husband and twins were at a circus in Bangor Erris, Terence was updated on the terror that had resulted from the Black and Tans' maiden visit to the parish. Antoinette described the tall, thin athletic looking Sergeant with the broad shoulders and smile-less narrow face. She described his high cheekbones, crooked nose and ice-blue eyes. He was a cold looking creature. He had the look of death about him.

The following night Terence took his wife to see the circus in Bangor Erris for its final performance before moving on to another town. They enjoyed seeing elephants and lions for the first time, and appeared as if they were the happiest couple on earth. They laughed aloud at the antics of the clown. Little did they know that the clown was there on a mission. This was no ordinary clown.

This was a clown that was heading for Ballycroy.

CHAPTER 22: NOVEMBER 1919

On a wet and windy night in the first week of November Agnes Bourke and her daughter Martha sat on their chairs either side of their fireside in which a pile of turf burned brightly. The light from the fire helped them to see what they were both knitting. On the mantelpiece above them was a picture of Batty Bourke in his army uniform. Patrick Bourke lay asleep in the loft upstairs and Andrew was at a friend's house playing cards.

All of a sudden above the noise of the lashing rain and whistling wind outside of their Aughness South home, they heard a loud knock at their door. The noise woke Patrick, and he climbed down the ladder from the loft as his wife opened the door. Their initial fear was that something had happened to Andrew as they normally never had visitors that late at night.

Bridie was met by the sight of a tall, foreign looking man with a long oval–shaped face and gaunt features. It looked like he had black rings around his hooded eyes. As he stood at the door with the water streaming down his oilskin outfit he looked a ghastly figure.
"My God. What on earth are you doing out on a night like this?!" said Agnes, "You are famished. Will you come in?" and the man entered slowly without a word. Patrick and Martha looked on open-mouthed.
"May the Lord bless us and save us. Let me take your gear off" said Agnes helping him take off his dark green oilskin jacket as a pool of water formed on the floor beneath him. From the rays from the fireplace the Bourkes could see that he looked about 40 years old. He had the appearance of miserable soul who had never smiled in his life. He also looked under nourished! The stranger finally spoke from his standing position and refused Agnes's request to take a seat and warm himself up by the fire.

"My English is not excellent" he said in a foreign accent, almost German-like.
"I am here with a message. You must not reveal that I visit" he added slowly.
"You have our pledge on that mister", said Patrick nervously.

The tall stranger reached into the breast pocket of his black shirt, and took out a leather pouch which contained a folded piece of paper. As the three Bourkes looked on with baited breath, he slowly unfolded the paper and handed it to Patrick to read. The embarrassed man nodded and pointed in the direction of his wife. As he was illiterate she had to do the deed and so the mysterious sheet was handed to her.

She sat by the fireside so that she had enough light to see the words, and began reading it silently, her hands shaking. As Patrick and Martha looked on in anticipation, Agnes let out a groan and started crying loudly.
"Thank you God! Thank you God most high!" she exclaimed before her tearful eyes looked over at her husband and daughter and she added "I knew it, I knew it – Bartholomew is alive!"

Patrick and Martha looked at each other in disbelief and the old man staggered over to his wife and threw himself to his knees in front of her. Martha looked up at the stranger from her invalid-chair. She struggled to find words:
"Who...who are you? Where is my brother? Where is he...now? Where has he been?"
The stranger just stared straight ahead as if he had not heard her. Her parents sobbed together in an embrace by the fireside.
Martha wheeled over and got hold of the letter and read it. It was typed. It was brief. It read:

"September 1919. Does the moon still shine in the loft? Please welcome my good friend Ecclesiasticus and listen to what he has to say."

The two codes meant something to the three. When he was young, Batty had always been fascinated by a white piece of quartzite which formed part of the stone wall in the corner of the loft where he slept. His father had told the young boy that that rock had come from the moon. The last thing the child Batty used to do each night was say goodbye to the moon on the wall. Regarding 'Ecclesiasticus', as a youth Batty had struggled with the pronunciation of that name when he was once required to do a reading from the bible in front of his classmates. He spent an entire week practising how to say it properly and he almost drove his parents insane! Both of the lines were instant proof to his family that he was alive. No impostor could have known the significance of this coded information.

As a gale developed outside, Ecclesiasticus made one step forward towards the fire where the three family members were sharing their tears of joy. This one step forward was enough for them to halt and pay attention.
"You will know me as Ecclesiasticus. For you only – I tell you that I am from Hungary. Your son is safe near Munich. You will receive a second message from Monsignor Rea very soon. I now depart. Please remain silent".

As he reached to take back his jacket Agnes rushed up from her chair and went to hug him but he politely raised his arm to prevent this.
"Please sir, stay here in our home. You cannot go out in that storm" said Agnes.
"Please, listen to her!" said Patrick, "You are more than welcome to stay here. It's no weather to be out in".
"I must leave. I must rejoin my circus" he said purposefully, heading for the door. The rain blew in the door as he opened it, and almost blew the precious letter into the fire! As Agnes and Patrick made one last plea for him to stay and even let the storm pass, he turned and coldly repeated that they were not to mention to anyone that they had met him. Then he disappeared into the turbulent night.

The Bourkes were in ecstasy. Each of them was bursting with happiness. Batty was alive and well! It was joyous news for Andrew to receive upon his return. They were so eager to spread their good news but made a promise to each other that it would remain in the family. Agnes prayed in thanks to God. And to the Angel of Mons. Of course they had lots of questions to ask but no answers, and hoped that Fr. Rea would bring some more news.

The tall Co. Sligo-based priest with the wild hair turned up two days later and there was great delight as he shared news of Batty's survival. He sat down with the four Bourkes and filled them in on what he knew.

"This is just the most magnificent news ever! I told you all along he was alive!" said Fr. Rea. "Remember at the mass, I refused to say he was departed. I KNEW in my heart and soul that that boy would make it".

"Thank our Lord most high – it's a miracle!" said Agnes, "There is no other word for it".

"The story I have" said the priest, "Is that he was captured and that the Germans convinced him to defect. The others captured with him were all killed. It appears that he had a good grasp of the German language and they used him for translation and such. Even though they lost the war, they want to hold onto him for the next war".

"The next war?" said Andrew, "Sure this war was meant to end all wars!"

"You can be assured that the Germans will regroup" asserted Fr. Rea. "It may take five years or ten years or twenty years, but they will seek revenge. They always do. The Huns will be back. And Batty's knowledge of the British Army and his language skills will be assets. Would you believe it – he is already married to a German!"

"Married?!" said Bridie incredulously, "Married?! What do you mean he is married?! Was he not one of these Prisoners of War or whatever?"

"Maybe initially" said Fr. Rea, "But he actually ended up fighting AGAINST the British. As I said, he defected".

"So he was actually fighting against the IRISH?" asked Patrick in disbelief.

"I suppose you could say that" was the reply, "But he probably had a choice – fight for the Germans or die".

"How do you know all of this, Father?" asked a curious Martha.

"I just know" was the meek reply

"The Vatican?" asked Andrew.

"There and many other places" said Fr. Rea. "Sure these confessional boxes are mighty altogether!" he laughed trying to move away from being questioned too much.

Getting serious again, the priest reiterated that not a word of this should leave the house. It would endanger the life of Batty and the life of the spy from Hungary. It was better to continue acting as if Batty were lost, as the British would be hell-bent on eliminating any defector. He even chillingly told the Bourkes that THEY would be massacred by the Black and Tans if it became known that one of their family had perhaps operated a machine gun against their forces during the war. The five of them said a decade of the Rosary before Fr. Rea headed back towards Enniscrone. They had all been invigorated by this wondrous news. It was a hard ask to contain it to themselves as they wanted to share their joy, but they knew that this was too risky. This Christmas would be their happiest in years. Who knows, perhaps their lost son and brother would be home with them to celebrate the following Christmas. Perhaps even with his fraulein!

*****

One person who was not in line for as a happy a festive season as the previous one was Mrs Alice Huckerby-McDonnell. Her dream of an idyllic rural life in the west of Ireland was turning into a nightmare. A nosy neighbour had gleefully told her that Terence had been seen cavorting with one of the young O'Brien girls on the night of the barracks fire. This was only confirming what the Surrey girl had expected. She rightly suspected that he had more than just one other woman on the go. He had stayed away from their Claggan home many nights and when he did come home it was late and he was abusive – both physically and mentally. Alice had no one to confide in other than her mother-in-law, and of course that had its limitations. She was actively trying to stash some money away by degrees so that she could make her escape. Her life was now one of utter misery. Many of her female neighbours were kind and tried to become friendly with the fragile little Englishwoman, but she was often afraid to answer their knocks to the door for fear they would see the bruises on her face.

Down at the centre of economic activity in the parish, Royston Carey was also having a bad time. He had become suspicious that something was going on between the mother of his children and her former boyfriend. Antoinette had become distant and agitated; and seemed to have a plethora of excuses ready in order to avoid being alone with him in their living quarters above the bar and shop. He had also noted that Terence seemed to be evading him, even avoiding eye contact when they happened to be in the bar at the same time.

In the last week of November old Peadar Glennon from Doona died and Royston and his father took charge of the arrangements as usual. For the past year they had drafted in Benny Hughton Junior an odd time to help them, as with the older man's ailing health and the younger man's demands from a young family they needed a contingency.

On the evening of old Peadar's removal from his house to the church Royston decided to take advantage of Benny Junior's availability and feigned a headache so that he could get back to Ballycroy Village early. His heart pounded as he drove towards his destination. He went upstairs to check on his family. As he suspected, his wife was not there and his sister Rosa was feeding little baby Royston as Louis and Charlotte did their school homework. When asked where Antoinette was, Rosa nonchalantly stated that she was down in the Post Office catching up on some paperwork.

Royston tip-toed out the back of their building and around by the lawn which was at the rear of the post office. As he took his position in the dark freezing night he thought his heart would jump out of his chest as he tried to control his breathing and listen out for any incriminating sounds. What he heard broke that heart. From inside the store room he could hear the familiar sound of his wife's orgasmic cries. His upper teeth bit into his lower lip as the sound grew louder. He clenched his fist in rage, and in minutes was swallowing a trickle of his own blood as his teeth dug deeper into his lip. Royston wanted his world to end. But he knew he had to keep control. Despite his agony at just confirming Antoinette's unfaithfulness, he resorted to the icy cold side of his personality and regained control of his breathing. About five minutes after the cessation of her moans of pleasure, the store door opened and out —as expected – stepped the figure of Terence McDonnell which he could easily identify from the street lantern rays. The man he wanted to kill with his bare hands ran across the lawn in the dark, and jumped the boundary fence with The Dispensary, and was off into the night like a rat.

Bitter tears streamed from Royston's eyes as he painfully watched his wife leave a minute later and head towards their home. Despite the turmoil going on inside his head, he was determined to stay calm and not do anything rash. Whatever had happened to him before this in his life, he had always found that he had a talent for gaining revenge and he knew that once he gathered his thoughts it would be no different this time. His tears were not for himself – but for his children. He was filled with hate for Terence. It sickened him to think that McDonnell had gained an advantage on him. His exact feelings towards Antoinette could not be categorised at that stage, but would be categorised eventually in his own good time. What he now had to become was a good actor, as he had to disguise his true emotions and act as if everything was normal.

The normality continued for a couple of days and he silently admired what a good actress Antoinette was as she too was behaving as if she were a dutiful and faithful wife. Then, one night in which she had gone to bed before her husband, she was awakened from her sleep in a shocking fashion. In the total darkness of their bedroom, she felt the long metal stem of a musket press past her lips and tongue. She tried to scream but couldn't because of the obvious obstacle that had her gasping for air. Her hands were stretched out and tied to the railings on the metal head-rails of the bed, one out to the right and one out to the left. Her first thoughts were that this was a raid by the Black and Tans and that she was about to be raped or even killed. As she tried to figure out what was going on and wondered who the figure astride her was, the voice that spoke out was horribly familiar.

"Listen here you whore!" whispered Royston. "One more move and this musket will fecking blow your fecking head into the wall". Antoinette gulped for air and let out a muffled groan. "Didn't I fecking say to shut up!" cursed Royston pushing the musket deeper into her throat as she froze in fear.

"Now. I know what you have been up to. You are a filthy despicable harlot. But YOU listen to ME. The affair stops NOW, or one of you dies. Do you understand?! It stops NOW!"

The terrified Antoinette nodded. That's all she COULD do.
"Good! It stops NOW! Now, we go on as if nothing happened, do you understand?" he said. Again, she nodded as she tried to untie her hands which were beginning to hurt more.
"Stop struggling woman!" he hissed. "Now, I am taking this gun away and there will be no more mention about this. If I have to take it out again it will spill blood. Now, we go on as normal. We are a normal happy family".

With that, he left the room and stored away his weapon, returning minutes later to his sobbing wife whose hurting hands were still stretched out like Jesus on the crucifix. Her husband lit a candle this time and acted as if nothing had happened. She was hyperventilating and could not speak to him even though she tried to. She could still taste the steel on her tongue. She noticed him smiling. She watched as he brushed down his best overcoat – a sign that he was about to head out. She wondered where he would be going at this hour of the morning, but she was unable to ask. She watched in horror and incredulity as he blew out the candle and left their bedroom, leaving her tethered. She heard him driving his car off in the Mulranny direction. It would be five hours later before he would return to release her. And for those five hours the traumatised Antoinette could do nothing but lie there helpless, with her wrists in agony, convincing herself that she was married to a dangerous psychopath.

Royston reached Newport Barracks by 4am, having been stopped three times along way, twice by IRA patrols and once by the Black and Tans. Each time he stated that he was on his way to Galway Docks to collect some coffin timber. He postponed worrying about what he would say on the way back when he was timberless! Upon entering the barracks he asked to speak with Corporal Gilberthorpe who was none too pleased to be raised from his bed. In the main interview room, the men had their first one-to-one encounter with each other. In his civilian clothes, the

Englishman looked even fitter. He had the appearance of an athlete.

"This better be good Mister Carey!" said Gilberthorpe grumpily as he prepared tea for himself, not offering any to his morning caller.
"Call me Royston – I am sorry if I disturbed you".
"Of course you did!" was the curt reply.
"I thought maybe that you were on shift or something" said Royston, "Sure I would be seen if I came here in broad daylight".
"You have more of a chance of being seen now actually", said Gilberthorpe. "Why are you here anyway?"
"Just to offer my support in any way I can" said the Ballycroy man.
"Your support? Explain!"
"Well" continued Royston, smiling nervously, "As you know we have an element that I am sure you would wish to eliminate".
"What do you mean?" snapped Gilberthorpe.
"Willie Kerrigan, the McDonnell brothers...I am sure you know them by now".
"I would eliminate the fucking lot of you if I could" snarled Gilberthorpe, "Including YOU, you little worm. You are all fucking pathetic peasant pisspots the lot of you!"
"I'll leave if it's a bad time" whispered a startled Royston rising to leave.
"EVERY time is a bad bloody time!" shouted Gilberthorpe.
"I'm sorry Mister Gilberthorpe" said Royston making for the door.
"It's fucking CORPORAL Gilberthorpe and not Mister Gilberthorpe, alright?! And sit down! Sit down you fucking weed!" and the sheepish Royston eased back to his chair by the table. Then the Englishman starting laughing sneerily and finished his mug of tea, before shocking Royston with the next part of his tirade.

"I know bloody well why you are here offering me up the McDonnells – it's because one of them is fucking giving it hard to your missus, isn't it?!" sneered Gilberthorpe.
"What?!" muttered a stunned and humiliated Royston.
"You heard me! Your missus is pulling up her petticoat for Terence any chance she gets. He is riding her all over your poxy parish!" taunted Gilberthorpe.

"See!" he continued, "I don't need fucking information from YOU. You piles of peasant shit are lining up to inform on one another. You are ALL pathetic!"

Royston was lost for words. He had expected to have been welcomed as an informant but felt even more worthless than he did upon seeing Terence leave the Post Office after being with Antoinette. But Gilberthorpe wasn't finished yet. He picked up a pair of boots from the floor and placed them on the table directly in front of Royston. Then he retrieved a rag and a tin of polish and threw them down beside his boots.

"Before you slither back to your miserable marital mattress, fucking give my boots a GOOD fucking shining you sad bastard. Leave when you can see the reflection of your pathetic paddy head from them!" said Gilberthorpe as his verbal victim sat rooted to his chair.
"I am heading back to my fucking bed. And next time you come here, you bring your whore of a wife with you, then leave and call back for her in an hour when I've finished with her – do you get me?!" roared the corporal, before slamming the door.

In a matter of days the Carey heir felt as if his dignity had been ripped out of him and dragged through the sewers. But as he drove back home in the dark morning he was as determined as ever to ensure he stayed strong enough to dose out his revenge. He was not going to let Terence get away with putting a gun to his head. He was not going to let him get away with ruining his marriage. Even if the entire parish knew about Antoinette's infidelity, he would keep his head held high. He resolved that NOTHING would stop him showing that he was better than Terence McDonnell. Nothing!

CHAPTER 23: ENTERING THE TWENTIES

Even though Terence was hated by his love rival and by his own wife, his stock had greatly risen with the Mayo IRA leadership. His skills as an organiser and drill instructor were admired by West Mayo Officer Commander Harry Heraty and his seniors. The Mayo OC, John Moore, was also impressed by what he heard of Terence and the two met in Castlebar just before Christmas 1919 when it was made clear that Terence may be required to carry out similar training in other parts of Mayo.

The training at Sheeaun Lodge involved the use of rifles, pistols and hand grenades. By the end of 1919 some 500 volunteers from all over Mayo had made their way to the peaceful green oasis in the middle of bogland between the butt of the Nephin Mountains and Bunmore. As well as instructions on arms and ammunitions, the men – most of whom had to travel for days through challenging terrain so as to avoid crown forces – received training on how to read maps; on how to use compasses; on how to use the night sky as a travel guide; on how to use flares; and on how to be resourceful in providing food. The latter included the setting of traps for rabbits, gutting salmon, killing hens, cooking deer and carrying water. For Mayo's IRA leaders, who were following their Munster colleagues in setting up flying columns, the benefits of what emerged from Sheeaun were priceless. The police and the Black and Tans never got to uncover the full extent of what went on in the grounds of Admiral Gay's remote estate in the back end of the back end of Mayo.

Activity against the British petered out over the Christmas period as the IRA awaited instructions from their national leaders for what the early months of 1920 should bring. In the discussions in Carey's Bar no conversation was complete without the names of Collins and DeValera being mentioned. Largely thanks to 'The Mayoman' newspaper, the ordinary people of Ballycroy felt they were as updated as anyone else in the world on what was going on. They could talk about the politicians Lloyd George and Winston Churchill in London; about Carson and Craig in the north; about the aviators Alcock and Browne; about the entertainers Barnum and Houdini; and about the great boxers such as Jack Dempsey and Gentleman Jim Corbett. They could rhyme off the names of the seven signatories of the 1916 Declaration of an Irish Republic who were now martyrs. They spoke about Big Jim Larkin as if they knew him. As the decade which had brought the Great War to their doorstep came to an end, many wondered openly what the next decade would bring.

Everyone was fully aware of the effects of the ongoing War of Independence, more commonly referred to as 'The Black and Tan War'. The parish was lucky enough insofar that it had seen limited action to date. The people had heard horror stories involving the British perpetrators from other parts of Mayo and Ireland, and were thankful that they had been spared. To date, this had suited Harry Heraty and his comrades at the top of the IRA as events in the major towns allowed the training activities in Ballycroy to go unnoticed by the crown forces.

Word reached Ballycroy of the atrocities in Munster. Churchill had decreed that any attacks on the Black and Tans should be avenged by violating the villages and homes of those who had produced or sheltered the suspected attackers. In Clare the town of Milltown Malbay was literally burned to the ground by vengeful Black and Tans after one of their members was killed. During the atrocity there, a union leader was executed in front of his horrified wife and child and his corpse was thrown into the flames of his burning home for good measure. In Limerick many innocent civilians were shot dead – some for no apparent reason. In Limerick City it was said that even a photograph of Britain's King George was smashed in one raid by his subjects. A street in which almost every house had supplied soldiers for the British in Flanders was not spared by the Welsh regiment based in the city when they went on a destructive rampage. The People's Park in the city was the scene of the murder of an Englishman who had settled there.

In one Limerick town the Black and Tans raided a family home and found nothing incriminating. However, two of the soldiers returned later to rob fifty pounds that they had spotted in their raid and they callously put a bullet into the skull of the homeowner after relieving him of the money. Stories emerged from Cork of alleged callous murders and rapes.

From closer to home, in Ballina, three prominent businessmen and republicans were forced to kneel in public and kiss the flag of Britain before being shot. A retarded man from the town was also dragged behind one of their Crossley Tender vehicles and after having his flesh and bones torn by the stony roads for miles was finally put out of his misery and shot and dumped in a boghole. Even closer to home, the houses of known republicans in Newport were burned. On one occasion in that town also, an innocent elderly farmer was tied to the underside of a cow by the laughing soldiers who then frightened the beast with a volley of shots, making it run through the fields with the unfortunate owner attached. Incidents such as these indicated that the British could act without fear of punishment, they were above the law and the poor of Ireland were at the mercy of these perverse soldiers. Rumours abounded that convicted murderers were being released from prisons in Britain on condition that they signed up with the Black and Tans for duty in Ireland.

As the war entered its second year, people wondered how long it would last. It was clear that the Irish were putting up a good fight and that the tactics of the flying columns had the British in disarray, but as always the question was if the Irish had the resources to hold out against the colonial enemy. Fight and spirit was one thing, financing weapons and feeding hungry fighters was another. There were also stories of disillusioned Black and Tans selling their guns and uniforms to the IRA before fleeing back to Britain. This was a strange war.

Nevertheless, the approaching decade of the twenties brought hope and promise to the downtrodden people of Ballycroy. The world looked determined to bring prosperity hand in hand with peace in the aftermath of the Great War. The success of Roland O'Grady a.k.a. Roger in America had been an inspiration to the younger people. Terence was the first emigrant ever to return from America to Ballycroy; and this showed that the ticket across the Atlantic was no longer necessarily just a one-way one, and this eased the pain of emigration. Although the parish was being constantly robbed of its young due to emigration, it was no longer being considered as a curse, but as a necessary opportunity. The people now leaving the parish knew that they could aim higher than just becoming a maid or a miner in Britain, America, Canada or Australia.

As Fr. Kinsella mentioned the names of Ballycroy's lost World War soldiers at midnight mass 1919, Patrick and Agnes Bourke squeezed each others hand in the packed church, hoping that the upcoming decade would reunite them with their son Batty. It warmed the congregation to see Sylvester and Terence McDonnell stand side by side in their IRA uniforms as they prayed with their fellow parishioners. There was applause as Fr. Kinsella announced that the parish would not need to worry about the cost of the church roof repairs as dollars had been received from one Jean Pierre Roland to cover this – and the provision of a new church bell. As usual, Willie Kerrigan prayed alongside his mother and they both shed a tear for John Peter on this night which always brought emotion.

As the people of Ballycroy gathered in prayer that night, just five miles away a Black and Tan patrol halted a hired car that was on its way out of the parish. It was a taxi, and the soldiers were surprised to hear the English accent from the sad-eyed but pretty lady who sat in the rear with her suitcase. A dispirited, demoralised and impregnated Alice Huckerby-McDonnell was leaving her heaven-turned-hell behind.
"I wish I were going back with you, Ma'am" said the Black and Tan as he waved the car onwards.

CHAPTER 24: BALLYCROY F.C.

In March 1920 Terence received a message to meet Harry Heraty at Dyra's house in Ballyveeney. He duly went there, even though he was surprised the West Mayo OC was looking for him so soon after a recent visit to Sheeaun Lodge. He also wondered why he had asked to meet him only and not Sylvester and Willie also.

By now Harry Heraty was top of the 'most wanted' list of the crown forces and he had no choice but to become acquainted with the backroads and mountains of his territory. By the time he received his warm soda bread and hot cup of tea in Dyra's he had spent two days and nights on the Nephin Mountains negotiating his way to Ballycroy. He also had to go on from there to visit his men in Achill. Although wet and weary, he lit up at the sight of Terence McDonnell entering the Dyra kitchen. Terence noticed that his commander was no longer the dapper figure he had come to know, but looked jaded and unkempt from his new way of life. After twenty minutes of a general chat with their friendly hosts, the two soldiers made their way to one of the caves that acted as a stable for the Dyra cattle. The cave was dug into an embankment along the beautiful Veeney River which flowed noisily by as the two men sat down on bundles of rushes opposite each other.

"Terence, I had to meet you on your own as I have a couple of important things to say to you" said Harry, "And to be honest I am very worried about your brother".
"In what way?" asked Terence.
"He's not right lad – is he?" asked Heraty. "The last day, I thought him very peculiar, very distracted. To me he looks like he has the shell shock".
"Leave it to me", said Terence, "I'll see to him. He will be fine for you. Leave it to me I say".
"Terence, he is not up to it. I need someone I can rely on. Sure he was perspiring and trembling the last day, he was a show, lad. Is he drinking?" asked Harry.
"Please Harry, leave him to me. I'll see to it that he pulls himself together" said Terence.

"I know it's awkward for you Terence as he is your brother, but I will have to have you leading the Ballycroy Flying Column, not him" asserted Harry.
"Ah please, he will be fine" said Terence.
"No! You lead the column. And that is an order" said Harry, before continuing "We can say he is still Training Commander. That should soften the blow. But you lead the column. Here, hand him this letter, lad, it covers it".
"Alright Harry, if you say so" answered Terence taking the folded envelope.
"So is your column ready?" asked Harry.
"It is" said Terence, "Six men as requested".
"Very good" was the reply. "You, Sylvester and Willie. And the other three?"
"Cecil Dyra from this house, PJ White from Aughness South and Eddie McArthur from Bunmore".
"Very good!" said Harry, "And a runner?"
"We have a runner in young Hughie O'Hora" replied Terence
"Is he anything to Paul the Butcher?" asked Harry.
"He is Paul's nephew" said Terence.
"Of good stock so!" said Harry, "Well done Terence. I will get your guns organised within the week".

"Surely you didn't travel two days just for this?" asked Terence.
"Sure this IS important" said Harry, "Ballycroy has been lucky enough so far but 1920 will not end without bloodshed here. You and your men are vital now, lad"
"We will be ready" said Terence. "I returned from America for this. I gave up my wife for this. I have given up my life for this".
"But you are right, Terence" said Harry, "I am here because there is something major afoot. And you are the only one I can confide in yet. And you must promise to keep this under your hat until I say so".
"Of course Harry" said Terence, "You know you can trust me".
"You just need to get your six ready. Willie is used to dynamite from the quarry so you are fine" said Harry.
"Sure I'm used to dynamite from the New Jersey railroad tunnels!" said Terence.

"Great Terence. When you get the signal in a few weeks, have yer sticks ready to blow up the road on the Bangor side and the Mulranny side as they will need to be cut off" said Harry.
"You say when and it shall be done Harry" was the reply.
"I can only give you the bare details as yet Terence" said Harry to his intrigued companion, "But we will be getting a shipment in".
"A shipment?"
"Yes. Arms and fuel. From Germany. Kindly funded by one of your 'Boys of Ballycroy'" smiled Harry, before spitting onto the cowdung-covered cave floor.
"Roger!" said Terence and Harry nodded assertively.
"Well fair fucks to him, fair fucks to him!" laughed Terence.
"When? Where?"
"Probably Innishbiggle" was the OC's reply. "Weather dependent. On a German U-boat. We managed to commission one that had been decommissioned!"
"You are joking me?" said Terence excitedly raising to his feet, "A fucking German U-boat coming to Ballycroy, unfuckingbelievable!"
"Operation Vandenburg to you and me, lad" said Harry smiling at how animated Terence had become.
"Did you hear me? Vandenburg?" added Harry as Terence struggled to contain his excitement in the cave.
"Yes, codeword Vandenburg, I'll remember that!" said Terence.
"Any significance in the name, do you think?" asked Harry to a perplexed looking Terence, adding "I think you'd better sit down again" and Terence placed his rear on the rushes again with his back up against the cave wall.

"Operation Vandenburg" repeated Harry, as Terence still didn't grasp the significance.
"Yes Harry, I have it" said Terence.
"Well. I just mentioned that one of your 'Boys of Ballycroy' is involved in this shipment, but it also involves a second 'Boy of Ballycroy'" teased Harry.
"A second? What do you mean?" asked Terence, evidently confused.
"Take a deep breath Terence" said Harry still smiling.
"Vandenburg is Bourke".

"What do you mean?" asked Terence after swallowing hard. "You mean it is named in his honour?"

"Terence, no!" said Harry. "Vandenburg IS Batty Bourke. Batty Bourke IS Vandenburg. He IS NOT dead!"

Terence turned pale and fell back against the wall. His mind struggled with what he had just heard. Harry rose to his feet and walked over to Terence and put his hand on his shoulder as tears came to Terence's eyes. He was overwhelmed. He did not know what to say. The friend he thought he had lost was still alive. He had never experienced an emotion like this. Finally he managed to speak.

"Harry. Is this real, really?" he asked. "Are you telling me Batty is alive?"

"Alive and in Germany. He defected during the war" said Harry.

"And you knew this all along?" asked Terence incredulously.

"God no" replied Harry, "I only found out last week".

"Unbelievable! Unfuckingbelievable!" repeated Terence. "Does his family know?"

"I understand that they do, but have been sworn to secrecy" said Harry, "And you must do the same, lad. Not even a word to your brother".

"Of course, of course…".

"If the Tans find out they will burn every house in Ballycroy" said Harry. "They will level the place".

"Of course" repeated Terence, still coming to terms with the news.

"You know Terence, our most dangerous enemy is the enemy within – not the British" said Harry as his companion nodded in agreement.

"Informers are Satan's Soldiers" added the Westport man. "We must always be on our guard".

It had been a pleasant surprise to hear of Roger's involvement, but Batty's involvement was astounding. Terence felt a warm glow of happiness for the Bourke family in Aughness South. He wondered if a reunion had been arranged. This was the best news ever! The blood rushed through his veins. His head spun. How would he be able to keep this to himself? The 'Boys of Ballycroy' numbered five again! He was so proud. His tears of joy were followed by tears of sadness as he thought of poor John Peter and

of poor Michaeleen. Stepping out of the Ballyveeney cave he raised his eyes skywards...
"You are looking after us from up there lads, God Bless you. God Bless you both".

Harry managed to calm down the excited Terence and get him to organise a bicycle and a curragh to transport him to Achill. He assured Terence that he would be in contact within the week with arms for the Ballycroy Flying Column and further instructions. Later that day Terence gathered his men together in the hedged field by Sheeaun Lodge and handed out some much needed money that Harry had brought. He placed his men on alert for the road explosions. He relayed that Harry had also instructed them to burn the replacement barracks – but that a date for this would be set for later in the year and outside help would be required. Terence told his men that they would have to immediately prepare for life 'on the run' as they would be targeted for reprisals. It was difficult for Terence not to impart the good news he had just heard, but his drive and enthusiasm rubbed off on his new charges. The BFC (Ballycroy Flying Column) was now in place and ready to play its part in the War of Independence. The Boys of Ballycroy were back in action – one of them even returning from the dead!

But things would never be the same in the parish. The enclave on Ireland's western periphery was about to be exposed to the bloody and brutal Black and Tan war.

CHAPTER 25: PROVOCATION AND PREPARATION

Three months passed and on the first Sunday of June Terence sat alone in his cottage and caught up on the week's edition of 'The Mayoman'. He and his fellow members of the column had met and trained regularly but they had yet to receive any definite indication from Heraty on when 'Operation Vandenburg' would come into play. All of them had kept a fairly low profile and were keeping out of the attention of the Black and Tans. The presence of the crown forces in Ballycroy was quite low – it was estimated that only about two policemen remained in the Castlehill Barracks and they were usually joined by about four soldiers who normally kept to themselves, probably being grateful to be away from the other areas in the county which were not so peaceful. Of course, the fact that Ballycroy was hardly featuring in the thoughts of the Black and Tans suited the IRA leaders as they awaited their shipment.

Terence smiled to himself as he read Toothy Lucey's article about Roger a.k.a. Jean Pierre Roland bringing his successful 'The Great El Ginto' play to a theatre in London's West End. It was amusing to think of members of the elite British theatre-going public funding ammunition that was to be used against their own army! Just a couple of yards away in his father's house, Sylvester worked on his bicycle to make sure it was roadworthy for the expected mileage ahead. He had been off the alcohol for almost three months now and was feeling much fitter. His shrapnel wound still ached but he felt that his leg was improving. A few miles further down the road in Doona, Willie reminisced with his brother Josey and mother Bridie about the exploits of the late John Peter. Today was sports day in The Master's Field, and the proud memories came flowing back. However, like their relatives in Claggan, they would not be attending this year.

It was an overcast day that threatened rain and a smaller crowd than usual gathered by the riverside for the sports day. There were no major stars to watch like there were several years earlier. John Peter was of course dead and Thady Finnegan had emigrated to join his brother in America. Bosco Darby had become bored of winning and had stepped aside to encourage some of his students to better themselves on the sports field.

Events were in progress for about half an hour when some lads up near the trees began shouting that a wagon was approaching. Then the cry of "Black and Tans! Black and Tans!" echoed. Sure enough, the running stopped and the crowd of about 150 hushed to hear the rattling of a truck in the distance, coming from the Ballycroy Village direction. As it drew nearer, loud English voices could be heard cheering and to a person everyone seemed to freeze for about 10 seconds before the sound of gunfire rang out. It was immediately followed by screaming mayhem as men, women and children darted in every direction to escape the field. The Crossley Tender came into view and the soldiers in the back were shouting obscenities. Within seconds the vehicle crashed through the admission gate and down the grassy slope into the field and as the driver revved up, screaming could be heard as the parishioners ran for cover.

A few of the soldiers jumped off and started running through the field, which was now almost empty save for a few startled ponies who were due to be raced, and their owners who were trying to bring them under control. To the horror of the terrified witnesses, two of the Black and Tans aimed their rifles at the ponies and started shooting. As the poor animals cried out and fell the British men laughed and cheered. The Crossley Tender was by now driving around the field in circles and making deep brown tracks in the green field, spraying muck everywhere. After a few more shots were fired at the animals, the sound of a whistle could be heard above the female screams as Corporal Gilberthorpe stood in the middle of the field and called his soldiers to order. Within minutes, all of his men had clambered onto the back of the vehicle, the top of which was covered by protective chicken coop wire. The entire incident lasted about two minutes; but to those who witnessed everything - it seemed as if it lasted two hours.

As the Black and Tans drove off out of the field an English voice could be heard shouting "Where are your 'Boys of Ballycroy', why don't they come out and fight us?" to a response of laughter. As they sped towards Ballycroy Village again, frightened families emerged from behind trees, whin bushes, rushes, rocks, river banks and even the water to return to the field to collect their belongings. There were tears of dismay and disgust at the sight of the four dying ponies. Children cried openly. Toothy Lucey tried to scribble a few notes and wailing could be heard as everyone gathered their bits and pieces and headed for home. Bosco Darby asked for help in organising for the un-won medals and trophies to be collected. To dampen spirits even further the skies opened and most people got soaked as they walked the road.

The truck load of Black and Tans stopped off at Carey's Bar where they caused more trouble by all entering the premises. A few of them jumped behind the counter and knocked Royston to the ground as they began helping themselves to free drinks. The last of them to enter the bar was the grinning Corporal Gilberthorpe who mocked Royston as he wiped blood from his face. He loudly asked where his wife was and if he could have twenty minutes with her. Luckily, Antoinette and Rosa had left the building once they heard the commotion downstairs, and had run to The Dispensary with the children through the rain. Gilberthorpe and two of his colleagues ran up into their quarters with rape on their mind but the only person they met was Roy Carey himself. The two soldiers with Gilberthorpe belted Roy with their fists and knocked him to the ground, and then kicked at him as the old man curled up on the carpet in front of the fireplace. They asked where his money was hidden and when he didn't answer, Gilberthorpe picked up a poker and violently prodded it into the crying man's ribs and shoulder blades.

Mercifully, the three of them then returned downstairs where they met a staggering Royston in the hallway. They all launched at him with kicks and punches for about a minute. His cries for help were heard by some of the drinkers who had scattered out into the rear yard, but no one was brave enough to enter and assist Royston. The sound of smashing glass and more boisterous cheering was quickly followed by the shrill of Gilberthorpe's whistle again, and within a minute they were all on the Crossley Tender again – all but Corporal Gilberthorpe. He repeated his

last performance of addressing an imaginary audience. As the rain lashed down on him, he shouted out:
"Dear subjects, we SHALL return. Thank you for the free wine. Next time we will take your free women. And thank your great heroes for not shooting us with their hurley sticks! God save the mighty IRA!" and to rowdy cheers from his own men, he hopped up beside the driver and the engine rattled into action once more and headed off towards Mulranny.

Tears of anger flowed as Antoinette and Rosa attended to the injured Roy and Royston, whilst at the same time trying to calm the petrified children. Word of both incidents reached the McDonnell and Kerrigan houses that evening and the three IRA men were seething with rage. That evening, all six members of the BFC met at Sheeaun Lodge. There was a strong desire to attack the Castlehill Barracks in revenge but the McDonnell brothers counselled against it. Eddie McArthur had said that his sister was shaking with fear and that they would have raped her had they managed to locate her. This visibly angered Terence but he managed to urge caution.
"This is provocation" he said, "They want us to take them on".
"Then we should!" said Eddie, "They are making us look like cowards".
"We will be dead cowards if we go near that barracks, it is a trap" said Sylvester.
"We are soldiers, we should fight and not hide out of sight" urged PJ White.
The six debated for an hour or so before the whistle of 'Silent Night' could be heard by the bushes. This was Hughie's arrival tune.

"A message from Captain Heraty" announced the runner, "Operation Vandenburg is near. Briefing is in order. Volunteer Terence McDonnell is asked to attend a convention in Mulranny Friday night at twenty three hundred hours. End of message"
"Operation Vanden what?" asked Eddie, and that was the prompt for Terence to give his men an outline of the plan for the German shipment to be brought in. He mentioned nothing of Batty Bourke - they did not need to know for now.

Terence cycled through the rain to Mulranny that Friday night and found the meeting house which was situated on the Curraun Road. He was soaked by the time he got there, but found that almost all of the attendees were likewise. He was ushered into the tree-sheltered house by one of the many IRA men who were discretely on guard to ward off any uninvited visitors. He was surprised that there seemed to be more than twenty people in the candlelit room. He received a handshake from the host Mr. Fitzpatrick and was immediately pulled aside by his former cellmate Colm Tierney and the two men embraced each other. "What the hell are you doing here Tierney?" laughed Terence, "I'm here for our share of the German loot!" was the jovial reply. "I thought ye had everything ye wanted in Ballina – leave the treasure to us poor sods!" replied Terence still laughing.

Harry Heraty welcomed Terence and introduced him to Connaught OC Quinn McWalter and Mayo OC John Moore. The three OCs sat at the top facing the others, and a blackboard on a stand was placed beside them. Terence did not recognise the ghoulish-looking man who quietly sat beside them and who did not rise from the chair when introduced to Terence as 'Ecclesiasticus from Hungary'. As everyone took their chairs Terence's hand was eagerly grasped by attendees from Erris and Crossmolina who were clearly proud to be meeting one of the famed 'Boys of Ballycroy'.

Proceedings began immediately and everyone introduced themselves. Harry Heraty was chairing the meeting and used Mr. Fitzpatrick's blackboard to draw a rough map of the Ballycroy coast, showing the borders with Bangor Erris to the north and Mulranny to the south. To the east were the mountains, and to the west the Atlantic Ocean, into which Harry chalked Achill Island with Innishbiggle and Annah Islands in between Achill and Ballycroy. He went on to state that the U-boat would be arriving off Innishbiggle of the evening of 23rd June, which was the feast of St. John but better known as 'Bonfire Night' as traditionally Irish people had used the midsummer's evening to burn unwanted waste.

Harry emphasised that the plans were weather-dependent, but that they expected it to be a warm summer's evening and that the unloading of the shipment would commence at 6pm. It would take approximately two hours and he already had men from the Achill and Ballina brigades lined up to work with several Innishbiggle Islanders to carry the arms and fuel and store them at the old schoolhouse. There would be a curfew on the island that evening, again patrolled by armed men from Achill and Ballina. He also said that he had plans afoot on how to get the arms off the island into the hands of the IRA soldiers of West and North Mayo, but that these would be divulged at a later stage. The main aim of this convention was to arrange the safe delivery of the shipment, and to ensure the British did not find out or jeopardise the operation.

Harry's presentation clearly impressed his seniors and indeed all of those present. It was obvious that he had put a lot of work into the project already and Terence was surprised at the level of detail. He was also slightly concerned that there seemed to be no role for the local Ballycroy activists, but he refrained from saying anything until he heard more at the meeting. He did not have to wait too long!

The West Mayo OC continued his presentation by saying that the Ballycroy Flying Column (BFC) would be expected that evening to use dynamite to bomb the approach roads from Bangor Erris and Mulranny. Ideally, the former at 4pm and the latter at 6pm. This immediately alarmed Terence but he kept silent for the moment. Harry stressed that it was important that no Black and Tan vehicles were able to access Ballycroy that evening, as those carried machine guns. He also said that it was his preference to leave the road explosions until as close as possible to the arrival of the U-boat, so as not to raise suspicion too far in advance. He accepted that there would be a small presence of policemen and soldiers at Castlehill Barracks but that they should not be a threat to the shipment.

He finished his presentation by referring to the sitting Ecclesiasticus, who he said would be working with three 'circus colleagues'. They would be linking by torch signal with the U-boat and would be strategically placed in the hills of Achill which overlook Innishbiggle. Ecclesiasticus would also be linking with Fr. Rea from Enniscrone to ensure the Bourke family were brought safely to and from Annah Island where a *rendez-vous* with Batty Bourke would be held. Again, Terence was surprised not to be party to this and believed he should have a role, but again he kept silent. Harry apparently had it all arranged. There was only one house on Annah Island which was situated very close to Claggan, and this belonged to Patrick Cooney – better known as 'Packie Tadgh' – who was now the sole resident on the tiny island and he had agreed that his house could be used for a secret reunion that evening. A curragh boat had already been annexed for the purpose.

After Harry finished his presentation the floor was taken by Quinn McWalter who heaped praise on Harry. He thanked Ecclesiasticus for his role but the sullen Hungarian did not move a muscle or bat an eyelid in response, but just stared glumly ahead at the wall. His presence cast an uneasy feeling at the meeting. McWalter went on to praise the courage of Batty Bourke, now a revered Major in the German Army.

"I know he is one of the heroic 'Boys of Ballycroy' with whom we are all familiar with. Indeed we are honoured to have one of them in our midst this evening. Batty is an inspiration to us all. We are humbled by his sacrifice. He is a true Irish patriot. His name will be up there with the likes of Emmett, Wolfe Tone and Pearse. We are privileged that we are living in the same time that he is" and a round of applause broke out and Terence received strong claps on his back as he sat amongst his comrades facing the speaker. McWalter continued his speech:
"Mick Collins was only yesterday asking me about Operation Vandenburg and asked me to relay his good wishes and thanks to you all". Again, a round of applause broke out as the green republican blood raced through their veins.
"But I am here tonight for one purpose and one purpose only. And that, my comrades, is to emphasise that this operation MUST be kept clandestine at all costs. The British must NOT learn of this. I urge you to do ALL within your power to keep this quiet. We must not arouse suspicion. We must not invite scrutiny.

Always beware that loose talk can cost a life. The enemy within is to be feared as much as the Saxon." He received gentler applause as he sat down and John Moore then rose to echo the importance of keeping Operation Vandenburg a secret – even after the U-boat has returned to Germany. He then invited questions from all those present, and Terence was first to speak from 'the audience'.

"Commanders", he said as he stood, "I must say I am concerned that my column is expected to carry out road explosions more than twenty miles apart within a two hour period. Can I ask for assistance in this matter?"
"We can discuss this later" said Harry, appearing uneasy that one of his trusted charges might embarrass him in front of his seniors.
"I can help out" offered Colm Tierney.
"You can join our discussion later so", said Harry, anxious to move onto another topic.

The meeting lasted about another 20 minutes before it was brought to a close and Harry gathered Terence and Colm in the Fitzpatrick kitchen. It was the first time they had seen Harry angry.
"What the feck do you mean Terence you need help, isn't there six of you plus O'Hora?!" he asked aggressively.
"I fucking need the six together and not split twenty miles apart!" replied Terence.
"What's wrong with three and three – one on each team to plant the sticks and the other two to keep watch?" asked Harry.
"I'll need two to plant the dynamite or gelignite" said Terence, "And one will not be enough on lookout, especially at the Mulranny end. What if something goes wrong, we'd be wiped out!"
"What can fecking go wrong lad, just blow the feck out of the roads and disable them and then position yerselves to shoot at the Tans when they attempt repairs!"
"That's exactly it", said Terence, "I can't have three and three taking on ten and ten. I need my men together – perhaps Colm here can supply a column for the Bangor side?"
"I can supply about four men but none with explosives experience" said Colm.

The three men reached a compromise. Colm would supply four men to work on a Bangor Erris explosion at 6pm on Bonfire evening. Willie Kerrigan – a skilled explosives user – and PJ White would join the four Ballina men, and after the bomb both of them would leave to regroup with the rest of the BFC at Crafton Lake. In Mulranny, Terence and Cecil Dyra would carry out the explosion at 6pm, and Sylvester and Eddie would keep sentry lookout from the hills as they awaited the reinforcements. After all, if the Black and Tans were to arrive in Ballycroy that evening it was most likely to be from the Mulranny side.

Harry, Colm and Terence shook hands on this arrangement and promised to link up again in advance of Bonfire night. As the attendees began to leave Fitzpatrick's house to begin their journeys back home in the midnight rain, Harry grabbed Terence by the arm and apologised for losing his temper with him.
"It's just that I've been under pressure over this, lad" said Harry.
"I understand fully Harry, no need whatsoever to explain yourself" responded Terence, "And you've done a fine job, you thought of everything. You even have food stocked up on the island for the Germans and the others".
"Thanks Terence. I should have paid more heed to your requirements though" said Harry.
"I'm just wary of being spread too thin" said Terence. "I need every man with me".
"I know, I'm sorry lad" repeated Harry. "Even though this is not a shipment sanctioned by the official German government, if anything goes wrong with this, it could re-ignite the world war, it's THAT important".
"It has potential alright" said Terence "A huge weight on your shoulders. But you will do just fucking fine, I know you will!" and he put his hand on the OC's shoulder.
"We cannot afford to let the Tans scuttle this on us" said Harry as he headed into the dark wet night, and his words echoed in Terence's mind as he cycled his way down through the windy roads towards his lonely Claggan cottage, the sound of the Atlantic waves lapping to his left and the dominating steep mountains to his right.

Bonfire night 1920 would surely be one to remember.

CHAPTER 26: TROUBLE IN PARADISE

June 23rd came around and the sky was cloudless. As the BFC held their final meeting together before Operation Vandenburg the mood was tense but exciting. They went through their plans and contingencies one final time. Terence now divulged all that he knew and the fact that a Ballycroy hero was returning in a submarine with arms for the national cause made the young members all the more determined to succeed. After their final meeting ended at midday, each of the column went home to tell their families that it was likely they would not be returning for some time. Of course they were unable to provide details of their operation to their loved ones.

In Claggan, Sylvester and Terence left their tearful mother Claire behind in the arms of their father Fintan. They assured their parents that they would return safely – just as they had done before the Great War. In Doona, their cousin Willie was in tears as he left his mother and brother behind and headed towards Bangor Erris with his rifle and his rucksack of provisions. He had already hidden the dynamite at the valley which dipped in the road about four miles the Ballycroy side of Bangor Erris. It was here that he would meet the Ballina four and PJ White and blow up the adjacent bridge to disconnect the road.

The runner Hughie spent his afternoon giving a final check to the three hideouts that had been chosen as contingencies to Sheeaun Lodge. He ensured that the arms cache in each location was securely hidden from view, and that tinned food was also buried. The locations were The Carthouse at Doona Sandybanks, the Shepherd's Hut on the north face of Bunmore Hill, and Crafton Lake which sat high in the mountains overlooking Ballyveeney. As he cycled throughout the parish he could not help but admire the rugged scenery as it soaked up the sun. The smell of freshly cut hay filled his nostrils and the singing birds filled him with joy. "The Germans will not want to leave here!" he said to himself as he faced into the cool ocean breeze near Doona. "Is this what they mean about the calm before the storm?"

At 5.55pm the people of Aughness North, Aughness South, Tarshaughaun, Logduff and Shranamonragh heard the sound of an explosion coming from the Bangor Erris direction. Willie Kerrigan had executed his job successfully, and now he and PJ left their Ballina counterparts in the valley and took the road into Tarshaughaun where they planned to make the long journey across bogland and mountain to join up with their BFC colleagues by Crafton Lake.

At 6pm Terence and young Cecil Dyra were on their knees in the water by the bridge that they were about to blow up. They had to be careful not to get their sticks of dynamite wet. Terence's hands trembled as he placed the sticks in between rocks beneath the road. A watery tunnel brought the rainwater from the high steep mountain under the road and out into the seawater of the bay. It was his intention to collapse the road into this tunnel so that the Black and Tans would be unable to drive into the parish. The bridge and tunnel lay about 100 yards from the huge railway bridge that crossed over the road. After having planted the explosives on the Mulranny side of the bridge, he ran across the road to plant more on the Ballycroy side where the water gushed out into the bay. Gazing down from the steep mountain overhead was his brother Sylvester and young Eddie McArthur. Both of them were positioned behind rocks and had their rifles ready. They also had a sack of extra bullets and two hand grenades each.

As Terence struggled to keep his balance and plant the sticks of dynamite, he heard a whistle blow high up on the mountain, followed closely by a shout to "Hide". His hearing was obscured by the sound of the flowing water, but from beneath the bridge he heard a shout from Cecil of "Truck coming, hide, hide!" Eventually, he could hear the unmistakable rattle of the Black and Tan Crossley Tender approaching from beneath the railway bridge further up the road. His heart pounding, he left his dynamite and threw himself into the tunnel beneath the road. It could barely accommodate him. He could see the outline of Cecil who had done likewise on the Mulranny side.

As both men lay belly-down in the water, they could hear the raised English accents chatting in the back of the truck as it

passed over them. The rocks beneath the road shook. Terence's heart raced and he thought he was going to pass out. The smell of the fumes from the truck entered his nostrils. He became filled with fear as he wondered what to do, and he cursed.
"Fuck! The Devil Blast them – they have fucking beaten us to it!" he said to Cecil.
But his sense of frustration grew tenfold and his heart beat even faster still as he heard a SECOND truck approach, again from Mulranny.
"Oh fuck no!" said Terence, "They are on to us! There is NEVER ever more than one truck. Oh fuck, what will we do?!"
"We can't do anything" whispered Cecil crawling up the tunnel towards his boss.
"We fucking HAVE to" said Terence. "They are on their way to intercept the U-boat! And WE will be blamed. I will be blamed. Damn! Damn! And damn again!!!"

With that, Terence ordered Cecil to crawl through the tunnel onto the Mulranny side and he himself emerged on the Ballycroy side to retrieve his rifle which he had laid by rocks there. They both jumped onto the road together and caught a glimpse of the rear of the second truck. Terence looked up at the rocks where Sylvester was standing with his hands outstretched as if asking what he should do.

Terence felt as if his heart was going to explode from his chest and if his brains would burn from the pressure he was feeling in his head. Even though less than sixty seconds had passed since the first truck was heard, he felt as if he had aged sixty years. He had a decision to make and make fast. His instinct was to let the convoy continue on but the phrase that bounced about in his head contained the words of Harry Heraty – "We cannot afford to let the Tans scuttle this on us".

That made his decision. And after one quick look up at his brother high up on the mountain above, Terence defied his instincts and took aim with his rifle at the rear of the slow moving second truck of soldiers, and fired a volley of shots. His actions were immediately followed by more firing from the two IRA men high above, who had both vehicles in their view and had a great advantage. The brakes of the trucks screeched and the second truck veered to the left of the road before crashing over the stone wall into the sea. There were shouts and screams from the convoy as Terence and Cecil knelt by the roadside bushes and kept firing. By now they could also see the first truck which had come to a halt and they could see soldiers scattering from it, some attempting to climb up the steep banks of the mountain. Terence looked up to see Sylvester moving to another rock to get a better position, and fire downwards at the men in the water. The tide was not in so the water was not deep, but painful screams emanated from the water as the Irishmen refilled their guns and kept firing.

Then, to Terence's left he heard another vehicle coming from the direction of the railway bridge and he instinctively took aim and fired in its direction. He managed to order Cecil to keep firing at the men in the water, and he fired more shots at what he had now identified as a car. The car swerved across the road and crashed into a drain, coming to a halt, with the rear of the car facing out into the middle of the road. Terence again turned his attention to the men in the water as well as the soldiers who were attempting to climb the base of the mountain. Two of the Tans fell onto the road, as he could see Sylvester again move up on the mountain face to take up an even more advantageous position. Then Terence felt a bullet whistle by him from the direction of the truck and he knew they were under attack. He shouted to Cecil to retreat but there was no answer. He ran up into the trees on the Mulranny side and felt another bullet fly by. He turned to look at the road he had just left to check on his comrade. To his horror, he saw the young man kneeling on the road with both hands clasped around the front of his neck. His rifle was on the ground. A gurgling sound came from him.

Terence braved the bullets and returned to the road. Cecil was now lying down on his back, still clasping his neck with both hands, and there was dark blood running down them. His face was as white as snow and he was staring skywards, eyes wide open, trying to speak. A bullet bounce off a rock behind them and Terence had another decision to make. He grabbed Cecil's rifle and hung it around his own neck. He dragged the wounded teenager to the side of the road and heard his brother's voice from up on high say "Get back Terence, get back!" Terence had to leave his young charge and dart again up towards the trees and rocks on the Mulranny side. The bullets were hitting the trees and he prayed that he would not be struck. On reaching a wide oak tree he hid behind it and prepared Cecil's rifle as the shooting continued below and above him. He came out from behind the tree and threw himself on the ground, and fired again at the Tans. In the corner of his eye he could see some movement at the crashed car he had fired at earlier, so he took aim and the sound of shattering glass was heard.

As well as the shouting from his brother and Eddie high up on the mountain, he heard an English voice below him shout "We will get you Terence, we will crucify you!" He thought that this must be Gilberthorpe. He fired in the direction of the Tans again and then ran further into the forest incline. He then heard the sound of machine gunfire come from the truck which was still on the road. He prayed that his brother would survive. He prayed for the dying Cecil and his parents. He prayed that the lad's suffering would not last. He feared for the worst as there seemed to be no response to the machine gun fire. He heard the distinctive sound of a pistol shot as he clambered through the forest, almost out of breath. He asked himself had he done the right thing. He assured himself that he had, that one truck was in the sea and the other would probably have to return to base with its wounded. He wondered if his bullets had killed anyone. He thought about the car he had fired upon. He wondered if that had contained their senior officers. Maybe it had not. But he convinced himself that he had little option but to fire as the car was dangerously close and he would have been an easy target from it.

He rested beneath a tree and looked around for where he might source water. His mouth was dry. He looked at his watch. It was 6.30pm. The U-boat would be unloading at this point. The convoy of Black and Tans could have reached the coast if he had not stopped them. He wondered if the British would come after him. The gunfire had ceased. He wondered if Sylvester was alright.

About a mile away on the way to Crafton Lake Sylvester was wondering about his brother. Eddie McArthur sat alongside him as they rested behind a large boulder. Eddie was panting heavily. He was shaking. He was starting to cry. Eddie had just witnessed one of his best friends being murdered. He had not seen Cecil fall from the initial bullet that struck his Adam's apple on the road below him. But as he hid from the machine gun fire being aimed up into the mountain he had seen Corporal Gilberthorpe approach the dying Cecil and fire a pistol shot down into his head to end his life. Eddie was distraught. Sylvester was much calmer; he surprised himself at how calm he was. He had witnessed the horrors of war at first hand on the continent. He had never thought we would witness it in Ballycroy. He knew that he had shot several targets. He reckoned he had killed four men at least.

"We will never be able to return home" said Sylvester. "They will want to avenge this". There was no answer from his shaking companion. Sylvester slowly rose to his feet and surveyed the mountainous terrain to see if they were being followed. He hoped his brother would come into view. He dragged Eddie up from the ground by the collar.
"Come on boy, we have to head for Crafton as planned!" he said. "Willie and PJ should be nearly there by now".

As the two IRA men approached their destination, from their heathery walkway they could see the pyramid of Slievemore Mountain out on the horizon miles away. In between, they could faintly see several bonfires send smoke spiralling into the clear summer sky. The place looked idyllic. But the sound of the shooting still reverberated inside their heads. And they shed tears for the loss of their comrade Cecil. They wondered how his heartbroken parents would cope without the young lad. Sylvester kept glancing backwards for a sight of Terence, but it was in vain. They settled by the mass rock and helped themselves to some bread and water. As evening fell they gazed down on Crafton Lake which was so still it looked like a fiddle-shaped mirror. It was beautiful as it reflected the red summer sky.

After about an hour they were joined by a tired Willie and PJ who were distraught at hearing what happened. With one dead and one missing in action it had been a horrific day.

*****

As night fell, up in the forest at the rear of Mulranny, Terence was sitting in a cave that had obviously been hewn into the rocks by dynamite by railway workers many years earlier. The entrance to the cave was now overgrown by bushes which obscured its view and was an excellent camouflage. It was dark and he now could no longer see the face of his companion who sat opposite him.

At 7pm that evening, as Terence emerged from a thicket were he had emptied his bowels he had felt the hard steel of a pistol stem come up against his temple from behind him. A Scottish accent had ordered him to drop his weapons as he duly did. The same accent then ordered him to remove his boots which he duly did. The voice then directed him to this cave with his hands above his head, and shoved him into it. As Terence silently prayed to the Lord that the faceless man would give him a quick and painless death, the Scot introduced himself as Joey Jarvis.

"Listen – I am on your side" said the Scot to the relieved Terence. "You just do as I say and you will be fine."
"Who are you?" asked Terence of the short balding man with the mischievous eyes and friendly smile.
"I am your guardian angel tonight!" he said smiling. "If Gilberthorpe comes upon us tonight, he will kill us both, but he will kill ME first, I tell you that".
"What do you mean?" asked a pale and terrified Terence.
"Well sonny, I was what you folks call a 'Black and Tan' but I am a deserter" said the Scot. "Heck, I'm even more wanted than you are Terence".
"How do you know my name?" asked Terence.
"Everyone knows YOU!" replied the Scot, "And of course that can be a bad thing as well as a good thing".
"But you could still kill me" said Terence.

"Listen, if I wanted to kill you I would have done it while you wiped your arse back there sonny. Heaven knows, I never want to see that sight again!" laughed Joey.
"I need to meet my colleagues tonight" said Terence.
"Maybe tomorrow" replied the Scot to Terence's dismay. "And no funny business, do you hear? No trying to disarm me or anything like that or you won't see the sun rise, do you understand?"
"I've had enough of guns for one day" said Terence. "Come with me to Crafton tomorrow".
"Perhaps" said Joey. "Sonny, that was a fair old battle ye had down there. Must be something happening in Ballycroy? I don't expect you to tell me nor will I ask".
"We lost at least one, hopefully my brother and the other lad are alright" said Terence.
"What, there were only four of you?!" said Joey surprisingly. "It sounded like the Somme down there. Heaven knows I heard about you Ballycroy lads before, but four men taking on twenty English, that's something else altogether sonny! I'm definitely sticking with you tomorrow!" laughed Joey and Terence laughed for the first time since the battle.

"Listen Terence, I admire you Irish. And the fight you have in you. Your sheer patriotism. When I signed up for this shower in London I did not know what I was getting into. I simply wanted a job after the war. I needed the money. I quickly found out that I was on the wrong side. We Scots should be fighting for our independence like ye. Since Bannockburn we haven't done a thing. After the way our ancestors were slaughtered there, there's no way the likes of me should be fighting alongside the English. Especially against ye. And me from a Glasgow Catholic family. And a Celtic supporter! I'm with you boys now".

As they tried to sleep in the cave tears fell from the eyes of Terence as he thought of poor Cecil. He wondered if Sylvester had survived the machine gun fire. He was in a bizarre situation now as he was essentially a hostage to an 'on the run' former Black and Tan but in a peculiar way he felt safe with the Scot. There was a chemistry between the two. They probably both needed each other.

As midnight arrived at Crafton Lake, the whistling of 'Silent Night' broke the silence. Hughie approached the four who were camped by the large rocks on the Ballyveeney side of the lake.

"The shipment arrived alright but there is WAR!" panted the runner. "Captain Heraty reckons the Black and Tans found out that Batty is alive but they don't seem to know about the U-boat. He said that Cecil Dyra was lost at the battle in Mulranny and one Black and Tan."
"One?!" said Sylvester incredulously, "I killed about FIVE myself. That's shite!"
"I am only quoting Captain Heraty" said Hughie "And it took me three hours to get here as the Tans are out in force for revenge".
"Any word on Terence?" asked Sylvester.
"No, I was hoping you would have word" said Hughie. "Anyway please let me continue. Admiral Gay and his family were all at Castlehill Barracks as well. Looking for your blood. His daughter and her chauffeur were shot dead in the Mulranny ambush and he is looking for your heads".
"Oh no, the car, the car. The fecking car!" said Sylvester. "Which daughter Hughie?"
"I understand it was his eldest, Esmeralda, returning from her business in Westport for Bonfire night", replied the runner.
"Oh no, oh no" said Sylvester. "Poor Esmeralda, the poor innocent. Feck it! Terence shot at the car. Feck it anyway!"
"If the Tans are on the rampage then we should be down there fecking fighting them and not sitting here on our arses with fecking guns by our side" said PJ White pointing to the villages of the parish below.
"Ye will be slaughtered if ye are seen tonight" said Hughie, "And it would be the Gays and the Dyras doing the slaughtering. Ye are under orders from Captain Heraty to remain here til morning. I am to report back to him with your numbers tonight. I will be here at 10 in the morning. And make sure to go nowhere near Sheeaun Lodge. Forget about that as a base from now on". And off he went into the summer's night as bonfires could be seen blazing away in the far distance.

The four men he left by the rocks were in total shock. The news had numbed them. It had been a bloody and barbaric day. A bad day for the BFC. But they had only heard half the story. The other half would reach them in the morning. An update from the Bourkes had yet to be received by Hughie. And a Scotsman who would change their lives was only miles and hours away.

CHAPTER 27: REUNION ISLAND

On the eve of bonfire night Fr. Rea and Ecclesiasticus had rowed Patrick, Agnes, Andrew and Martha Bourke across the narrow but dangerous channel of water between Claggan and Annah Island. Packie Tadhg made the Bourkes welcome; and allowed them free reign in his house as he worked on repairing boats as usual in his back yard.

When 6pm the following day arrived there was nervous tension. The Bourkes were flummoxed by the emotions they felt. The father, Patrick, was of course very relieved that his son was alive but could not understand how he had come to defect and was now working for the hated Germans. Similarly, his wife Agnes's prime desire was to see her beloved Bartholomew again. She did not particularly care whose side he was on as long as he was alive. She was a religious woman and deplored all violence but was just so grateful that her desperate prayers to return her son had been answered. Andrew was just looking forward to seeing his brother again. Martha had brought her pencil and copybook as she excitedly updated it with all of the questions she had for her long-lost brother. Other pages contained little reminders of recent stories from the parish that Batty might be interested in.

For example, she would update him on the career of Jean Pierre Roland that she was closely following, that he was now in London with 'The Great El Ginto' and that a movie was being made in Hollywood not only on that play but on its follow-up swashbuckler 'Lothario of the Loch'. She would tell Batty of the scandal of Terence McDonnell's supposed affair with Antoinette Carey and the departure of his wife. She was also sure that Batty would be glad to learn that Royston Carey had recently inherited his uncle's hotel in Castlebar and was supposed to be moving there with his wife and children to run that business and set up a new funeral director service in that town. Benny Hughton Junior had become engaged to Rebecca Carey who was now teaching in St. Kieran's and word was that Benny Junior would take over the running of Carey's Bar. She would also tell Batty that one of the Deeneys was about to graduate as a lawyer in Dublin, and that the widow Cooney was to remarry – the lucky man being the one and only Toothy Lucey! It was a love story that boosted the parish in the midst of war and hardship.

It is difficult to describe the scenes of emotion at the jetty on Annah Island that evening as Ecclesiasticus and Fr. Rea brought Batty Bourke in a boat to reunite with his family after over six years. All but the cold Hungarian were in tears as the soldier was hugged by his overjoyed parents, who clasped him so tight they never wanted to let go. Andrew respectfully stood back to let his crying sister get her moment of joy with Batty before he got his opportunity for a bear hug.

Andrew was surprised at Batty's appearance. His hair had gone grey despite him being only 30 years of age and he had a huge bushy grey beard. He looked more like 50. The hair had the effect of making his head too big for the rest of his body which certainly did not appear as muscular as it was once, it now seemed just thin. Batty's skin looked very dark, and Andrew was not sure if it was a tan or just dirt. He put it down to the sweat and dust of being stuck in an underwater vessel for weeks. Batty's face looked thinner and this had the effect of making his teeth more prominent; and his teeth were now yellow and stained. When he hugged Batty he could not help but notice the stench of sweat from his brother, but of course he was just so overwhelmed to see him that he did not care.

Ecclesiasticus kept looking around and observing his surroundings as Patrick Bourke led his reunited family on the warm midsummer's evening to Packie Tadhg's for a feast of sausages, bacon, pudding and warm brown bread that Agnes had prepared in her host's kitchen. Everyone noticed how hungry the soldier was as he greedily devoured the food and swallowed the warm tea. He had been cooped up in a warm tin with over a dozen smelly Germans for over a month after all. He was starving, and could not wait to change have a wash and soap scrub in the island water and shave later on. But first, following his wonderfully welcome meal, he knelt with his family as an emotional Fr. Rea led five decades of the joyful mysteries in thanks for bringing back Batty to his family.

Batty was transformed as he changed into a fresh khaki outfit and reappeared clean shaven after his dip in the water by the jetty. It was then time for Martha to set her copy book on him, but Andrew noticed that Batty's attention span seemed greatly diminished. He would appear interested in each story their sister had, but then his eyes seemed to drift. And his eyes seemed much sadder. The glint seemed to have gone. And sometimes when his mind wandered off from Martha's chatter he seemed to pick a spot on the wall and fix his gaze on it, and after a few seconds his smile would disappear and his mouth would turn downwards. Patrick and Agnes noticed this too but they had prepared themselves better than Andrew. They both knew that Batty must have endured some of the horrors of war in his six year absence; he had not been on a holiday. He had been in the thick of the cruellest conflict ever unleashed on this earth. They knew that the old Batty would never return, but they thanked the Lord for bringing their flesh and blood back to them.

His eyes lit up for a moment when he spoke of his daughter Agatha and his wife Ruth, and Martha was delighted to see the photograph of both. Tears rolled down Agnes's cheeks as she saw her first grandchild for the first time.
"They will come with me next time for sure", said Batty, his Mayo accent replaced by a German one.
"They are just beautiful", said Agnes, "I would so love to meet them".

Packie Tadhg, Fr. Rea and Ecclesiasticus made themselves scarce as the family caught up with each other. The Hungarian had reminded them that they only had two hours. He was not going to give them a minute more or a minute less. Just a mile or so up the coast the unloading of arms and fuel from the German vessel was continuing as planned as German and Irish voices mixed in the common goal to defeat the British. Harry Heraty's plans were executed efficiently. It was one of his finest hours to date.

Whilst the female Bourkes wanted to find out more about Batty's wife and child, the males were more interested in finding out how he had come to switch sides in the war.

"I had no choice father. The three captured with me were executed. I was spared because I was the only Irish one. And even then, they made it difficult for me". What Batty could not bring himself to tell them was that the Germans had forced him to execute his captured colleagues one by one, as they knelt on a concrete floor in a cell with their hands tied behind their backs, begging for their lives to be spared for the sake of their wives and little children back in England. One by one, amid heartbroken pleas from grown men with tears flowing down their cheeks as their minds pictured the sad faces of their loved ones, the Boy from Ballycroy – in order for him to be allowed keep his life – had to send a bullet through each of their skulls. Each bullet brought a chorus of Lucifer's laughter from their German captors. The sound of the Englishmen's cries, the sight of their teardrops hitting the concrete floor, and the image of the blood splattered walls haunted Batty for every hour of his life. But he could not talk about it. He just was not able to put that horror into words. He could remember the exact plea, word for word, from each of his sobbing comrades that awful day.

He was able to tell the Bourkes about the time he spent in Munich, where he sharpened his German language skills. There too he began working to teach German military recruits about the history between Ireland and Britain. He was also expected to give an insight into the British way of thinking. Part of his duties involved the teaching of regularly used phrases and highlighting the variety of British accents. His students were being prepared for lives as spies. All of the Bourkes were fascinated. They also listened agog as he described the beauty of Munich. The music, the art, the fine buildings, the river Isar. They tried to picture it.

"But I have yet to witness the beauty that is this evening" he said in slight German tones. "Beautiful Achill on one side and beautiful Ballycroy on the other side, competing on which looks better in the mirror of the inlet waters below them" he added poetically. "This is worth the fight".

"And of course you. My family. You all look so well. You all look so happy. I have missed you so much. And I am sorry for the pain I have caused you. But I am fine. I shall always be fine. You know now not to worry any more. I am a soldier. I am strong. I will survive. Look after yourselves". The joy of the reunion was about to be replaced by the heartbreak of parting again. The five Bourkes embraced each other in a ring, and again knelt by Martha to say more prayers. They were interrupted by the door opening and the foreign accent of Ecclesiasticus saying "We have no more time. We must go. Immediately!"

After their two hour get together, Batty departed from the jetty, this time accompanied by two German colleagues who had arrived in a rubber boat for him. Fr. Rea was staying behind for now. As was Ecclesiasticus. He was communicating by signal with his counterparts high up on the mountains. He would not be evacuating the family until it was safe to do so. And by 8.30pm the signals were that there may be some distress. That it certainly was not safe. But he did not relay this to the family. They could not tell from his demeanour that there was anything to worry about. He always had the same serious expression. This helped him to be the excellent spy that he was.

As the U-boat left from the waters surrounding Innishbiggle at 9pm and headed out into the Atlantic, Major Bartholomew Vandenburg ordered that it resurface for a moment so that he could have one last valued view of his beloved Ballycroy. His German colleagues joined him on deck as he peered at the bonfires in the distance that were illuminating the parish in the foreground, with the towering outline of the Nephin Mountains as the backdrop. He tried to focus in on his home village in Aughness South, but the smoke from the blazing bonfires obscured his view.

Little did he know that the smoke he saw coming from Aughness South was not from a bonfire. It was from the Bourke family home. As Batty re-entered his vessel to disappear deep into the bowels of the ocean, Corporal Graham Gilberthorpe was looking on smiling as the Bourke house blazed. A dozen of his vengeful colleagues cheered as the flames went higher into the cloudless night sky. The hay was now being doused in fuel to be set alight as well. From a nearby willow tree blood was dripping onto the grass below. It was coming from the mouth of 15 year old

Seaneen White. He had tried manfully to stop his neighbours' home being burnt by the Black and Tans. He was now hanging dead from the tree. His family did not yet know that their second son had just been murdered. Gilberthorpe did not care. The boy would just be the first victim in revenge for had just happened in Mulranny three hours earlier.

Gilberthorpe had earlier received confirmation from his Dublin HQ that Batty Bourke had not been killed in the war. He had survived. But he had fought with the Germans. Against Gilberthorpe and his country. Treason. The Bourkes were now fair game. There were rumours that he was possibly back in Ireland. This one of the 'Boys of Ballycroy' was now high on the British enemy list. He or anyone that harboured him were legitimate targets. They would be executed without trial.

There were screams from the mother of Seaneen White as the armoured car containing the shouting Black and Tans left Aughness South and headed for Newport Barracks. On the way the vehicle stopped briefly on the road outside of Carey's Bar as a bonfire blazed nearby across the road from Paul the Butcher's. There was commotion in the bar as the vehicle was spotted and everyone heeded the shout from Royston Carey for everyone to dive to the ground. Drinking glasses smashed on the floor, and children who had been standing by the bonfire ran for cover and dived into the adjacent field. One of Gilberthorpe's men turned the machine gun on the back of the truck towards the bar and shop. After about twenty seconds a round of rapid machine gun fire was launched on the premises and the windows shattered as they were hit. Screams could be heard from within the bar and the shop, and from the frightened children in the field. After about 30 seconds the firing stopped and there was silence. Then a whistle sounded. Gilberthorpe stepped from the truck. There was no Ballycroy person to be seen but he knew that he had an attentive audience. For a third time he gave an address outside of Carey's Bar.

"I have plenty of more bullets for you, you peasants!" he shouted. "For every one of my men you get, I will get ten of you, I assure you. This is fucking WAR! To the McDonnells – I will fucking dice you into cubes! To Royston – start making plenty of fucking coffins! Fuck you! Fuck you all you papish bastards!"

His words were met with silence. Then to the relief of the terrorised locals, the truck revved up and sped away, accompanied by the usual thuggish cheers from its occupants. It was a miracle that no-one had been hit by the machine gun fire. Royston and his sisters surveyed the damage. The frightened children cried by the bonfire.

Many of the IRA men coming from their work on Innishbiggle had heard the sound of the gunfire. They heard the sound of the Crossley Tender speeding off and they pedalled furiously to Ballycroy Village, expecting to find a scene of carnage. They were relived to find that no one was injured. But they were furious at the terror that had been brought. Harry Heraty listened to some of the children as they repeated what Gilberthorpe had said. He and Colm Tierney tried to calm some of them and reassure them that the IRA would protect them from the Tans. As they sat by the bonfire with the kids, a breathless young lad from Aughness South dismounted his bicycle.

"They've hung Seaneen White, they've hung Seaneen White! And they've burned the Bourkes out of it!" he panted. The West Mayo OC and the North Mayo OC looked at each other's faces in the light coming from the blaze. Their blood boiled. Only half an hour earlier they had heard in Doona of the deaths near Mulranny.

Bonfire Night had brought them their arms shipment, but it had also brought blood. Innocent blood.

CHAPTER 28: MOUNTAIN MUTINY

At 6am on the morning of June 24th the dawn lit up Crafton Lake. It was a corry lake, about half a mile long and a quarter of a mile wide. It was fiddle-shaped, with the circular end situated under steep mountain edges. During penal times the lake had been the location for illegal masses, where Catholics gathered to avoid persecution by the dominant British forces of Protestantism. There was a mass rock situated on the Mulranny side of the lake, where the priests of the time had celebrated those secret masses. Legend had it that one of the priests had been drowned by the redcoats there, and that he had taken a golden chalice into the lake with him to avoid the British getting their hands on it. In the interim years, many young adventurous Ballycroy youths had spent time diving deep into the lake, hoping to find the treasure!

The lake was nestled in the mountains high above Ballycroy, about three miles from the nearest house in Ballyveeney below. It was difficult to access. As he admired the reflection of the surrounding heathery inclines in the still water from his observation point at a rock on the Ballyveeney side, Sylvester McDonnell felt a strange calm. Although he was worried about his missing brother and had not slept a wink because of this, he felt a connection with the people of the past who had defied the British authorities by convening by that very lake to pursue their faith. He felt he was now continuing their good fight. He was proud to be at the forefront of the modern fight against the hated occupiers. And he had personally ensured that some of the aggressors would be returning to Britain in coffins. He looked at his sleeping companions, and then cast his eyes over the waking parish of Ballycroy below. He looked out into the sea and wondered what it must have been like for his old friend Batty returning and then heading back into the deep ocean.

Suddenly he heard some movement high up on the Mulranny side of the mountain overlooking the lake and he looked up to see the outline of two figures walking on the horizon. Against the blue morning sky he could see them. He darted over to his colleagues and shook each of them to wake them, saying that there was someone coming. The startled men then hid behind the rocks before they heard the familiar whistle of 'Silent Night' again. This time Sylvester recognised the whistler immediately. It was his brother Terence! With a mixture of relief, delight and pride he ran towards him and embraced his smiling sibling. He was of course, distracted by the small, stocky, smiling companion in a khaki outfit, carrying a bayonet rifle and a sack of belongings.

"Who is your friend Terence?" he asked as the rest of the BFC gathered round.
"This is Joey Jarvis, he's on our side" was the reply as the Scot smiled at the contingent.
"Pleased to meet you Joey" said Sylvester reaching out to shake his hand.
"Likewise I'm sure" said Joey clasping his hand.
"You're Scottish?!" exclaimed PJ White.
"Aye", said Joey "Is it THAT obvious?"
As Willie gripped his hand PJ and Eddie looked at each other, and then PJ addressed his captain.
"Terence, can you explain? How come we have a Brit with us this morning?"
"Joey is on OUR side now" said Terence.
"NOW!? NOW!? What do you mean by that? Was he on the opposite side until NOW!?" asked PJ raising his voice, before the Scot interjected.
"Aye. I came over not knowing what I was getting into. But now I'm on the run from the Tans as well" he explained, but PJ was having none of it.
"This is fecking unbelievable!" he shouted. Eddie decided to back up his friend.
"What's this, you get a Ballycroy man shot and you replace him with your Scottish boyfriend?" he ranted at Terence.
"What did you fucking say?" snarled Terence angrily, "I fucking dare you to repeat that".
"How can you do this?" asked Eddie, turning to the others. "Lads, why don't you agree? How can he bring a Tan in amongst us?"
"He will bayonet us in our sleep" said PJ. "Once a Brit, always a Brit!"
"McArthur, I dare you to fucking repeat what you fucking said!" roared Terence. "Withdraw your remark or I'll have you fucking shot!"

"I will not withdraw it!" shouted Eddie. "Go on! Shoot me! Go on! Go on! Shoot me! Shoot your own and lick up to the Tans!"

Terence ran towards Eddie and PJ in temper, but was wrestled to the ground by a combination of Joey and Sylvester. As he cursed at Eddie and struggled to fight off the men who were holding him, Willie had to help restrain him as his face grew purple with rage. The young recruits had gone too far to back down now. The damage was done, so they went for the jugular.

"Let him shoot me!" shouted Eddie. "Shooting Ballycroy men and women. Isn't that all you are good for Terence?"
As the incandescent leader struggled to fight off the three who were restraining him, Sylvester decided he had heard enough and he sprung from the melee on the ground and like a charging bull aimed his head at Eddie's midriff, flattening him to the ground. He followed this up by belting three successive right hand punches into the face of his dazed victim. PJ tried to force Sylvester off Eddie, but was met with a left handed punch from the rising Sylvester which floored him also. Within seconds Sylvester was standing over PJ with a pistol pointing down to his face as he gazed skywards from the flat of his back. Terence had taken a similar position over the bleeding Eddie.

"Lads, lads, cool it! Cool it!" said the Scottish accent. "You Irish are always fighting amongst yourselves, cool it for a minute please!"
"Shut up Joey!" panted Terence, wiping the sweat from his forehead with his left hand whilst aiming his gun at the moaning Eddie on the ground.
"Now McArthur" he continued. "Many's the time I fucked your sister, but I am going to fuck your fucking skull with a bullet if you don't apologise within ten seconds. I fucking mean it!" he roared.
"Don't kill him Terence!" begged a worried Sylvester, knowing what his brother was capable of in a rage. "Please Terence, think of what you're doing".
"I'm sorry Terence!" cried Eddie from the dew covered heather. "I'm sorry; I'm just upset over Dyra. I didn't mean it!"

"What did you say sorry for?!" shouted PJ from beneath Sylvester's pistol. "Sure you did nothing wrong Eddie! Sure it wasn't YOU who brought a Tan to our hideout. It wasn't YOU who killed Esmeralda Gay".

Silence struck the group as their leader absorbed what he had just heard.
"What do you mean, Esmeralda Gay?" asked Terence, looking over at his brother ruefully.

The next few minutes were spent explaining to Terence what news Hughie had brought the night previously. The group calmed down and Sylvester allowed PJ up off the ground as Terence sat back on a rock and placed his head of curly black hair between his hands. He was distraught. He had just been told that he had killed two innocent people at the Mulranny ambush. He tried to take it all in. After several deep breaths, and pats on his shoulder, including one from a seemingly apologetic PJ, he stood and walked towards the edge of the high bank looking down on the lake. As he gathered his thoughts, it crossed his mind that he should blame the deceased Cecil Dyra, but it was likely that Eddie had witnessed him firing at the car from his mountain perch. The others waited in silence for him to speak. They expected the usual curse. Maybe even a prayer. But as usual Terence surprised them.

"Esmeralda Gay. I lost my virginity to her!" he exclaimed. The others did not know whether to laugh or cry!

As Terence sat back on his rock, the Scot decided to capitalise by addressing his audience.
"Listen lads. I totally understand yer reaction. I came over with the Auxiliaries thinking we were fighting scum. I quickly realised that WE were the scum. That I was fighting on the side of the same tyrants who made the lives of my family a misery in Glasgow. I quickly realised that I had more in common with ye. So I stopped taking their money, and am on my way back to my sister in London. She is all I have left. And if they capture me, I'll be hung for treason. No question. So I'm just passing through on my way to Sligo. But I'll help ye out for a few weeks if I can,

before heading on that way" he said as he pointed in the Sligo direction. There was total silence.

"I'll be honest with you. I will tell you the full story some night by the fireside. And I know I cannot prove myself to you. Yet. But I'm on your side I assure you. I just want a safe passage through them mountains and I'll repay you in return by telling you anything I can about the British. I assure you, if they rounded all of us up I'd be the first man hung. But I understand your situation. I will have to earn your trust."

"That man saved my life last night" said Terence. "The place was crawling with Tans looking for me and he kept me hidden. He could have shot me if he wanted to. He's a Celtic man for God's sake".
"But he would say that, wouldn't he?" said PJ. "How can we trust a Tan? Really, in all honesty?"
"You can shoot me if you want, Lad" said Joey marching towards PJ and offering his gun. "I hope you don't but you can".
"Go back Joey!" said Terence. "Willie, bring him down to the lake and see if there is anything in the net. The Scots should be good with all of their lochs" he laughed.

After all of the tension had died down Terence received a briefing from the rest of the men. As they all had some bread, cheese and barely-cooked rabbit meat, they looked down over the beautiful morning sky over the parish. After a while they noticed a figure approaching them through the brown bog. They recognised him as Hughie. As he drew nearer he looked pale. He looked very tired. Sweat was pouring from the runner. His clothes were soaked.

They gave him some bread and water as he drew breath. He threw his sack of food for them to the ground. He sat down with his back up against a rock, his chest heaving.
"My feet are killing me" he said kicking off his boots. He pulled down his sweaty socks to reveal purple blisters, one of them seeping with yellow pus. He was still hyperventilating.
"Lads. Ye must all sit. I have terrible news" he said. They all looked at each other and gathered around. They noticed that

Hughie was not making eye contact with anyone. This must be really bad. He tried to control his breathing. Terence, Sylvester, Willie, PJ, Eddie and Joey all waited in anticipation.
"Who is he?" he asked pointing at Joey.
"Never mind, he's one of us" said Terence urging Hughie to reveal his news.

"I'm sorry" splurted the runner, "But the Tans attacked Bourke's and Carey's last night. Bourke's was burned to the ground".
"Are the Bourkes safe?" asked Sylvester anxiously,
"The Bourkes were kept on the island and Batty got away, but I've bad news still" said the young O'Hora, beginning to choke on his words. He slowly looked across at PJ who was crouched waiting for the news.
"PJ. PJ, they got Seaneen!" said Hughie as a tear came to his eye.

They all looked at PJ as his face turned as white as a cloud. His brother was dead. He was paralysed by the news. He tried to rise to his feet but stumbled, and fell over on top of Eddie.
"Oh no!" said Terence. "How Hughie?"
"They hung him. He tried to stop the burning at Bourkes. They found out that Batty was still alive and with the Germans" said the tearful runner.

PJ White stomped around in circles. Hands to his head. Pulling at his own ginger locks. He was muttering incoherently to himself. Terence noticed that he was frothing at the mouth. "Get him some water! Quick!" he ordered.

Within a minute PJ the young volunteer had flown into a rage and again Willie, Sylvester and Joey were the restrainers. Unable to hit out at anyone physically, the strong young lad commenced a vitriolic assault at the McDonnell brothers and their cousin.
"Ye feckers! Ye feckers! Ye useless feckers! I told ye last night that we should be fecking down there. But no! We lay here with tonnes of guns whilst my baby brother fought the Brits with his bare hands! Ye feckers. YE are the cause of him dying! Murderers! Ye feckers! Ye feckers! Ye just murder women and cows and young fellas! And YE are supposed to be fecking heroes"?!

Everyone was shocked. They tried to understand his rage. Terence stared at the ground. The three continued to restrain PJ. "Let me go! Let me go! Let me fecking home to Ma and Da! Let me fecking go!" he roared before breaking into a loud and sorrowful outburst of tears. "Seaneen. Poor Seaneen! Seaneen! Oh no! My little brother. What have ye done to Seaneen?" he wailed. The three stood back and allowed him to drop to his knees. His head bowed in sorrow. His good friend Eddie was also crying and knelt beside PJ. He put his arm around him.

"We are sorry!" said Sylvester sensing that Terence had chosen the right option in not opening his mouth to further inflame the situation. "The poor lad. We will get them for this"!
"Awful" said Willie. "May he rest in peace. May his death not be in vain".
"I will have to head to Aughness with him" said Eddie lifting his head up.

Terence bit his lip. He stared at the ground, trying to control his emotions. Joey put a friendly arm on his shoulder. Sylvester came over and whispered:
"We will have to let them go, Terence" he said. "There is no way we can keep them here. They'll kill us all just to escape".
"There will be four of us left" said Joey. "Ye can count on me. We will manage. They can rejoin us after the funeral". Terence kept staring at the ground. But there was more to come from Hughie.

"They sprayed Carey's with bullets but no one got hit, thank God. It was a miracle. Gilberthorpe announced to everyone that he would kill the McDonnells. He said that he would kill ten Irish for every one of theirs. And Admiral Gay has declared war on our column as well. And, one more piece of news. The crown has admitted that they lost more than one yesterday".

"Didn't I tell ye?" interrupted Sylvester, "Didn't I tell ye there were more?!"
"Sergeant Clive died too" announced Hughie and all heads raised again.

"Sergeant Clive?" asked Willie in a surprised tone. "How? Was he in one of the trucks?"
"They say he got trapped beneath the one that keeled into the bay and was drowned" said Hughie. "They are now saying they lost three altogether".
"That means they will kill 30 of us" said Eddie.
"THREE is shite too!" said Sylvester, "We got a lot more of them than that, I am telling you. The truth will come out yet. On my solemn oath it will".
"They always downplay their losses and exaggerate the gains" contributed Joey.

By now PJ was back on his feet and one by one they hugged the sobbing red head. Terence gave his sympathies and discharged the two men. He made sure they had a pistol each and asked them to meet up with the column on Bunmore Hill at The Shepherd's Hut exactly 24 hours after the burial, whenever that would be. He told them to be careful and to be good soldiers. He told them to think with their heads and not with their hearts. PJ was in bits. They all expected one final outburst from him but he could not find the energy. The six footer looked as if he had just been shrunk by the news. All of a sudden Eddie looked taller than him. Hughie put his boots back on and followed the two friends as they headed out slowly for Aughness South. Despite his blisters, the runner assured them that he would return that evening with a further update.

The four remaining men gathered together by the side of the lake and three of them undressed and entered the icy cold water. Willie stayed on sentry duty. There was no laughing, no cheering, no horseplay. They immersed themselves in the water in shock and silence. Terence tried to gather his thoughts. Images of Esmeralda bounced around in his mind. Her sultry smile. Her soft skin. Her freckles. Her posh accent. The sound of his bullets hitting the car. The shattering of glass. The thud of the car crashing to a halt. The blood pouring from Dyra's neck wound. The sound of the ensuing gunshot which finished the youth. The smile on Seaneen White's cherub face when he welcomed him home from America. The night Sergeant Clive wished everyone in Carey's a Happy Christmas. The scare that Antoinette must have got when the bar was peppered with bullets. The horror that the parents of Cecil and Seaneen must be going through.

On the heathery embankment with his rifle perched by his side Willie counted on his fingers. Cecil, Esmeralda, her driver, the sound Sergeant Clive, the two dead Tans, Seaneen. Seven dead in one day.

Surely it was the bloodiest day ever in Ballycroy's long history?

CHAPTER 29: TAKING STOCK

In Newport Barracks, a sweaty Graham Gilberthorpe paced around the meeting room on his own. He had a headache. He was stressed. His ears were buzzing from the admonishment he had just received from his superiors who had come from Dublin. He had lost five of his men, one RIC man, and a truck on the Mulranny Ballycroy border. Yes, six men altogether. This embarrassing figure was to be kept from the newspapers. Not only that, but it was now known that one of the 'Boys of Ballycroy' had returned in a German U-boat on his watch, to hand out weapons and bullets to be used against the British. The location of the arms was as yet unknown, but it had been made clear to the corporal that he was now expected to retrieve them from the hands of the peasants.

It had also been made clear to Gilberthorpe that he was now to focus solely on Ballycroy. It had previously only received peripheral attention, but everything had now changed. He was to bring as many staff as he could to the new barracks at Castlehill. He was to ensure that the McDonnells and their cousin and the rest of their band of bandits were hunted down. He was to ensure that their heroism was to be put to an end. He was expected to be effective, ruthless and efficient. But above all he was expected to redeem himself and win.

He was joined in the room by his counterpart in charge of the Belmullet area. He empathised with Gilberthorpe, and said his men would support his in any way they could. Already he was making efforts to ensure that two Alsatian dogs trained in man-hunting were to be brought from the hillocks of Cavan and Monaghan where they had been successfully used. Gilberthorpe thanked his colleague, and they headed off to see the five coffins of their men.

It took a lot to bring a tear to the steely man from Deal in Kent, but he wept at the sight of the bodies of his five men in the mortuary. Each of them had been killed by a McDonnell bullet. Soldiers Napier, Robinson, Pritchard, Hillyer and Clement. He clenched his fists and swore to avenge them.

Raised on the south eastern English coast, from his home he could see the French coastline on a clear day. He swam the icy waters there daily in his youth, and won many competitions in that sport. He had been one of those British lucky enough to survive the bloodshed at Gallipoli during the Great War, and had won a medal for bravery. After his return home, he and his wife divorced and it was a welcome distraction for him to take up his assignment in Ireland to fight the Irish rebels. He had not though, expected the ferocity of the natives, and their skills in guerrilla warfare. He had expected a facile victory. He certainly had not expected to be sending five of his men back to Kent dead. He now had to improve his performance. He had to be more thorough in his planning. He had to try and get inside the minds of the Irish.

Getting inside the minds of the British was something that Joey Jarvis helped the BFC with as they contemplated their next moves. He was certain that Ballycroy would now receive much more attention. The British would feel humiliated and would be seeking revenge. Rules of war would mean nothing. Everyone and everything in Ballycroy was fair game.

He urged Sylvester, Terence and Willie to think carefully about attending the Dyra and White funerals. The Black and Tans could be waiting in the environs of the wake houses or at the graveyard. They would want to make an example of the 'Boys of Ballycroy' when the opportunity arose. He said that in other areas the British had abducted local hostages and carried them in their convoys to dissuade the Irish from firing on them. The biggest danger though, in his opinion, was informers who would sell out their fighters if it meant that their own properties and families were ignored by the British. "Informers", he said, "Are Ireland's curse".

Terence knew that the people of Ballycroy were hurting. He knew that a large section of them would be angry with him and his men. He knew that they too had to redeem themselves. Sergeant Clive had been a moderate. Despite his position and rank, he had been liked and the parish could have ended up with much worse. In relative terms, he had been well-respected. He had often turned a blind eye to questionable activities. Admiral Gay and his family had always been popular despite their background. They had always been generous to the locals. The unfortunate death of his daughter had now alienated a family who had supported the Irish cause. And it had also cut off their main congregation point. The death of the innocent driver would also win the BFC no friends, even though the killing was not intentional. The Dyra and White families would also obviously be deeply upset. Fr. Kinsella would be upset at having to bury two youths from the parish, and would undoubtedly denounce the column from the altar. The Careys and their clientele would be upset that for a third time, Gilberthorpe had been able to let his men run riot there and give one of his vitriolic addresses without a Ballycroy gunman to be seen to defend the locals. Their reputation was at stake. The words from PJ and Eddie haunted the column leader. What HAD Terence ever done other than kill a cow, a woman and her innocent companion? Of course Terence knew that he had done a lot more than this, but he was intelligent enough to realise what the perception must be.

If he had any doubts in asking these questions of himself, they were put away when he got to meet Harry Heraty when he accompanied Hughie to Crafton Lake late at night and asked to meet Terence alone. The West Mayo OC gave him a verbal lashing on a number of fronts. He was clearly infuriated. What the hell was a Scottish Tan doing in the group? Why did he fire on Esmeralda Gay's car? Why did he allow Hughie break the news of Seaneen's hanging to PJ in front of the whole group? Was it true that he had left Dyra to die on the side of the road? Why hadn't he bombed the bridge in time?

Terence tried his best to counter, but Heraty was in no mood to listen.
"We have three fecking funerals in my home town on Sunday evening because of you!" he shouted as the others listened by the fireside twenty yards away.
"And the Tans have young Dyra in a morgue in Castlebar and they won't release his body back to his poor family – no doubt they are doctoring it. And young White is lying in a coffin. And the Gays,

our most valuable allies, have turned on us. All because YOU fecked up!!"

"How did I feck up?!" answered Terence, "Sure you got your shipment?"

"No thanks to you!" roared Heraty. "And that's another thing, lad, the Bourkes are STILL stranded on Annah and cannot even attend their neighbour's funeral. And we have to try and find them a safe house in Achill now! A fecking safe house for a family of four including a handicap – how fecking hard a job is that?!"

"But surely you knew there would be lives put at risk?" tried Terence.

"Shut up Terence! You are putting us ALL at risk now with that Joey fella. If he turns on ye YOU will roast in hell!" exclaimed Heraty.

"He's an asset", said Terence before Heraty continued his volley.

"Get your act in order, lad. Make sure you get your two men back after the funeral and keep the Brits at bay from the Mulranny side. I have to get the shipment distributed and you better help me!"

"But sure Hughie said Castlehill Barracks is full of Tans already, they're already in!" said Terence.

"You just keep them at bay, keep them occupied!" replied Heraty. "I went to school with Johnny Ryan and now I have to meet his widow and three children tomorrow because you shot his car. And Clive went to school with me".

"Fuck Clive!" shouted Terence. "He was on his way to intercept your shipment. I fucking saved your shipment from him Harry".

"He did not know about the shipment that evening" responded Heraty. "Gilberthorpe had only found out Batty was alive, so they were just on their way to burn the house, which they ended up doing anyway in spite of you. They only found out about the shipment after that".

"And who told them about Batty?!" roared Terence defiantly. "It certainly wasn't one of MY men. And OF COURSE they knew of the shipment. Why two trucks? It doesn't take twenty men to burn a house! They were on their way to engage ye. DON'T treat ME like an amadán! DON'T try to lay the guilt on ME! I'm fucking warning you Harry! And I tried to drag poor Dyra with me but they were firing on me. Perhaps you would be happier if I died alongside him!"

"Shut up lad!!" replied Heraty. "Just get on with it now! Keep the Tans at bay and not by your bed".
"There's only fucking four of us. I need help!" pleaded Terence.
"I'll see what can be done", said Harry calming his tone. "But for the moment you have enough food. And you've enough bullets to keep them at bay. Occupy them. Fight them".

With that, he headed off into the darkness with Hughie. A chastened Terence walked slowly back to join his brother, cousin and Joey by the fire. It was all very quiet.

At 6am the following morning the four of them came down from Crafton. They passed through the forest at the base of the mountain and followed the river down to a spot near Dyra's house. They then headed across the marshy bogland towards Bunmore Hill. This was a different route, which added mileage to their journey. They had now to avoid Sheeaun Lodge, so they had to alter their plans. By 9am they were settling into their new position on Bunmore Hill. The Shepherd's Hut was built on the sheltered shoulder of the north facing side of the hill. It overlooked the five houses of Bunmore village, and beyond that the line of houses that formed Shranamonragh village could be seen. One could see Aughness South and North, and beyond that again lay Erris and the Mullet Peninsula.

The thatched roof on the hut had almost collapsed, but they had previously done some work trying to repair it. Some of the stones had crumbled from the gables but both were still solid, and one of them had a fireplace and chimney. There was just one small gap in the wall which acted as a window, and the wooden door had rotted away so they discussed how they might replace it. The Scot was fascinated, and he observed the surrounding fox and badger holes. The hut had been built on a patch of green that seemed out of place in the surrounding heather.

"Apparently it was built for a herdsman but he never lived long enough to move in" said Willie. "It was built before the famine, and it's said a few famished here".
"Amazing!" smiled Joey. "We'll have ghosts for company so! It's so sheltered. And close enough to the top too. Perfect!"

After retrieving some hidden food the men headed up to a patch near the summit where they took up a position looking down on Ballycroy Village. They knew a crowd would be gathering soon for the funeral mass of Seaneen White. As Joey stood and looked around at the surrounding spectacular scenery, his three companions took turns peering through his binoculars. They had never handled a set before. They answered all of Joey's questions as he pointed out various islands and headlines and asked their names. He was particularly fascinated by Black Rock Island which could be seen far out into the ocean. He then sat down with the three as they observed that the Black and Tans had indeed men guarding all approach roads to the church and graveyard. Their presence would increase tensions with the locals for sure.

Over the next couple of hours, the four men maintained their position. The day was bright and sunny, although there was some cloud. They took turns looking through the binoculars and could see Roy Carey's horse drawn hearse parked by the church gates. They watched as the coffin was carried to the graveyard gates and up the incline to where the large crowd gathered to bury the hanged youth. The wind that whistled around the hill, even on a clear enough day, prevented the four from hearing anything from below.

As they rose and prepared to head back to the hut, Terence gave one final look through the glasses at the graveyard. He noticed movement in the crowd there. But it was running. Not just walking.
"Lads, something's happening down there!" he said and his companions stalled in their tracks.
"People are running, there must be a shooting or something!" he exclaimed.
"We did not hear shots. We would have heard the shots" said Joey grabbing the binoculars. "Och aye, something has disturbed them alright".
"What shall we do?" asked Willie.
"Well, the place is crawling with Tans" said Sylvester.
"Back to base for now, back to base!" directed Terence feeling helpless. "Hughie will be here soon to update us".

But as they came close to the Shepherd's Hut the reason for the disturbance appeared. Heavy black smoke could be seen rising from Aughness South in the distance.

"Oh no!" said Terence. "The bastards have burnt Whites. They have fucking burnt Whites!"

"The feckers!" raged Sylvester. "The cowardly feckers. What shall we do?"

"Burning a house while the family are burying their son. Bastards!" said Willie.

"I told ye" said Joey, "There will be no mercy now. It's absolute war".

"There's nothing we can do for the Whites yet" said Terence trembling. "We could head for Aughness but it could be a trap. I want to head but we must be patient."

"Poor PJ" said Willie. "He will go fecking mad".

"We are ALL fecking mad!" said Terence. "But let me think, let me think a minute!"

It was a long day that the four spent camped on the side of Bunmore Hill. They hardly spoke a word all day. Each man was alone in his thoughts. What was their purpose? What would they do? What COULD they do? It was as if they were rooted in fear and confusion. How could they prevent burnings like this? If they moved closer to the villages they could be captured. They were greatly outnumbered. The realisation hit the Ballycroy men that they could only ambush on their terms, and not on British terms.

Hughie arrived that night with more food and more news. His hosts tried to remain calm as he delivered his latest update.

"You will have seen the burning" he said. "They razed Whites. During the funeral mass. No one thought to stay behind and guard the place. They could not even bury Seaneen in peace."

"How is PJ?" asked Terence.

"That's what I'm here with", replied Hughie. "He and Eddie were arrested this evening by the Tans. They were got close to the barracks. They had their guns on them. They had no chance but to surrender. There were dozens of them".

"Oh fuck!" said Terence.

"Oh fuck is right" said Hughie.

"It's execution or the prison ship for them" said Joey. "I hope they are spared".

"It looks like they were on the way to attack the barracks themselves" said Hughie. "But ye are right to hold yer fire. They are trying to smoke ye out. It's YE Gilberthorpe wants. He thought he would get ye today."

"We had no choice but to hold back" said Terence. "I hope Heraty gets us help".

"Ye will need it" replied Hughie. "Word is that the burning today was the work of the Belmullet Brigade"

"I knew it!" said Terence. "Sure we would have seen the convoy passing the church had it been Gilberthorpe. We would have seen them coming down the road".

"We should have kept watch on the Bangor road too" said Willie.

"How can four of us watch every fucking direction?" snarled the angry Terence.

"You're right" said Hughie. "I should have orders from Captain Heraty tomorrow. He is in Westport tonight. The wakes are on there. For Esmeralda, Ryan and Clive. And he's in Castlebar tomorrow as they're trying to get Cecil Dyra's body back from the coroner. They say it's needed for an inquest or something".

"The fuckers!" said Terence. "They're only trying to take the bullets from his body to save themselves. God blast Gilberthorpe anyway!"

"And by the way" added Hughie recapturing their attention, "Father Kinsella denounced ye today in the church. He asked where the defenders were when a rope was tied around Seaneen's neck".

"I suppose he didn't fucking ask why they were putting a rope around his neck in the first place, did he?" roared Terence rising to his feet from the stony corner. "No. He wouldn't ask that, would he? The bastard! He would probably greet Gilberthorpe with a cup of tea from his best china if he met him. And he curses us!"

As Hughie slept in his warm bed the following morning, the Gay family gathered in the Church of Ireland cemetery in Westport to bury their beloved Esmeralda. Half a mile away the just-widowed Molly Ryan stood alongside her three crying children as their

Daddy's coffin was lowered into his grave. Two miles further away the RIC community bid their final farewells to Sergeant Clive as his widow and daughter leaned on each other and shed their sorrowful tears of loss.

Tears fell in Ballyveeney too as young Cecil came home to the Dyra house for the final time. The distraught young family thanked Harry Heraty for getting the corpse home to them, but asked for no IRA presence at the wake house. As well as being broken-hearted, they were bitter. Neighbours gathered and asked Heraty for arms so that they could defend another house from being scorched during a burial. He promised to help in any way he could.

As the day became showery the McArthurs made room in their house for Sean and Nora White who were now homeless – and sonless. One of their sons was lying in his eternal resting place. The other was in an army truck being transported to Dublin in handcuffs. Tied beside him was Eddie McArthur. The two families united in grief in the Bunmore house.

Little did they realise that the men they were cursing most were only a quarter of a mile away in the camouflaged hut looking down on the McArthur farm, at the end of Bunmore village. Before the rain came the men had been busy trying to make repairs on the hut for the long winter. Now they were inside cleaning their rifles and waiting for orders.

June 1920 was coming to an end, but the Irish War of Independence certainly wasn't.

CHAPTER 30: A DIVIDED PARISH

On the morning of Cecil Dyra's burial, Willie Kerrigan and Joey Jarvis emerged from the caves by the banks of the Veeney River on Dyra's land. They had crept into them in the darkness of the night before, without being spotted. They were there with their rifles to fire at any Black and Tan vehicle that would approach to repeat what they had done in Aughness South and burn the homestead of the grieving family. There was no guarantee that there would be such an attack of course, but they were following orders delivered by Hughie from Harry Heraty.

Hiding elsewhere were the McDonnell brothers. They had positioned themselves on the outside of the graveyard perimeter fence. They crouched there in the nettles in their uniforms with their rifles resting against the wall. They were located at the top of the graveyard, where they had spied the grave of their column member being dug close to the top wall.

The rain came down as they heard the funeral procession arrive in the cemetery following mass. They were glad it was raining as it normally meant the Black and Tans were in shelter! Of course, they were taking a risk being there. As well as the threat of capture, they would probably have to deal with the ire of the Dyras and their families. They tried their best to be motionless. They had planned to make their appearance just before the coffin was lowered. For now, they would have to join their fellow parishioners in five decades of the sorrowful mysteries, which was being led by Fr. Kinsella amidst the wailing of Cecil's heartbroken mother and sisters.

Just as the second decade began, a cracking sound reverberated in the grey skies. Terence and Sylvester looked at each other as they sat with their backs to the wall. Then more shots rang out. They realised at once what was happening. The Dyra home was under attack and Willie and Joey were engaged in combat. There was more shooting. As it was coming from about three miles away as the bird flew, it was faint enough but it scared the funeral goers who gasped en masse. Some even threw themselves to the ground thinking the shooting was much nearer.

The adrenaline raced through Terence and it was too much for him to contain. He rose to his feet in excitement and leapt on top of the cemetery wall with his rifle, closely followed by his brother. There was a collective gasp of surprise from the crowd. They were already unnerved by the sound of the shooting, and now the sight of the two armed IRA men looking down at them from the wall was truly frightening. Again the crowd gasped as the sound of shooting from Ballyveeney continued.

The McDonnells surveyed the crowd and were heartened to see their parents and their sister. Their aunt Bridie was there too. They received nervous smiles from them but that was not the general sentiment as the crowd began to react to the shock of what they had just heard and what they were just witnessing. It was if two hundred people wanted their voices to be heard simultaneously.
"Put those damned guns away! Have you no respect?" uttered Fr. Kinsella in disgust.
"Yea, show some respect!" sneered Royston Carey in his black suit. "Have you not caused enough damage? Have you no shame?!"
"At least we fight, not like you Royston!" shouted Terence as he caught a glimpse of Antoinette in the startled crowd.
"I would rather not fight than kill innocents" shouted Royston as his elderly father moved to calm him down.
"Get away from this sacred ground!" shouted Fr. Kinsella to the McDonnells, "Have some respect for the Lord's dead!"
"It is our graveyard TOO!" shouted Fintan McDonnell, their father, as he rushed towards the priest before being grabbed by Mr. Dyra.

All of a sudden there was a fracas in the rain as several people started swearing at each other and pushing each other. The McDonnells were stunned to see parishioners fighting amongst themselves as the coffin lay by the open grave. It was impossible to hear all that was being said but it was clear the BFC had both opponents and friends in the crowd. The sound of shooting from Ballyveeney had stopped. The McDonnells looked at each other again, before Terence pointed his rifle into the air and fired a shot to get everyone's attention. Children cried and some people threw themselves to the ground. For the vast majority, they had never been this close to a gunshot and the sound almost deafened them. Terence took a deep breath and began his oration.

"We are fighting for YOU! Not for ourselves. For YOU! We are sorry to have lost our comrade and we express our sympathy to the Dyras. And to the Whites. But remember – we forced no one to join the cause. Cecil joined of his own free will. I regret that I could not drag him to safety. But this is a war. And we need your support. The Tans are reeling. We will win the fight."

"Go home Terence! You are no Michael Collins!" interrupted his nemesis Royston. And several others shouted out in support of the undertaker, including Cecil Dyra's father:
"Please Terence, be gone! My son is about to be buried. Show respect to my family!" But Terence had not finished.

"What did you just hear? Did you not hear the gunshots over yonder? My men are fighting off the Tans from burning Dyra's farm! We are prepared to die for the cause. And we will! And Royston, WHEN we have won our victory, then the likes of you and your father can bravely step forward and become parliamentarians. Why don't you fight with us Royston? Why don't you?"

"Because he is a coward!" shouted Bridie Kerrigan loudly. "He dares to criticise my sons who have made sacrifices for the likes of him. You should be ashamed Royston!" and as she finished more insults started to be exchanged among the agitated crowd.

This time, it was Sylvester who shot into the air to silence the crowd. He was proud of his brother's speech, and of what his aunt had just said, and he felt it was his turn to have a say:
"People of Ballycroy. You ALL welcomed me home from the trenches" he shouted. "Now please. Welcome the fight I am now undertaking. Support what we are trying to do. Let Cecil's sacrifice not be in vain. I am prepared to limp through this war with my shrapnelled leg to make sure we turf out the British. We

will die for our freedom. Cecil and Seaneen died for our freedom!"

"And did Esmeralda die for our freedom?" shouted up Benny Hughton Junior, trying to impress his boss Royston. "You shoot at women and not at Tans!"
"You know well that was an ACCIDENT!" retorted Terence. "You know well there are always innocent victims caught in the crossfire. Fuck you Hughton! Fuck you and your likes. Talkers! That's ALL ye are!"
"Go on then, shoot me!" taunted the grinning Hughton.
"He can't!" shouted Royston, "Sure you're not a woman!"

Terence was raging. He jumped down from the wall and paced towards Royston and Hughton:
"Look here you heathens!" shouted Terence, "Are you deaf?! Could you not hear the shooting just now?! Do you not know how many Tans we shot in Mulranny? Not another word from you two or they will be digging two more graves tonight!"
"Enough! Enough!" shouted a furious Fr. Kinsella, his cape flying behind him as he darted towards the confrontation. "You should all be ashamed. You are all degenerates!"

As he spoke, a voice in the distant was heard shouting "Tans! Tans!" and the crowd dispersed in all directions. Terence and Sylvester took their crouching positions at the outside of the walls again. After the initial consternation there was silence. Terence stood up. In the distance he could see the Crossley Tender come into sight after it had passed the church and was heading in the Bangor Erris direction. Everyone waited until it had gone out of sight.

Then shortly after, everyone reconvened as the rosary for Cecil was calmly concluded. The McDonnell brothers stood by their parents, sister and aunt in silence as the young man was lowered into the ground. There were no more internal hostilities on this occasion, but there was great tension. After the burial the brothers had a quick chat with their family members. They waited until almost everyone was gone before they headed for Bunmore Hill. It was now clear that they could not trust all of the parishioners not to betray the fighters to the enemy. They had to be extra careful.

They were joined in the Shepherd's Hut that afternoon by a delighted Willie and Joey. They excitedly described how they opened fire on the Black and Tan truck that was making its way up the sandy road towards Dyras. They had forced a retreat, and had hit at least two soldiers who had jumped off the rear of the truck on hearing the first shots. Joey was delighted as he felt he had proved his loyalty to his new comrades. Willie was awestricken by Joey's marksmanship, and described how he had hit each target unerringly.

Hughie arrived in the hut that evening and confirmed that one Black and Tan was confirmed dead. Captain Heraty had sent a message of congratulations. This had been a better day.

Two days later, as the three IRA men admired their own work on repairing the stone work and thatch work on the hut, their Scottish friend called for silence. He thought he had heard the sound of an engine. He was right. It was a Crossley Tender, and it was on the Bunmore road! He had predicted that McArthur's house below was a likely target, and he was being proven right. The four men gathered their guns and raced down the hillside towards a high point on the windy road on their side. They had earlier identified it as a suitable ambush point should a vehicle drive that route. The humming sound grew nearer as they settled into their positions. Within minutes they could hear the British voices as soldiers conversed above the sound of the noisy engine.

Joey Jarvis was lying on his stomach and had his rifle pointing to the turn in the road. Willie was in a similar pose just a few feet away. The McDonnells stayed back taking up covering positions, poised to join the shooting if called upon. Willie's heart beat rapidly as he waited for the front of the vehicle to come into view. As soon as it did, Jarvis fired and the sound of breaking glass could be heard. Then the screeching of brakes. Then an agonised cry of an English accent followed by much shouting as the soldiers realised they were under attack.

There was some firing back from the Black and Tans but the Irishmen could hear the order to "Retreat! Retreat!" come from the vehicle. They could hear the wheels spinning as the truck tried to turn and face outwards towards the main road again. The English were in disarray and the McDonnells ran to catch a view. They each had a pistol in their hand, and as they saw the truck drive away again they fired into the rear where the soldiers were, and then dived into the heather.

The truck continued driving and disappeared from their view as it sped past O'Grady's house. The four men checked each other to see if each was unharmed. They were ecstatic. They had not expected the truck to head off without a fight. Joey was beaming. He was fast becoming a hero. He was fast becoming accepted.

"I definitely hit one of the front boyos with my first shot. I hope I've killed him!" he exclaimed.
"Fuckers! On their way to torch the McArthurs" said Terence. "We gave them some fucking surprise, didn't we?! It was they who got torched! Well done lads! Well done Joey!" The four of them headed to The Shepherd's Hut. Joey asked for a whiskey and was given one for his exploits.

He had indeed hit someone. The someone he had hit was Corporal Gilberthorpe. That evening he cursed in pain at the military hospital in Castlebar as his wounds were sutured with a hot knife. Joey's bullet had smashed through the windscreen and hit the base of his left thumb, almost severing it and the index finger. In pain, he had ordered the retreat. By the time he reached Castlebar he was in agony and the medical team had to amputate what was left of his thumb and index finger. He now had only three fingers remaining on his left hand. He was livid. He had survived the hell of Gallipoli unscathed but not a trip into Bunmore! He had just received a permanent reminder of his hated Irish which would be with him for the rest of his days.

That evening, a buoyant Terence decided to head to McArthur's house. He brought Joey as a lookout. Terence braced himself for the reception he was about to receive, but he hoped that his earlier defence of their homestead would earn him some credit. How wrong he was!

Of course, until he arrived at the door he had not realised that the McArthurs AND Whites were both there now. They were in no form for a cosy summer's evening chat with the commander of the column which had not looked after their sons. Terence's arrival was met with fury. He tried to repeat his graveyard speech about both youths volunteering, but the parents were having none of it. The headmistress Mrs McArthur had never tried to hide her dislike of Terence since he courted her daughter Antoinette. Now, as far as she was concerned, he was to blame for luring her Eddie away and getting him imprisoned. He could even be executed. Her husband did not need to speak as Mrs McArthur batted away Terence's reasoning like a cow's tail swatting a fly. The younger McDonnell had quickly realised what a mistake he had made, that he had gone against his own counsel to think with his heart and not with his head. He realised that he had gotten carried away with the successful ambush on the Bunmore road. Perhaps his visit to McArthurs was subconsciously an effort to impress Antoinette again.

Sean White also unleashed his ire. He was grieving for his buried Seaneen and the captured PJ.
"You look for praise for defending us – where were you when my son was hanged?!" he cried.
"We cannot be everywhere" replied a subdued Terence.
"Everywhere?!" asked White in disbelief. "You were not ANY where!!"
"That is not the truth Mister White" said Terence.
"No. I know! The TRUTH is that you and your antics have left me and my wife child less. And home less. You have DESTROYED our lives. Why did you not just stay in America or continue blacksmithing or whatever? Why?! No! You HAD to draw the Brits upon us. You HAD to ruin everything. God Rest his Soul Sergeant Clive kept everything peaceful. He kept everything in order. The war would NEVER have touched Ballycroy! But you HAD to cause him to die too, didn't you McDonnell?"

The desperate Terence tried to scramble a defence, but there was no point. He may have won the earlier roadside battle but he was not going to win this, with four angry parents up against him.

"The British would have conscripted your lads if we hadn't fought them off" declared Terence.
"Maybe they would still be alive if they had!" shouted White. "Your brother survived the war and now we hear Batty did. Sure it was probably safer there than what it is here in this parish!"
"Now off with you!" shouted Mrs McArthur. "And NEVER step foot inside my gate again!"

Terence felt like saying they should have allowed the Black and Tans to burn them but he wisely decided to head away and join Joey up in the field. The door was slammed behind him. And the McArthur dog tried to bite his ankles.

As he trudged back up the hill towards the hut, he wondered silently to himself what this all was about. Was he doing the right thing? Had he lost the run of himself? What was he doing by walking side by side with a Scot? He had lost one half of his six men already – was he able for this responsibility?

As midnight passed and brought the four 'on the runs' into July 1920, the familiar whistle of 'Silent Night' was heard as their messenger Hughie arrived. As was becoming the custom, he was the bearer of bad news.

"Terence, they've burned your cottage!" said Hughie.
"Little loss!" was the surprising reply. "What about our home place?"
"Your father fired a few shots at them and they went away, but they said they would be back. Captain Heraty sailed two men over from Achill to guard the house tonight" said Hughie.
"God blast them!" said Sylvester.
"Sure we had to expect this kind of thing" said Terence.
"Gilberthorpe wasn't in Claggan, so they backed away easily" added Hughie. "Word is that he was wounded in Bunmore and is in hospital".

"Bloody brilliant!" exclaimed Joey and Sylvester ran across the floor to congratulate him. "But pity I did not bloody finish him!"
"And more news" said Hughie, "Roy Carey is dead".

It was the end of an era for the people of Ballycroy. Royston Carey Senior had died just weeks after the death of his hotelier brother in Castlebar. Despite considering himself 'a step above' he had spent most of his life ensuring that there was enough food, fuel and fluid in stock to keep the parishioners happy. Then, when they expired, he had been on hand to provide their coffins, wreaths and headstones. His empire was now being passed onto his son who was simply known as Royston. Although he passed to the next world suddenly in his sleep, there was general agreement that the terror the Black and Tans had visited upon him and his premises had contributed to an earlier than expected demise.

"I've been thinking about Roger all day" said Terence, "I don't know why, it must be because he used to play around here as a boy. When I was leaving McArthurs I didn't mention saving them from being burnt because – as Roger would say – it would 'inflame' the situation! I wonder now what clever-ass thing he'd say about the coffin maker ending up in a coffin?!"
"It would be a Latin or a Greek phrase or something like that" said Sylvester. "*Mortis Mortuaris* or something!"
"There'd be a Shakespeare quote thrown in for sure!" laughed Willie.
"Yea!" added Terence, "Something along the lines of 'live by the sword, die by the sword'".
"Tell me more about this Roger!" said Joey.

That night was spent updating the Glaswegian on the rags-to-riches tale. He was spellbound. A lad from a simple holding within a stone's throw of their hideaway hut had conquered the vastness of America in his chosen career.

Terence lay in his corner and smiled as he listened to the stories. The parish was divided, it seemed, but one thing was for sure. Each and every one of the people still loved Roger. Theatre was obviously more rewarding than freedom fighting!

CHAPTER 31: LIFE ON THE RUN

July passed quietly, mainly because the injured Gilberthorpe had returned to Deal for a break. There was heavy fighting in towns like Claremorris, Ballyhaunis and Kiltimagh and British reinforcements had been deployed there. The lull gave Harry Heraty the chance to organise the dispatch of the German weapons to where they were needed. It also gave the McDonnells, Kerrigan and Jarvis the chance to prepare for the onset of winter. They stored what they could in their hiding places at The Sandybanks, on Bunmore Hill and at Crafton Lake. At night, they were able to retrieve most of what they had stored in Sheeaun. A bitter Admiral Gay had withdrawn all of his co-operation with the freedom fighters.

Batty Bourke's family had to remain in Achill, and the trauma had a devastating affect on young Martha. She deteriorated rapidly. Fr. Rea visited her and was alarmed by her rapid decline. Batty was back in Germany arranging a second shipment, this time destined for the Donegal coast.

Fintan McDonnell had managed to fend off another attack on the family home in Claggan but his forge by the cemetery was firebombed and was now a burned out shell. His sister Bridie was suffering from ill health. Her eldest son Josey was an emaciated alcoholic and was of no use to her on the farm. She was missing Willie's help badly. She had never recovered from John Peter's death.

Toothy Lucey proudly showed off his new wife at mass each Sunday. He still worked for 'The Mayoman' but he had handed his postal duties over to his new step son David Cooney. His young successor had a torrid first fortnight on the job as he was twice held-up near Mulranny by the McDonnell brothers, who relieved him of the sack full of letters that he was bringing to the post office in Mulranny for mailing. Sylvester and Terence did not harm the brother of their drowned good friend, of course. All they wanted to do was check all of the post to see if it would reveal any informants in the parish. There was obviously someone feeding information to the British, one such example being 'Operation Vandenburg'.

The Whites and McArthurs in Bunmore were visited by the nomadic Harry Heraty. He promised he would do all he could to fund a new house for the Whites. He had dollars from Roger that would be made available. Both families were still trying to come to terms with the fact that their sons were Irish republican prisoners in Wales.

In Ballycroy Village, the Careys were adjusting to life without Roy. Rebecca was due to marry Benny Hughton Junior at Christmas. He was by now doing most of the serving duties in their public house, as well as helping Royston with the undertaking business. Rosa was helping out whenever and wherever she could. Royston was driving to and from Castlebar regularly. He was investing a lot of money into improving the hotel he had inherited, which was situated by the cricket lawn, across from the Court House. Royston was planning to hire additional help to help run things in Ballycroy, as it was his intention to eventually move his wife and four children to Castlebar on a permanent basis. He felt less exposed there to the lawlessness of the Black and Tans, despite there being a considerable presence of them in Castlebar.

At the Castlehill Barracks, there was an increased presence of what were now known as 'National Police' and they were accompanied by about six Black and Tans. Gilberthorpe had promised an injection of extra resources in September and therefore an increased focus on wiping out the republican element. So for the moment, the forces of the crown tried to keep a low profile and they spent a lot of their time playing cards inside and playing football outside.

Young Hughie O'Hora had to be commended for the clandestine role he so excellently carried out as a messenger. He had not come to the attention of the authorities in any way. His success did not go unnoticed by Harry Heraty. He helped smuggle some pickaxes, shovels and mortar to the three IRA men as they prepared 'fox holes' to hide in as shelter from any attacks. It was essential that they had hiding places they could rely on, places with a commanding view.

Joey Jarvis continued to bond with his new companions. He wrote a coded letter to his sister in London assuring her that he was safe and that he would be in touch. Although he had plans to move on, he felt so comfortable in his new situation. He loved the scenery. He loved fishing on The Veeney River. He loved hunting. He loved seeing the hunger disappear from the faces of his friends as they devoured his roasted rabbit, venison, lamb and trout. He was a chef of some experience, and none of the Irishmen complained when he insisted daily on carrying out the cooking chore. The only thing that worried him was an ugly ulcer on his instep. It was constantly either bleeding or seeping pus. It was also painful, but he tried to smile on through it. He even dipped it into the holy well in Bunmore in the hope of a cure.

By the time August came and went it appeared that he had the full trust of Sylvester, Terence and Willie. The former was probably the most suspicious of him and never relaxed as much as the others did in his company. There was no tension, but Willie often wondered about Joey's motives.

The Scotsman did like talking and finding out as much as possible about his new environs. This in itself could have been a justified cause for suspicion. His chattering helped pass the time. Sylvester even reckoned that the IRA men were starting to develop a Scottish accent! Some of what he said amused them.

"Can you explain something to me?" he asked one night. "That's Bangor Erris there to the north and that's Mulranny there to the south. So why do you always say 'we went down to Bangor' or 'we went up to Mulranny'? Surely it should be 'up north to Bangor' and 'down south to Mulranny' lads?" They all looked at each other and laughed.
"I think it's because the road to Mulranny is mostly uphill and the road to Bangor is mostly downhill!" said Sylvester.

He also seemed to know as much about Roger as the rest of them did, thanks to what they had told him.

"He was right about the Irish always dividing and making themselves easier to conquer" said the Scot.
"*Dividi et empero*" said Willie, "I think that's what he called it".
"Don't fucking start that Greek quote shite again!" said Terence.
"You ALWAYS make it so easy for the English" replied Joey. "For the Great War, sure didn't half of you join them and half stay here? It comes naturally to the English - splitting you lot - they don't even have to try! Now it seems that half of you want the independence on offer and half of you don't. If you get independence you will probably fight each other to see who will take over and the English will laugh at you. What is it about you always killing each other? Sure as soon as I arrived in Crafton I caused a split in your group as well! Does the concept of 'United Irishmen' mean anything to ye?!"

That particular night on Crafton, Willie decided it was time to turn the tables.
"You talk about the Irish and us all the time, Joey, but you hardly ever tell us anything about yourself" he said.
"I've nothing to hide!" was the defensive reply. "Go on sonny! Ask me anything you need to know and I'll tell you".
"Alright. Where did you live and what did you do?" asked Willie.
"I lived in the Govan area of Glasgow. My father was a shipbuilder but he was also a heavy drinker. He was sacked and he died in a sanatorium. We could not afford to pay our bills and were thrown out by the Prods who moved a new family into our house. I had to work in a dockside kitchen and earned enough money to send my folks down to my aunt in London. I later joined them and then enlisted. After working in the food camps on the front I returned to them in London. My mother had died and Eleanor was alone. I enlisted again for Ireland and here I am folks!" he smiled.

"I see! Good. You told us you would tell us 'the truth' about leaving the Tans" said Willie, "Isn't now as good a time as any?"
"Aye, I suppose" said Joey as the small cackling fire flames projected onto his face. "There's not much to it really".
"Go on Joey!" said Terence, "We need a good bedtime story tonight. Just as long as there are no ghosts in it like last night's! Jaysus, I could hardly sleep after what you told us".

"Well, it did not stop you fecking snoring!" retorted Willie.
"No ghosts tonight sonny!" said Joey. "Well. I was based in a town in Sligo and me and my friend Blair were asked to escort the truck that was transporting all of our wages to Sligo Barracks. As we did so, we came under attack from the IRA column and in the darkness I managed to escape to a nearby church. Of course I made sure that I had the bags of money with me!"
"Really?!" exclaimed Willie. "It was that easy?"
"Not exactly Willie lad! Blair got hit and was to go on and expire a couple of days later, poor devil. Your lads obviously thought he was the sole escort. So I hid in the church attic for a few days before re-appearing at my base. My story was that I was dazed and could not remember what had happened. The gaffers started asking about the money of course and I said that the IRA must have had it. Of course, they did not believe me. Over one hundred men were without their month's salary! I was taken to Castlebar where they planned to court martial me – even though they have not a wisp of evidence, lads. I managed to escape and here I am. Slowly on my way back to the hidden stash!"

"Unbelievable!" said Terence. "Unfuckingbelievable!"
"So the only one who knows the church at the end of the rainbow is....ME!" laughed Joey.
"But you WILL tell us, won't you?" said Terence.
"Ha ha!" laughed Joey. "I love you lads but not THAT much! You or the English can torture me as much as you want, but I'm no good to any of you dead if you need to dip into that treasure trove".

It was the IRA men's turn to be fascinated. What a story! It all made sense now. He must be an embarrassment to the Tans. There was no way they would take him back in. That was, of course, IF his story was not conjecture.

"It's my ambition to set up my own little hotel lads" he continued. "And the stash will help me if I survive this war. I had always imagined it would be somewhere in Scotland or in the south of England, but now I want it to be in Mayo, near a river, near the sea. I will bring Eleanor over to help me. On my opening night you will be all invited to stay in my wonderful rooms and to dine

from my special menu! There will be a salacious selection. You will be able to choose between mussels, cockles, oysters, lobsters, hake, swordfish, pike, pollock, salmon, cod, mullet, herring, mackerel and squid".
"And perhaps some fish as well?!" laughed Willie.
"Indeed!" grinned Joey. "That is my dream. My crock of gold lies over there beyond them Nephin peaks there. And don't worry; I will not forget my good friends when I get my hands on it again".

They all slept with a smile on their faces that night, and dreamt of what they would do with the loot. But with Gilberthorpe and his deformed hand *en route* from his sojourn in Kent, the recent nights of peace and harmony for the men on the run were coming to an end.

CHAPTER 32: THE BUTCHER

Within his first week back on duty, Gilberthorpe was planning a vicious assault on Ballycroy. He was aching to avenge the loss of his men – which now numbered six Black and Tans. His first target was the McDonnell family home in Claggan and he briefed his men on the plan of action. They were NOT to fail this time.

As his truck revved up to leave Newport Barracks on the deadly mission, the corporal was called aside. There was bad news to be broken to him. His face grew pale as he was informed that the Gilberthorpe family home and family business premises had been burnt to the ground in Deal, Kent. None of his family had been injured, but the damage to both buildings was irreparable. His parents had lost their home and their livelihood. The fire that destroyed the butcher's shop where he had learned his trade from his father had also spread to damage neighbouring buildings.

Because both buildings were about a mile apart, it was clear that it was a targeted arson attack. He immediately knew that it had some connection to his activity in West Mayo, and he suspected that there was Ballycroy involvement. He was correct. He was not to know that the work was that of the man known as Ecclesiasticus, who was acting on orders from Major Vandenburg, who wanted to avenge the loss of his family home which upset him immensely. As the flames from both buildings lit up the dark September sky in the scenic coastal town on the English Channel, the Hungarian calmly walked along the seafront unnoticed as fire-fighters frantically tried to contain the damage. Aughness South was being avenged in the south of England!

A furious Gilberthorpe knew he would have to return to Kent to check on his parents and siblings, but first he jumped aboard the Crossley Tender and ordered the driver to get to Ballycroy as fast as he could.

Whilst they were driving the twenty two miles, Willie and Joey were calmly sitting by the riverbank near Ballyveeney Bridge. They were surrounded by bushes and trees, and immediately behind them stood the ruins of the burned barracks. Both men were calmly going through the contents of Davy Cooney's mailbag. It had become a regular affair, so much so that the young postman was helping them!

"We better hurry, lads, I need to be in Mulranny by five and I want to avoid the teems that will come from those black clouds" said Davy.

"Alright", said Willie, "Nothing much in here today either although I do wonder where the O'Briens get all of these dollars from!"

"By the way", said Davy, "Toothy said to mention a couple of things to you whenever I meet you, I keep forgetting".

"What things?" asked Willie.

"Let me see, just give me a moment and I'll remember. Oh yes, the first one is the name Huckleberry or something like that..."

"Huckerby?" asked Willie curiously.

"Yes, Huckerby, that's it".

"What about him?"

"Well, Toothy says that you should know him and that he is with the Black and Tans in Munster. Toothy says that he is supposed to have murdered three or four innocent people down there."

"Are you telling the truth, Cooney?!" asked Willie incredulously.

"Well, that's what Toothy told me!" was the reply.

"My God!" exclaimed Willie. "That son of Satan. We can be thankful he is not stationed up here. He is a born murderer."

"Who is Huckerby?" asked Joey.

"I will tell you again. But you don't want to know him, believe you me!" replied Willie.

"So Davy, what is the second piece of good news you have for me?" he asked sarcastically.

"Let me think, let me think. It will come to me". As the postman paused the two IRA men looked at each and smiled.

"Oh yes, I have it. Toothy said to tell you that two men who used to dwell in Ballycroy are supposed to be with the Black and Tans, in Munster as well, in Tipperary actually. He said that you would know them well".

"Who does he mean?" replied Willie. "Sure no Ballycroy man in his right mind would join the Tans!"

"The Brophy brothers!" stated Davy.

232

"The Brophy brothers?! Black and Tans! Sure they are NOT Ballycroy men. They were a shower of 'blow-ins' who were rightly blown right back out!" and Willie started laughing and turned to Joey. "Well, if the best the Tans can do is to recruit the Brophy brothers, then you made the right decision in switching to US Jarvis!"

Davy walked away from the laughing men and threw his mail sack into the basket on front of his bicycle, and pedalled off in the direction of Mulranny. Even though the clouds threatened rain, Joey convinced Willie to stay there a while longer as he had placed a net across the river, and reckoned it was untouched as of yet. The two men lay back on the grassy banks and rested.

After nearly an hour, their rest was disturbed by the sound of truck engines coming from the Mulranny direction. They rushed up and took positions in the riverbank bushes looking directly onto Ballyveeney Bridge. Their hearts pounded. Sweat rushed from Willie's forehead.
"We HAVE to fire" he whispered to Joey.
"I know!" replied the Scot, pointing his rifle, "Let's give them a bit of metal and they'll back off".
"We HAVE to fire", repeated Willie, as if trying to convince himself. "Heraty's last message was that we were making life too easy for them."

As the vehicle approached Ballyveeney Bridge, Gilberthorpe had planned to direct the driver to veer left towards Claggan once the bridge was crossed. Just as he was about to speak a volley of shots shattered the windscreen and he could hear his side of the truck having its steel armour punctured. He tried to dive for cover as the vehicle swerved momentarily before the driver regained control.

"On straight ahead! On straight ahead!" shouted Gilberthorpe as the truck picked up speed. His main aim was to get out of the range of the firing guns, and it would have been suicide to veer the truck in the direction from which the bullets came.
A mile further on, the truck stopped and Gilberthorpe did a check on his men. No one had been hit. The ten in the rear of the truck

were unscathed. He informed his men that there was a change of plan. They would avoid Claggan for now, but head to Doona instead.

Little did Willie Kerrigan realise that the shots they had fired had just fatefully sent the troops in the direction of his family home instead of his cousin's family home. As Joey gathered in his fishless net, the men decided to head for Crafton as previously planned, instead of pursuing the truck. They had hoped it was merely going to Castlehill Barracks. But their hopes were not realised.

None of the Black and Tans had ever seen their corporal so animated. They had never seen him so hell-bent on revenge. He used his bandaged left hand to wipe the sweat from his brow as he ordered the driver to pick up speed.

Bridie Kerrigan and her son Josey were bringing their final sheaves of oats into their barn before the rain came. The sickly lady and her even sicklier son were not to know of the horrors just about to be inflicted on them. It was better that they did not know what was ahead. Just as they headed for the comfort of their kitchen the rattle from the Crossley Tender reached their ears. As the rain started to spill down, a dozen British savages smashed through their gate in their noisy truck. The first bullet shot the beloved family dog, who yelped in agony as the Kentish cheers rang out. Within minutes the fresh sheaves of oats were ablaze along with the hay they had struggled all summer to save.

In another shed the wiry thin Josey had a pitchfork up against his neck and was being stripped by the laughing soldiers. In the house Bridie Kerrigan was screaming as she was punched to the floor and repeatedly struck with the handle of her sweeping brush as she cowered. Her already broken heart shattered as she watched a Black and Tan take the precious photograph of her beloved John Peter from the wall, and smash it into the ground. Her crockery, her cutlery, her ornaments, her religious statues, her coins and her food went flying in every direction. Several laughing Tans started passing around their bottles of whiskey and gulping from them. As she tried to pray she looked up from the ground to see one of the English shamelessly urinating down on the shattered picture of the son she had lost fighting with the English. This was hell for the widow. As she tried to comprehend what was happening a boot was driven into her shoulder and she roared out in pain. As she began to pass out, she could hear the desperate cries of her eldest son from the shed, calling out for John Peter and Willie to help him.

No Irish eyes would want to see what happened to the Kerrigans that evening. No Irish ears would want to hear the blood-curdling cries of pain that emanated from them.

By the time Gilberthorpe blew his whistle and his dirty dozen were all on board the despised truck, the family home was also ablaze. As the sound of their boisterous laughter went out of earshot, neighbours gathered and observed in silence the sorry sight of the house and two barns blazing. They were dumbstruck at what they found.

Blood trickled from under the family dog that was sprawled lifeless by the gable. The pale white skinny corpse of the naked Josey lay by the burning barn. Not far away lay the motionless Bridie Kerrigan, lying face down in the mud, her dress gathered around her waist, her naked posterior exposed for all of the neighbourhood to see. Some of the Doona people managed to grab hold of a few buckets of water to try and douse the flames but it was futile. There was no way they would stop the fires that were raging. Even the heavy rain that arrived had no effect.

This atrocity numbed the people of Ballycroy. How could the British be so cruel to a family who had sacrificed their son for the British cause? Surely his service to the crown should have counted for something. Was nothing sacred anymore?

But their numbness was nothing compared to what effect it all had on Willie. Having received the awful news from Hughie, it fell to Terence to break the news to his cousin as he entered Willie's sheltered cave looking down on Crafton Lake, a small fire smouldering in the corner. Willie's mournful cries echoed between the mountain ridges as he learned of what had happened. His brother was dead. His mother was at death's door. Their home destroyed. Their cattle and dog shot. Their barns and everything within incinerated.

Terence, himself in tears, tried to calm his cousin down. But he could not. Sylvester heard what was going on and he tried to enter Willie's cave but was forcefully pushed away.
"I HAVE to get to mother, I HAVE to see her" wailed the heartbroken Willie.
"There's NO WAY you are going down there tonight, we can all go in the morning" shouted Terence. Willie pushed him aside to gather his belongings from inside the cave. Hughie and Joey looked on from several yards as the cousins physically grappled with each other.
"Do not head down tonight!" Hughie shouted over. "They will be waiting for you!"
"They will be waiting to get you" echoed the Scottish accent, "Wait here tonight sonny".
"I'll fecking wait nowhere!" shouted Willie as he struggled to escape the clutches of Terence. Taking the most desperate of measures, Sylvester swung back his right hand before propelling it forward into the side of his cousin's head. Willie's head went back and his legs buckled beneath him. As Joey and Hughie gasped in unison, Willie fell to the ground unconscious.

"I HAD to do that" said Sylvester regretfully.
"I know. The poor sod" said Terence. "He's so close to Bridie..."
"You did the right thing" said Hughie, "They are smoking you out again. They were incensed to be fired upon at the bridge".

The next morning, Gilberthorpe finalised his arrangements to return to Kent to check on the welfare of his family. He did not spare a thought for the family he had just destroyed. But he was not finished. He would continue his revenge on Ballycroy in a week or so when he returned. In the meantime he made a peculiar order to his men. He ordered them to stay within the confines of the Castlehill Barracks, and not to show any presence at any funerals. No one questioned his orders. No one questioned his motives. But it was clear that this was personal. He wanted to be there himself when the 'Boys of Ballycroy' were captured. He wanted to inflict as much suffering as possible, and to witness it for himself. He did not want to hear of it second-hand.

There would be no joy in that.

CHAPTER 33: LOST FOR WORDS

As the devil incarnate set out for Kent, the shell shocked people of Ballycroy gathered to bury Josey Kerrigan. He had been stripped of his dignity in death, and they wanted to ensure that his funeral made up for it. As usual Royston Carey was solemnly professional and did all an undertaker possibly could in such circumstances.

Bridie Kerrigan was being cared for at a neighbour's house. She had not spoken a word since she had been pulled from the mud and resuscitated. She was in a constant tremble, not even the Doctor Skelton's pills could do anything for her. Her eyes looked as if they were frozen and they stared directly ahead, barely blinking. She had not slept. She had not eaten. Her distraught brother Fintan wanted to bring her to his warm home but he was advised against it as logic dictated that his house would be one of the next targets. He tried to get her to communicate but the best he could do was get her to sip some icy cold water.

The locals wondered if Willie would make it down. They wondered if he was aware of what had happened. They wondered if he had been got too. The last person to see him was Davy Cooney and he was fearful that perhaps the truck load of Black and Tans that he had passed on the Mulranny Road had got Willie and Joey, especially as he had heard gunshots.

Josey Kerrigan was waked in Carey's Hall. Many of those who filed past the coffin were wet; having travelled in the rain from Achill where they had attended the funeral of young Martha Bourke who had succumbed to her illness. It had been considered too dangerous to bring the Bourkes back to Ballycroy to bury her in her home parish.

As the customary queues formed to pay their respects, there was some noise and shuffling when Willie arrived and led his two cousins into the hall. Royston Carey was none too pleased to see his immaculate carpets ruined by the muck from their boots, but his wife Antoinette squeezed his hand to prevent him from making a scene.

She barely recognised her ex-lover whose curly hair was overgrown, and who was sporting a rugged black beard. His uniform was drenched. She gazed at him from behind as he stood by the coffin, blessing himself with his right hand and holding his rifle upright with his left hand. Beside him stood his similarly unkempt brother Sylvester; whilst the sobbing Willie leaned over the coffin and kissed the ice-cold white cheeks of his dead brother. He put his hands on the rosary beads that Royston had secured in between the lifeless hands. Rainwater dripped from his bushy brown locks down onto the gaunt corpse.

Outside, many in the queue tried to identify who the small stocky soldier was keeping watch. He followed Terence's orders not to reveal his accent. He remained silent and did not have too long to do so, as the three IRA men did not wait inside for long. It was too dangerous to loiter, with a full barracks just up the road. Outside, Terence had a quick word with his father Fintan, who directed him where to find Bridie. Fintan proudly hugged his two sons and the four men went in the direction of Doona on foot, into the night darkness. Even in the short few minutes he was there, Joey noticed how awe-stricken the locals had been to see the three IRA men in the flesh. Young boys and girls in particular seemed to be gob-smacked at seeing them.
"Ye are definitely heroes in these parts" bellowed the Scottish accent as they paced along the road, led by Terence's weakening flash lamp, "I don't know what ye do be worrying about lads, they all love ye!"

In Doona, Willie fell to pieces when he saw the state of his poor mother, lying in the foetal position on the bed that lay by the wide open fireplace of their neighbour's house. The only acknowledgement she made of his presence was a fresh stream of tears from her bloodshot eyes. Her sorrowful condition also affected her nephews, who swore revenge for Gilberthorpe's handiwork. They asked why the doctor had not been able to stop her constant shivering. They were horrified by the bruising on her face and the cuts to her hand. When the friendly neighbour removed the sheets to try and get rid of the stench from the room, she washed Bridie from a basin and took the opportunity to unbutton the back of her dress to reveal the black and purple lash marks that the Tans had left on her. It looked as if the poor woman had been whipped by the Cat O Nine Tails. Orangey pus seeped from the wounds. Her feet were almost black in colour, as if the blood had all clotted in her veins.

Willie wept openly as he tried to get his beloved mother to speak. She did not react to his begging. He turned and asked Terence if he could stay, but a sombre Terence beckoned him to leave. As Joey looked inside from outside of the door, he heard the man of the house respectfully ask Willie to leave. The poor man knew that his house would be a valid target if the British discovered who was being harboured there.

Willie was a broken man as he bade farewell to his mother. Terence cajoled him by saying they would return soon when she improved. Sylvester rubbed Bridie's cheek gently as he said goodbye. He had witnessed soldiers shake like that in France as a result of the trauma of war, but had never expected to see a female do so, never mind his own flesh and blood. His aunt was literally dying from a broken heart.

The four stayed in their hut on the Bunmore hillside that night. Willie pined all night for his mother. It was a pitiful sound. The following morning he looked down on the graveyard through Joey's binoculars as his brother was laid to rest beside their father. His companions did what they could to support him, but they were limited in their options. How could anyone have foreseen that a Ballycroy man would have to witness his brother's burial from a mile away?

Despite a warning from Harry Heraty, carried via Hughie, not to seek immediate revenge and get captured like PJ and Eddie had, Terence decided to capitalise on the dry days that followed and let the Tans know that the fight was far from over. The night of the burial, Willie and Sylvester entered the grounds of the Castlehill Barracks as Terence and Joey perched high on the trees across the road on the Lettra side. Fuel was spilt in and around the two army vehicles that were parked outside of the front door. When one of the soldier's dogs started barking, a flame was lit by

Sylvester and at the same moment Willie aimed a hand grenade at each of the upstairs windows. Fire rose from the ground and engulfed both vehicles, as the arsonists headed across the road for the trees where the other two were.

Within moments, the wildly excited dog was joined in the front yard by several figures that rushed out of the front door and roared in alarm. Joey and Terence took aim from their unsteady positions, and it was enough to send the policemen and soldiers scurrying back in into the building, most of them crawling. The two men aimed their shots as best as they could but it was difficult to be accurate atop of the swaying trees. Seeing that the top two rooms of the barracks seemed to be ablaze from Willie's accurate throwing of the hand grenades, the gunmen fired a final round of shots at their target before joining their colleagues on the ground and running uphill further into the village of Lettra. In their wake, they could hear the loud noise of the exploding fuel tanks of the trucks as the blaze that raged behind them lit up their sandy path ahead.

There was mixture of pride and fear the following day as many locals gathered to observe Castlehill Barracks in the aftermath of the attack. The burnt carcasses of the trucks lay in the front yard. The gable that was once all cream-coloured was now scorched brown. Bullet marks were visible on the gable and on the façade. The upstairs windows were gone and the sky was visible through the damaged roof above them. It had not been destroyed like Ballyveeney Barracks down the road, but the damage was considerable nonetheless. And there were no prizes for guessing who had inflicted it.

The foursome knew that replacement vehicles would be a priority for the British. Terence and Willie made a daring raid on their old patch in Sheeaun that night to retrieve some hidden dynamite. As dawn arrived, they planted it under Ballyveeney Bridge and congratulated each other minutes after the fuse had been lit, as they observed the debris that had exploded into the river. There was now no bridge and therefore a huge gap for the Brits to negotiate. And they were not finished.

As they had anticipated, an army truck headed for Castlehill Barracks from Newport. The four laughed as it came into view from their mountain vantage point that overlooked the first straight stretch of road that any traveller would encounter having left Mulranny. There were two houses along this stretch of road in the area known as Claggan Mountain. Terence had earlier visited both houses to instruct the dwellers to remain inside and to keep away from the windows. Of course the frightened homeowners took heed.

Because of the destroyed bridge, the truck had no option but to do a u-turn at Ballyveeney and drive back towards Mulranny. The four were lying in wait. They grew excited as it came into view again, and tried to ascertain if it still contained the same amount of men as it did when it was heading for Ballycroy just half an hour earlier. It did not. There were only three on it now, as the others had crossed the Veeney River on foot on the wet September day. There was one driving; one armed soldier was accompanying him in the front; and there was one at the rear looking after the valuable machine gun there. This third man was busy surveying the mountains but in the mist he did not spot the four who were about to take aim.

Joey, Sylvester and Willie responded to Terence's command to fire and the soldier accompanying the driver in the front slumped backwards. The truck picked up speed and Terence could see the soldier in the back of the truck tumble as he lost his footing. The Tan tried to get control of the machine gun and aim it towards the mountain ledge from where he was been fired at, but he could not stay on his feet. As this was happening, Joey cursed as his gun jammed. Willie and Sylvester kept firing, purposely selecting their shots so as not to endanger the households below. But the vehicle roared towards Mulranny at an amazing speed, and was soon out of sight.

As the Irishmen congratulated each other, the Scot was frustrated and cursed his rifle. He reckoned he could have killed them all had his luck not ran out.

"We could have had that fecking machine gun! We could have had that truck to ourselves, there were only three of the bastards" he said.
"And the one in the front is - as Roger would say -'worm's meat', that's for sure!" said Sylvester.
"Time for salmon!" laughed Terence as he ordered his men back to Crafton Lake, while he himself went down to check on the two houses to make sure the occupants were safe and had not been victims of stray bullets. When he joined his men for the feed of fish he told them about the track of blood he had seen which dotted the yellow sandy road. As they ate, Willie remembered to inform him about the news he had heard about Huckerby and the Brophy brothers. Terence was amused!

A person who was far from amused when he arrived back in Newport was Graham Gilberthorpe. He had just given his life's savings to his parents to help rebuild their home and business, but he would need much much more. His family were reeling from their loss. His mood was black as he tried to make himself a sandwich in the kitchenette of Newport Barracks. He flung his knife to the floor in frustration. The simple task of buttering bread had become a headache with only three fingers remaining on his left hand. But his mood was to become pitch black as he learned that he had lost another soldier in his absence. Not only that, but he had lost two valuable vehicles and his Ballycroy base had been badly damaged. And hundreds would have to be spent repairing Ballyveeney Bridge. This was so serious that his superiors visited from Dublin.

The day after his return he received a verbal lashing from both Majors. The 'bogmen' of Ballycroy were making a laughing stock out of him. He had lost seven soldiers and one policeman. The 'Boys of Ballycroy' were still un-captured. The desperate man from Deal pointed to where his left thumb and left index finger used to be and told them about what had happened to his family in Kent. But it was in vain. The Majors threatened to remove him but he pleaded for last one chance.
"I will get them, I promise Sirs" he asserted. "Please give me one last chance. I have the Alsatians now and I'll have their heads for

you within days. Please Sirs, just one more week and I will do you proud".

His seniors left the room and promised to return with a verdict. After keeping him waiting for almost an hour they returned to the sweating Englishman. This time they were accompanied by a new person, smartly turned out in his black and brown uniform, fresh looking, perfectly groomed, dashing-looking and smirking. Gilberthorpe recognised the person he had heard so much about. He was lost for words.

"Corporal Gilberthorpe, I introduce the honourable Corporal Ifor Morris from the King's Welsh Regiment" stated the tallest Major. "He shall join you for one week in your enclave. Before returning to his assignment in Sligo, he will report back to us and we shall make a decision in accordance with his recommendations. I trust that I shall be hearing of progress in the first week of October, Corporal Gilberthorpe. Good luck to you both".

Ballycroy was now faced with TWO of the cruellest men God ever placed on this earth. Hell was about to be unleashed.

CHAPTER 34: BUTCHERS IN ARMS

Gilberthorpe and Morris were an uneasy partnership, but they had one common aim. What they also had in common was the fact that they were both egotistical. On top of this, they were also both butchers by trade!

The Alsatian duo named Caesar and Brutus helped the Welshman and the Englishman to bond. Word seeped to Harry Heraty that Gilberthorpe had new support and on a cold October night Hughie brought an update to the four 'on the runs' up by Crafton Lake. He told them that Bridie Kerrigan was now sitting up and was beginning to eat bread, but was still trembling constantly and not speaking. That news was warmly received, but the next piece of news wasn't. Once Hughie mentioned the name of the Welshman, Joey Jarvis jumped to his feet.

"No way! No fucking way! NOT Ifor Morris! NO!!" he exclaimed with a look of dread.
"What do you mean?" asked Terence, "He cannot be any worse than Gilberthorpe".
"That bastard makes Gilberthorpe look like a fucking ballerina!" said the Scot. "Listen lads, I'm out of here if he's on the scene. The best thing about leaving Sligo was knowing he was there, and if he's no longer there then I'm heading for Sligo tonight!"
"Hold on, hold on!" pleaded Sylvester, "What's the rush? I thought you knew no fear, Joey".
"Oh yes I do! And I fear HIM!" said the Scot with his eyes wide open. "He is the devil himself. What that animal did to harmless women and children in Sligo, you do not wish to know. He is the devil himself I tell you!"
"Calm down!" urged Terence. "If he was that bad, why did you not mention him before?"
"Because I tried to forget about him!" shouted the Scot, angry for the first time in their company.
"What did he do? Give us an example" gulped Willie.
"Nay. You don't need to know" said the Scot as Hughie looked on with the hairs standing on the back of his neck with fear. No one had expected to see the cheery Scot spooked in this way.

Joey resisted the requests to divulge stories on Ifor Morris but it was clear that he had been affected by whatever he had seen and heard. Willie kept sentry as Hughie headed home and the McDonnells went to sleep. Joey lay awake for most of the night as he contemplated the next phase of his journey to Sligo. The only thing that stopped him leaving immediately was the fact that his instep was hurting and bleeding incessantly. He was simply too sore.

As the darkness left the cold October morning, Joey prepared a breakfast for the four from his cave. The moon was still visible as it approached 9am, and the four prepared for another day of nomadic life. As they gathered by Joey's cave, they all noticed that Willie looked happier because of the news about his mother. He was definitely more upbeat.
"Sylvester, will you come down to the forest with me? I'm sure there is a deer stuck in our trap there, there was a lot of rustling by it" he stated.
"Better go and get it lads, we could do with some fresh meat!" shouted the chef.
"We won't be long" smiled Willie before the duo trudged upwards from Joey's cave on the edge of the lake shore.

From the summit of the incline they had just climbed, they could see the forest trees below them on the other side, about a quarter of a mile away. There was indeed rustling, and the men thought they could hear the groans from their struggling prey as they neared where the animal had become entrapped. As they made their way downhill, Sylvester stopped. He asked Willie to do likewise, but his cousin was too eager to reach the deer and finish him off with his pistol in the brightening morning.

"I thought I heard a growl" shouted Sylvester, "Maybe there is a fox in there, or even a wolf!"
"Or even a bear!" laughed Willie turning back towards his cousin, expecting to see him smile. But all he saw on Sylvester's face was an open-mouthed look of sheer horror. And when Willie looked towards the forest again, he could see the reason! Two Alsatian Dogs were emerging from the trees. Saliva dripping from their jagged teeth.

"Oh fuck!" said Sylvester as he turned and raced back towards the summit.
"Jesus!" shouted Willie as the vicious dogs ran towards him. He aimed his pistol at one of them and fired and the beast fell onto the boggy ground, yelping in agony. Willie tried to fire at the second dog but the animal was quickly on top of him, having pounced on him and knocked him to the ground with his weighty stomach. Willie began to cry out as the giant Alsatian mauled him, biting deeply into his neck and shoulder. Willie's pistol lay on the bog as he tried to fend off the Alsatian with his bare hands, but the dog just bit into the tendons of his hands.
"Help me Syl...." cried Willie in pain and desperation. "PLEASE help me!"

By this stage Sylvester was half way back up the summit, cursing himself that he had left his weapons in his cave. He was aiming for a cluster of rocks on the summit within which lay a fox hole he had prepared. He had a gun hidden there too that perhaps he could use to help Willie. A breathless Sylvester turned back to see not only his cousin grappling with the giant brown beast, but a line of about twenty soldiers come out of the woods. It was like a scene from hell. He asked himself if he was dreaming it. Was he in the middle of a nightmare? Unfortunately this nightmare was for real.

Sylvester continued his scramble up the hill towards the rocks, as he heard the English voices below, including an order to fire. He dived to the ground as a volley of shots flew past him. Below him on the heathery incline Willie cried out in more pain as the Alsatian continued mauling him. The flesh was being torn off of him. On the other side of the incline, down by the lake, Terence and Joey looked at each other in horror at the realisation that they were under attack. Their heavenly oasis was being invaded by the two devils and their hellish animal.

"Here, here Brutus!" said Gilberthorpe as he called his savage dog to heel.
"You can add to your list of victims at last, Graham, Caesar looks dead!" sneered his companion Ifor Morris.

"The poor dog" replied Gilberthorpe, "Tommy - put Caesar out of his misery".

As the men advanced to the crawling and mauled Willie, Sylvester disappeared between the rocks at the top of the incline. He had reached his target and he searched for his hidden gun in the foxhole, which was barely big enough to accommodate him. He was shaking. But not as much as poor Willie. He knew his time was up as he looked at the gathering army of men around him, all laughing at the bloodied frightened IRA man. He knew there was little hope of escaping this.

"Get up and run!" ordered the grinning Gilberthorpe. "Run now like you always have done; let's see how far you can go now!" The dazed Willie turned towards the top of the incline which seemed like a million miles away. He was suffering unbelievable pain, as the muddy water began to enter his deep bleeding wounds. The British laughed at his failed efforts to rise, as he then tried crawling on his bloody hands and knees in his torn clothes.

"I see the standard IRA uniform isn't up to much!" said Ifor Morris to laughter as Willie continued his pathetic efforts to crawl, and Gilberthorpe restrained Brutus by the collar, continuing to pace behind the victim. The sound of another shot rang out as the Tan Tommy applied the *coup de gras* to the Alsatian that Willie had wounded. The hiding Sylvester peeked from the rocks to see the action below him, and he sweated like a pig as his heart raced. He tried to control his trembling hand on his gun. He wondered what he should do. There were too many of them. If he fired he was revealing his foxhole and even if he killed one or two of them, there was no way he could kill them all or save Willie.

Down by the lake shore, the two there shook with fear and argued over whether or not to hold their position. They had heard the barking, the screaming and the shooting and so knew the situation was dire. They knew that they were likely to meet certain death if they emerged. Of course they wanted to climb up to the summit and fire at the Tans but they would be easy targets if the enemy got to the summit first.

"I have to go and save my brother" said a desperate Terence.
"You'll save no-one if you're a corpse!" said Joey restraining him.
"They are just waiting out there to pick you off on the heather, sonny".
"But Sylvester...our Sylvester...and our Willie..."
"Hold yer head, I say hold yer head. We HAVE to wait here, Terence. If they come to the water we can attack then, but don't commit suicide. Just wheest now 'til we hear what's going on" ordered Joey.
So, all three of Willie's comrades were helping to seal his fate by not coming to the poor man's aid. He desperately gazed ahead to see if his cousins were coming to his rescue. He was in so much agony.

"Now soldiers!" shouted Gilberthorpe. "We have our man for today. Mister Kerrigan. Thank you all. Back to the trucks with you and bring Brutus. Ifor, Tommy and I will stay here and finish the job. Give us some rope please".
"Use the rest of the rope to bring that trapped stag back on the Tender" said Morris, "We shall dine finely tonight!"
"And so shall Brutus!" laughed Gilberthorpe pointing to Willie who had just about ceased his crawl in front of them half-way up the incline, seizing up in pain. The group were now within earshot of the hidden Sylvester.

As the rest of the soldiers headed for the trees, Morris asked Gilberthorpe why he was not pursuing the other IRA men.
"One at a time, one at a time!" was the reply. "This is a good sport, isn't it Morris?! We should do this EVERY day! Let us leave one or two of them for the morrow!"
"I do so enjoy hunting!" laughed the Welshman.
"And such beautiful surroundings" said Gilberthorpe looking around before fixing an angry glare on the sad figure below him.
"Turn around, Kerrigan!" he ordered but Willie remained face down, laying flat on the wet bog with his hands and legs spread out.

The Tan named Tommy stepped forward and gave the unfortunate IRA volunteer an almighty kick in the groin which yielded a high pitched scream. The chilling sound reached his three comrades and made them shudder. Tommy then went beside Willie and used his boots to push him into the face up position Gilberthorpe wanted.

"Fuck you!" muttered Willie up to the three Black and Tans, lying now on his back. "Get the fuck out of my country!"
"What's that you say?" sneered Morris sarcastically. "You ought not to waste your final words like that!"
"Fuck you!" repeated Willie as the three stared down at his bloody face. "Burn in hell!"
"Burn, yes, just like your home!" said Gilberthorpe to more chuckles.

Gilberthorpe ordered his companions to stand on Willie's wrists, one either side as the suffering IRA man stared up into the blue morning sky and yelled out in pain again. He decided to cry out a prayer to his brothers and father as the British continued laughing. It was now time for the cruel Gilberthorpe to exact some revenge for the killing of his men, for the attack on his family and business, for the loss of his thumb and finger, for the attacks on his convoys, and for his loss of face with his superiors. He pictured the five bodies in the Newport morgue in their coffins. He pictured the tears of his father. He pictured his gutted butcher shop. He remembered how he used to use his left hand to sexually satisfy his women. He remembered fallen colleagues at Gallipoli. He remembered his wife's infidelity. A rage grew within him. He was to be humiliated no more. This was his moment to shine. His moment to show he needed no help to do his job.

He reached for his knife and sliced a finger from the right hand of the captured IRA man. He cowered over the screaming Willie and dangled the severed extremity in front of his eyes.
"See now. How do you like that, you Fenian Bastard!" he taunted.
"Please no! Mammy help me!" wailed Willie.
"Please...why...Mam..."
"MAMMY cannot help her little boy now!" he grinned as he sliced off another right finger to send Willie into excruciating pain. Then he cruelly cut two more from the writhing left hand.

"Mammy! Mammy HELP me!" cried Willie as the eyes rolled around in his head and his hiding companions froze in fear in the distance. "My fingers...Mammy...my fingers!"

"MAMMY indeed!" snarled Gilberthorpe as his companions continued to stand on the struggling wrists of Willie, the rest of his body convulsing in unimaginable agony.
"MAMMY gave us all a great ride in Doona, she has a fine arse on her!" sneered Gilberthorpe to the amusement of his comrades, but the utter horror of the tortured Willie.
"Sure we even let Josey have a go on her before Tommy here put him out of his misery!" laughed the English Corporal, his behaviour now even beginning to disturb his colleagues.
"Finish him off!" urged Tommy.
"Not at all!" was the reply, "What's the hurry? Do you KNOW how long I have been waiting to get one of these mythical 'Boys of Ballycroy' Tommy? I am going to make THIS last! And I am going to make THIS peasant SUFFER!"

"Back to your mother" he continued to the drained face of Willie who was now struck silent.
"Yes, she loved what we did to her. She really loved it. We must call back. And it is a pity your brother isn't around for more naked fun and games. At least he did not die a fucking virgin! And I am sure your OTHER brother the HERO would have liked Tommy's pole too!"

Willie was now frothing at the mouth. The look on his face was one of sheer terror.
"Get it over with Graham!" said Morris, "I'm hungry".
"Yes, finish him off!" added Tommy. "You have your pound of flesh now".
"May I have my bayonet please, gentlemen?" asked Gilberthorpe mockingly.
"Here, take it!" said Morris trying to maintain his balance on Willie's wrist which by now had been driven into the ground.
"Now stay on his wretched wrists!" ordered Gilberthorpe. And he took a position standing above the fallen freedom fighter, towering over him, with his boots between his spread-eagled thighs, staring down at him.

"Now you Irish shit, look at my face, the last face you will ever see!" he panted. "Go on, look at my face you bastard". The frothing Willie looked up at him through his tears.
"Now, any final word from the Shinner?" asked Gilberthorpe.
"Fuck you!" muttered Willie whose mouth was caking with dried froth and blood.
"Fuck Bridie? Of course I will!!" he snarled, tapping the sharp point of the bayonet downwards onto Willie's chest.
"She will be ALL alone now tonight, but I will visit her and comfort her" said Gilberthorpe with the cruellest of smiles.
"Just think of that now as you die, you fucker! YOUR mammy and ME. Just think of that now Kerrigan!" he said as he leaned his flat solid stomach onto the butt of his rifle and slowly inched it downwards into Willie's heart. The Boy of Ballycroy yelled out in breathless pain as Sylvester bit his tongue and sobbed like a baby just thirty yards away in his foxhole.

Tommy and Ifor Morris looked down at Willie's rolling white eyeballs. As the British bayonet twisted deep in his heart, he struggled to murmur his dying words:
"Mammy...oh mammy...the pain...the pain...they're killin' me...they're killin' me..."
They felt the struggle beneath their boots give up. The English corporal groaned as he finished driving the sharpened steel into the Irish chest. Blood splurted up onto their uniforms. Willie's chest was still heaving but his head was motionless. His legs threw out a dying kick. Gilberthorpe slowly pulled up the scarlet glistening bayonet but struggled because of his injured hand. Then, without warning, he plunged the bayonet quickly down into Willie's stomach, and more blood squirted up.
"Just to make sure!" said Gilberthorpe to his comrades.
"He's dead alright. Sure Brutus did most of the work!" said Morris. "Now, where's that rope? We need to bring Brutus his steaks!"

As Tommy and Ifor tied the rope around Willie's ankles, Gilberthorpe headed for the summit. Sylvester clasped his weapon and prepared to shoot. The Black and Tan was now on an emotional high, having just had some of his bloodlust satisfied.

Sylvester slithered onto the base of his foxhole. He wondered if his final moments had arrived. Terence and Joey gripped onto each other in Willie's cave. A beaming Gilberthorpe stood proudly on top of a rock as he gazed down on the beautiful lake below. He held his bloody bayonet rifle in his right hand. He was just ten yards away from the quaking Sylvester. As if he had not the full attention of all in the vicinity, he blew into his whistle and commenced yet another speech.

"Your darling Willie is dead! What a freedom fighter! What a man! Like a true Irish hero he cried out for his Mammy! His Mammy will cry out for ME tonight. My friends and I will be back for the rest of you peasant patriots. It will be a tremendous sport hunting you little animals down. I will fillet each and every one of you! Willie first – of course! God save the bawling 'Boys of Ballycroy'. God save Ireland, ha ha!"

Off he went, following his colleagues who were dragging the lifeless body of Willie behind them. He hardly broke pace as he stooped to scoop up Willie's abandoned pistol.

The murderous snakes were slithering out of paradise.

CHAPTER 35: SEARCHING

The savage brutality of Willie's murder devastated his cousins beyond belief. What a way to spend your final minutes on earth. Hell itself could not be near as bad. Sylvester plunged into uncontrollable despair as he tried to comprehend what had just happened. When Terence pulled him from his foxhole he was a shaking, sobbing mess. As the stunned Scotsman looked on, Terence tried to calm his brother. Terence himself was as white as a sheet, the blood drained from his features. But although in a state of shock, he was in control of himself, he HAD to be. And despite his angst at losing Willie, he was relieved Sylvester was spared.

As Sylvester curled up by a rock, Terence walked over to where Willie had taken his final breath. It was not difficult to locate the exact spot. Blood dripped from the heather and mixed with the mossy juice of the mountain. As Joey gazed down on beautiful Ballycroy by the sea below, he struggled to reconcile God's gift with what the devil had visited upon this patch of earthly heaven. He cursed aloud as Terence fell on one knee, cursing as well before he recoiled up into an upright position in horror having sighted one of Willie's severed fingers on the ground. He immediately started to vomit on the spot, as Joey spotted another two discarded fingers.

As Terence emptied the contents of his stomach, Joey trudged down to where the body of the dead Alsatian lay. It struck him that it was like seeing a slayed dragon from one of the books he read as a child. There was no sign of Willie's body. He walked back up to the summit overlooking the lake where the McDonnell brothers were locked in an embrace by a boulder. It took a while for any of the three to speak.

Each of them felt a strong guilt that they had not come to Willie's aid. Each of them felt a coward, especially his cousins who had grown up with him. But each of the three knew that they were lucky to be alive, that they would not have survived an encounter with such a large body of men. At least that's what they tried to convince themselves.

Joey spoke of how they should not blame themselves. This was war, but Gilberthorpe had overstepped the mark with his inhumane treatment of a captured fighter. And he would do the same again without hesitation given the chance. Joey also spoke of how the flying columns were designed for attacks on larger groups, but not for defence from larger groups. His words did little to console the brothers.

In the following hours as they tried to come to terms with what had just occurred, there were no immediate recriminations. No one was in a position to blame the other. Their main focus now was to recover from this ordeal and focus on retrieving their dead comrade's body so that he could be given a Christian burial.

The McDonnell brothers knew that this news would finish off their aunt. She would not survive this. Joey convinced them to join him for some cooked trout even though no one felt like eating. Willie's agonising final cries haunted them. Gilberthorpe's triumphal and cruel words made them feel sick.

"Lads I told ye, Ifor Morris IS Satan" said the Glaswegian.
"It was Gilberthorpe who did the murdering, I heard it all" whispered a hoarse Sylvester.
"The fucker gave poor Willie one hell of a cruel death. The fucker. He will not leave these shores alive, I promise you that!" said Terence. "But we were cowards. We should have helped him. We should have fucking helped the man".
"None of that now, lads!" came the Scottish brogue. "We were sitting ducks for them if we showed our faces. And in any case, I'm still trying to figure out why they did not want to hunt us all down. Why? Why settle for one of us when they could have had us all? They could have had us all hanged by noon! *Finito!*"

It was a question that had the McDonnells had also asked themselves. It was as if the British were toying with them, like a cat playing with a mouse for hours and tiring him out, before finally killing and eating him.

"They will be back for us soon" said Terence. "We must get out of here. Bunmore it is".
"But we need to search for Willie" insisted Sylvester, "We cannot go back down without him!"
"You're right I suppose" replied Terence. "Let me think. Isn't Hughie due up soon?"
"Aye, we better wait for him and get word to yer captain" said Joey. "I suppose we'd better chance the woods below and see where they left him".
"If they left him at all!" said Terence. "The Lord only knows what those fuckers are capable of".

Terence was right. The search they commenced that afternoon yielded nothing but trails of his blood to a clearing near where the road began, just yards from Dyra's house. From the fresh wheel tracks in the sand, the IRA men deducted that the body was loaded onto the lorry there. Joey suggested that the blood could have been that of the deer but they all knew that Willie had been taken.

The search continued for a couple of days as news of the gruesome murder spread. An angry and desperate Harry Heraty asked a Westport priest and nun to act as intermediaries with the Newport Barracks in an effort to get Willie's remains back. Their official reply was that it had been left in the woods. When it was pointed out that all searches had yielded no corpse, Gilberthorpe suggested that perhaps foxes or badgers had beaten them to it. He curtly told the religious representatives in their final meeting that he could do nothing more to assist them and that he would not entertain any further approaches.

Bridie Kerrigan relapsed pitifully from word of the murder of a third son. She had not spoken a word since the night the Black and Tans drove into the Kerrigan yard and unleashed hell on her. A mournful groan came from deep within her and she keeled back onto her neighbour's bed as her brother Fintan broke the sorrowful news.

The wider community of Ballycroy were aghast at what they had heard. And THEY had been spared from the full gruesome details. They gathered at the church praying for Willie's body to be granted. But their prayers went unanswered. There was a theory that he was lying at the bottom of Crafton Lake but the McDonnells knew this was not the case. As the parish reeled from the loss of a third Kerrigan son, Joey tried to help the McDonnells to focus on their mission. But he himself was greatly distracted, and on the verge of taking his next steps towards Sligo. However, he did not wish to abandon his new friends when they were most in need of him.

In Newport Barracks, Graham Gilberthorpe sat through a meeting that Ifor Morris had arranged. A team of ten Black and Tans sat around as the Welshman laid out his plans. The McDonnell family home in Claggan was to be burned. Their adjacent forge was to be burned. Fintan McDonnell was to be captured, alive if at all possible. They could do what they like to his wife. As long as she ended up dead.

Luckily for Mrs Claire McDonnell, British intelligence had not known that she had a daughter Beatrice living with her husband's family in Castlehill, and she was about to give birth. That night, Claire would be away from the family home at the McMahon house helping to bring her first grandchild into the world.

Fintan hammered away in his forge as usual that dark October evening as the Crossley Tender left Newport for him. As the soldiers made their journey, Gilberthorpe tried to disguise his anger at his Welsh counterpart. After their meeting in the barracks, when Ifor Morris headed down the town for some tea and scones, Gilberthorpe had taken the opportunity to enter his quarters. He was raging to have found an incomplete report the Sligo-based corporal had written for their commanding officers in Dublin Castle. In the report, to the detriment of Gilberthorpe, Ifor Morris had taken all of the credit for eliminating IRA man Willie Kerrigan. He had also taken all of the credit for an incident the previous day in Mulranny in which the Black and Tans had intercepted a local by chance, who had been transporting three German guns from the shipment that had arrived in Innishbiggle. In his report, Ifor Morris had described his own brilliant 'detective work' in apprehending the guns and the courier, who was now in jail waiting to be hanged. And he had not been slow to highlight the shortfalls he had observed 'under the current regime'. Gilberthorpe was seething.

As planned, the ten Black and Tans disembarked at Ballyveeney Bridge which was still under repair. They crossed the low river by foot. Under the bright moon on a cloudless early October night, Ifor Morris organised them into five rows of two abreast, and he and Gilberthorpe led them on a jog towards McDonnells. The sound of their boots clattered the sand and pebbles on the road as they ran past the ruins of Ballyveeney Barracks towards Drumgallagh School. Just before the school they took a sharp turn to the left and up the steep road towards their tree sheltered destination over a mile away. Gilberthorpe gritted his teeth in the darkness as his fellow corporal egotistically shouted "I-for, I-for" as a command for the others to follow the slow pace he was setting. The hum of "I-for, I-for" a la "left right, left right" continued until they came within 200 yards of McDonnells, where Ifor Morris whispered a final briefing.

As the team approached, the ever vigilant Fintan heard the sound of road pebbles being disturbed and he darted from the forge with his pistol. He hid in a bush and tried to control his palpitations as he witnessed several dark figures run towards his candlelit forge and house. His dog started howling and he heard the English accents. Even though he was scared, he was relieved that his wife was not in the house, and he decided not to fire and thus give away his position. He kicked off his boots and ran towards the nearby shoreline where the moon lit up his curragh. He pushed it out into the calm water and then jumped into it, lying face down but trying to move his body so as to bring momentum to the boat and sail it further out into the sea.

Behind him he could hear the voices grow louder as the Black and Tans searched for their prey. A few of them entered the McDonnell home and started smashing pictures and ornaments. Others were hungry and started bagging whatever food they could find. The stable and barn were checked but they could not find anyone, and they began to despair.

"I'd say he is in the cottage" said Gilberthorpe, pointing up the pathway to where Terence's burned home was.
"Let's check it so!" said Ifor Morris and the two of them ran, stooping, clasping their weapons in their right hands, wary that Fintan may have his gun poised for their arrival.
"He's not here!" exclaimed Ifor Morris emerging from within the roofless walls to where Gilberthorpe had stopped outside the door.
"Pity" said Gilberthorpe calmly as he lifted his right hand and blasted a shot from Willie Kerrigan's pistol into the Welshman's temple. Ifor Morris was dead before he hit the ground.

Gilberthorpe raised his pistol up towards the shining moon and shouted "Take cover, take cover, he's firing!" and fired two more shots from Willie's pistol skywards. As he looked down at the lifeless shape on the ground below him, movement in the water caught his eye and he rushed towards the shoreline. Fintan was in the boat. But Gilberthorpe calmly decided to say nothing. As he had hoped, within sixty seconds, someone else had spotted Fintan. "Take aim at the boat. He's in the boat!" an English voice shouted as a hail of bullets was released in Fintan's direction. By now he was about twenty yards out to sea but his painful yells could be heard in the middle of the gunfire. "Keep firing, keep firing!" ordered Gilberthorpe as he went back towards Terence's cottage. The flames starting to come from the thatch on the McDonnell family home lit up the crumpled heap on the ground and two of the Tans shouted at the approaching Gilberthorpe.

"Ifor's been hit! Ifor's been hit Sir!" shouted one.

Gilberthorpe feigned an appropriate reaction and ordered the men on the shoreline to keep firing at their target. They cheered as the punctured boat disappeared into the water. And there was no sign of its occupant on the sea surface. Gilberthorpe started blowing his whistle and the men reconvened by the burning house. One of them had finally managed to get the forge blazing as well.

"Alright men!" shouted Gilberthorpe. "We've got to carry Ifor. Did McDonnell hit any more of us?" Everyone else appeared to be unscathed, and the corporal gave a quick headcount.
"Alright", he continued, "Make sure you have your fill of food, drink and whatever and off we go. Did ye get the wife?"
"No sign of her" was the reply.
"Fuck it!" said Gilberthorpe. "Let's head for Bessie. We've got to get the casualty attended to right away".

By the time they had reached their lorry nick-named 'Bessie' it was clear to everyone that Ifor Morris was dead. Blood poured from his temple, ears and mouth as they lifted him onto the rear. As the driver started the truck and drove towards Mulranny, Gilberthorpe smiled to himself. On the rear of the truck, despite having the corpse of a colleague with them, the Black and Tans congratulated each other as they admired the spectacular blaze they could see in the distance.

The blaze could also be seen by the wet and wounded Fintan McDonnell as he crawled towards the front door of Packie Tadhg's house on Annah Island, leaving a trail of blood in his wake. Just as the bewildered islander answered the weak knock on his door, the Claggan man fainted in front of him.

Back on the mainland, it took less than an hour for the screaming Claire McDonnell to appear at the inferno that was once her home. The hated Black and Tans had finally got them. She despaired as her neighbours searched frantically for Fintan. They feared the worst as the following morning they followed the trail of blood from Terence's cottage to Ballyveeney Bridge. It appeared that he had met with the same fate as his nephew, and the Tans had taken his dead body – never to be seen again. All that was left behind of him was his boots. Everything else was destroyed. Even the poor dog had been dragged into the forge by his leash and shackled to a metal loop where he was burned alive.

Word reached Bunmore Hill of the latest atrocity. Young Hughie O'Hora was becoming hardened to breaking bad news. He tried to knit hope into his revelation that Fintan was missing but presumed dead. But it was still difficult for him to witness grown men emotionally disintegrate right in front of him. The McDonnell brothers were distraught. Not only had they lost their home and business, but their beloved father. And it was difficult for them to be able to welcome the arrival of their baby nephew Fintan William McMahon. Unbeknown to them, the baby had saved their mother's life. Hughie had to warn the revenge-hungry brothers to stay on the hill as the Black and Tans had patrols set up at several locations. They were waiting for them to emerge from hiding.

The next evening, after the longest of long days in the Shepherd's Hut, Hughie finally got to be the bearer of some good news as he was able to inform the brothers that their father was alive and recovering on Annah Island! They rejoiced in each other's arms as Jarvis poured some celebratory whiskey that he had stashed. Hughie was hugged and kissed! Sylvester and Terence prayed to the Kerrigan brothers above for guarding their father. Below them, the parishioners of the oppressed parish immersed themselves in the miraculous news. Just like Batty, Fintan had come back from the dead. They had a new hero to look up to. A new legend was born. He had emulated his Fenian ancestors.

His popularity rocketed when news came out that the despised Ifor Morris was dead. The acclaim for this was showered upon him, even though he himself knew that he had not fired a shot that night. But he accepted the accolades. Who wouldn't? Life rarely brought such opportunities! The people of Sligo wanted to canonise Fintan. Joey Jarvis became an instant disciple of the man he called 'Saint Fintan'! The IRA propaganda team were elated.

Though wounded on both arms and on his stomach, Fintan was recovering fast. News of his survival irked Gilberthorpe when it reached him several days later, but he was not surprised, he knew that there had been no certainty that the McDonnell patriarch had been killed. But he was not overly disappointed. He could try again. In any case, he had achieved his main aim that night. He was able to rip up the report that Ifor Morris had commenced but had never got to finish. He was able to close the coffin on his unwelcome rival. He was able to bask in another murder without the nagging worry that someone might turn and testify against him. He was now able to take the credit that Ifor Morris was lining up for himself.

He was able to assertively state that he was achieving his mission. That he was the man to sort out the rebellious parish once and for all. After all, the renowned Corporal Ifor Morris had not even survived one week in the wilds of Ballycroy!

CHAPTER 36: A HARSH WINTER

The McDonnell brothers kept up their assault on the Black and Tans by hijacking a lorry load of coal and logs that was *en route* to the Castlehill Barracks. The unfortunate driver was held up at gunpoint on the narrow twists of the Claggan Hill mountain road, and forced to dump his entire consignment over the sea wall and into the lapping waves. And within days of Ballyveeney Bridge being repaired, Terence blew it up again.

A delighted Harry Heraty had a *rendez-vous* with Terence in Tiernaur, halfway between Mulranny and Newport, in the grounds of the idyllic castle owned by the Fitzwiltons which overlooked tranquil Clew Bay there. He urged the three remaining members of the column to keep antagonising the Black and Tans. There was still over three quarters of the German shipment to distribute. He realised that there was only so much the depleted column could do. He confirmed that the Tierneys of North Mayo had deployed a column to operate at the northern end of Ballycroy to keep any troops who tried to enter from the Erris side at bay. The column included a young footballer recently recruited from the Ballycroy GAA team, who was being trained-in.
Harry Heraty was a weary man. The war had aged him. Life on the run was adversely affecting him. He had lost many's the good volunteer. He deeply regretted what had happened to Willie, and was visibly anguished when Terence revealed the real story of what the British had done to him. When he heard all of the details, including the positions the BFC were in when the assault commenced, he understood why Willie's three colleagues had been powerless to assist him. But Willie's murder made him all the more determined to pursue his goals and to rid Ireland of her conqueror. The tale of how Ballycroy was heroically doing more than its fair share was a great fillip for the cause.

The sacrifices that the parish had to make, though, were coming at a cost. After being moved between several safe houses, the destroyed soul of Bridie Kerrigan passed into the next world on her 56th birthday on October 20th. It was a mercy for the woman, who had come to look as if she was in her eighties. She had suffered so much in her final weeks, and had not spoken since the night she was attacked in her home. The suffering she endured could never be imagined. A hard working and religious woman, all she had ever wanted to do was to keep her husband and three sons happy. She had outlived all her men. This world had been cruel to her. Most war victims die from wounds from guns or daggers – but not Bridie Kerrigan. Her poor heart has been sliced at until there was no more to slice.

Her only sibling Fintan did not shed a tear when he heard the sad news. He had no tears left to shed. "Hell could not be any worse for her", he said. He was striving to put a roof on Terence's cottage so that he and Claire might have some shelter for the promised snowy Christmas. As he continued on working an hour after hearing of Bridie's death, he was thrilled to see his sons appear from the trees. The McDonnell family had an emotional reunion. There was little time for delay. It was even too dangerous for the new uncles to visit the house of their sister and meet their nephew for the first time. Despite being delighted to see their parents and sister in Claggan, it ripped the hearts out of Sylvester and Terence to see the sad sight of their gutted home and forge. Fintan quickly showed them his healing wounds, before they embraced and kissed both their parents and ran to rejoin Joey who was on sentry.

The following evening, Terence insisted on walking to Carey's Hall where his aunt was being waked. Sylvester and Joey had begged him not be so foolish, but Terence was determined to pay his respects. The two others stayed behind in the Shepherd's Hut, and cursed his folly.

In the funeral home, Terence's appearance surprised and excited the parishioners who had gathered.
"You should not be bringing that in here!" said Fr. Kinsella, looking at Terence's rifle.
"I won't be too long, Father", said Terence in hushed tone as he bowed his head in prayer. His heart panged to see how gaunt the once-beautiful face of his aunt had become. Her lips were black and cracked. There was a smell of rotting flesh from her.

"What's that?!" snarled the observant priest, spotting that Terence had deposited something into the coffin by her side. "It is only a ball of wool, Father. She loved knitting" was the reply.

As Terence darted out of the crowded room towards the graveyard, he felt relieved and happy. Relieved that there was no sign of any crown patrols. Happy that he had just dropped the four severed fingers of Willie into his mother's coffin to join her for eternity.
"That puts an end to the fucking curse of the stupid white cow!" he muttered, "Willie WILL be buried in Irish soil".

As he climbed up Bunmore Hill in the darkness, his father was taking the backroads to travel from Claggan to Doona, where he wanted to pay the Brennan family for looking after his sister in her final days. He then planned to travel to Ballycroy Village via Knockmoyleen to act as chief mourner. He never got to the funeral. As he was walking by Drumslide School, six Black and Tans jumped onto the road from behind the school wall. He never stood a chance of resisting the arrest, especially with his bullet wounds still hindering him.
"Gilberthorpe will be delighted with this catch!" snarled a Liverpudlian accent. Within minutes, a dispirited Fintan was on the back of a truck and on his way to a cell.

His wife feared for the worst when he did not turn up at the wake or the burial the following day. Several of the football team, who had played with his son Sylvester in bygone days, turned up at the Castlehill Barracks and started shouting, demanding to know where Fintan was. All they got was abuse from the Black and Tans. Hughie brought the worrying development to the attention of the three men on Bunmore Hill. The brothers sank back into a worrying depression. They did not know what to do.

The following Saturday night, there was still no sign of Fintan and at evening mass the locals prayed for his safe return. But deep down they feared that he had joined his sister. Harry Heraty sent his religious contacts again to Gilberthorpe to try and discover his fate.

As the McDonnell brothers grew demented with worry, Joey headed into the darkness at 11 at night, saying he had to get some medicine and bandages for his deteriorating foot ulcer. This was the second Saturday night in a row he had trekked down the marshy mountain to Ballycroy Village to break into The Dispensary and steal what he needed to ease his pain.

And for the second Saturday night in a row, he hid himself behind the cemetery boundary wall onto which backed the empty shell of McDonnell's second forge. And for the second Saturday night in a row he listened aroused as he heard two illicit lovers fornicate inside the gutted building. He did not see them or know who they were. But they were passionate! He was thrilled to have stumbled upon their love making. His life had been devoid of pleasures of the flesh for so long. Their moaning reminded him that there was more to life than scraping for food, trying to sleep in harmony with nature's elements, and looking down the length of a gun.

His next step now was to establish who the lovers were. He had heard each of them call out the others' name, but he wanted to find out more. He figured that they were secret lovers – "A married couple would not generate such passion!"

Back in the hut later that week, the brothers were so preoccupied by their father's situation that they did not pay attention to the peculiar questions that the Scot casually dropped into conversations.
"The night of Josey's funeral, I thought I heard a man being addressed as 'Bosco'. Surely there is not such a name in this country, I had to mishear it, surely?" he said.
"What? Isn't there a saint called John Bosco, sure it must be common enough" replied a distracted Sylvester.
"Really", continued Joey, "So ye have a few of that name in Ballycroy? I know of none in Scotland!"
"Well, I know of only one in this parish, and he's an outsider" said Sylvester.
"And who is he?"

"Bosco Darby, a teacher that came down from Leitrim a few years ago" said Sylvester.
"A teacher! I see" smiled the Scot, happy that he seemed to have solved the first half of his puzzle. "Married I suppose?"
"He is married, yea. Why do you…" was the irritated reply from Sylvester before Joey quickly changed the subject!

Two nights later, he continued his probe on the unwitting brothers, this time by tapping into Terence's reservoir of knowledge, without raising suspicion.
"If you had a baby daughter, a beautiful baby daughter, what would you name her?" asked the smiling Glaswegian.
"That's a strange sort of question" answered Terence, "Why do you ask?"
"Just passing the time, I suppose. I've been thinking all day of a lovely girl I used to know in Govan, Rosa was her name. I love that name. I think I would christen my daughter that" said Joey.
"Name your daughter after a fucking fancy woman. Strange!" said Terence.
"Do you not like the name?"
"It's alright I suppose" replied Terence.
"Is there any of that name in these parts?" asked Joey innocently.
"Only one that I know of - Rosa Carey from the bar. Roger's woman!" laughed Terence.
"Really? I did not know he had a lady friend. Did she marry since?" asked Joey.
"No. Looks like being a spinster to me" said Terence. "I always liked her though, dancing eyes she has, I'd fucking ride her now if she came looking! Jesus, I'd even ride YOU now it's been so long!"
"Keep that dirty smelly arse of yours away out of my sight!" said Joey and for the first time in a few days they laughed together.
The ex-Black and Tan had just completed his puzzle!

*****

The following Saturday night, just after Hughie had visited the hut and assured the brothers that Harry Heraty was doing all he could to find out what had happened to their father, Joey headed in the direction of The Dispensary again. His foot had improved greatly from the ointment and clean bandages. This time though, his purpose was not to steal. It was much more sinister. He grew aroused as he approached the scene of the lovemaking, and recalled what he had heard. The testosterone raced through him as he took his usual hiding place behind the wall and anticipated the arrival of the teacher and barmaid.

As usual, the male was first to arrive and Joey trembled with excitement as he heard Bosco light up a cigarette under the moonlight. The cheating teacher stood between the outside gable of the forge and the inside border wall in the dark. Rosa would be along shortly. Their clandestine routine was well established. Bosco would not have been expecting the shock of sensing a figure emerge from behind him. Instead of the pleasure he had sought, he met with a sharp pain as his head was intentionally banged into the forge wall with such force that it knocked him out. As he lay face down on the ground motionless, the Scot pulled a rope from the sack he had always brought to fill with medical supplies. The unconscious Bosco's hands were tied behind his back. His legs were tied even more tightly. A third piece of rope with a handkerchief knotted into it was placed around his frothing mouth.

Joey panted. It had been easier than he had thought. Now he would have the lady all to himself. Now he would have a piece of the action that he had coveted. Now his lust would be satisfied.

After several minutes, the female figure appeared and entered in through the door of the burnt out forge.
"You've been smoking again!" she whispered excitedly. As she tried to find her lover with the lantern she had just lit, she called out his name.
"Bosco, answer me. Stop messing you rogue!"

The poor girl was on the ground in pain within seconds as she was pounced upon by the intruder. In no time, he had her pinned to the hard floor, face down, and was tying her hands together with more rope. The dazed Rosa gasped for air as he roughly pulled at her hands and fastened them behind her back. She felt her lip bleed from the force of the attack, and knew that her knees were also cut. She could hear his hyperventilating and knew that this was a stranger. She was in so much shock that she struggled to find words.

"Please, please – do me no harm!" she begged.
"Be quiet lass and you'll be alright!" replied the Scottish accent. "Just do as I say, and you'll be just grand". He then turned her over so that she was face up.
"What did you do to…"? She could not finish her sentence.

"He will be grand too, lass" said Joey. "Don't you worry about him. Just do as I say, the both of you, and there will be no more word of this". Rosa was unable to reply.
"Now, part your legs, good lass" he added having raised her dress up from her ankles to her waist.

As the moon shone down on them through the huge gaps in the burned roof, the distraught barmaid did all she could to fight off her attacker. In frustration he held a knife to her shaking jaw and threatened to slit her throat if she did not relent. The crying Rosa had little choice. With only her quenched lantern at her side on the cold unforgiving floor, she tried to close her eyes as the rapist pounded into her from above, hurting her with every thrust. He warned her not to scream or he would murder her and Bosco. "What a scandal that would be!" he panted as he continued raping her. The terrified Rosa prayed to her father and mother that her life would be spared. The seconds seemed to last for hours as the Scot continued his wicked violation.

After he had satisfied himself, he rolled off her and lay gasping for breath on the stone, gazing up at the moon and murmuring thanks for the pleasure he had just received. His pretty victim begged to be released; her wrists and elbows were in agony behind her. She was sore from his thrusting.

Jarvis ignored her pleas and as they began to hear moans outside, he rolled over beside her and produced his knife again which caught the reflection of the moonlight.

"Now lass, we'll do this one more time! If you promise, I'll free your hands this time but only if you promise to keep them both on my back" he whispered.
"Please no, please stop. I don't want to be with child. Please!" she begged.
"I'll not stop til I have some more of you, lass!" he said, ripping her blouse apart before asking:
"Now, will you promise that you'll keep your hands where I can feel them?"

The broken girl nodded and he cut her hands free. He got on top of her again and began plunging in and out of her again as she wept. She could hear Bosco's groans from outside and hoped he would come to her rescue. But even though he was regaining consciousness he was helpless. Tears came to his eyes as he heard the painful cries from his secret lover, amidst the breathless demands of the rapist.
"Put your bloody hands on me backside!" shouted the Scot as he continued.
"That's a good lass! That's a good lass!" he panted. "I will be done soon. You're one good lass, doing this for me, I won't be much longer".

Rosa gagged from the stench of sweat from his shirt and the vile odour of his cheesy breath. After what seemed like an eternity he rolled off her a second time and put his trousers on.
"Thanks. You're a great lass!" he repeated as she rolled on her side and vomited. "I did not mean to hurt you. It's just been such a long while, so long since I was with a lass, and that's unnatural. I had to do that".

After Rosa finished throwing-up, Joey tugged her behind him as he brought her outside to Bosco's shaking figure. He cut the ropes from his legs and mouth but as he continued to lay down Joey drew two kicks into his ribs, causing a sharp cry.
"Leave him alone!" shouted Rosa. The Scot turned around and slapped her cheek. "Now listen to what I say! This is how the story plays out" he hushed. "I drag him out there onto the road. You go for home. I cut him free. You say you were awoken by

noises. You alert everyone. Blame one of his scholars. No one speaks of me. Everyone is happy. Story over!"

He dragged the moaning teacher onto the road and cut the ropes from his hands. As Rosa ran down towards her home above the bar, her rapist ran in the opposite direction towards Bunmore Hill.

At Sunday mass there was shock amongst the parishioners as they learned that Bosco Darby was attacked after leaving Carey's Bar the night before. They learned that he was in a bad way. They learned that his wife and three children were distraught. Early indications were that it was the Tans who robbed him. The mass-goers also suspect a couple of his former pupils. Whoever did it, it was a terrible thing to happen to such a fine athletic young man. It was a terrible thing to befall the lovely Darby family.

Rosa managed to conceal her cut lip and hide her bruises beneath her outfit. The traumatised girl had to suffer her ordeal in silence. She suffered recurring hellish nightmares of the degrading acts inflicted on her person.

That same Sunday morning, the McDonnell brothers received the dreaded note from their Scottish friend that he had left for Sligo. In it, he thanked them for their hospitality and said he hoped to meet them again after the war is won. Even after Hughie brought word of the attack on Bosco Darby, they did not make a connection between it and Joey.

As the parish faced into November 1920, none of the parishioners had been able to find Fintan McDonnell. His sons managed to meet their mother and their nephew for a stolen hour. Doctor Skelton told Mrs Darby that it appeared that her husband had suffered permanent brain damage and would have to live with the constant shaking in his left hand for the rest of his days. His teaching career was in jeopardy. His pension was in doubt. The lives of the entire family were whirled into chaos.

In a filthy dungeon beneath Louisburgh Barracks, a starving Fintan McDonnell fought with rats for scraps of food thrown down to them by laughing Black and Tans. One day, a hateful Graham Gilberthorpe sneered down at him and taunted the father of the men he intended to hunt down.

"Look at the shit on him!" laughed the Kentish corporal, pointing down with his disfigured hand. "His 'Boys of Ballycroy' will be proud of him when they see him tied to Bessie tomorrow. That's if their hurleys don't arrow a bullet through him first!"

The next phase of Gilberthorpe's winter revenge was about to commence.

CHAPTER 37: HUMILIATION

Friday November 4th 1920 would have been the 45th birthday of Miss Esmeralda Gay. It was a sad day for her family, but they decided to turn the negative into a positive. Her elderly parents, her three sisters and her brother set up several tables on the cobblestones in front of Carey's Bar. With the help of some Westport people who had worked for Esmeralda in her bakery shop there, they laid out a splendid array of buns, tarts and pastries. There was also a wide variety of sweets. And to keep everyone warm in the cold November air, there was hot whiskey and soup available. All of this these treats were provided free of charge for the parishioners of Ballycroy, kindly funded by the Gay family of Sheeaun Lodge.

It was their way of saying thanks to the local population for the good will and prayers that was showered upon the family in the aftermath of the tragic and unfortunate death. The family were deeply touched by the warmth that had been shown to them, and in the middle of their grief they decided to mark her birthday this way. Being Roman Catholics, the Ballycroy people had been forbidden from attending her funeral in a Protestant Church. Even though he was understandably resentful about the circumstances surrounding his daughter's loss, Admiral Gay showed that he was not holding the Irish responsible. He even went as far as asking the two Schoolmasters and one Schoolmistress in the parish to allow the children to finish their classes an hour early to get their share of the goodies on offer.

It was a challenging task to make sure all of the hungry girls and boys got a fair share that wintry afternoon! A few of course were determined to exploit the generosity of the gentry, but all in all it was being managed well by the Gays. There was a large picture of Esmeralda on display, and the white bearded admiral gave a short speech in which he thanked everyone for coming. He became emotional as he described how much they were all missing their firstborn. One of her staff from the bakery business she ran in Westport also gave a speech. There was a white silken handkerchief with the initials EG embroidered into it handed out to every family. Esmeralda's family did an excellent job in lifting the spirits of the people.

But their day was spoiled just after the speeches. When they were about to take away their stalls, the dreaded sound of a lorry engine was heard in the distance. The crowd, especially the youngsters, began to scatter and some of them started screaming as they feared a repeat of the bullets of Bonfire Night. As a light drizzle descended, the yobbish sound of the shouting soldiers came closer and after a few minutes the Crossley Tender roared across the cobblestones before braking sharply.

The sight that greeted those who were brave enough not to leave was one of disgust. As the laughing soldiers descended onto the street and Gilberthorpe started blowing his whistle, the locals recognised that the man who was standing upright on the back of the vehicle and tied to its chicken-coop wire was one of their own. But he was barely recognisable. He was battered. He was bruised. He was naked but for a pair of soiled female bloomers. He was dirty. He was bearded. He was shivering from the cold and rain. He was looking desperate. He was being humiliated. He was Fintan McDonnell.

There he was, on display by the Black and Tans, who gathered around and poked him with their rifles. The father of Sylvester and Terence stood high on the truck, trying not to make any eye contact with any of his fellow parish people below. He stood helpless with his hands tied to a combination of the wire and a narrow girder. It was a pitiful sight.

As the locals looked on stunned, and frightened drinkers peered out from the pub window, the tall Graham Gilberthorpe blew his whistle again to get everyone's attention. He was about to begin yet another address.

"Now, Peasants! SILENCE! See here the great Fintan McDonnell, father of the even greater McDonnell brothers, wanted by his majesty for cowardly attacks on his forces. See what we can do to so-called freedom fighters. See what we can do to those of you who think that..."

Suddenly his speech was interrupted by a loud "Stop!" from the elderly man who stepped forward from the crowd gathered at the Post Office door, approaching the speaker and the truck. Gilberthorpe looked irate to have been disturbed in full flow.

"How dare you!" snarled the corporal. "Who do you think you are, old man?!"
"How dare YOU!" replied Admiral Gay. "How dare you humiliate this gentleman! Release him immediately! Get him down from there!"
"I shall do nothing of...of the sort!" stuttered the embarrassed Gilberthorpe.
"I am First Admiral Simeon Octavius Gay of The Royal British Navy. I order you, in the name of the king, to release that gentleman from his shackles. If you do not I shall inform the Lord Viceroy immediately. Get him down, you scoundrel!"

Gilberthorpe was clearly shocked and embarrassed, and looked at his men for some kind of support but they all had their faces facing the cobbles. He tried to counter.
"You cannot order....."
"I know the terms of Article 12 of the Convention of Geneva and so should you!" interrupted the admiral in a stern and strong voice. "You have no right to humiliate this gentleman like that. Now, I give you one final command. In the name of Brittania, RELEASE HIM!!"

As he spoke, a clearly distressed Claire McDonnell ran out from the Post Office where about fifty had crammed upon hearing the truck arrive.
"Oh Fintan! Thank God you are alive!!" she cried running to the truck and reaching out to touch his legs. "My goodness, what on earth have they done to you?"
The sight of his loyal staff member being so upset at the condition she had just found her husband in made Admiral Gay all the more determined to have his way and he walked right up to Gilberthorpe and stared upright at the shocked looking Kent man.
"Release Mister McDonnell now and be off!" he instructed, his white eyebrows gazing crossly upwards. "You and your fellow

scoundrels have spoiled my daughter's memorial. You are a disgrace to his majesty's crown! You are a disgrace to the realm! Now, BE GONE!"

Within minutes, the truck was pulling away towards Mulranny without its prisoner. Gilberthorpe looked sheepish. He could not even blow his whistle. The team of Tans had been shown up by the old man of the sea. As they disappeared from view there was a loud cheer and everyone started to gather around Admiral Gay. The children emerged from behind walls and trees and began dancing excitedly. The very upset Fintan hugged his sobbing wife who asked Rosa if they could bathe him upstairs and borrow some clothes. McDonnell was just happy to be back in Ballycroy and out of the cruel clutches. He had been certain he would not survive. They had starved him and beaten him. Two of his bullet wounds had become infected. He looked as if he had lost half of his bodyweight. There was a vile smell off him. He was happy to stand by and make way for a new hero. This time, the accolades all went in the direction of the 75 year old admiral. For the first time since Bonfire Night he was able to laugh.
"Essie would have been proud" said his wife, hugging him.
"I suppose she would!" he replied tearfully, "I suppose she would!"

*****

Later that evening Hughie arranged a reunion for the McDonnells at St. Kieran's school in Shranamonragh. Although furious to have found out about the inhumane treatment their father had endured, Sylvester and Terence were just delighted and relieved to see him again. In the school too, Fintan got to meet his grandson for the first time. It was an emotional thirty minutes. That's all the time they had. Barely ten minutes after Sylvester and Terence left in the mist for the side of Bunmore Hill, four Black and Tans from the Castlehill Barracks arrived at the school. Someone had obviously given them information that the McDonnells were there. The four checked the building and returned to their base without attempting to interfere with Fintan, Claire, their daughter, son-in-law and grandson. Hughie was able to tell the brothers that night of the near-miss.

In the following days, the McMahon family in Castlehill ensured that Fintan and Claire had a roof over their heads, as they finalised the necessary repairs on Terence's cottage in Claggan. That was the easiest of the burned buildings to repair and to have ready for Christmas.

Alternating between Bunmore Hill and Crafton Lake, Sylvester and Terence continued some firing at the passing Crossley Tenders, as instructed by Harry Heraty. Their actions helped distract the British from the smugglers who were taking the German weapons and ammunition out of the parish via mountains, road and sea. They missed Joey Jarvis, especially his cooking! They wondered if he had managed to retrieve his hoard.

In Newport Barracks, Gilberthorpe was forced to concentrate on the situation there where his men were being decimated by the local columns. Fresh with the new firepower from Vandenburg's submarine, the Irish were winning the war.

In Castlebar, Royston Carey was still in the process of renovating his new property. His wife was reluctantly preparing for town life. She hated the thought of leaving the McArthurs behind, but she had not much choice. Her brother Eddie was still a prisoner in Wales with PJ White.

On the last day of November an incident in Tuam, Co. Galway was to have a direct effect on Ballycroy and its war. As he walked from a funeral parlour, the Head IRA man in Mayo, John Moore, was hit by a Black and Tan sniper's bullet. He stumbled backwards and fell into a doorway, into a sitting position; holding is head in his hands as blood gushed from his mouth and nose onto his uniformed knees and boots. A brave colleague rushed over to join him in the doorway and whispered an act of contrition into his ear. John Moore groaned as his head then fell forward and revealed the entry wound on his skull. He was dead within five minutes. The 35 year old left a wife and three children behind.

On the day of Moore's burial in his native Ballyhaunis, Harry Heraty was told that he was now in charge of the IRA in all of Mayo. The job as OC for the West was being given to Frankie Phelan of Newport.

"What of Terence McDonnell?" asked Harry of the man who had just 'anointed' him as they sheltered from a hailstone shower in an Abbey Street alleyway. "I thought he deserved the West after me".
"You can have a deputy for the county" was the reply. "It is your choice. Feel free to take Terence for that role if you so please. I hear he is one of our best."

These words came from the mouth of the national Commander-in-Chief of the IRA – one Michael Collins.

CHAPTER 38: TOWARDS THE END OF THE LONGEST YEAR

A harsh December afflicted the West Mayo coastline as a fitting end to what everyone considered 'the longest year'. That title came from an article Toothy Lucey had written about the losses that Ballycroy had experienced in 1920. His piece wasn't just about the loss of human life, but of the loss of houses and livestock. About the loss of dignity. About the loss of innocence as war brought its wickedness into the heart of the bogland. "Even in prosperous times", he wrote, "My people know of nothing but hardship. What are we to ever gain from a war? The turf will still have to be saved, the sheep sheared and the cowdung spread. All it seems that this conflict is bringing us is less of a population to do this work. Only our coffin maker could point to any economic benefit, and alas even that poor gentleman has gone to his eternal reward this year".

The Black and Tans kept a heavy presence at the Castlehill Barracks, but unless Gilberthorpe was around to stir them up, they kept to themselves. And he was still reeling from being faced down by Admiral Gay. Many of the Black and Tans were becoming demoralised at this stage. They could see no immediate end to the war. Many of them simply wanted to return home to their loved ones. News had reached them of riots in British cities because of unemployment, and perhaps they could consider themselves to have a good wage, but nevertheless they had enough of Ireland. They were losing the war. The columns were beating them. And they had little sign of ceasing their onslaught. And every Auxiliary soldier posted to West Mayo had lived through the sobering experience of sending colleagues home to England, Scotland or Wales in a wooden box. Sometimes, with body parts still left behind on Irish boreens and ditches.

The war was almost two years old and the Black and Tans were more unpopular than ever. The events of Bloody Sunday in Croke Park when some of their numbers fired indiscriminately on GAA followers slaughtering over 20 people was a low point. British MPs in Westminster argued openly about the incident and very few were able to justify what had happened. There was increasing political pressure there to find a solution to 'The Irish Problem'. It was becoming a major source of embarrassment internationally for the United Kingdom. A relative of an MP happened to witness an atrocity by the Black and Tans in Castleconnell, Co. Limerick in which an innocent barman was one of three ruthlessly killed – for no apparent reason. This relative himself had to return to England disguised as a woman as he became a target of the Tans for daring to reveal the truth. Just miles away from there, three more unarmed republican sympathisers were rounded up and shot in cold blood in the middle of the bridge that connects Killaloe, Co. Clare with Ballina, Co. Tipperary. As was normally the case, no Black and Tan was ever charged with the callous crimes.

Word reached Ballycroy of many of the awful happenings nationwide. In 1920 Cork had lost one Lord Mayor to the Black and Tans and his successor to a hunger strike. Limerick City was to also lose a sitting Lord Mayor and a former Lord Mayor to an Auxiliary assassination squad the following year. The story of Kevin Barry's martyrdom in Dublin was another to spur young Irishmen into joining the fight against the colonial power. Dozens of innocent civilians all over the land were losing their lives.

As far as the republican leaders were concerned, they were winning the war and they expressed this publicly. But they had private worries that their men were running out of ammunition and would not be able to cope with the threatened reinforcements on the British side.

Countries such as America and South Africa were deploying envoys to seek peace talks. They wanted peace between the neighbouring islands as Europe was trying to recover from The Great War.

The men most exposed to the harsh realities of war that winter were the IRA men on the run. Harry Heraty had not had an opportunity to offer Terence his new role, as he settled into his new exalted position. One of the reasons is that for most of December 1920 Terence and his brother were holed up on

Bunmore Hill in the heavy snow. From within their stone hut they could see the vast whiteness spread out for miles and miles in front of them. One could not be but awe-stricken by the beauty of the white carpeted landscape, sparkling beneath a grey-blue sky with the silvery inlets of Blacksod Bay intruding from the left. On the right, the towering peak of Corcliabh of the Nephin Mountain range, with its mound of stones at the summit, overlooking the parish like a protective arctic giant.

But that snowy scenery had its downside, and that was the freezing cold nights that Sylvester and Terence had to endure in their hillside hut. To keep warm, they had to snuggle together at night covered by their stolen blankets and sheep fleeces. Of course this heat also attracted the rodents and ants. The men's teeth chattered with the cold. Their skin broke out in rashes. Their nostrils clogged. Their toes became frost-bitten. Their indoor fire was hard to keep alive when the wind was blowing and when the turf and firewood were buried under a foot of snow. Using their iced fingers to claw for fuel in the snow or frost was not a pleasant experience.

Of course they were occasionally able to visit some safe-houses for a good night's sleep. Many's the child who had to yield his or her bed to make way for the McDonnell lads or any gun-runner they were helping to escape from the parish. That young boy or girl usually ended up sleeping with daddy and mammy for the night whilst 'the men with the guns' were guests. Sylvester and Terence were always mindful not to loiter and thus endanger these hospitable families. The thought of getting some warm milk or a piping hot feed of salmon and floury spuds kept the men going when they faced into freezing nights in the hut.

Those same families were not slow to wash clothes for the men or darn their socks. Grandmothers were particularly helpful in knitting good woolly socks and hats, especially if the men were able to provide the raw materials in the shape of a fleece! Terence in particular developed a liking for sleeping in cowsheds as the warmth from the animals and their hay helped. But the downside to this was the itchy headful of hay-lice. He had never gone such a

long spell without having a woman to sleep with. Sylvester had remarked that he was surprised Terence was not 'on heat'.
"Sure my bollocks have been fucking frozen up on me!" he laughed, "Maybe they will thaw out by Easter and I will be back in the saddle again!"

Despite the laughter, Terence was becoming increasingly worried about his older brother. He seemed to be becoming weaker and stiff in his joints. He craved alcohol and suffered from its scarcity. He had begun to slur his words a lot. Most nights he shouted aloud in his sleep, roaring Willie's name. It was clear he was having nightmares about what his cousin had been subjected to. He was also suffering flashbacks from his time in Amiens.

Christmas Day arrived but the snow remained on the ground. The brothers sat outside of their hut and looked down on Bunmore village.
"That was known as 'Knockathample' long ago" said Sylvester.
"I know!" replied Terence. "Roger used to tell us that story, and I was here when you told it to Joey, remember?"
"It's hard to believe, there was a monastery down there nearly 1000 years ago" continued Sylvester pointing to a section of the McArthur land at the end of the village. "It was probably the only building around. Everywhere else must have been pure wilderness. It must have been so peaceful back then".
"Sure didn't Roger tell of the Red Pedlar murdering the woman by the holy well down there?" said Terence. "It mustn't have been THAT peaceful!"

"Jarvis. I wonder what he's doing now" said Sylvester, changing the subject.
"Probably lying with an expensive lady of the night in London somewhere!" replied Terence, "Wouldn't I love to be in his shoes!"
"You'd be no good to the lady with your frozen bollocks!" laughed Sylvester.
"Jarvis, he was on our side after all" reflected Terence. "But for one awful moment that morning Willie died, I felt he would turn on me within the cave. He restrained me, and probably saved my life – again".

"He was genuine alright" replied Sylvester, "Even though there were times I was uneasy around him".
"Come on" said Terence. "Let's head for O'Gradys. They'll have the sow half-cooked by now!"

The famished brothers had an enjoyable meal with Roger's family. Some welcome dollars had arrived specifically for the Christmas celebrations. The finest of food and whiskey was available for the freedom fighters. The brothers were joined that afternoon in Bunmore by their parents, sister, brother-in-law and nephew. Everyone enjoyed themselves in front of a roaring hot fire.

Just back the village, the Whites were still guests of the McArthurs and they prayed together for their incarcerated sons. Seaneen White's grave was visited that afternoon.

Up in the Castlehill Barracks the four on duty played cards for the day and wished they could be with their families. Corporal Gilberthorpe WAS with his family, having been given special dispensation to visit his parents in Deal who were still homeless. As part of his plea for Christmas leave, he had undertaken to visit the grieving family of the late Corporal Ifor Morris near Swansea. He dutifully carried out the task without a slightest pang of guilt.

In Sheeaun the Gays recalled tales of happier Christmases with Esmeralda. In Achill the Bourkes did likewise as they remembered Martha's life. They also contemplated what to do with the money Batty had sent them to put towards a new house. Neighbours of the Kerrigans visited their lonesome grave and then paused as they passed their ruined farm on the way home. Toothy Lucey enjoyed his first Christmas as a married man and kept his new family entertained with his tales from America. "You'd swear he was three decades there and not three weeks!" laughed Davy Cooney.

In Ballycroy Village the Carey family were busy preparing for the St. Stephen's Day wedding of Rebecca to Benny Hughton Junior. It helped distract them from the loss of their father. Rosa took a break from the preparations and sat alone on her bed and cried.

She was missing her lover Bosco Darby. But he was at home with his wife and children, and he was suffering still with the after effects from his assault. He could not remember exactly what happened, but he knew he and Rosa were finished. He knew he was fortunate that their affair remained secret.

Rosa rubbed her tummy. Only she knew that she was not alone in her room; that a baby was growing inside of her. She tried to write to Roger for help and advice but she wasn't able to finish, so before long several scrunched up pages lay on the carpet by her dainty feet. How she would love to have him there now. Though gone over eight years, she still felt close to him. She smiled at his Christmas card through her tears. What would she do? How she missed not having her Dad around. She needed him now. As the giggles and laughter echoed from downstairs, she never felt so alone.

Just a couple of hundred yards away, someone else was also suffering in silence. Fr. Francis Kinsella had been a good man. He had joined the priesthood twenty five years previously because he believed in goodness. He believed he had something to offer. He believed he could lighten the burden on the oppressed and help them bring God into their lives. Now, it had all gotten too much for him. He gazed out on his white lawn. A robin redbreast caught his attention by the hawthorn bushes. Even the robin looked depressed.

Father Kinsella tried to focus on the happy wedding he had to officiate the following day. Surely that would cheer him up. But no, he kept falling back into the deep pit of depression. This year had been the worst ever. There was no escaping the blackness, despite the glow from the whiteness outside. He had buried too many people. He had seen too many families ripped apart by war. He had seen too many eyes full of pain and hopelessness. He had heard God's will questioned so many times, he was now doubting his own faith. He had seen blood soak the sand. He had heard of human bodies being butchered. He had seen the slaughtered remains of poor hens, dogs, cows, sheep and horses. He had seen a young teacher and his family having to cope with the prospect of losing their livelihood – due to unprovoked violence. He had seen the Kerrigan family wiped out. He had seen a man being paraded almost naked by his captors. He had seen hungry and cold barefoot children in the shacks called schools. He had baptised little babies whose parents had dreaded bringing into the world. He would not be able to face another year of this.

He quenched the fire he had just worked so hard to light an hour previously. He went to his bedroom and left his bible on the middle of his bed. He took his revolver from the drawer, and closed the door behind him. He calmly walked out of the house, again closing the door after him. He had one last look at the church to his left and to Bunmore Hill up to his right. He knelt on the snowy edge of his front lawn, and looked at the wondrous giant triangle of Slievemore in its brilliant white directly in front of him. It was the last vision that his eyes absorbed before a bullet pierced his skull.

The gentle priest had been so considerate; he had purposely carried out his final deed on the lawn to save his housemaid from having to clean up a mess inside. He had died as he had lived – putting others first.

The loud sound of the gunshot startled the nearby residents of Ballycroy Village, who feared that the Black and Tans were about to ruin everyone's Christmas Day.

Royston Carey was the first to discover the body of the priest on the blood-soaked snow. He would have to quickly inform his sister that she would have to get a priest from a neighbouring parish to marry her. The longest year had yet to come to an end.

The distraught couple ended up postponing their wedding by a week and the sombre ceremony went ahead in the pulverised parish on January 1st 1921. That was also the date that Terence was asked by Harry Heraty to join him as a Special Operations Officer at the head of the Mayo IRA.

The year that had brought the number of remaining 'Boys of Ballycroy' back up to five – and then down to four again - was over. Hopefully this coming year would see no more of them lost.

Terence believed that accepting this post would help see that hope realised. Harry had promised the deployment of some Erris, Achill and Mulranny new recruits to help guard either side of the parish.

Sylvester now had help. And Terence was heading for bigger and better things.

He hoped.

CHAPTER 39: THE WAR GOES ON

Father Timothy Roland from Crossmolina settled into his new assignment in Ballycroy, replacing the tragic Father Kinsella whose flock still grieved for him. A long lost cousin of Roger, Roger's brother Liam O'Grady was one of the first to welcome him to the parish and this made him feel at home. But the forty year old priest had inherited a dispirited place. In his first sermon he tried to find positives in facing 1921. He predicted that the current war would end. He predicted that their most famous son, Jean Pierre Roland, would return for a long overdue visit. He predicted an end to the unforgiving weather and a year in which the turf and hay would be handily saved. He was determined to raise the spirits of the picturesque parish who had just lost their old priest to suicide. He pointed to the young kids and said everyone had to try their best to ensure that a brighter year lay ahead. And that there was more to life than the gun or the emigration ship.

There were rumours that a ceasefire was being sought in the war. The downtrodden individuals hoped that this was so. Like the priest they lost, they had more than enough.

Again, a beacon of hope to the Ballycroy people was the ever-growing success of Jean Pierre Roland. He was now a major player in the movie industry, and his cousin wasn't shy in displaying pictures from America in the main porch of the church, showing the smiling Playwright and Film Producer alongside famous names such as Eisenhower, Barrymore, Ruth, Pickford and Rockefeller. These images inspired the youngsters that they could rise above their station. That fame and fortune could be found beyond the mountains, bog and sea shores that surrounded them. Roger had sent money to Rosa and Royston Carey for the purposes of setting up a mini cinema in their hall. Every Saturday night after mass, the excited parishioners gathered to watch the film reels. Images from all over the globe were projected onto the walls of Carey's Hall, which they enjoyed from their comfortable chairs, all bought from the gratefully received dollars. This was escapism at its best. And they now felt that they were a real part of the wider world.

Terence McDonnell however, did not have to watch a film reel to experience action. He was seeing it for real in his new role. His job took him all over Mayo where he did much of the donkeywork for the new Mayo OC Harry Heraty. He linked with the columns in places such as Carrowteigue, Ballycastle, Moygownagh, Kilfian, Keenagh, Glenhest, Balla, Kilmaine, Tourmakeady, and Ballindine to ensure that there was no let up in the guerrilla war against the fading British. He had to ensure that the entire county was doing its fair share for Ireland. Terence's organisational skills became a valuable asset and were applied effectively in the first few months of 1921.

Harry Heraty's replacement as West Mayo OC though, Frankie Phelan, was struggling to fill the boots of his predecessor. He was more short-tempered and his gruff, impolite and impatient ways were not going down well.

Back in Ballycroy, Sylvester felt isolated without his brother, despite having columns of support to the north in Bangor Erris and to the south in Mulranny. Morale in the columns wasn't great as they felt they were not getting the resources or intelligence they required from Frankie Phelan. Sylvester was still very much a wanted man, and so he had to stay 'on the run'. He would have liked to join his brother, but was under orders to act as an experienced link between the columns at either end of his parish. He was perturbed to arrive at his hillside hut one March evening to find that his belongings had been disturbed. He didn't sleep much that night as hurricane-like winds howled at his hut, and he curled up in a freezing corner wondering who had intruded into his hideaway. He decided that it was best to head for The Sandybanks the next day and he gathered some cans of food, bread, cheese and brandy to carry with him. He also topped up his sack with bullets.

As he sat out for the Bunmore Road below, he froze momentarily in horror as he sighted what seemed like hundreds of soldiers advancing towards him from that road. His ears were numb from the cold and he cursed himself for not being more alert. As he turned towards his hut and darted back up the hill, he could hear shouts of "Surrender" from below in English accents. He was their target. He took a look back behind to see the enemy, who were spread out about five yards apart, all armed and marching menacingly in his direction. Sylvester realised that he had only minutes of freedom left, and his instinct took him past the Shepherd's Hut and up the steep incline to the summit of Bunmore Hill. "Stop! Surrender! Or we will shoot" was the cry from below but he just kept on climbing frantically. His aim was to descend on the other side.

However, to the hero's horror, from the summit he was met with the sight of an advancing battalion climbing from the Gortbrack side. He was being surrounded. He was trapped. He looked around in a panic for ideas, his gun clasped in his shaking right fist. He saw nothing. Nothing, until seconds later the hellish hound that had mauled his cousin on the mountain ran into view, running straight at Sylvester with his jagged teeth bared. Sylvester took aim but his gun jammed. And before he knew it the dog had pounced on him and had knocked him to the ground, and was tearing at the flesh under his chin. As Sylvester screamed in pain he could hear "Brutus, good boy Brutus!" being shouted and as he fought with the beast his lower earlobe was torn off by the razor sharp teeth. He tried to force his arm back the Alsatian's throat but then received a painful bang on the back of his head and he fell onto the ground.

His face was now on the wet heather and all he could see in front of his bloody nose was a pair of muck covered boots. He heard Brutus being called to heel and the gathering clatter of English accents around him. He thought he was about to be killed. He waited for the clicking of a bullet chamber. But instead he received another blow to the back of his head, and then felt the heavy weight and soreness of a knee digging into his lower back. Then a pair of hands grasped him around his neck from behind and pulled his head upwards sharply. Sylvester felt as he was about to be decapitated. He shrieked in pain. He expected his neck to snap.

"Got you at last you bastard!" snarled Gilberthorpe, pushing Sylvester's head into the wet boggy ground so that muck and moss began entering his mouth.
"I wish I could fucking finish you here!" continued the corporal, "But you are wanted in fucking Dublin Castle where there is a thick fucking rope waiting for you, you peasant piss. I will get my promotion from you. But I will make sure you suffer before you reach that fucking rope. You will be fucking begging to be hung by the time I am finished with you, Sylvie Boy!"

Sylvester reckoned he passed out from the pain as he could not remember the descent from Bunmore Hill. They must have carried him. As he lay in the dungeon beneath Louisburgh Barracks which had held his father just some months previously, the disorientated IRA man tried to recall how he had got so many of the wounds that covered his aching body. Bit by bit, it all came back to him...

He remembered the appalled faces of the people outside Carey's Bar as he passed them, tethered by his outstretched hands to the rear of Crossley Tender, which drove slowly but fast enough to ensure the captured and barefoot Sylvester had to keep up a decent pace to stop from collapsing onto his knees. He remembered the sneering faces of the laughing Tans who spat at him from the back of the truck as he tried not to fall. He remembered one of them pissing from the moving truck on top of him as they edged through the winding pathway near Mulranny. He remembered having to urinate in his torn trousers as they refused his plea to stop by a bush. He remembered the pain of the sharp stones piercing the soles of his feet. He remembered the agony he felt as bits of sand and rock entered his foot wounds and stung him. He remembered the pain he felt in his lower side, and the cacophony of laughter from his captors as the driver deliberately picked up speed going up the bray near Mulranny so that Sylvester would have to run faster or risk falling and being dragged along the road.

By the scars on his knees, he reckoned that he must have eventually passed out and been dragged for a while. As he surveyed the scores of cuts, he had a strange feeling of calmness.

His father had survived this same hellhole and he was certain that he could too. He was sure that his brother would be working on an escape attempt. Unlike his father, who felt that any minute could have been his last, the prisoner felt that at least he knew the plan was to get him to Dublin. He was valuable to Gilberthorpe. In fact he wondered why Gilberthorpe had told him this. Perhaps the corporal was playing with his mind? But what he had said made sense.

In Ballycroy the McDonnells were praying that their captured son would survive. They too were hoping that Terence and his men could somehow rescue his brother from the jaws of the British lion. Father Tim, as he liked to be called, prayed at mass for Sylvester's safe return. The GAA team which he had captained before The Great War convened and sent an official appeal to the British authorities for his immediate release. There were rumours that several GAA parish teams were planning to launch a rescue attempt at Louisburgh Barracks, where they suspected he was being held.

This was a challenge to Frankie Phelan and he urged the GAA to desist from any such action. He, Harry Heraty and Terence were already working on a plan. There was no way they wanted Sylvester to reach Dublin Castle. Even though his hanging would make him a martyr, they did not want Gilberthorpe to get the plaudits that were lined up for him. If he had been seen to kill a second of the 'Boys of Ballycroy', his star will have risen, at their expense. Publicly executing such a rebel would boost the morale of the British in West Mayo. The men took a risky decision. A high stakes rescue attempt would be made before Sylvester was to be moved from the county. There was a high chance that he would not survive it and that others would be lost also. But if he were to die in Mayo, at least a spin could be put on it. They could control events there better than they could in Dublin.
Terence had no choice but to go along with the plan. Harry Heraty insisted that Terence be kept at the periphery of the actual operation. He did not want to lose both brothers in one day.

CHAPTER 40: OPERATION STATION

The new Mayo OC, Frankie Phelan, knew that he was not meeting the standard expected of him but he was his own harshest critic. He was a dedicated and determined republican who wanted to see every last Briton removed from the isle. He had led one of the Newport columns with a fair degree of success. In his new role, he had found it difficult to 'spread himself' throughout the region he was supposed to command. He saw the rescue plan to retrieve Sylvester McDonnell, named 'Operation Station', back from the British as an opportunity to reclaim his reputation.

"Terence, I am willing to die for this" he told the prisoner's brother. "I am literally putting everything on the line".
"I know" acknowledged a tense and nervous Terence after the final plan had been gone through one last time. "I know you will try your best. But you should never have left my brother so isolated in Ballycroy like that. May God be on our side".

One of Frankie Phelan's strong points was that he had a well organised network of spies. He had connections everywhere through his previous job as a bread delivery man. The stocky, crooked-nosed, balding barrel of a man had always been a jovial, popular figure. But in fighting this war his demeanour was deadly serious.

On the eve of 'Operation Station', as expected Corporal Gilberthorpe had arrived at Westport Rail Station to inform Station Master Falconio that his men would be bringing a prisoner to Dublin on the next 8am train. Falconio nodded his head as the Englishman laid out his demands – that they would have the last carriage to themselves, and that seats would be reserved in the front carriages for some of his men. Falconio, the man with an Italian father and a Roscommon mother, had little option but to nod in agreement. Even though throughout the country, particularly in the south, some rail workers had rebelled and refused to carry personnel or supplies for the Black and Tans, there had never been any major issue of this sort in Mayo.

Gilberthorpe was aware that during the two years of the war to date, a number of attempts had been made in various counties to rescue prisoners from trains. Some had succeeded spectacularly, but most had failed. Fighters and innocent civilians had all been casualties throughout Ireland in these incidents. Gilberthorpe took every precaution he could think of to ensure he would thwart any rescue attempt. He had himself and two others assigned to guard Sylvester in the rear carriage until he was to be handed over at Athlone Station to the Leinster brigade. He had four others planted in the other carriages. On top of that, he had an additional two delegated to act as sentries that March morning. Nine men in total.

Of course, Falconio had fed all of the information to the IRA leaders. The IRA had sixteen men ready for action that morning. This was Frankie Phelan's biggest test to date. He had managed to pay a quick visit to his wife and baby son the previous day. When leaving them behind, he wondered to himself if it was the last time he would ever get to see them.

By 7.50am, Frankie Phelan was perched alongside Harry Heraty on the grassy slope overlooking Westport Station, the terminus station on the Dublin to Westport railway line. They had two of their own men covering their backs. They could see the smoke coming from the engine below as it warmed up to take its five passenger carriages and one cargo carriage – at the very end – to Dublin, stopping at 14 stations *en route*.

The two IRA leaders noticed a Black and Tan climbing aboard the cargo carriage at the rear end and checking the rocks it was carrying in case any rescuer had been hidden there. It was a dark, overcast morning and visibility was poor, but they could make out that Sylvester was indeed in the rear passenger carriage with three soldiers guarding him, the final passenger carriage situated directly in front of the load of rocks.

Phelan and Heraty could see that there were a couple of armed Tans standing in front of the station on the road, ready to return to their barracks in the waiting Crossley Tender. When Falconio blew his whistle for the train to leave the station at 8am exactly, the IRA leaders in the grass were relieved to see the Crossley Tender drive away, having completed its task.

The train revved up and a puff of pitch black smoke shot into the early morning sky. In his carriage, the bruised Sylvester McDonnell was in the corner seat, by the window but with his back to the rear carriage wall. His bound hands lay on his lap in front of him. Immediately beside him sat a burly armed Tan. Directly across the table, facing him, was a second Tan. Sitting across the aisle from those three, nervously holding his handgun was a fidgety Gilberthorpe. As he had directed, the rest of that carriage had 'reserved' signs on the tables meaning that the four had it to themselves for the moment. In the carriages ahead, four Black and Tans in civilian clothes took their places at various different points and were preparing themselves for action in case the train was attacked in transit.

Back in the rear passenger carriage, Gilberthorpe breathed a deep sigh of relief at the sound of Falconio's whistle as he knew they had their prisoner and their men all *en situ* and positioned to fight off any ambush.

As the engine pulled away from the station, the hiding IRA men sprang into action and ran to their pre-arranged positions by the track. Before Gilberthorpe had a chance to realise what was happening, he spotted several men in peaked caps surround the carriage on the outside, with their rifles pointed at the four men inside. Gilberthorpe grew red with rage as the reality of what had just happened hit him.   The engine had pulled off just bringing four of the passenger carriages! The section carrying the cargo of rocks and the four men had been unhooked and left behind! Gilberthorpe had checked everything he could, but failed to spot that Phelan had disconnected the final two carriages from the rest of the train.

As the Tans in civvies tried to blend in with the other passengers in the front carriages and look like normal travellers, they were blissfully unaware that they were travelling towards Dublin without their high-value hostage and three of their men. Harry Heraty stood on top of the slope and elatedly gave the thumbs up sign to the men guarding his back. The plan looked like it had worked. But 'Operation Station' was not yet over...

Sylvester quickly copped that a rescue attempt was occurring but he knew his life was in grave danger. He looked at the tall panicking figure of the standing and cursing Gilberthorpe whose face was changing colours by the second. The two other Tans looked at each other open-mouthed and then looked to their leader for guidance. But he was too busy trying to count how many IRA men were surrounding the carriage and he was weighing up the diminishing odds of winning a shootout.

"Put your hands up Gilberthorpe!" shouted one of the men by the tracks. The helpless Sylvester could not take his eyes off the corporal as he tried to figure out what the English would do next. Then, at the other end of the carriage, came the shout of "Don't shoot! Don't fucking shoot!" as the stocky figure of Frankie Phelan bravely boarded the stagnant carriage, pointing his pistol at the corporal. Behind him was another IRA man who quickly leapt on top of the nearest table and fixed his rifle at the two other Tans.

Gilberthorpe knew he was in a hopeless situation. He had just been outwitted. Big time. He figured that the best he could do was get out of the situation alive and un-captured. Although he was tempted to fire a bullet through the hostage's skull, he knew it would result in certain death for him and his men. He considered trying to play for time in case some of the Tans on the train or on the truck would realise what had happened and return, but there was no way the IRA would give him that time.

"Put DOWN your guns!" came the harsh order from the Newport man. "Put DOWN your fucking guns IMMEDIATELY!" Gilberthorpe had one last look around. Sylvester gulped and could not avert his gaze from the right hand of the corporal which was still holding his gun.
"One last time, put DOWN your fucking guns!" shouted Phelan as some of the men on the outside impatiently shouted to "Hurry up! SURRENDER!"

To his eternal relief, the three Brits did as they were told and their guns bounced off the floor. By now there were three IRA men at the opposite side of the carriage behind the lead gunman.
"Now. Untie the prisoner and let him off!" commanded Phelan. "He stays with us. He is a prisoner of his majesty!" replied Gilberthorpe boldly to the disbelief of everyone in the train. Even his two colleagues knew they were not going to win this battle!
"You harm Sylvester" snarled Phelan as one of the Tans loosened his binds with trembling hands, "And there will be blood on the floor of Number 20 Elizabeth Carter Road!"

Those words stunned Gilberthorpe. His face turned grey. That was the house his homeless parents were staying at with their old friends – in Kent.

"Yes, you heard me right Gilberthorpe. George and Edwina will be executed this morning if you harm our man" said Phelan. Gilberthorpe was reeling. His knees went weak. He had a vision of his elderly parents kneeling at the end of IRA rifles, terrifyingly contemplating their fate. He was on the verge of fainting.

As Sylvester clambered to freedom from his corner, the three Tans lay down as ordered and had their hands tied behind their backs. The liberated prisoner aimed a spit at the back of his captor's neck, before being shoved towards the rear exit door to his freedom by Phelan. An aching and stiff Sylvester then joined his fellow IRA men outside, who were proud of a job well done but still in alert mode. They ushered him quickly away to a waiting safe house as planned.

A thrilled Frankie Phelan was the last IRA man to leave the carriage, leaving the three Black and Tans bound, gagged and gun-less. It was still only 8.05am!
"You are lucky to be alive all three of you!" stated Phelan. "We promised only to kill if any of our men were harmed. You are fucking lucky that we are Irishmen and not Huns". And off he leapt.

The execution of the plan took only five minutes but it was Frankie Phelan's finest hour. Mayo had another hero, and word spread quickly through the towns and town-lands of the daring feat. Sylvester had been rescued safely from the Tans without a shot being fired. Terence was joyous and wrapped his arms around his brother and Phelan. Mayo people laughed when reports emerged of the confused Englishmen at the platform of Castlebar Station that morning who had just realised that they had left their most important train carriage behind in the last town!

The Bard of Burrishoole pondered about how he could possibly describe the latest heroics involving the 'Boys of Ballycroy'. Their legend now knew no bounds.

The incident was a huge embarrassment for the British commanders in Dublin Castle. Instead of the high profile prisoner they were expecting, all they got from the West was a story of immense humiliation. Michael Collins and Eamonn De Valera were amongst those to send their congratulations to Harry Heraty and his Mayo men. Frankie Phelan was relieved that he had regained some credibility, but he realised that the fight for freedom was not yet over. They had won a battle, but not yet the war. But for the moment, he was just glad to be able to hold his wife and child again.

The incident marked the end of Gilberthorpe's reign in Mayo and he was summonsed to Dublin Castle and assigned menial tasks there. But not before a severe dressing down from his superior officers. He was hurting to have been mugged by 'the peasants'. He found out later that his parents in Kent had not been held at gunpoint, but obviously the IRA had a spy over there and the information Phelan revealed on the train had the desired effect. Phelan had intended to use that information only if Gilberthorpe had resisted arrest or held his gun to Sylvester's head, but thankfully the stranded man from Kent had realised that any stunts like that were futile.

On Easter Sunday of that year, with the Tans in Ballycroy leaderless and in disarray, the McDonnell and McMahon families were able to come together at the parish church in Ballycroy as baby Fintan William McMahon was christened by Father Tim. It was a proud day for everyone, and the wide-eyed little child brought joy and hope to his doting relatives present as holy water soaked his tiny head.

Some of that joy and hope became realised when in mid 1921 a truce was called between the Black and Tans and the Irish. Negotiations would begin on self-governing and possible independence for the Ireland.

There was huge relief in Ballycroy but as ever the Irish began to divide. The majority of rebels felt that the war should continue until the British were driven out. In boxing parlance, they felt they had the British 'on the ropes' and it was only a matter of months before they would retreat from the country. These fighters felt that agreeing to a truce was a sign of weakness.

Several months previously, Terence may have felt the same as his brother and father did, but his role with Harry Heraty had shown him that, using boxing parlance again, the Irish were 'punching above their weight' and were doing well to be where they were at. But that effort was unsustainable in the longer term. The arms supply was almost exhausted. Stocks were running low. Senior IRA officers were aware from international intelligence that the British were planning one last major effort to crush the Irish ruthlessly. Tens of thousands of reinforcements were being prepared on the mainland for action in the Emerald Isle. Most of the IRA men at the top of the organisation knew that their people could not hold out for much longer. They feared for the civilian population. They felt that now was a good time to negotiate with the British. They felt that they were in a strong position to gain independence for the first time in 700 years. Five years after the 1916 Rising, the dreams of those executed could be about to be realised. The men who had fought in the Great War and in the Irish War of Independence had shown that Ireland was now ready to "take her place amongst the nations of the earth", which Pearse had aspired to.

Sylvester and Terence started re-roofing their parents' home in Claggan. They were free to return. They could leave Crafton, Bunmore and The Sandybanks behind. They were no longer 'on-the-run'. They set about re-establishing their blacksmith business. They were heroes to the people of Ballycroy, as was their father. The brothers decided to capitalise on their popularity. Terence did it by having sex with as many as possible of the willing women he met. He retraced his steps throughout Mayo to make up for lost time! Sylvester capitalised by drinking every last drop of the ale and whiskey that was sent in his direction by grateful fellow imbibers. After experiencing the hardship of being at the forefront of the war, no one begrudged them their opportunity to enjoy themselves.

But as one black cloud disappeared, another was on the horizon. As the end of 1921 approached there was division as it became clear that the negotiations in London that followed the truce were not going all the Irish delegation's way. The prospect of another tragic divide in Ireland's history loomed. Civil War between supporters and opponents of the Treaty signed in Downing Street was a very real threat. Families and factions began to split, as people argued amongst themselves on whether what was on offer from the British was enough.

Those who supported Collins on the pro-Treaty side claimed the offer of a 26 county Free State with six Ulster counties remaining in the union was a stepping stone towards an eventual united Ireland. It gave an immediate opportunity to establish an independent Irish parliament – albeit for just 26 of the 32 counties. Those who fell in behind De Valera and his stance claimed the Treaty was a sell out. They were particularly annoyed that under the Treaty terms, the taxpayers of Ireland had to fund the pensions of the RIC men and Black and Tans who had terrorised the natives and inflicted so much pain.

That Christmas Eve in Carey's Bar Sylvester and Terence McDonnell promised each other that their family would not split, no matter what. They had already come through so much together.

It was a promise that would be severely tested.

CHAPTER 41: REVELATIONS, ROMANCE AND RETRIBUTION

As rural Ireland tried to mend the scars of the war just ended, there was some employment for the locals in rebuilding houses, roads, bridges and ditches that had been damaged. The McDonnells had their home habitable again, but there was still much work to be done. Terence's cottage was fully repaired. They had extensive work yet to do on their forges in Claggan and Ballycroy Village. Fintan McDonnell, being the closest relative to the deceased Kerrigan family, inherited their Doona farm and encouraged Sylvester to rebuild the burnt house there for himself. He and the rest of the clan had become increasingly concerned by Sylvester's drinking, and they figured that this project would keep him away from Carey's Bar.

Also returning to a property that had been destroyed by the hated Black and Tans were the Bourkes of Aughness South. With the aid of money sent from Germany, they decided to build on a new site and Andrew did most of the work. Their friends and family were glad to welcome them back but could not get over how Patrick and Agnes had aged so much since losing Martha.

Just down the road, German money also helped the Whites build a new house. Batty had felt terrible that they had lost young Seaneen forever and that PJ had been captured. The truce allowed PJ's return but he did not stay long as he had fallen in love with a Dublin girl and wanted to be with her there.

In Bunmore, Eddie McArthur returned from the prison in Wales to a warm welcome. After his experience of war and being a prisoner, the young man had decided that he wanted to join the priesthood. The family were delighted and sold most of their livestock to kick-start his education fund.

Over the road in O'Grady's house, Liam was the proud owner of only the fifth car in Ballycroy, following the trend set by the Gays, the Careys, the Lyalls and the Fitzwiltons. Of course his purchase was funded by his wealthy brother. Roger's latest movie production, a comedy named 'Five More Minutes' was another success, and received its Irish premiere in Carey's Hall on Christmas week. It was shown for free all week, and people from Belmullet, Glenamoy, Bangor Erris, Crossmolina, Mulranny, Achill and Newport trekked the wintry miles to see the film.

Roger's cousin, Fr. Tim, was determined that the parish would enjoy a better Christmas to the last one they had to endure. The movie-showing helped achieve this aim, as did the beautiful carol singing of the newly-formed Ballycroy Church Choir. He also organised a Christmas Fair outside of Carey's where local produce such as Christmas cakes, black pudding, rashers, eggs, candles and knitted garments were either bought or bartered.

As usual, crowds crammed into the church for midnight mass on Christmas Eve, where special prayers were said for those who had been lost to what was being referred to as 'The Black and Tan War'. Two of the surviving four 'Boys of Ballycroy' again stood side by side during the ceremony. Between them, the McDonnell brothers had directly killed several of the Tans. Terence had played a vital strategic part in ensuring what was now being clearly claimed as a victory over the British. It had taken nearly one hundred men to capture Sylvester, yet he was still standing there in the church! The brothers were a testament to Irish freedom. But in the cold days and nights on the mountains, they had often wondered if they would survive to make midnight mass for Christmas 1921. They had beaten the odds and succeeded. In the row behind them proudly stood another man, much younger, who had played his part in making sure that they succeeded. He was the lean smartly dressed future parliamentarian Hughie O'Hora.

Fr. Tim had his Christmas dinner with the O'Grady family in Bunmore. William's health had been deteriorating but he enjoyed the occasion, especially the fun being generated by his grandchildren.

The Carey family gathered for some pre-pheasant sherry on the only day of the year that their business closed. It was Benny Hughton Junior's first time sitting down with the Careys for their Christmas meal. And it was one he would not forget!

It didn't take him long to realise that there was some tension between Royston and Rosa. Of course Royston had been spending a lot of his time establishing his new businesses in Castlebar, and was only in Ballycroy once or twice a week. Rosa too had been 'away' for a lot of the year. Benny had not been paying much attention as the combination of the bar work, undertaking duties and acclimatising to married life had kept him more than occupied, but he caught up with what he had been missing on Christmas Day.

Royston had been short-tempered with the children all morning, and was particularly critical of the crying baby Robert in the cradle. Charlotte, Louis, Royston Junior and Philip had individually felt his wrath at some stage as the noise that they created with their new toys caused him annoyance. Both his wife Antoinette and sister Rosa had defended the children, much to Royston's disdain. Rebecca did not become involved and whispered to her husband to steer clear of the tense Royston. Benny simply put it down to the stress that the businessman was understandably experiencing in Castlebar with his new ventures. But as they neared the end of their meal, with nine sitting around the table and the infant crying nearby, a row erupted when Royston took exception to what he perceived was a snigger from Rosa.

"What the feck are you laughing at now, you cow?!" he shouted across the table.
"Don't you dare speak to me like that!" responded the shocked Rosa.
"I will speak in any fecking way I like!" roared Royston as his wife pleaded with him to refrain from swearing in front of the children.
"You're an ass!" shouted Rosa as she stood up to leave the table.
"An ass?!" asked her brother with his eyebrows raised. "An ass?! Well I suppose I must be, mustn't I? I must be a real donkey doing all that I have done for you, you stupid cow!"
"All YOU have done for ME?!" replied Rosa incredulously.
"Working all the hours God gave me to keep YOUR pockets full,

and all for a few measly shillings a month?! How dare YOU! How dare YOU!"
"You would be in the gutter but for me!" came the reply from the sinister looking Royston, his face contorting with rage. "You and your lousy children would be in the gutter..."
"Stop Royston PLEASE!" begged Antoinette as she ushered the four frightened children from the table and into the living room.
"You bastard!" said Rosa. "You rotten bastard!"
"Let's leave" said Rebecca to her husband Benny, grabbing his arm.
"No" interjected Royston. "Stay! I am sure Benny would like to hear the TRUTH about the angelic Rosa, the 'virgin' with the heavenly halo, in whose mouth butter would not melt".
"You shut UP!" snarled Rosa, nearing tears, to her tormenter.
"And why should I shut up?" asked Royston, by now the only one left sitting, as he gulped some more sherry. "This is MY house! This is MY food and this is MY drink. I can do and say what I like. And you will not tell ME what to do!"
"Dad said this is our family home" sobbed Rosa, "And that we could all use it whenever we like".
"And you certainly ARE using it" laughed Royston sarcastically, "Filling it with your litter".
"Shut up Royston!!" shouted Antoinette.
"You bastard. You bastard!" repeated Rosa. "You absolute bastard from the depths of hell".
"You might as well find out now, Benedict" said Royston turning to his brother-in-law and beckoning at him to re-take his seat. "Snow White here is the reason my wife and family have not yet joined me in Castlebar. She has landed us with another bastard – and she dares to call me one".
"Stop! I'm begging you Royston" urged Antoinette as Rosa ran to the cradle, picked up the crying baby Robert and ran out of the dining room in tears. But Royston was in no mood to cease.

"Yes Benedict. Rosa is Robert's mother. And not my wife, as you had been led to believe. I'm not the little creature's father. No one knows who the father is. But for a second time she has lumbered us with the fruit of her womb".
"Be quiet Royston" whispered Rebecca as she averted an attempt from her shocked husband to make eye contact.

"Yes Benedict. You heard me correctly. Let the truth come out! Nearly ten years ago she also lumbered us with her firstborn. Yes, young Louis 'Carey'. But at least we KNOW who his father is, don't we?" he said smiling.

"Who?" asked Benny.

"The great Jean Pierre Roland of course!" he exclaimed. "And do you think he has sent even ONE dollar from his MILLIONS our way?! Nah!"

"That's because he doesn't know!" said Rebecca, looking nervously at Benny as she wondered what his reaction to this revelation would be.

"Oh yes. The mighty Jean Pierre Roland and his great El Ginto are raking in millions, when my wife and I are killing ourselves to keep the mess he left behind at his wake fed and educated along with our own lot. And now the cow has spread her legs again and we have another bastard to care for! And she calls ME a bastard?!" said Royston as he rose from the table and reached for his tobacco.

Rebecca led Benny to their bedroom, and tearfully apologised for not revealing everything to him sooner. She explained that when both Rosa and Antoinette found out they were pregnant in 1912 the decision was made to have the children, born within two months of each other, reared as twins. A story was concocted that one of the babies was sick and required hospital treatment, when in fact Rosa was being kept at her uncle's home in Castlebar. Everyone in Ballycroy fell for the story that Antoinette had twins, when in fact she only had Charlotte. Louis was the result of Roger and Rosa's last night together in Ballycroy before he left for America. Roy Carey Senior had ensured that a scandal was avoided by convincing a reluctant Royston to go along with the plan. As part of the deal, Royston would not name the boy Royston as was the family custom; and the rightful heir would be the first boy that he and Antoinette would have together. For her part, Rosa made everyone promise that Roger would not learn of his son. No one outside of the family was to know. She did not want to wreck Roger's dream to conquer America. It was agreed that the truth would be revealed to Louis on his 18th birthday. Until then, he and Charlotte would be raised as twins. As far as the boy was concerned, Rosa was his aunt.

She then went on to reveal how Rosa had again fallen pregnant in the past year but that she would not reveal who the father was. Not to anyone. Antoinette had offered to fake pregnancy to again act as cover. Rosa took her up on the offer and again no one noticed that she was with child. This time, Royston had not his father around to coerce him into a second deal. He did not want to cover for Rosa a second time. He was annoyed at her, especially for keeping the father's identity secret. Antoinette's actions in portraying to the public that baby Robert was her fifth child angered Royston. He had wanted Antoinette and the children to join him in Castlebar, even before Robert's birth. And Antoinette had always made excuses, the main one being the fact that her parents needed her in the absence of her prisoner brother Eddie.

The new pregnancy was used by Royston's wife as another reason not to leave Ballycroy. He figured out that she did not really want to join him at all. And he blamed Rosa for influencing Antoinette. Now it had come to a major clash. Royston was adamant that the six month old should be reared by Rosa herself. He had covered enough for her in the previous ten years. He did not care if there was a scandal. The family honour did not mean as much to him as it did to his father. As far as he was concerned, the baby was her problem and not his. He had enough of his own problems to attend to.

Of course, the harsh truth was Rosa did not know for sure herself who the father was. It pained her greatly to have to keep the details to herself, but she could not reveal anything, even to her dear sister and sister-in-law. She was sixty per cent sure the child was the rapist's. There was a forty per cent chance that it was the child of her married lover Bosco Darby. She suspected that the truth would emerge in the features of young Robert as he grew older. That Christmas Day, she locked her room door and bawled her eyes out at how Royston had treated her. She wanted to leave but she had nowhere to go. She was full of hate for her brother now.

She gazed at baby Robert who was now sleeping. She adored him. She wished she could be with Darby at that moment. She wished Roger would walk in the door and whisk her and the two boys away forever.

Bosco Darby was with his wife and three children that Christmas Day. He was not aware that there may possibly be a fourth child of his just a few miles away. His hand was still shaking so badly that he could not dress himself or clean himself without the help of his doting wife. He put any thoughts of Rosa to the back of his mind and thanked the Lord that he had such a wonderful wife. How could he ever have been unfaithful to the wonderful woman? Of course, she did not know of his affair. Had she known it is doubtful she would have been so quick to shave him, scrub him, and dress him. The once proud athletic running champion was now a pitiful sight.

As Royston tried to shake off his hangover to face one of the bar's busiest days, St. Stephen's Day, he thought of the four young boys in the house. He thought about them every waking hour of every day. He thought about the fact that he was only certain that one of them was his. Royston. Louis and Robert were Rosa's. And the thing that pained him most: he was quite certain that the curly-haired Philip was not his, but Terence McDonnell's.

Terence and his brother took advantage of the fine bright day that was St. Stephen's Day to work on mortaring the walls of their Claggan forge. The plan was to work hard until about 3pm; then have a feed of pheasant; and then head to Carey's for the music and craic. Just as a couple of wren boys left the McDonnell home with a few coins, the sound of a motor car could be heard crackling the stones on the approach to the forge where the brothers were working. A white delivery-type vehicle appeared from the trees and rolled up beside the workers. Terence and Sylvester could not believe who had arrived.

"Fucking hell! Will you look who it is!" shouted Terence.
"Who? Who? Who is it Terence?" asked Sylvester.
"It's Joey!" replied Terence. "It's fucking Joey fucking Jarvis!"

The smiling Scot climbed out of the van which had the words 'Kerrigan's Kitchen' written on the side in green writing against the white background. He opened his arms as Terence embraced him and lifted him off the ground.
"Joey. It's so fucking good to see you" he said.
"And you too sonny" replied Joey almost suffocating from the squeeze he was getting.
"Jesus Joey, thanks for coming" said Sylvester as he took his turn to hug their old comrade. "You are some welcome sight to see".
"And I see you got your treasure trove" laughed Terence as he admired the van, before being surprised to see a red haired female emerge from the passenger side. "And, and, you got yourself a wife too?!"
"Not so, sonny!" laughed Joey, "Eleanor is my sister. You remember me talking of her".
"Welcome Eleanor" said Terence reaching out to embrace her too, although he refrained from the temptation to lift her off the ground.
"Pleased to meet you" she smiled as her brother made the introduction. Sylvester was immediately smitten with by her long curly red hair, smiling face and friendly eyes. She was short like Joey, but not as heavy.
"Eleanor, it is my pleasure" said Sylvester as he took her hand and gave it a gentle kiss. There were smiles and laughs all round.

The siblings from Glasgow enjoyed their feast of pheasant. Claire McDonnell had cooked lovely potatoes, carrots and onions to accompany the main dish. Fintan McDonnell made sure there was plenty of brandy and whiskey flowing. It was such a difference for Joey to enjoy such luxuries with the brothers in such comfortable surroundings. It was a world away from their days on the run. They all had great fun as incidents and situations were recalled. After stuffing themselves with food and drink, Joey piled them all into the back of his van and drove them to Carey's Bar where the drinking continued and before long they were all joining in the singing and dancing that took place. Joey's cured foot was no longer a problem!

Fortunately for her, on this occasion, Rosa Carey did not get to meet the man who had raped her. Because of the row the previous day, she refused to work alongside her brother and so she stayed upstairs with her baby. If only she had known that the person who had brought her so much grief was drinking his fill in the bar below, and was the owner of the white vehicle that everyone was admiring outside.

Joey and Eleanor stayed at McDonnell's for a couple of days, before heading back to Ballinrobe. Joey had explained that he had set up a business there, a little café, in which he served fish that he had caught and other food that his sister helped him source and prepare. His dream was coming true. He was loving his new life. And the venture was going well.

He explained that he had adopted the name Joey Kerrigan. This surprised Fintan a bit, until Joey explained that it was partly out of respect to the Kerrigan family, and partly because he had to hide his real identity as he was still wanted by the British for treason. He had come to accept that he could never return to Britain. Ireland was now his home. And Eleanor was here now as well - for good. Ballinrobe and the surrounding rivers rich with salmon were treating them well.

Sylvester fell in love with the Scottish woman and this became obvious to all. Terence kept a respectful distance and made sure he did not sabotage it! Although he found her quite attractive, he could see that his brother was mad about her. She would be a good distraction for Sylvester, and help to give him something else to think about besides ale. In any case, Eleanor was more attracted to Sylvester. There was something about his vulnerability that drew her closer to him, whereas she considered Terence as being slightly cocky, and she did not like his habit of cursing. She also liked Sylvester's long hair, which he had grown to hide his ear – disfigured by the Alsatian.

As the white van drove away from Claggan, Sylvester resolved to follow up his promise to visit her in Ballinrobe within a month. But there was another visitor *en route* who would disrupt this plan. This time the visitor came by bicycle. From over sixty miles away. He arrived in Claggan on December 29th in his black vestment and dog collar. The visitor was Fr. Rea from Enniscrone.

After receiving a welcoming cup of tea and some warm scones from Claire McDonnell, the bushy-haired priest sat on a wall outside of the repaired McDonnell home, beside where he had parked his bicycle.

"You must have some news for us" said Terence. "You didn't cycle half of Connaught for our mother's scones!"
"They were worth the journey!" joked the priest, before addressing the real matter.
"Indeed, I do have news. News you may be interested in. It concerns a certain Graham Gilberthorpe".

The brothers looked at each other and tried to digest the despised sound of his name. They felt the good feeling of the past few days disappear with the arrival of that name.
"Gilberthorpe. Yes, go on" said Terence in anticipation.
"Gilberthorpe. Colm Tierney tells me that his location may interest you boys" said Fr. Rea. "So that's why I'm here. He is in my parish. He is in Enniscrone".
Again the brothers looked at each other. They had assumed he was back in England.
"Enniscrone?!" said Terence in disbelief. "What the fuck is he doing in Enniscrone?"
"Easy with the tongue!" urged Sylvester, mad that his brother could not refrain from swearing in front of a man of the cloth.
"He's with a woman there. And her son" said Fr. Rea. "She's the widow of an RIC man. Hynes. He was shot in Donegal. She's back in Enniscrone with the boy. And Gilberthorpe has moved into her house. He goes under the name of 'Gilbey'".
"Gilbey? The fucking bollox" said Terence as his brother again tried to stop him from swearing. But the priest spoke up for himself this time.
"Please, Terence, must you swear so much?" he said. "It is my wish that you stop".
"Sorry Father, sorry" uttered Terence. "But that beast is the antichrist. You should see what he did to poor Willie. And to Bridie

and Josey. And to the Whites. And to poor Cecil Dyra. You would not put down an old dog the way he shot poor Cecil".
"And according to Joey Jarvis yesterday" said Sylvester, "Word is that Gilberthorpe had Willie's body filleted and fed to the Black and Tan Alsatian that attacked him and me. How can anyone be that evil, Father?"
"Tierney mentioned that he was bad alright" said Fr. Rea. "So now you have it. You know where to contact me. I shall help in any way I can. So will the Tierneys I'm sure. St. Patrick got rid of the snakes, and it looks like you may have to do something similar!"

The brothers tried to convince their messenger to stay for the night but he insisted on cycling to Fr. Tim's. He would stay there until the morning, and recommence his long journey back to the pretty coastal town in Sligo. The brothers sat on the wall as the priest pedalled from view.
"Enniscrone here we come!" said Terence. "Thank God he is within reach".
"Death is too good for that bastard!" replied Sylvester.
"Now now dear brother, no cursing!" laughed a sarcastic Terence.

The Black and Tan war was over but scores still needed to be settled. This was an opportunity the vengeful brothers could not resist. They oiled their bicycle chains for the long cycle.

They were determined to ensure that Gilberthorpe did not leave Ireland alive.

CHAPTER 42: EN ROUTE TO A SHOOT

It was the first week of February 1922 before the brothers set out on their bicycles for Ballina, which was their first designated resting place on the way to Enniscrone. After a fine feed of porridge that cold morning, Sylvester and Terence said goodbye to their parents. Their first stop was at the graveyard in Ballycroy where they visited the grave of Bridie Kerrigan, her son Josey and her husband. Of course there was no grave for Willie, and Terence took the opportunity to reveal to his brother for the first time that Bridie's grave held Willie's severed fingers. This brought tears to the eyes of Sylvester and when he had finished his prayers he pledged revenge.

They then walked the short few yards to the graves of their grandparents. They knew that old Fintan and Nappie would be so proud of them both, and would be willing them on from above to accomplish their mission of avenging the horrible murder of their other grandson Willie. Just before they exited the cemetery, the lads touched the monuments to Michaeleen Cooney and John Peter and prayed for their guidance.

On their journey, the brothers spoke of Sylvester's new love. He revealed that he planned to make it to Ballinrobe for St. Valentine's night. He received a gentle ribbing from Terence. In a moment of seriousness, Terence wished his brother well and said that he hoped Sylvester's romance with Eleanor would end up better than his did with Alice.

Although there was a biting breeze from the north, the sky was clear and the IRA men admired the rugged scenery as they cycled through Bangor Erris, Bellacorick and Crossmolina. They had to rest a few times for Sylvester to massage his aching war wound from France. Darkness was descending on the banks of the Moy as the weary brothers reached their destination, St. Helens, the grey two-storey home for retired priests in Ballina. It was there that had been chosen as a meeting place by Colm Tierney.

One of the housekeepers there ensured the Ballycroy men were given tea, soup and sandwiches as they recovered from their long cycle. They were shown to their bedrooms and they changed into fresh clothes for the meeting later that evening. They sat together in the main communal room where a couple of old priests were resting. Sylvester made conversation with them as Terence thumbed through 'The Mayoman' newspaper.

After a half an hour, the figure of Fr. Rea appeared at the door of the large room. "God bless ye Ballycroy Boys" he laughed.
"Well how are you Father?" said Terence rising, with Sylvester copying him.
"Ye must be famished!" said the priest as the brothers insisted that they were being treated like kings.
"Well, I have a little surprise for ye" said Fr. Rea, still standing by the door in his black attire and dog collar, before stepping aside to reveal who he was talking about.
"Batty! My God it's Batty!" shouted Sylvester in shock as Terence struggled to find words. "Fuck, fuck Batty it's you!" was all he could manage.
"I shall forgive the cursing this one last time" smiled Fr. Rea as he watched the three men joyously wrap their arms around each other in front of the bemused priests and the housekeeper.
"Reunited friends" explained the Enniscrone monsignor to the others. "Just like in the bible, the lost sheep has returned to rejoin the flock!"

The reunion cheered up everybody as the joy became infectious, and everyone was seen sporting a smile, even the Tierney brothers Colm and Ignatius as they arrived for the meeting. The three 'Boys of Ballycroy' had so much to catch up, but that could wait until later; and as Fr. Rea ushered them to the meeting room he assured them that he had a few bottles of altar wine hidden for afterwards!

There were seven in total gathered in the room which had a long rectangular oak table in the middle. Two towering candles were all that lit the room. Colm Tierney sat at the top of the table. On his left sat his brother Ignatius, Fr. Rea and the local runner identified only as Felix. On the right sat Terence, Sylvester and Batty. Each of them had a tumbler of water in front of them, and Colm started the meeting by introducing everybody officially.

"We are here for one reason tonight, as we all know" he stated.
"Let me run down through these few points:
Number one – we know that Gilberthorpe using the alias 'Gilbey' is living in my brother's territory of Enniscrone. He lives with the widow Hynes and her son.
Number two – he swims daily at Enniscrone beach, anytime between 6am and 8am.
Number three – we have carbine rifles for you which Felix has left at the sand dunes where your observation point will be.
Number four – we ask for a clean execution and no daft stuff. A bullet to the head will suffice.
Number five – we want you not to come to the attention of the Enniscrone locals or constabulary there.
Number six – we want no innocent victims caught in the crossfire.
Number seven – we want you back here for debriefing within four hours of the execution being carried out.
Number eight – here is a photo of your target, just in case!
Number nine – we wish you well in your operation. Críost libh".

"May I add that it is imperative that my parishioners are sacrosanct in this and only the legitimate target is harmed" stressed Fr. Rea.
"Understood, Father" said Terence. "We are grateful for your support and we will do all in our power to respect your conditions".
"You need to do more than that!" said Ignatius Tierney speaking for the first time. "Enniscrone is MY patch and I want NO botching. Just a quick, clean job. We know he mutilated others but I want none of that. A quick clean job".
"Understood" said Terence as Sylvester nodded in agreement.
"Young Felix is the key man here" said Colm. "He knows the place inside out. He will keep an eye on everything".
"Batty, are you taking part?" asked Ignatius from across the table.
"It is my intention, if that is in order Comrade" he replied.
"Very well" said Ignatius. "We will organise a third carbine so".
"I HAVE my own gun. No need thank you" came the firm but polite reply.
"Good luck. We will see you back here when Felix convenes us" said Colm.

"Meeting over so?" asked Terence.
"Well, the main part is", replied Colm. "I just have a few questions to ask, general questions".
"Go on" said Terence warily. "I know what your questions can entail!"
"Can I ask whose side ye are on, Dev's or Collins'?" asked Colm with a wicked smile.
"That's an awful question!" laughed Terence.
"Surely you must know by now?" said Colm.
"Gentlemen, don't start. Sure we are all Irishmen" interjected the priest.
"Well, my brother here is turning Saxon on me by going all pro-treaty on me" said Colm. "I'm hoping ye Ballycroy men have more sense!"

"In fact, Sylvester here is leaning that way but to be honest we have not decided" said Terence nervously afraid to jeopardise the Ballina co-operation.
"But what do YOU think, my old cell mate?" asked Colm leaning on the table gazing at Terence.
"To be honest, I think Collins is right in saying the treaty gives us 'the freedom to achieve freedom', but I need to read it fully before making a decision" said Terence hoping that would round off the uneasy conversation.
"Shite!" said Colm in a raised voice as everyone edged towards the door. "Collins is selling us out. Sure Ballycroy is FULL of Ulstermen. He is leaving Ulster to the Brits. How can ye possibly support him?"
"Because he is not a coward like DeValera" interjected Batty firmly.
"What do you mean?" snarled an increasingly agitated Colm.
"DeValera sent Collins to London to do his dirty work. Why did he not go himself? Because he is a coward!" asserted Batty, staring directly at Colm.
"Ah gentlemen, come on, I have wine waiting!" said the Fr. Rea trying to diffuse the tension.
"Feck the wine!" said Colm. "I'm fecking disgusted. Three of the famed 'Boys of Ballycroy' here and it looks like they ALL want to swear allegiance to the fecking crown!"

"It's not like that!" shouted Batty. "Did you not fight for the crown in Flanders, Colm?"
"That was different! I fought for small nations, not the crown!" roared Colm.
"Did you or did you not fight on the side of the British army?" asked Batty defiantly.
"Ah shut up!" said Colm, his voice starting to tone down.
"Be careful of what you say to me!" said Batty, looking for eye contact from the North Mayo OC. "I do not take kindly to lies or insults".
"I am surprised with you" replied Colm. "You are with the Germans against the English but you want to bow to the throne?!"
"I want to bow to no-one and nor shall I bow to anyone!" shouted Batty in his German accent. "All I am saying is that the most pragmatic solution is to take what is on offer and work from there at a later stage!"
"Prag-what?" replied Colm. "Ah feck ye. Feck ye and yer big fecking words. Keep yer words, ye will need them all when genuflecting to the King!"
"You speak no sense" stated Batty, "There is no point in trying to be rational with you".
"RATIONAL! That's a big fecking word for a Ballycroy man!" said Colm sarcastically.
"Come on lads, come on lads" repeated Fr. Rea. "We are ALL Irishmen. Let's not fall into the trap of splitting again, so soon after a great victory over the Tans!"
"Have I read things wrong?" asked Colm. "I thought ye were here to KILL a Tan and not KISS a Tan!"
"Enough now!" said Terence smiling and reaching out to place his hand on Colm's crouched shoulder. "You got the little row you wanted, that's enough for now!"

The priest and the runner managed to calm the situation down but Colm did not wait for the wine and stormed out of the building. It was typical of the growing tensions over the treaty debate. There was another general election on the horizon and pressure was growing to declare for either the Pro-Treaty side or the Anti-Treaty side. It was unfortunate that the evening had been scarred by the short but heated outburst.

The wine ran out at midnight and Batty and the McDonnells found their way to their bedrooms. They had just enjoyed a great night of recounting stories. It had been an emotional evening. But they had only a short rest as Felix had them up and ready for Enniscrone by 5am.

Another long day lay ahead.

CHAPTER 43: ANOTHER IRISH SPLIT

It was a wet, drizzly morning and the humour was not great by the time the four hid their bikes in the high grass of the sand dunes that overlooked the wondrous strand at Enniscrone. The combination of saddle soreness, wet clothes, lack of sleep and wine hangovers had proven to be not a merry mixture! Felix provided the two McDonnells with their rifles. He left them to lie on the sand dunes and pointed out to the path down which Gilberthorpe usually ran. He headed away and said he would return soon after.

The mood deteriorated as three hours passed and there was no sign of Gilberthorpe by 10am. The whispering wet men had gone over their plan, that Terence would disable him with a rifle shot and then the three would approach him and finish him off with a handgun.

"I've waited for this fucking day so long" said Terence.
"Same here" replied Batty. "He destroyed my family. I will never forgive that".
"Tell him what he did to Willie" said Sylvester, shivering, "And tell him that Dad never fired a shot that night they burned our place, that it was the fecker himself who must have finished Ifor Morris!"

Batty listened in horror to what had been inflicted on poor Willie Kerrigan, before he was disrupted by a hush from Terence. He had spotted their man. The three excitedly settled into their pre-planned positions. But their plan fell into disarray that Sunday morning as they spotted that Gilberthorpe had company. There was a boy with him, skipping along the sand beside the semi-naked Englishman, heading for a morning dip.

"Fucking hell" said Terence, "It's the fucking ten year old. The devil blast him. I thought he always swam alone!"
"God blast it!" said Sylvester.
"All this for nothing, what a waste" said the German Major.
"What do you mean?!" snarled Terence.
"I mean, it's a waste of a trip. We have to leave it", replied Batty.

"No fucking way!" said Terence, "I'm fucking taking aim!"
"You must NOT!" said Batty, his voice raising.
"Shut up! For God's sake be quiet!" urged Sylvester.
"You heard what the men said last night" said Batty, in a lower tone, "No innocents and no locals!"
"Fuck off!" said Terence. "It's only his step son or whatever. I won't fucking hit the boy!"
"You will hit NO-ONE!" said Batty, rising from his position.
"Get down to feck!" cursed Sylvester. "Do you want us to be fecking spotted?!"
"Cease!" urged Batty, as Terence took aim. "Cease now! And that is an ORDER!"

Terence was infuriated. He turned angrily back to face his long lost friend from their boyhood.
"Listen here Batty", he said in a hushed but angry voice. "You may be a fucking major in Germany but you are NOTHING here. You cannot fucking order ME to do ANYTHING!"
"Quiet, lads!" said Sylvester. "Just be quiet!"
"NO shooting!" said Batty. "Not with the boy. We return tomorrow!"
"We'll fucking do no such fucking thing!" replied Terence. "I'm not leaving this beach 'til that fucker is lying lifeless on it!"

The latest Irish split had just occurred and as Gilberthorpe and the boy splashed in the icy water in the distance, Sylvester had to physically intervene to stop his brother aiming an angry punch at Batty. The furious Batty grabbed his bicycle, but had the last word as Terence continued his volley of vicious vitriol:
"We cannot do this to the boy. I will have no part in this. Do what you like but I will have no part in this." And he headed away on the bumpy path on his bicycle.

Sylvester managed to calm his brother down. "We'll get him tomorrow" he said. "It's not worth the risk. The Tierneys will kill us".
"And how do we know the boy won't be with him again? Do we wait here and catch our fucking death of cold until he turns up alone?" asked Terence.

"If we have to", said Sylvester. "And it will be worth it. Please. Anyway, tomorrow is a Monday so the boy should be getting ready for school".

By noon Gilberthorpe was at home with his woman and her son and Felix had returned for an update. He was surprised to hear that Gilberthorpe was not alone, but he said that Batty had made the right decision. This did not go down well with Terence but he bit his lip. Felix undertook to bring fresh food and dry clothes to the McDonnells and said the afternoon weather was promised better. He said he would try and track down Batty.

As the McDonnells spent a wasted day lying on the wet sand dunes and trying to shelter from the dull drizzle, Batty spent a few hours in the comfort of his old bedroom at the Enniscrone Parochial House. He was still annoyed with Terence. Later that evening he went for a cycle into Ballina, where he wanted to meet an old acquaintance from his days working in Enniscrone.

Just after 6pm he was pushing his bike towards Vickery's Hotel when he noticed a tall, thin man with high cheekbones in a long black overcoat walking across the road and entering the hotel, puffing on a cigarette. He could swear it was Gilberthorpe! His heart pounding, Batty instinctively decided to enter the hotel where he saw the man taking a seat at the counter in the bar, having just ordered a drink, and still puffing from his cigarette. He was not yet 100% sure it was Gilberthorpe, but Batty quietly ordered a whiskey from the red-faced rotund barman whilst the tall man browsed through the newspapers, having not spotted him. Batty tried to catch a glance of the man's left hand to see if there were fingers missing, but he did not want to be caught staring.

Batty took a seat and sat by the window, which looked out onto the street. After several minutes, the tall man started a conversation with the barman about an upcoming poker tournament to be held in the hotel.
"Count me in Paddy" said the English accent.

"I'll put your name down so, Gilbey" was the reply, confirming that it was indeed the man who had burnt Batty's family home, hung his young neighbour, and butchered his good friend Willie.

Batty calmly contemplated his next move. Would he simply stand and aim a shot from his pistol? Would he wait until he went to leave and get him on the street? Was Gilberthorpe armed? Had Gilberthorpe spotted the stranger in the bar? He grew excited as he thought of what it would be like to break the news to the McDonnells that he had got their man.

As he pondered to himself, the tall Gilberthorpe got up from his stool and arrogantly strode by him. He had left his coat on the stool by the counter and was heading for the outhouse at the rear to relieve himself. Batty instinctively decided to follow him out and get him there. There would be less chance of witnesses out there than if he were to shoot him in the bar or on the street. He counted to sixty seconds and rose, heading for the rear yard in which the outside toilet was. He could hear the Englishman whistling inside the door of the toilet cell. Beneath the nearby hanging lantern, he could see the top of his head. He took deep breaths to gain control of his breathing as he heard Gilberthorpe get ready to come out. He tried to keep his hand from shaking as he aimed the pistol towards the top of the door from beyond which the Tan would emerge. The door finally opened.
"This is for the Bourkes of Ballycroy" said Batty just before he pulled at the trigger as the wide-eyed Englishman gazed at the weapon in shock.

But - to Batty's utter horror - the pistol jammed. He looked at it. Then at Gilberthorpe who still looked frozen with fear. Batty shook the pistol, then aimed it again and tried the trigger a second time but still nothing happened. Gilberthorpe was having a lucky day!

There was no way the Black and Tan was going to give the German army man a third chance to shoot him, and his steel capped right boot was quickly smashing into the teeth of Batty. The Ballycroy man fell back onto the yard wall in shock and before he hit the ground the left boot of the Englishman had driven a second kick into the side of his head. Gilberthorpe then picked Batty's weapon from the yard floor and whacked him several times on the head with it, cursing aloud in rage: "You-fuck-ing-bast-ard-peas-ant!" he roared, pistol-whipping the fallen Ballycroy man with each syllable.

Batty was so injured that he could not even bring his hands up to try and protect his skull, and the vicious Gilberthorpe took full advantage. One, two, three times he drove his boot into Batty's head, sending blood squirting onto the wall of the yard. The only thing that stopped Gilberthorpe was the sight of the landlord's blunderbuss gun pointing at him, and the sound of the screaming daughter upstairs who happened to witness the entire incident. "Get the hell out of here or I will shoot you, Gilbey! Now!" shouted the shaking landlord. Gilberthorpe cleared his throat and spat down at the motionless would-be-assassin on the ground, before heading away, with Batty's German gun in his hand. He marched out into the street. He was breathless. He was raging. But he had always known that it was likely his past would catch up on him. Back in the hotel he had just left, the traumatised Vickery daughter continued screaming as a pool of blood formed under Batty's head on the cold yard floor.

Within an hour word had reached the Tierneys and they visited the comatose Batty in the nearby hospital. His head had swelled to nearly twice its normal size. He was unrecognisable. His eyes were surrounded by purple circles and his lips were black. His right jaw looked as if it had simply caved in. There were dents visible on his skull from where the pistol had made an impact.

The sight of the pitiful Batty brought a howl of sorrow from Fr. Rea. Mr. Vickery explained to the men what had happened. His daughter had seen it all. After consulting with Felix they decided not to tell the men who were lying in wait at the beach. They prayed that Batty would survive. The hospital doctor told them that it was unlikely he would make the night, his skull had several fractures.

As Fr. Rea sent for the Bourkes to visit their gravely injured son and brother, the McDonnell brothers slept on the slopes of the slippery dunes.

A mile away, Gilberthorpe was still shaking in his bed. He knew he had escaped death once that day, but had not realised that he had escaped it twice.

CHAPTER 44: FROM THE MOUNTAIN TO THE SEA

At 7.30 the following morning the McDonnells greedily swallowed some corned beef. It was raining lightly, and they were both freezing, but knew they had survived worse weather. They peered anxiously at where the sandy path led to the strand over to their right. That was the path their target always took on his way to his daily dip. They prayed that the boy would not be with him this time.

At 7.45 Gilberthorpe appeared at the Enniscrone sand dunes. Alone. The brothers breathed a sigh of relief, and took up their positions. The tall wiry former Black and Tan was blissfully unaware that his hour had come. All that was on his mind was the indescribable sensation of diving into the fresh waves of the cold Atlantic. Ever since he was a boy in the pretty coastal town of Deal, a swim was his daily ritual. He ran towards the crashing water, but he was never to reach it.

Terence's first carbine rifle shot echoed through the icy Sligo air and made a connection with its target directly on the left elbow, shattering the joint and causing Gilberthorpe to spin around with the impact. As he span, Terence's second shot entered his lower back on the right and exited through his stomach, sending blood and guts spewing onto the wet sand. Gilberthorpe fell to his knees in a combination of shock, agony and sadness. He knew he had been got. He was now having to painfully pay back for his sins. The cruelty he had inflicted was being avenged. On a Monday morning. On an empty unspoiled heavenly strand.

He took his eyes away from looking at his crimson entrails on the sand, and tried to look around to see who was killing him. He saw the two brothers, their long overcoats flowing behind them like black capes, racing from the dunes in his direction, their right hands gripping their carbine rifles. He recognised them both. His time was up.
"You fucking cowards!" he panted, "Shooting a man in the fucking back, you fucking Irish peasant cowards!"

Terence was now only yards from Gilberthorpe and slowed down to quickly assess the damage from his first two shots. He could almost pity the kneeling Englishman when he saw his left forearm dangle from its elbow limply, just the skin surrounding the destroyed joint keeping his lower arm and upper arm together. Then he focused on the bloody crater in the white vest. And the mess on the sand. Most of his work was done. He looked at his brother. They both gulped. It was not in their nature to take a life, but they had to. Despite all of their hate for Gilberthorpe and what he had done, the act of murder was not something they relished. It was just not in their make up. The look of sadness and desperation on the Tan's face hit deeply within their inner selves. But they had no option. There was no going back now. They were doing this for family, friend and fatherland.

"Are you happy with me doing it?" asked Terence. Sylvester just nodded. All of the built-up anger that he had been expecting to vent at the Cretan, it had just frozen.
"Go on! Finish me off you coward!" said the Englishman, still kneeling, looking up trying to make eye contact with his assassin.
"I'll decide when to finish you, you cripple, not you! Your orders mean nothing now" said Terence calmly, clasping his pistol in his right hand after tossing the carbine onto the sand.
"Fenian bastards! You will burn in hell!" said the weakening English accent. Terence stood over Gilberthorpe and pointed the pistol at him. He was starting to cough up blood and gurgle.
"Say goodbye to this world 'Gilbey'!" said Terence putting some pressure on the trigger.
"This is for the Kerrigans!" uttered Sylvester. They were the last words Gilberthorpe would ever hear. There was a loud crack from Terence's pistol as a bullet entered the corporal's skull. Within seconds, he had keeled over onto his right side onto the sand, his smashed left arm flopping across his stomach.

The sound of the shot still reverberated around the sand dunes as the dying Tan exhaled his last few breaths on the blood soaked sand. What had happened on the mountain by Crafton Lake had just been avenged by the sea.

"Come on, let's go!" said Terence as Sylvester stood and stared. The older brother could not believe that all of his bravado had evaporated. He had planned to stuff the man's mouth with sand, even sever a finger, to make him suffer as Willie had. But he had simply been incapable of it. As he trudged back to the dunes he wondered why. Had it been the long wait? Had it been the cold numbing him? Why couldn't he be as ruthless as Terence? He just could not understand it. He had cycled for miles and had waited for hours to gain this revenge, but he had copped out. He had just felt empty. Maybe he just wasn't bad enough a person? But he had killed others in the past. Maybe it was the premeditated manner that got to him? Why couldn't he rouse enough angst? After all, this man had him on his way to be hanged. Had set an Alsatian on him. Had tortured him and his father. Had burnt everything they owned. Had mutilated and mercilessly murdered his cousins. Had boasted about raping his aunt. Had shot Cecil to death. Had hanged PJ's brother. Why did it not feel right to kill him?

Terence was quiet too as they cycled to the hayshed where Felix said he would be waiting. He was glad to have completed the grim task, but he was not ecstatic in any way. He just felt serene. He was thankful that he had been up to the task. Be it human or beast, ending another life was never easy on the mind. But he felt more at ease now with the spirits of Willie, Bridie, Cecil, Seaneen and Esmeralda.

However, when they learned from Felix what had happened to their friend at Vickery's Hotel, they both felt like returning to the beach to chop Gilberthorpe into pieces. And when they got to see the state of the unconscious battered Batty they were livid. They did not get to spend much time with Batty, as Colm Tierney had summoned a meeting at St. Helens. They grasped the hands of the numbed Bourkes who were maintaining a bedside vigil, before leaving the hospital and promising to return.

At the meeting Colm Tierney commended the brothers and Felix on a job well done. Gilberthorpe's body had been spotted about an hour after his death. It was now in the Sligo morgue. The constabulary now had officers working on the case, and Colm advised the men to stay with the old priests for a few days and keep a low profile.

Fr. Rea was still upset over what had happened to Batty, but refused to blame anyone.
"He should not have confronted the demon by himself" he said.
"I know" said Terence. "Poor soul. He put the boy first. If the boy had not been there yesterday none of this would have happened and Batty'd be here with us now".
"At least Gilberthorpe has gone ahead of him" said Sylvester.
"But he did the damage before he went" replied Terence, still raging. "Pity ye did not tell us this last night, we would not have given the fucker such an easy death!"
"Please lads", said Fr. Rea. "There's not much than can be done now. Please God the doctors will be able to save him. His poor parents. And his poor wife and child in Germany".

Sylvester sneaked into the hospital the following night. He was delighted to see that Batty had regained consciousness. But he could not stir or speak. All he could do was move his eyes and moan a little. Patrick, Nora and Andrew reached over at him at various stages, and stroked his purple bruises. Sylvester did not take much notice of the tall, mournful looking man standing in the corner. He just thought he was a driver for the Bourkes or an attendant of some sort. Sylvester decided to lean forward and whisper into Batty's ear.
"We got the bastard for you. He died on the sand. The crabs had a feast!"

As Sylvester was leaving to return to St. Helens, he felt his shoulder being grabbed in the hallway. He turned back in alarm to see that it was the tall, deathly looking man from the room.
"Are you a McDonnell?" he asked in an accent Sylvester thought may be German.
"Who wants to know?!" he snapped.
"I am known as Ecclesiasticus. A comrade of Major Vandenburg" he replied.
"Oh yes, I heard of you" said a relieved Sylvester, but he was quickly on the defensive as the Hungarian tried to commence an interrogation.

326

"Why did you not protect him?" he asked crossly.
"Protect him? How could we protect him – he ran away on us!" explained Sylvester.
"He does not run away. What happened?!" asked Ecclesiasticus aggressively.
"There was a row. There was a boy with Gilberthorpe and Batty did not want us to endanger him. My brother wanted to go ahead....and, hey, why am I telling you this? You could be an informer?! Leave me alone!" said Sylvester, pulling away.
"Come back!" demanded the spy.
"Feck off! I don't answer to you!" said Sylvester, running away into the night.
Terence took his turn to visit the next day and explained the whole situation to Ecclesiasticus. He did not mind telling him, he trusted him, and in any case the main thing was that Batty was beginning to improve and was murmuring a few words through his smashed teeth. He was sipping some water too.

For the next few days, Batty slowly continued his recovery much to the relief of his family and friends, and to amazement of the medical staff. The McDonnell brothers spent a restful few days playing cards with the elderly priests and entertaining them with stories from places as diverse as Broadway, Boulogne and Ballycroy! Terence even managed to seduce one of the housekeepers, a 50 year old local woman, and spent a day in bed with her as a colleague of the woman acted as lookout. Even in what was a virtual monastery, Terence was having his fill of love-making! As the retired priests read in the oak panelled communal room, they wondered what the creaking noises from upstairs were!

Terence's brother was just anxious that he would make his Valentine's Day date with Eleanor Jarvis, and sent anxious requests to Colm Tierney as the day drew nearer as to when it would be safe for the brothers to head for home. The Ballina man not only gave the go-ahead on February 14th, but arranged for Sylvester to get a lift to Ballinrobe, on a truck bringing seaweed to a factory in Headford, Co. Galway. Sylvester was delighted, and before he tossed his bicycle onto the truck, he paid one last visit to Batty. The following day, Terence did likewise before setting out for the return journey to Ballycroy, having completed the mortal mission.

"It was so good to meet you again" whispered Batty, sitting up on his hospital bed, an array of ghastly colours and wounds dotting his shaved skull.
"It certainly was. And we will meet again soon" smiled Terence.
"I am not so sure" said Batty. "If I make Germany I will be happy. I just want to see my two girls one last time".
"Will you stop with that fucking shite!" urged Terence. "You will be fine. You are doing great. You're as strong as a fucking horse. Your strength will stand to you".
"Much damage is done. I know it" said Batty, sounding authentically German.
"You're improving everyday" asserted Terence. "You will forget about this in no time. All that will ever remind you are the broken teeth!"
"You're as funny as ever" smiled a weary looking Batty. "You have always been a good friend. I am sorry we argued Terence".
"It was nothing!" laughed McDonnell. "All forgotten about. But IF you had listened to me you would not be in this fucking hospital!"
"Ha ha!" laughed Batty. "As Roger would say *ab irato*'. Don't listen to an angry man. You were an angry man that morning!"
"Wouldn't you be too after having a red raw arse from cycling all the way from Claggan?!" cackled Terence. "And having had NO sex for a week!"
"A WEEK?! Stop Terence! You are hurting my jaws!" laughed Batty trying to control himself, as tears of laughter rolled from his eyes.
"Well, I made up for it in the retirement home! LOADS of riding there!" smiled Terence.
"Stop! Please stop!" shouted Batty trying to suppress the waves of laughter that were beginning to cause him pain. "You were with priests, yea?! Not nuns! Yet you find a dame there! In need of sex. Unbelievable! Only YOU can do that!"

After the laughter calmed down the good friends clasped hands as Terence prepared to leave. There were still tears in Batty's eyes, and now they were about to be joined by more.

"Goodbye my good friend" he whispered. "Thank you for all you have done. You have been a true friend. You are a good man".
"Will you stop! We will laugh at this in Carey's some night!" replied Terence.
"Go now!" cried Batty, "And look after yourself Terence. Please!"
"Batty, you will be fine. You've defied the docs. You WILL be back!" said Terence.
"TOO much damage. I can feel it inside my head. Just say goodbye!" replied Batty.
"Bye Batty" said Terence, reaching down to kiss his yellow forehead. "We had some good times, hadn't we?" and he felt tears well behind his own eyes.
"We did for sure!" sniffled Batty. "The Sandybanks will always be heaven to me".
"You have me crying, you fecker!" said Terence, wiping his eyes. "For God's sake we WILL be together again".
"Not on this earth, I fear" replied Batty. "Please go. You have a long cycle ahead. Please mind yourself".
"Goodbye so Batty. May God bless you. Give my regards to your wife and little girl. Long live the 'Boys of Ballycroy'!" said Terence, before heading for the hallway.
"Yes. Long live the 'Boys of Ballycroy'!" sobbed Batty, before breaking down alone as his friend disappeared from view.

Within a week, Batty was on a merchant ship that had docked in Sligo, preparing for the long sail to Bremerhaven. Sylvester was back in Ballycroy with news of his engagement. Terence was re-opening the forge in Ballycroy Village. And Gilberthorpe was lying under six feet of heavy soil in a wet English graveyard that looked over the channel dividing England and France. Ireland was forever rid of the hated Black and Tan.

CHAPTER 45: LIFE DURING THE CIVIL WAR

April 1922 marked the 10th anniversary of the sinking of the Titanic and a special mass in honour of Michaeleen Cooney was held in the cemetery, where crowds gathered around the anchor memorial. The event re-opened wounds for his family, but they were delighted that so many turned out to remember the tragic boy.

A marble plaque from Roger was unveiled, which had the following engraved:

"The Boy Michaeleen – He Loved the Sea,
He Sailed it so that he Might See,
Betterment for his Irish Family,
Whose Hearts were Broken Literally,
By News of Their Boy's Deity,
Who Put Others before Whitey,
And Ensured Unlikely Safety,
For Some from Titanic Tragedy,
And Now He Lies Far From this Cemetery,
At the Bottom of the Icy Sea,
But Don't Despair as we Pray for Thee,
'Cos the Boy Michaeleen – He Loved the Sea".

Some thought it lovely. Others not so. Another example of Celtic dividedness! But all agreed that the marble looked magnificent.

The Carey family laid on tea and sandwiches for everyone in their hall later and there was a special showing of a Pathé film reel about the Titanic Tragedy, which exhilarated most who attended.

The Careys had overcome their internal problems by Royston agreeing that Antoinette and the children remain in Ballycroy for another year, and that the pretence continue that Robert was their baby. Rosa was making secret preparations though, and was trying to set some money aside so that she and her boys could move away. She knew that their continued presence in the longer term would only lead to more family strife. In any case, Rebecca was now pregnant so the homestead was becoming a bit too crowded.

Meanwhile, a new home in Doona was getting its final touches as Sylvester McDonnell was preparing for married life. As well as falling in love with her Irishman, Eleanor Jarvis had fallen for the beauty of a little church near Cong and so the marriage was arranged for there. It gave the McDonnell family an opportunity to view Joey's new business venture for themselves, as the reception was held in his little restaurant. The marriage took place on Easter Monday, and Terence stood proudly in his new national army uniform as Best Man to his beloved older brother. The ever-smiling Joey gave away his radiant sister to one of the men he had become great friends with on the hills and bogs of Ballycroy.

The happy couple moved into the old Kerrigan home in Doona. Sylvester was determined not to become involved in the looming Civil War. His plan was to create a new little family of his own with his Scottish beauty.
"I've done TWO wars now. I'm 35 years of age. Let the younger generation step forward for the next one – I've served my time as a soldier. My life is now Eleanor's" he had said in his wedding speech.

But there was no such option for Terence. He had agonised desperately on what side to take. His instinct was to go against the Treaty. He had no desire to see his country remain linked to the empire. He was against the idea of Irish elected representatives swearing allegiance to the crown when taking up a seat in the new Dáil. He did not want to see his country divided into two distinct parts. He did not want the British to retain naval bases. And above all, he did not want a civil war – with Irish man fighting his fellow Irish man.

But the war just passed had made him a realist. Despite it deepening his hatred of the English, he realised that they would not give up Ireland overnight. They were going to make it extremely difficult for Irish self rule. He believed that Collins had been 'set-up' by DeValera and placed into a hopeless situation. A no-win situation. As Collins had said just after penning his name to the treaty, he had signed his own death warrant. However, he believed that the treaty was a major stepping stone towards complete independence. It might take 10 years, 50 years or even 100 years to break off the shackles completely, but this was a good start. A good opportunity. His father Fintan was against the Treaty but said he would respect the decisions made by his sons. He just wanted a clean break from the British. But he knew it was not that simple.

Terence's main influence in making his decision to join the Pro-Treaty side was Harry Heraty. 'The Boss' convinced him that any war would be over within three months, such was the majority of senior IRA and Sinn Fein people in favour. He said that the new Free State Army would have significant resource advantages in terms of personnel, equipment, arms and transport. He said that DeValera would be exposed very quickly, and would have no option but to cede to public opinion who would want an end to any bloodshed. Seeing Harry so definite that this was the right thing to do impressed Terence. On top of this, Harry promised Terence a key role in the team he would be putting together. "I'm taking you out of the mountains" he had said.

It was just as well Roger was not present to see another tragic split painstakingly rip through Irish society. Like almost every parish in the country, communities, families – even couples – were torn apart. The Anti-Treaty supporters began to call the other side 'Traitors' and 'Tan Lovers'. The Pro-Treaty supporters revelled in calling Anti-Treaty forces 'Irregulars'.

In Ballycroy it quickly became apparent that the divide was probably about fifty-fifty. Understandably a majority wanted to stay as neutral as possible. Prominent Pro-Treaties were the Careys, the Hughtons, the McArthurs, the Bourkes and the O'Gradys. Vociferous in their Anti-Treaty views were the Whites, the Coxes, the O'Briens and the Dyras. Remember – the Whites and the McArthurs had lived under the one roof together for over a year. The large Cooney clans seemed to be split. The GAA club seemed to be split too.

In other areas, Newport's Frankie Phelan joined the Irregulars. He saw the Treaty as a shameful sell-out. He was prepared to take to the mountains again. There was a bitter split between Colm Tierney in North Mayo who was on DeValera's side, and his brother Ignatius in South Sligo who was on Collins' side. On the Inishkea Islands off the coast of Belmullet, the north island was for the treaty and the south island against it. It was indicative of how the British had engineered another Irish divide.

The first shells of the Civil War hit the Four Courts building in Dublin in June 1922, and the country was in conflict again. Collins had reluctantly authorised an attack to retrieve the important buildings back from the Anti-Treaty forces. His main reason for turning weapons on fellow Irishmen, who just over a year previously had fought alongside him, was to appease the British who were threatening to tear up the treaty if he had not dealt with the occupation of the Four Courts which had lingered for over three months.

The war was a bitter one. Thankfully though, as far as Ballycroy was concerned, it did not bring the bloodshed that the War of Independence did. It was as if the people had realised how close to the precipice they had come. They were fearful that more strife would push them over the edge. They would have absolutely nothing. As it was, everyone was barely able to get by. There might be conflict between Dublin and London and even much closer to home, but a community spirit had been entwined into the parish. This spirit of togetherness had helped the generations survive one challenge after another down through the years. Bad harvests, floods, blizzards, storms, famine, emigration, disease, war, poverty. They had all visited. And only neighbourly love had helped pull people through.

And not everyone had been able to pull through. The Kerrigan family were one such example. If a Ballycroy DeValera man had killed a Ballycroy Collins man – what difference would that make in Dublin? Would it even be quoted as a statistic? Whereas the local suffering it would cause would be immense.

Fr. Tim was a gift from God in this regard, as he asked these types of questions. From the altar he urged his people not to turn on each other. He fostered a spirit of togetherness. He begged everyone to look after each other and not satisfy the bloodlust of others. Others that they were never even likely to meet. Others who would never even go to the bother of setting foot in their picturesque parish.

Carey's Bar witnessed some skirmishes between rival supporters but it was mainly down to intoxication. A few youths, anxious to express their rebellious side and vent their emotions, went to the trouble of attacking Shranamonragh Lodge and Lyall Lodge. They believed that these gentry houses were valid aristocratic targets, symbols of Englishness. But the damage was minimal. This time there was no shootings. No robberies. No bombing of bridges. There was a lot of angst. A lot of arguments. A lot of bad blood. But thankfully that was about it for the duration of the war, which lasted just over one year.

It probably would have ended quicker had it not been for the killing of Michael Collins in August 1922. The Free State General died after an attack on his convoy in his native Cork. For many, after seeing such a fine man and hero die, it took away the stomach for the fight. But for others, it deepened bitterness and unfortunately there came a renewed determination from both sides to win in the aftermath of his huge loss.

One Ballycroy man though who did see a lot of violence was Terence McDonnell. Even though he was an important soldier to him, Harry Heraty had to dispatch Terence to Dublin at the start of the campaign as Collins had asked each county to send one man of proven calibre to Dublin, which was seen as crucial to ultimate success for the Pro-Treaty side. They succeeded in taking control of the capital city early on, and this gave them an advantage that they never relinquished. Terence was involved in leading a unit that operated in the Stonybatter area. He never revealed much about his Dublin activity but claimed to have met Collins one day at Grangegorman.

After Dublin was taken, Terence was dispatched to Limerick City where both sides had captured a former British Baracks each, and a tense stand-off was in place. The glorious Shannon River wasn't the only thing dividing the city. Limerick, whose Treaty Stone from 1690 was one of its main hallmarks, was now having to deal with another treaty. Terence played an important role in the negotiations which eventually resolved the situation. But it kept him occupied and away from his native parish for the most part of the war. The delicate nature of his mission, in a city whose motto means 'well versed in the art of war', meant that his every step was treated as his last one. It was a sniper's paradise, and his reputation from Mayo meant little in these parts. Again, Terence did not divulge much of what his experiences in Limerick were. But like most people, it pained his heart greatly to see the Irish fighting amongst themselves.

In Munster, he was exposed to a lot of what his native county was spared. It was a cruel, bitter conflict there. Many old scores from the past were being settled under the cover of 'war'. More worrying, many new scores were being created. The legacy of these would be a heavy burden for future generations.

The fighters for the Free State were winning the war, but they wanted desperately to end it so that they could focus on the task of building a new state. The cost of a war at the nation's birth was so regrettable. Exiles such as Roger and Batty despaired to see what the country was doing to itself. And the ministers in the new government decided that they had to act fast and cruelly to crush the internal enemy. They sanctioned the execution of 77 captured irregular officers. This was a stunning development. It was a merciless development. But it showed the determination of the fledgling Free State government to get the country up and running, to make the most of this opportunity for independence, and to extinguish the resistance.

As well as those official executions, an influential move came in the form of an official dictat from the Catholic Church, in which they gave recognition to the authority of the Free State government to run the country.

There were also many unofficial executions. The murder of eight irregulars by the Free Staters in Ballyseedy in Kerry was a major turning point. There were no British around to be blamed for that atrocity. It was Irishmen tying fellow Irishmen to a landmine and blowing them to pieces. It was a dark day in Eireann's long history. But it was days such as this that finally convinced the Anti-Treaty side to call a halt to the war. In May 1923, six weeks after the ceasefire had been agreed; DeValera stated to his followers that "Further sacrifice would be in vain. Let victory rest with those who destroyed the republic".

Such words came too late for the thousands of families who had lost loved ones in one of Ireland's most tragic periods. A consolation for the people of Ballycroy was that no one had been directly lost to it. Four of the seven 'Boys of Ballycroy' were still alive. For Christmas 1923, those four were to be found in two parties of two.

In Germany, Batty, Ruth and Agatha hosted a very special guest – his old friend Roger. Jean Pierre Roland had spent most of December in France, where he was a celebrity and treated as one of their own. He officially opened his 'The Great El Ginto' play in Paris near the famous Moulin Rouge, and was mobbed by photographers and journalists. But in the middle of the glamour and the acclaim, he made sure he did not forget his friends of old. He visited the grave of John Peter Kerrigan, under one of millions of white crosses which act as a reminder of the horrors of war. He then visited the nearby Menin Gate in Ypres to pay his respects to all who had fallen in the Great War. It was an emotional day as he recalled the special times - the innocent times - he had shared with his boyhood friends. Now one of them was lying beneath the Flemish clay along with thousands upon thousands of others who had made the ultimate sacrifice.
"Little did we realise" said a sombre Roger to his bodyguard, "That when we innocently played soldier games on the dunes of The Sandybanks, that some of us would end up fighting real battles in the bunkers of Belgium. Real bullets. Real bombs. Real blood".

336

Roger then made his way by rail to Germany, a country trying to rise from the ashes of war and defeat. It was the warmest of embraces he shared with his long lost friend Batty when they got to meet after almost twelve long years. They shared a treasured Christmas together.

In Ballycroy, yet again at midnight mass the McDonnell brothers had defied the odds and survived another war to stand side by side. Facing Fr. Tim on his high altar, Terence stood on the right and Sylvester on the left. To Terence's right he had his proud parents Fintan and Claire. To Sylvester's left he had his wife Eleanor, their 11 month old playful son Noel, and their one week old daughter Josephine.

It was a happy Christmas Day meal that Eleanor hosted in Doona. The McMahons were there too. And Joey Jarvis arrived from Ballinrobe for the meal. After much food and wine, Terence managed to have a quick word with his Scottish sister-in-law.
"I've never seen Sylvester look so happy" he said.
"That's nice to hear", she replied, "But don't you think he looks a bit thin?"
"A bit" said Terence, "But that's no harm. He'll be fine, our Sylvester will be fine".
"I really hope so", said Eleanor, "But I'm worried about him. He wakes screaming every night. I'm not sure how I will manage him AND the children. He suffers awful flashbacks. He keeps waking the house up".

Terence tried to talk to his brother about his trauma later on in the day. But Sylvester played down the concerns. He was embarrassed. And he didn't want his brother to be fussing over him. He assured Terence that he would be alright. But secretly he wondered if he would ever exorcise the nightly images that haunted him. The mangled bodies strewn on the fields of Amiens. Gilberthorpe firing a bullet into the helpless Cecil. The falling bodies of the Tans he had shot in Mulranny. The Alsatian mauling him on top of Bunmore Hill. The last desperate look in Gilberthorpe's eyes before he died. And worst of all, the recurring nightmare that was the haunting pitiful screams that came from the tortured and dying Willie.

The Careys had a peaceful argument-free Christmas as the growing band of children took centre stage. Rosa in particular was in good form, as her annual card from Roger had brought her the news that he would be visiting Ballycroy in February, on his way from Germany and England. They also had news of this in Bunmore, where Liam O'Grady was hoping that his ailing father would live long enough to see his second-born return home. Liam's three children were counting the days until they would meet their famous uncle for the first time.

1924 promised much. It promised peace. And it promised excitement. It was welcomed in with eager expectation.

CHAPTER 46: THE ANVIL

Rosa Carey was a realist. She never held out any hope of ever marrying Roger. It was almost 12 years since they had their final night together. She received cards and dollars each year for her birthday and for Christmas. Sometimes he had a note enclosed. She had wondered why he had not married in America, but thought that he was probably just too busy. She was excited about his upcoming visit. She had decided that she would try and get him alone. She had decided that it was only fair to tell him that 11 year Louis Carey was his son. Their son. What she dreaded most was his denial. The thought that he would think it was a plan to get at his wealth. She would rather go penniless than for that to happen. But she was counting on her intimate knowledge of her former love. She knew he had a kind heart. He would not disown his own flesh and blood.

By mid January, old William O'Grady was deteriorating by the day, as he lay in his death bed in Bunmore. Liam prayed that Roger would arrive in time. Fr. Tim contacted an old seminary friend based in London, to ask him to try and meet Roger around the West End and to get him to expedite his trip to Mayo.

The schoolchildren of the parish grew excited as they made American flags and 'welcome home' posters for Ballycroy's most famous export. Houses were white-washed and the grounds of the church got a makeover. An influx of media was expected to accompany the world-renowned producer of shows and movies. Toothy Lucey gleefully relished the opportunity to be the journalistic link with the outside world. This would be a huge moment in his long career.

On January 17th, as they worked together at the restored forge by the graveyard in Ballycroy Village, word reached the McDonnell brothers of the sudden death of Frankie Phelan. He had died of a heart attack whilst playing with his children. They made their plans to attend his burial in Newport. Despite being on the opposite side to him during the Civil War, Terence wanted to pay his respects to the man who had rescued his brother at Westport

Rail Station. It went without saying that Sylvester wanted to pay his respects as well.

After the burial, the brothers went for a drink in one of Newport's fine taverns. They joined the locals in toasting the life of the hero Frankie. There were some tensions, obviously, it being so soon since the divisive war, but people were careful not to disrespect the dead man by starting any trouble.

Leaving the bar after two drinks, Sylvester spotted a brown teddy bear in a toy shop window and went in to buy it for Noel, who would turn one on the following day, January 19th. As Sylvester was doing his business, Terence was approached by an old man outside of the shop.
"Are you McDonnell from Ballycroy?" he asked.
"I am indeed" replied a smiling Terence. "You're Alfred, aren't you?"
"Bejaysus you know ME!" chuckled the old man.
"I remember you from the fairs long ago" said Terence.
"Well now, isn't that something" said Alfred, pushing back his cap and rubbing his forehead. "Well, it is a pleasure to meet you. I have heard a lot said of you!"
"I'm not so sure I want to hear what you heard" laughed Terence. "Is there something I can do for you, Alfred?"
"Indeed there is. Indeed there is" said the old man looking down on the cobbles. "It may be nothing, but an old anvil has come my way and someone was saying that it might be your father's"
"Really?" said Terence.
"Well. It has 'FMCD' etched into it. Someone was saying that it might be your father's. That the Tans stole it".
"Well!" said Terence, "Isn't that some news. Come here Sylvester! Old Alfred here thinks he has Dad's big anvil! Can we have a look?"
"Indeed you can" replied the smiling Alfred. "Call to me in an hour or so. Branch off the Mulranny Road onto the Furnace Road, heading for Skirdagh, you must know it, and I'm the house on the right with the red gate and red door", and off he went.
"Unfuckingbelievable!" said Terence. "Dad will be delighted!"
"How did old Alfred end up with it?" asked Sylvester

"Who knows! Who cares now!" came the reply. "Come on; let's go back in for more porter. He said it would be an hour!"
"I can't go into the bar with this!" exclaimed Sylvester showing his brother the brown bear toy he was holding.
"Just put it in the bicycle carrier and it will be fucking alright. Come on!" instructed Terence. And he was right. When they emerged two pints later the bear bought for young Noel was still there smiling up at them!

The brothers reached Alfred's house and parked up their bicycles. They knocked on the red door but there was no answer. They called out Alfred's name a few times but there was no reply. There was no sign of a dog or a cow, nothing. They noticed that the shed door was open, and they decided to go in. That's probably where the anvil was. They were right. As they entered the shed, there it was, on the ground in front of them. They did not need to read the etching to know it was theirs. They recognised its every scratch and dent. They had worked on that since they were toddlers. It was like a part of the family to them.

The brothers smiled at each other. Then the silence was shattered by the deafening sound of two shotgun blasts from behind, and a painful shout from each of them as both of their sets of legs buckled. They had never felt pain like this. Their flesh burnt.

Before they could take in what had just happened, they were belted across the head with blackthorn sticks. Each fell to the ground. Each with an attacker standing over them raining down hard, agonising blows that broke their bones and pierced their skin.

After two minutes of this incessant severe punishment, the stunned brothers barely realised that they had become shackled by the wrists by cuffs to steel rings in the shed wall. Steel rings used for tying cows. They looked up to try and see the faces of their attackers but the blood gushing from their head wounds blinded them. The shed was dark and the light coming in the door only served to dazzle them. They shouted out to each other and for help but no-one but their attackers heard their cries. The blows from the sticks continued to come down on their battered bodies. The shotgun wounds tortured them. Their minds tried to cope with the pain, as well as why they were being attacked. The stick beating stopped only to be replaced by a severe kicking as their laughing attackers competed to see who could inflict the most pain and yield the sharpest scream.

Mercifully, after a few minutes of pure hell, the out-of-breath cursing attackers took a break and left the shed, leaving the traumatised brothers behind them in the darkness, each of them shackled to the wall and crying in agony. After a minute, they shrieked in unison as the door opened again and a thick Mayo accent spoke.
"We're far from finished with ye, ye weasels! We're just waiting for the main man now. THEN ye will see what pain really is, ye weasels!" The door was slammed shut again.

Terence squirmed on his patch, trying to find a position that would ease the stinging coming from behind his left knee. He circled his dry tongue around the inside of his mouth, trying to gauge how many teeth he had just lost. Trying to suck blood from the roots of the teeth so as to quench the thirst of his tongue. His demented mind tried to decide which part of his body was aching the most.

Sylvester beside him was gulping. He was trying to spit out the mixture of cowshit and his own blood he had swallowed. His left eye was killing him. The agony was indescribable. His calf muscle burned from the gunshot. He wished he could die that very moment.
"Who they fuck are they?!" Terence managed to utter. There was no reply from his brother, just wincing as his body tried to cope with the horrific beating.
After about an hour or so, which felt like a century to the suffering brothers, Sylvester managed to murmur a few words:
"We are dying, brother"
"Sylvester, stay strong. For Noel and Josephine. Stay strong. We could be rescued yet.." whispered Terence, gasping for water.
"No...no brother...this is it. They have us..." came the weak reply, followed by "My eye is bursted, the...the pain...I'm bleeding to death here Terence..."

"Come on please – stay strong for Eleanor – and the kids!" urged Terence.
"I just can't…I…" said Sylvester before slipping into semi consciousness.
"I bet it's fucking Huckerby!" whispered Terence again, not sure if he had an audience or not. "The fucker has come back. I…I never told you Sylvester that I had a near miss with the fucker in Dublin last year. Did I? Came to my fucking hotel so he did…tied up the poor hotelier's family…but I copped something was not right and stayed out of my room and hid in the laundry closet…but didn't the fucker turn up to do me?! He's back to finish me now…"
"Why?" came the weak reply.
"Because his step-sister probably told him that I abused her or something. That's why. God only knows what she has been saying about me. He hates the Irish anyway. Sure…sure down in Limerick…down there they had awful stories about what he did there as a Tan. Just a murdering bastard he is…"
"I'm dying" repeated Sylvester.
"Listen! Someone's coming!" said Terence.
The door opened and two oil lights lit up the room. Each lamp was been held by a smiling brother with broken yellow teeth. Terence recognised them. It was the Brophy brothers! They were back in Mayo. The ugly brutes who had tried – and failed – to better the Kerrigans on Shranamonragh Bridge years earlier. Terence tried to make out who the tall figure in between them was. The glare from the lights was dazzling him. He waited to hear the English voice of Patrick Huckerby return from the past. A voice came from the figure alright, but it was not an English voice. It was a very familiar one.

"Well. Well now. Would you look at the state of the 'Boys of Ballycroy'!" snarled Royston Carey. "Look at them. The two of them. Wouldn't I love them to stand up in the church together now like that, as proud as peacocks!"
The Brophys laughed. The suffering and shocked McDonnells squirmed.
"Find yer Daddy's anvil?" Royston taunted.
"Fucking Royston!" shouted Terence. "Decided to fight NOW, when the war's OVER?"

"No more smartness out of you!" shouted Royston, belting his victim across the head with a stick. "Lads, I see ye've beaten the shit out of them, but not their smartness. Ye will have to beat the bastards a biteen more!"

The oil lamps were put to the ground and the pitiful wails rang out again as this time three of them laid kicks into the captured brothers. The Brophys and Royston laughed and cursed as they knocked yells out of the men.
"I don't want them to die just yet" panted Royston. "We will wait til dawn. Aren't soldiers normally shot at dawn?"
"How would you know?" asked Terence defiantly before receiving a painful kick into the groin for his trouble.
"I'll silence you yet, McDonnell" said Royston. "You're going to have a long slow death, I'll make sure of that. And as for poor Sylvester here, he's nearly expired already. No more for him tonight lads. Here, give him his little bear" and Noel's first birthday present went flying into cowshit, landing at Sylvester's trembling head.

"Now Terence. Just remember as you lie here on your last cursed night on this earth. NO ONE messes with Royston Carey and gets away with it! NO ONE! You can kill women and soldiers and cows and whatever, but you won't get away with messing with me!"
"With your wife you mean?!" whispered Terence.
"Fucking NEVER mention my wife again!" snarled Royston bringing the blackthorn stick crashing down onto Terence's shoulder.
"She was some ride!" roared Terence in defiance. "Lovely breasts on her!" and his taunt was met with frantic strikes of the blackthorn until one of the Brophys interrupted the latest attack, saying "You'll finish him Royston, hold back 'til morning!"

Terence could speak no more. The pain was too much. His brain could not formulate the words. It was trying to deal with the convergence of pain from so many different areas of his body.

Royston stepped back from Terence. He took pleasure from the sight of the cowering bloodied and battered body. He was content that he had exerted enough physical torture for now. But he had one round of psychological torture left in his cruel armoury for Sylvester. He knelt down beside the sobbing elder McDonnell, who was staring at the bear in front of him on the stable floor. "Do you know that your brother has been riding your wife?! Yes, he has been sticking it up her. As often as he can. She preferred his to yours after all. Maybe the two little scoundrels are not yours at all Sylvie. Maybe you are just their uncle?!" he whispered.

Both McDonnells heard the words but both could no react. The pain was too much. Of course what came from Royston's mouth was not the truth, but he was just tormenting them, rubbing salt into the wounds. Trying to cause division, just like the Brits had always done. There was no division amongst the guffawing Brophy brothers. These were just brutes. United in thuggery.

The door slammed and the lights went out as the brothers and the teddy bear were left behind in the shed on the freezing January night. The coldness actually helped numb their wounds. But the brothers just wanted their worlds to end. They could not endure this for much longer. Dawn could not come quickly enough.

At about 3am on the morning of the 19th, Sylvester seemed to get a 'second wind'. His eye was completely closed at this stage, but for a ten minute spell he seemed alert again. Terence's teeth were chattering, as he heard his brother say that they had to think of a way of escaping. It was as if a new person, an energised positive person, had taken over his body. He recalled who the Brophy brothers were and said that they might accept money to release them. But it seemed that Sylvester was hallucinating. It wasn't long before he started to lose consciousness again. His brother started to talk, in a dual effort to keep his own mind focused and to keep Sylvester tuned into their situation.
"Don't go to sleep Sylvester" begged Terence. But there was no answer. "It's, it's young Noel's first birthday today. He will be waiting at home for his present. He will be waiting for you, for you – his Daddy. Don't go to sleep on him. Please! Just imagine his little smile when he sees the teddy bear. He will be so happy. Just like I was with Sammy the sheep when I was small.

Remember? Do you remember that Sylvester?" All he heard in response was a murmur. Then a cry of pain. Terence continued his monologue.

"Little Josephine will be waiting too. Her eyes will light up when she sees you. And, and of course Eleanor. She'll have a tart ready. She'll be waiting for her man. But it will be Noel who will be looking out the window. Waiting to see you come into view Sylvester. Waiting to see you come down the road. And he will give you a lovely hug and a lovely little kiss on your cheek. And he will LOVE his little teddy. He really will. And Dad. Dad will be so glad to get his anvil back. And Mammy, poor Mammy. Oh no. Oh no. Our poor Mammy. What will she do, Sylvester, what will she do? Oh no...."

Terence continued crying for a while. His felt as if he hands would sever at the wrists. He could not feel his legs. He hoped this was not the end. Surely it couldn't be? Surely, after all that he had put himself through, it wasn't going to end in a shed. At the hand of Royston. He wondered if anyone had heard the shots. He wondered if Harry Heraty would come and rescue him. Or perhaps Batty. Or perhaps John Peter in his army uniform? He too was beginning to hallucinate.

Reality arrived at dawn as Terence heard the voices approach the door. He was hoping of course that it was a rescue party, but it was only the three torturers.

"Oh – yer still here!" said Royston sarcastically to laughter from the idiots with him.
"Please Royston", whispered Terence but he was not allowed to finish his sentence.
"Oh here comes the begging!" said the cruel businessman.
"Listen lads, listen. This will be good. One of the great 'Boys of Ballycroy' begging ME of all people!"
"Please" repeated Terence from his bloody patch of the stable,
"Your gripe is with ME. Do what you want to me. But Sylvester, he's...he's done nothing to you. Let him home. It's his boy's first birthday. Let him live".

"We may be a bit too late for that!" said Royston, prodding a foot into the motionless Sylvester, who was curled up in a heap. He moaned faintly in reply.
"Oh, he's still alive! Well, not for much longer. Go and get the truck backed up to the door Billy!" ordered Royston before addressing Terence again.
"I've not forgotten your brother prodding his gun into my temple at the rear of my own property – he is not the innocent you claim. He's a great man when he has a gun. Let's see how great he is now. He's paying the price for threatening Royston Carey, I tell you. NO ONE messes with me and gets away with it, NO ONE!"

Terence listened as he heard the sound of the truck's slow arrival as it reversed up to the stable door, blocking out whatever natural light had been coming in through it. The frozen man could do little as the trio removed his numb hands from the ring on the wall and dragged him towards the back of the truck, and chained him to the rear. As he could not walk, his hands were stretched out in front of him to where they were bound to the back of the Crossley Tender. His neck could not support his head which limped downwards so that he was staring at the ground. He could barely feel his useless legs on the ground behind him. He prayed for a quick release. He expected to be joined at the back by his brother, but they just tossed him onto the floor of the truck overhead. Sylvester was already at death's door. To be dragged behind one of the actual trucks used by the Black and Tans on his final journey was part of the special punishment being dealt to the womaniser. An angry husband was exacting his revenge.

"Just to let you know" said Royston as he prepared to board the truck. "Me and the lads here had a nice night making sure those two Ownsworth spinsters down at The Demesne did not go to their graves without a good ride. My God, these two Brophys hadn't had any action in ages! They were like little bulls. Rampant they were. Anyway, the two Ownsworths were robbed, rode and riddled. And guess whose bicycles we left by the river beside them? I'm telling you, there will be no memorials for ye two boys. They'll build a memorial to Gilberthorpe before they build one for ye!"

This time, it was not concocted psychological torture on Royston's part. He was telling the truth.

"You will die for this Carey!" muttered Terence as the next stage of his crucifixion was about to begin.

"Maybe so – but you won't be around to see it!" replied Royston with a smirk.

We can only hope that the arctic air that hovered over the bumpy road that led into the Skirdagh Mountains helped numb Terence's pain that morning. We can only hope that he did not feel the stones, sand and mud enter his torn wounds, as the Crossley Tender dragged him for over two miles through his final dawn. We can only hope he did not hear the laughing or the taunts of his fellow Mayo men who were giving him a gruesome death. We can only hope that his mind was hallucinating and that he was seeing different images other than those of his dying brother being thrown into a large boghole that morning. We can only hope that he did not see the rope tied to his brother's ankles being threaded through their father's precious anvil and onto his own ankles. We can only hope that he did not see the satanic eyes of Royston look down on him as he choked him with a rolled up union jack flag. We can only hope that his earthly pain was ended by the time he reached the bottom of the deep boghole where his father's anvil would weigh him and his beloved brother down forever.

Sylvester and Terence McDonnell were dead. Murdered viciously. Their bodies never to be found. Not only did they have no dignity in death, but their reputations were tarnished as planned by being associated with the bloody find in The Demesne. The new Irish policemen had no other leads. The two protestant sisters had been savagely attacked, violated and murdered. Newport was in shock. The sisters were the gentlest souls that could ever be met. There was an outcry as local men gathered with the intention of heading to Ballycroy to exact revenge. The priests in the respective parishes had to use their every skill and energy to urge calm and avoid a confrontation. Local woods were searched. The men of Newport and the surrounding areas were understandably furious. They would have killed the McDonnells with their bare hands if they had happened to find them.

But they never did. Only a year later did Toothy Lucey dare to publish his theory on what happened in 'The Ownsworth Case'. Like all who knew the McDonnells, he knew that they would never have committed such an atrocity on two innocent women. There had to be some logical explanation. But, for now, the story spread that they were seen drinking in Newport, and that they had gone on a drunken violent rampage, leaving their bicycles near the scene of the crimes.

Word reached Roger of the murders of the sisters and the disappearance of the brothers. He was convinced that there was something more sinister at play. And he was determined to get to the bottom of it.

As for the McDonnell family, they went insane with grief. Fintan and Claire mourned their disappeared sons. They knew someone had got them. Their main suspect was Huckerby. Next perhaps, vengeful relatives or associates of Gilberthorpe. They knew their boys were innocent of the accusations being made against them. They desperately tried to organise searches in the Newport area for their bodies but there was no sympathy for the McDonnells there, and any searchers were quickly hunted back to where they came from.

Eleanor cradled her two infants. The three of them missed Sylvester terribly. Noel waited by the window every night for months waiting for his Daddy to come home.

Only one person was suspicious of an involvement by Royston Carey. And she dared not speak a word, for fear of losing her own life. She was his wife, Antoinette.

January 1924 was a black month. Only two of the 'Boys of Ballycroy' now remained alive. And one of those was packing his bags in London for a first return home in a dozen years.

CHAPTER 47: HOME IS THE HERO

As the ferry bringing him from Britain sailed into Dun Laoghaire on a sunny February morning, Roger leaned on the deck railings and admired the view of Dublin's coast. His bodyguard and loyal friend, the towering Carlo, stood smiling by his side. As the harbour drew nearer a seagull perched on the railing several feet away. Then it inched closer to Roger. It had caught his eye the moment it landed. He was fascinated. The bird came further still, until it was right beside his hand. The gull looked up at him, and chirped. Then it looked around a few times. Roger reached out and stroked it. It didn't fly away.

"That's totally amazing!" said the American voice of Carlo.
"That's my Dad. He's gone" replied Roger as the bird finally upped and flew into the blue sky.
"What do you mean? You're crazy!" laughed Carlo.
"I'm telling you. That's a sign. I've missed him. He's gone. That was him saying goodbye" said Roger calmly.

He was right. When he reached Castlebar the face of Toothy Lucey gave the story away. William O'Grady had died when his son was *en route* to see him. He was just one day too late. Roger did not shed a tear. He just thought of the bird. He was glad he had managed to stroke him. Carlo looked at him open-mouthed. He could not believe this. What an introduction to Ireland!

What was supposed to be a joyous homecoming was tempered by the passing of Roger's father. Fr. Tim and Toothy reminded the excited locals that respect had to be shown. The O'Grady family needed space. It was not a time for celebration and flag-waving.

Dozens of journalists and cameramen descended on Ballycroy that memorable week. Many of the locals were annoyed at this intrusion. They had never seen an influx like this before. As well as the international press, hundreds of people from all over Ireland came to the parish to catch a glimpse of the star. They wanted to see the type of transport he used and the style of his clothes.

Many of the locals were surprised by the gaunt appearance of the man they once knew as a cheery, chubby lad. He was still tall, and his belly still protruded, but he was much thinner around the face. His cheekbones were now prominent. His smiling eyes looked a bit larger. He was greying around the temples and his brushed back hairline was receding. Some whispered that he looked like he was wearing make-up, especially around the eyes as they looked darkish. Others put it down to tiredness after his journey. More alarmingly, he carried a walking stick and seemed to lean on it quite a bit – it was not just for show. The shine off his maroon shoes won plenty of admiring looks, as did his beige sheepskin coat. But most of those who had known him when he was growing up were just delighted to see his warm infectious smile back amongst them again.

Whatever about Roger, the appearance of his bodyguard caused many female palpitations. Carlo stood even taller than his boss, and had the typical dark Italian features. He was very handsome, had well groomed shiny black hair, and was an imposing figure. For the main part he retained a stern expression, but when he smiled his sparkling white teeth couldn't help but impress. The rumour spread amongst the excited Ballycroy people that he was a movie star, and he could easily pass as one.

The Italy-born but New York-raised Carlo was busy keeping the media at bay as Roger was reunited with his only brother at the wake-house in Bunmore. Tears were shed as they hugged at the front porch, before standing together at William's coffin. Roger shed more tears as he stared at the lifeless face of his father. The old man had aged even more than expected, but he looked at peace. As he touched the stone cold hands that had a rosary beads wrapped around them, Roger's mind glanced back to the bird on the ferry deck. He took a deep breath and resolved to cry no more for his father. Their relationship had never been a close one. He felt sad that they did not get to have one last conversation, but he knew that it would probably have been a curt one in any case. Roger blessed himself and turned to meet his sister-in-law and nephews and niece for the first time. It was time to look ahead – and not backwards. It was consoling for him to see the house now – despite the loss of William O'Grady - full of youth, love and exuberance.

Throughout that evening and the burial mass the next day, Roger received a mixture of welcomes and sympathies from the parishioners he had got to know so well in the first twenty years of his life. He greeted each familiar face with a smile and a firm handshake. When he met younger faces, he asked each person their name, looked them in the eye and gave them an individual greeting. He was back amongst his own. And even though they were treating him like royalty, he was determined to treat his fellow Ballycroy folk in the same warm manner as he had always done.

Fr. Tim was particularly proud to be seen with him. His former cell mate Mongey came from Castlebar to offer his condolences. Roger became emotional when he met the families of his former comrades in the 'Boys of Ballycroy' - the Cooneys and the McDonnells. There was no sign of the Bourkes, and as the funeral mass commenced for William O'Grady, the crowded church soon found out why.

Fr. Tim cleared his throat and announced to his captive congregation that he had bad news to impart on this February morning. His voice trembled as he informed everyone that Batty Bourke had collapsed and died whilst carrying out training duties with the German army. The church was stunned. Roger gripped his walking stick and thought of how upset poor Ruth and Agatha would be. His mind was still fresh with the happy memories of the idyllic Bavarian Christmas they had just spent together. He knew that Batty was never the same after his Ballina beating, but he had not expected this sad news. Gilberthorpe had struck one final blow from beyond the grave. Batty Bourke a.k.a. Major Vandenburg was dead.

Of course the majority of the shocked congregation had not got to see Batty since he marched off to war in 1914. Because of his defection, he had to keep a low profile on the trips he had since made to Ireland. Most of the sympathy was for the much-loved

Patrick, Agnes and Andrew Bourke, who were devastated at his passing.

Immediately after his father was laid to rest, Roger asked to be driven to Aughness South where he sympathised with the grieving Bourkes. In the midst of one of their darkest hours, Roger brought rays of brightness by describing the fun that they had enjoyed just seven weeks earlier. It was a consolation to them that Batty had spent a happy final Christmas with his wife, daughter and friend. Andrew cursed the rotting corpse of Gilberthorpe. He was certain that the sudden death was caused by the brutal beating.

Roger offered to pay the Bourke travel fare to attend the funeral. But the German Consulate had beaten him to it, and the arrangements were already made and paid for. The three remaining Bourkes were making the poignant trip to bid farewell to their son and brother.

As Roger was preparing to leave the Bourke house, a steady stream of sympathisers began arriving. A car carrying Fr. Rea from Enniscrone pulled up as the visitors from America were getting into their car. The priest recognised Jean Pierre Roland from newspaper articles and dashed over to greet him.
"So privileged to meet you. I'm Agnes's brother – Father Rea" he said.
"The Rebel Republican Reverend Rea! The privilege is mine I assure you Father" replied Roger. "And I am sorry for your tragic loss".
"Thank you Roger. I know. So sad. I'm none the better of the news yet" said the priest. "And sure it is your loss too; you were a fabulous friend of whom he always spoke highly".
"He's a loss for all of us, I guess" said Roger. "Sorry Carlo. Please meet Father Rea. Father Rea – this is Carlo from Italy - a member of my staff".
"And you were with him for Christmas Roger" said Fr. Rea shaking hands with the bodyguard.
"Yes. We were. He was in fine form. Even though he still was in a lot of pain, he was doing alright. And did he love little Agatha or

353

what! His eyes lit up whenever she was around. I can't stop thinking of her and Ruth".
"It's a tragedy" said the priest. "I hope to get over to meet them both".

As Carlo drove Roger from Aughness to Carey's Bar, the realisation hit Roger that he now was the only one of the 'Boys of Ballycroy' still alive! So far, none of them had come near the age of forty. And he secretly knew that the likelihood was that he would not reach that age either. He also thought about 'The White Cow Incident' and the prophecy made on that cursed afternoon. Michaeleen was lying at the bottom of the ocean. John Peter was lying in Belgium. Batty would now be lying in Germany. The other three of the six dead had never reached any graveyard. Roger also secretly knew that the likelihood was that his own remains would not lie beneath Irish soil either, but in America. The cow had been right! The mystical world had collided with the real world on that fateful afternoon that he could never erase from his memory. The sound that came from that beast's mouth still haunted him to this day. No script of his could ever capture that experience.

At Carey's, Rosa was waiting to greet her old boyfriend as he stepped from the magnificent silver car. She threw her arms around him and he kissed the side of her neck.
"Roger I'm so happy to see you!" she cried as the smiling Carlo looked on.
"Me too! Me too, Rosa!" replied the laughing Roger. "Gosh, it is so good to hold you again!"

Bulbs flashed as the gathered photographers took pictures of the reunion. But they did not get to spend more than a minute together as Roger was ushered away to visit the mini-cinema and meet the rest of his family for a post-burial meal in Carey's Hall.
"I'll be in the bar tomorrow, we'll talk properly then!" shouted Roger as he was led away from the waving Rosa.

Roger and Carlo stayed in Newport House that night. It was a luxurious hotel regularly used by the very rich. The next day they drove to the McDonnell homestead in Claggan. The parents and

sister of the missing men were still distraught, and extremely angry at the false accusations emanating from Newport.
"There's no earthly way they would do such a thing" repeated a distressed Fintan. "You know them, Roger, they would NEVER do that, I don't care what anyone says!"
"Of course they wouldn't" assured Roger, "We all know that. It's some kind of set-up. They have been framed. Someone shot them and disposed of them. Probably the same folk who killed those two protestant ladies".
"It has to be something like that. That Huckerby step-brother of Terence's wife, I reckon it was him. Sure he tried to rape and murder a woman in Bangor Erris when Alice first came over and almost caused the loss of her child. He was an animal. And Terence reckoned he murdered people in Limerick for no reason at all after that. It MUST be him".
"I'll do whatever it takes to track him down Fintan" said Roger.
"Are they searching for them now in the Newport area?"
"No. They won't let us. We're dogshit as far as they are concerned. They all think my boys murdered those two poor ladies. No way, Roger, no bloody way!"

Two visitors to the McDonnell house in Claggan that day were to influence how Roger would react. The first visitor was Harry Heraty from Westport, their former OC. It became clear to Fintan that Harry and Roger had remained in close contact throughout the years, such was the comradery and familiarity between them. However, they did not dwell on the greetings too much out of respect to the McDonnells, who needed their help.
"We have no definite intelligence as to what went on", said Harry, now an elected TD for the Dáil. "But I will ensure that Newport is appeased and my men are already working on convincing the locals that the McDonnells are actually as much victims in this as the Ownsworths were. Leave that to me".

After Harry had left, the second visitor arrived in his white van. It was Joey Jarvis. Gone was his smile as he grieved for his brother-in-law and friend. He was having to support his inconsolable sister and her two young children. He was angered not only by the disappearance of the brothers, but of the slurs wrongly tarnishing their heroics. Unlike Heraty, he had his own intelligence but he only wanted to speak to Roger about it, he didn't want to upset Fintan further by his revelations.

Joey and Roger had never met before but had heard about each other. The missing brothers were their bond at the moment.
"Joey. Is there ANY possibility they're in a barn somewhere?" asked Roger as the two of them sat on McDonnell's stone fence by the house.
"I'm afraid not. They're gone. Buried somewhere. Maybe even chopped up and fed to the dogs like what happened to Willie!"
"No! They did THAT to poor Willie!" said Roger reeling in shock. But what he heard next about the current case had him reeling even more.
"Royston Carey is involved in this, Roger" whispered the Scot. Roger was astounded.
"Are you sure?!" he gasped.
"Him and two others, not yet identified. But I'm working on it. It was they who also robbed and killed the women. And made it look like the lads did it" added Joey.

Roger tried to digest what he had just received. This was more intriguing than any plot he had come up with!
"Royston! Royston Carey! Why would he do such a thing?" asked Roger.
"Because his wife still loved Terence, and they were lovers" replied Joey. That made sense to Roger, he knew of the history there.
"My God you are right!" he exclaimed, but in a low voice. "Carlo, come over here! I have a job for you! But before that, please get me some water. I need a drink!"

That afternoon Carlo drove Roger, Joey and Fintan to Carey's Bar for a few drinks. The place was quite busy because a lot of people were hanging around waiting to see the famous Jean Pierre Roland. Roger planned on having just one quick drink and then popping upstairs for a private chat with Rosa, but he could see that she was busy in the bar, so he stayed on drinking. He reached in behind the bar and gave her a bundle of dollars. He told her that the cost of all drinks that afternoon in the bar was to come from that. She nodded and kept working as the demand from the other side of the bar was huge, and she had only her brother-in-law for help. Roger cast a quick look around for Royston. He tried to prepare himself to keep calm whenever they met. He whispered to Carlo that he would point out Royston to him if he appeared.

As they spoke, Joey Jarvis squeezed his way past the other customers to the bar counter for his third drink. He was so busy trying to shove the customers clambering for free drink to move out of his path, that he did not pay attention to who was serving the alcohol. He leant in over the top of the bar and shouted towards the ear of the brown haired female who was busy trying to satisfy the demand. "Two more ales, that's a good lass" he roared.

The barmaid looked up in horror. She recognised that voice! That Scottish voice! The voice that had come back to haunt her every night as she tried to get rid of her demons. It was the voice of the man who had raped her! Her eyes met his. It took a few seconds for him to realise who she was. Then, as he recalled their previous encounter, he smiled. The sight of the smile pushed Rosa over the edge. Hearing his voice again had felt like a punch to her stomach, but the knowing sinister smile caused her to faint.

The sound of glass smashing echoed around the pub and Benny Hughton shouted for help as he attended to the collapsed woman. Just at that very moment, Royston appeared behind the counter. "What the feck has happened?" he shouted. He looked at the guilty-looking Scot. "What did you do to her?!"
"I did NOTHING!" responded Joey.
"You said SOMETHING to her, I saw you!" said Benny from his knees, gently slapping his sister-in-law's face, anxiously trying to revive her.

Royston leapt onto the counter and jumped down onto the Scot. He started to rapidly punch his customer, as excited yelps came from the onlookers. Joey was dazed by the reaction and was slow to throw a punch back. But just as he did, the tall figure of Carlo pushed his massive frame in between the bodies of both men.

"Hey guys. This is totally unnecessary!" shouted the Italian. A shocked Royston stared up at him, his face contorting with rage. "Who the feck are YOU?!" he roared at the stranger.
"Stop! Please! This is totally unnecessary!" repeated Carlo. "A misunderstanding, that's all, we're leaving now…and we DO apologise!"
"Get the feck out of my bar!" roared Royston. "How fecking dare you!" He cast a look over at Roger and the two men exchanged stares, but no word was exchanged. As Roger gently pushed his way towards the exit to follow Joey and Carlo, Royston was back behind the bar helping Benny to carry Rosa upstairs.

In the silver car, Roger asked Joey what had happened but he said that he did not know.
"You ask anyone beside me, I just asked the lass for two ales and she got a weakness. Just collapsed in front of me!"
"Is it ALWAYS this exciting in Mayo?" laughed Carlo.
"Well, you got to see Royston close up" said Roger. "Hope you got yourself a good look!"
"I got a good look alright. He was the funeral undertaker guy, right? He's kind of got a face made for punching!" said Carlo.

In her room upstairs, it didn't take long for Rosa to respond to smelling salts. Again though, she had to suffer on in silence. Her annoyed brother was not satisfied with her reason for having the weakness. She denied that the Scot said anything to her. She said she could not even remember the Scot!

But as she cried herself to sleep all of the horrid emotions came back to her. The physical hurt, the degradation, Bosco's injury, the putrid smell from her attacker, the loneliness, the pregnancy, the painful birth and the recurring nightmares. She asked herself what this evil creature was doing in HER bar. Why – as Royston had said – was he along with Roger of all people?! What was the connection there? Her skin crawled. How had the man she once loved brought that rat into her home building?

It was a day Rosa wanted to forget forever, but it was a day she never could.

CHAPTER 48: A MEMORIAL

The following morning an event was held in Carey's Hall which had been organised by Toothy Lucey, and choreographed with Carlo's help. About 100 invited guests were there, but 100 more gathered outside. There were priests, politicians, photographers, reporters and the likes there to hear Roger address them inside.

He thanked everyone for their kind support throughout the years. He talked of some of his experiences growing up in Ballycroy. He talked of the curse of emigration, but said that it could be a positive thing. He announced that he would continue to support the Ballycroy mini-cinema, and he stared again at the sitting Royston as he thanked him and his sister for running the service. The Careys received a round of applause in response to this public accolade. He approached the end of his speech by talking about the recent wars which had scarred the parish.

"You do not need someone to come from America to tell you what has happened. YOU have borne the brunt of the suffering. Fine men like the three Kerrigan brothers have been lost. And Seaneen White. And Cecil Dyra. And a woman in her prime – Miss Esmeralda Gay. And now it seems, my two great friends Sylvester and Terence. Undoubtedly their loss is some way connected to some misguided gripe from the wars they bravely fought".

As he spoke these words, Roger stared at Royston in the audience. But there was no reaction on the businessman's face. Roger continued his emotional address:

"IF these brothers had stuck to their blacksmith business and pretended not to hear the call to arms, they would be here today. But they did NOT pretend. And they are NOT here. They volunteered to serve their people and they put themselves at the front. To fight for US. To paraphrase Edmund Bourke 'All it takes for evil men to prevail is for good men to do nothing'. These good men did SOMETHING. And much more. They slept in the snow. They lived off berries and pocketfuls of oats. So that WE can someday raise our own flag. And yet they will not be around to see that glorious day when it arrives. I can only pray that God is good enough to yield their sacred bodies so that they can be buried alongside their proud Fenian grandparents. That someday, Fintan and Claire will be able to join their boys who gave their lives for OUR freedom. That someday, young Noel and Josephine McDonnell will be able to proudly visit their father's headstone".

By this stage, the sound of crying could be heard amongst some of the audience as the outside crowd began to filter into the hall from the rain outside. Roger had requested that they be let in to join everyone else. He had one final part to his stirring speech: "In the past ten years the world and Ireland has called for heroes. I ashamedly admit that I did not answer that call. But I am proud and honoured that friends of mine did. Friends of mine of whom I am not worthy. For the likes of me - spared to enjoy the freedom they fought and died for - I humbly request the politicians gathered here to ensure that NO obstacle is placed in the way of the memorial I plan to fund for those lost. A simple white cross to be placed at the summit of my beloved Bunmore Hill. A white cross that can be seen for miles. A beacon of freedom. A white cross to honour them, and remind us all that we are free from foreign shackles only because of their bravery. An ORDINARY symbol of gratitude for their EXTRAORDINARY sacrifice.

In case they should EVER forget, it would remind future generations that it was streams of blood, sweat and tears that won this island back. It would remind future governments that it was the ordinary hard-working, weather-beaten people of Ireland that fought the fight, and not the privileged classes. It was the men of creed – not the men of greed!"

A noisy round of applause broke out and the speaker received a standing ovation as he left the stage. People gathered around him to praise his speech and congratulate him. Carlo used his considerable physique to make sure the situation did not become uncomfortable for Roger.

A tear rolled down the cheek of Rosa. She was moved. And so proud. But her sitting brother remained unimpressed. He was the only one in the entire place that looked unhappy.

"A fecking white cross!" he said to his sister in a hushed but cross tone.
 "Will you STOP please and show some respect!" she whispered back.
"A memorial to the great men who hid in the mountains!" continued Royston sarcastically. "The great men who were nowhere to be seen when the Tans freely attacked us and our father. The great men who were nowhere to be seen when they sprayed our place with a machine gun. The great men who drowned a cow! The great men who shot Esmeralda and her chauffeur in cold blood. It's Esmeralda who should get the memorial – not them!"
"You better keep well out of the way later when Roger calls if you are going to be in this humour!" hissed Rosa.
"Don't worry, I will!" replied Royston. "But I hope he leaves some of his yankee dollars for the cost of rearing his child!"
"You're just impossible!" stormed Rosa as she left for the exit door.

Roger spent over an hour chatting with those present. His speech was well received and many old friends were anxious to have a quick word. As all of this was going on Toothy was furiously scribbling some notes for his article. He wanted everyone in Mayo to read every word that had come from his hero's mouth.

It was well into the afternoon before Roger was sitting in the Carey living room, just he and Rosa. She had asked her family members to afford her some privacy for an hour. They had an enjoyable conversation by the warm open turf fire, sitting across from each other, sipping steaming tea and nibbling at some biscuits.
"So, where are you bodyguards today?" asked Rosa after twenty minutes of catching up.
"You mean 'bodyguard' Rosa" replied Roger, "I have only one, Carlo. He's in the car. I think!"

"I thought you had more. The lads said there was a Scottish man with you the other day?" asked Rosa.

"Oh the guy that made you weak at the knees!" laughed Roger and Rosa faked a smile. "He's not my staff. He's Sylvester's brother-in-law".

"What's his name?"

"Joey Jarvis".

"So how was he with YOU?"

"We picked him up in Claggan, at the McDonnells, we had gone there to check on how Fintan and Claire were doing" replied Roger. "I had never met him before. Had heard of him though".

"Heard what?" asked Rosa curiously.

"That he spent some time with the guys on the mountain. He had deserted the Black and Tans. He became good friends with them both".

"And where does he live now, why isn't he back in Scotland?" asked Rosa.

"How do I know? Gee, this guy has freaked you a little, hasn't he?" remarked Roger. "I don't know much about him. Think he mentioned having a café up in Ballinrobe".

"Ballinrobe?"

"Yes, Ballinrobe Rosa. I'm sorry, but did he insult you or something" asked Roger, putting his cup down and coming over to kneel in front of his former love. "Just tell me if he did, really!"

"No. It's nothing. He just looked weird" she whispered, looking into the fire.

"Rosa, you're trembling. Please. Please tell me if he upset you. I'll deal with him. Anyway, I thought you hadn't seen him?" asked Roger curiously.

"Forget about it. I'm being silly. I'm just getting dizzy spells lately. My mind plays tricks. Forget about it" said Rosa, before changing the subject.

"So what's the story with the stick, and the weight loss?" asked Rosa.

"Isn't it obvious" replied Roger walking back to his chair. "I haven't been well. I have surgery due when I get back on this" he added, pointing to his belly.

"Really? Is it serious?" asked Rosa with a concerned look.

"It is. Dear, I'm not sure if I can talk about it right now. Maybe I need something stronger than tea!" laughed Roger.
"Wait, I'll get you a brandy..." offered Rosa rising from her chair.
"No, no, I don't mean now! Perhaps tomorrow evening. I'll take you for a nice meal, alright? I'll get Carlo to pick you up at six...."

He was interrupted by the twins rushing in and forgetting that they were not supposed to intrude. A flushed looking Louis and Charlotte smiled and offered an apology but Roger called them back.
"And who are these cool kids?" he asked. "These must be the twins! Come here, let me see you"
"Roger, this is Charlotte" said Rosa as the man from Bunmore rose to shake her hand, "And this here is Louis".
"Fabulous French names – just like mine!" laughed Jean Pierre Roland.

They both shook his hand and answered his friendly questions about their age and school. As he dug his hand into his deep pockets to retrieve a five dollar bill for each of them, they thought they would explode with excitement! Rosa inhaled a deep breath as she watched Roger chat with his eleven year old son. If only they both knew who they were speaking to! At that very moment, it would have been her idea of heaven to have them both as part of her own little family of four.

They were quickly joined by Antoinette who ushered the children out of the way, before enjoying a brief clinch with Roger, her friend and Bunmore neighbour from days gone by. They shared a short conversation and promised a follow-up as Antoinette took leave of the couple to allow them finish their meeting. But just as they were about to recommence, the noise of men arguing in the stairwell leading down to the pub could be heard and they rushed from the fireside to see what was going on. It was Carlo and Royston, in a stand-off on the stairs!

"What's going on?" shouted Rosa.
"Oh I just found 'Mister Totally Unnecessary' here on his way up to my home!" shouted Royston. "I don't like shit like this on my expensive carpet!"

"Please!" said Carlo ignoring the insult and looking up at Roger at the top of the stairwell. "I was just coming to collect you. I did not mean to cause trouble".
"It's alright" said Roger. "Just go back to the car and I'll be down in a moment".

"Royston. Just say nothing. Just say nothing!" scolded Rosa as Carlo disappeared as directed.
"I'll keep my mouth closed so" came the surly reply as he brushed past Rosa and Roger at the top of the stairs, resisting his natural urge to cause more trouble.

Roger gave Rosa a gentle kiss on the cheek and finalised the dinner arrangements for the following evening, before rejoining the Italian in the car.

That night Rosa promised herself that she would reveal to Roger the following evening that he had a son. The time felt right.

CHAPTER 49: BROTHERS

As Rosa prepared her outfit and hair for her big night out, the father of her son wasn't even thinking of the meal. He was busy in Ballinrobe where he, Carlo and Joey were having a discussion on what they should do for the McDonnell family. As they drifted on Joey's boat on beautiful Lough Mask, a plan was put into place.

Rosa was picked up by the handsome bodyguard at six and driven to the marvellous restaurant at Newport House overlooking the Black Oak River. She looked stunning in her pink silken dress. Roger was smartly dressed too, but the follow diners could not help but join him in admiring the Ballycroy barmaid. They spent the evening continuing their chat from the previous afternoon. They felt so comfortable in each other's company, as they feasted on oysters and smoked salmon, washed down with immaculate Italian wine.

Rosa was beginning to breathe heavily in anticipation of revealing her secret to Roger. He had no intention of revealing HIS secret to her. How could he? He admired his own calmness and callousness as he thought to himself that while he was gazing at the delectable lady across the table from him, he had been arranging revenge on her brother just hours earlier on the lake.

But Rosa was disconcerted by the steady stream of sweat that rolled from his forehead all through the meal. She asked him again about the operation. He took a few deep breaths and another sip of wine before composing himself to answer her.

"I know this sounds like something from one of my movies, but unfortunately it is true. Rosa, I may not survive this surgery. But I have no choice. I am being literally eaten away, so they have to cut me up and take this out", he said, pointing to his stomach.
"What...what do you mean...'not survive'?" she asked hesitantly, being already afraid of the answer.
"I mean, exactly that!" replied Roger.
"And...And what about your stomach, they have to remove your entire stomach?" she asked before taking a mouthful of wine.

"Pretty much" came the response. "Rosa. I'm going to die. It's just a matter of whether it is a year or a month!"

Rosa felt tears come to her eyes as an icy cold feeling ran up her spine. Then she felt herself go weak again. But she managed to compose herself.
"You're going...to die? Already? How...?" she stuttered.
"I am ALREADY dying" Roger replied calmly, before pointing downwards again. "It's this cursed thing. Bugged me all my life, now it will kill me. Just as my father predicted".

Rosa's head filled with thoughts of young Louis. She knew that she could not now reveal her secret tonight. She gulped some more wine. She was now starting to perspire too. After taking a handkerchief offered by her former lover she wiped her brow, and tried to take deep breaths so as not to faint again. She managed to regain control of herself, but the next part of his story plunged her into a downward spiral that brought her crashing to the floor.

As she lay across his lap in the back of the travelling car, *en route* back to her home, she tried to come to terms with what had made her faint. Roger stroked her hair and patted the ice cold handkerchief on her hot forehead.

"Is this a dream. A nightmare? One of your movies?" she whispered as they were driven along the bumpy road.
"I wish it was" replied Royston gently. "I am so sorry. You told me that you were having dizzy spells. I should not have said anything. I am so sorry for ruining your night".
"No, I ruined YOUR night!" she insisted, before she made him repeat what he had just told her twenty minutes earlier, before he had to call Carlo to carry her from Newport House to the car!

Roger repeated that he had *fetus-in-fetu*. It was a medical rarity. A one in twenty million occurrence that baffled the science world. Rosa's mind whirled as he explained what it was. His protruding stomach was carrying the mutated foetus of his twin brother! It had been there since before his birth. It had possibly contributed to the death of his mother during childbirth.

No matter how much he tried to lose weight down through the years, his stomach kept getting larger and larger. Then in later years, in the height of his success, it started becoming sorer. Eventually, after suffering from an agonising gnawing pain, he was admitted to hospital where the deformity was found. The foetus of his twin had somehow attached itself to his insides. There, for over thirty years, it had continued to exist and grow, feeding off his internal organs.

The shocked doctors who cut him open said that the living organism had even grown some hair and teeth! It had died during the initial surgery, but had become attached to some of Roger's vital organs so they were afraid to risk removing it. The doctors had to stitch him back up again and break the news. The foetus was now decaying inside of him and was in danger of poisoning him. But expert surgeons were now lined up for the second surgical operation, in which they hoped to remove the twin and try and repair the damage it had caused to the host. But the chances were that much of that damage was beyond repair. He had only a 25% chance of survival.

Rosa was in absolute shock. How could this be happening? Was she cursed too? Roger was calm but of course he had much more time to accept what had happened. And he had an interesting footnote for Rosa as they pulled up outside of her bar.
"I always wondered why that cow cursed eight of us that day, when there were only seven of us on the strand. I had assumed it was Michaeleen's dog the beast was referring to, but now I know it was my twin inside of me. Amazing, isn't it Rosa. Truth is indeed stranger than fiction. If I put that in a movie script I would be laughed out of Broadway!"

Roger spent the entire next day in bed at luxurious Newport House. The demanding few days had drained him, and he had to prepare for his gruelling final day. He was low on energy, and feeling quite weak. The medication he was taking was very strong. Carlo spent some time by his bedside discussing their plans.

Roger would have loved to enjoy a final glance at The Sandybanks where he had spent so much of his youth. He would have loved to have had the energy to climb Bunmore Hill. He had planned to get Carlo to drive him to the end of the Mullet Peninsula where he would have pointed out the idyllic Inishkea Islands where he had worked, but he was just too weary. He could not even bear to think of the long sea voyage ahead of him. The thought of chancing a transatlantic airplane trip did not appeal to him or his stomach!

Their first stop on his final day was at the cemetery, where he bowed his head at the fresh grave of his father, who was now lying beside the wife he lost the day Roger was born. The bitter wind coming from scenic Achill numbed the playwright's face as he prayed for his parents. He wished that he could be laid to rest beside them, but did not dwell on that wish as he knew it could not be a reality. He thanked them both for bringing him into this world and prayed that they would be there to welcome him into the next one. On his way out, he stopped and prayed at the memorials for Michaeleen and John Peter. He looked up at the impressive Bunmore Hill and imagined how a gleaming white cross would look on top.

Carlo then drove him the short journey to Bunmore, where Liam's wife had laid on a grand breakfast of boxty. Carlo remarked that he had never tasted anything so pleasant in his life. The children played noisily and the O'Grady brothers joked that this departure to America would not be as silent as Roger's previous one!

After eating, the brothers sat alone by the well and had a final chat. Roger did not want to tell Liam about his *fetus-in-fetu*, he had asked Rosa to explain to him at a later date. But he did want to tell his brother that he would not be coming back.

"What do you mean, Roger?" asked Liam
"The medics tell me I have about a year. I have stomach problems. My internal organs are wasting away and there's nothing that can be done", replied Roger solemnly. His brother looked down at the ground in shock.
"Can't they do ANYTHING?" Liam asked slowly.

"I've tried everything, Liam. This is the one thing my dollars can't buy" Roger sighed, "But I will make sure you are looked after. I've made my will and even though I haven't as much as I should I, I...."
"Will you STOP about money!" interrupted Liam, getting teary. "Doesn't all of this go to show that money doesn't matter? God, I'm thankful now that Dad is gone for this".
"Me too" said Roger. "And I'm thankful I have no wife or children to worry about. Thank God for that small mercy."
"My youngsters – I can't tell them. How can I tell them?" cried Liam. "They look up to you so much. They were so excited about you coming. My God, how can.....and me, of course I will miss you too..."

Liam held his head in his hands and cried at the thought of losing his only brother. He had just lost his father. Now he was going to be the last of the little family to survive. Roger put his hand on his older brother's shoulder.
"The O'Grady bloodline is safe, thanks to you" said Roger.
"You've done well. Your wife is wonderful. The children are fantastic. You have the place going well. We are all proud of you Liam".
"I'd rather have living people proud of me" came the tearful reply.
"Will we bring you back here? Why don't you stay here altogether? This is your place? Surely you are not going to continue working?"
"I simply cannot. Please don't ask me. It's complicated" replied Roger, managing to remain composed and tearless, although it was breaking his heart to see his beloved brother upset.
"So, so, so is THIS it? Today? And NEVER again?" asked Liam looking up with his watery bloodshot eyes.
"Today is the day. I'm sorry Liam. I truly am. But this is the hand dealt to me".
"Some hand! Oh God, what am I going to do?" sobbed Liam.
"And I have one favour to ask you" added Roger, "Please visit Rosa tonight and give her this note. I cannot say goodbye to her today either, I just cannot put the girl through it. She is not well these days, collapsed on me the other night so she did" said Roger.

The brothers concluded their conversation by the well before hugging each other tightly and returning silently to the others. Carlo bade farewell to the O'Gradys and Fr. Tim who had just arrived, before starting up the car. Liam's wife was surprised at how upset her husband was. She was expecting tears but not as much as he was now shedding. She hugged her brother-in-law tightly as he kissed her goodbye, the poor woman not realising it was for the final time. Fr. Tim took his turn to have a couple of parting words, before Roger fetched three wrapped gifts from the car and gave them to each of his two nephews and niece. Then each of them received a twenty dollar bill and Roger told them to be good for their parents. He was surprised at how well he was holding himself together, despite being surrounded by crying loved ones.

But that suddenly changed at the sight of Liam emerging from the porch throwing holy water at him and the car. It was as if Roger was seeing his father again. It was like sighting a ghost. All of a sudden he was overcome by sadness and he grabbed his brother and hugged him tightly, drawing him in tightly to his body. Even though it was hurting his stomach, he did not mind and for a fleeting moment he felt like telling his brother that there were actually three of them in that embrace. But his instinct was that this strange news would spoil the departure, and prolong it, so he heeded his instinct. Roger's tear ducts, though, had just gushed open.

"Good bye my Liam" he whispered down into his brother's ear as they interlocked by the running engine. "You were a great brother, and you looked after me when I needed you. When I was a little boy with no mother. And no father worth speaking of. Thanks so much. I love you. Forever I love you brother".

Liam just cried uncontrollably into his younger brother's chest. The poor lad was distraught to be losing his only brother. He did not want to let him go. He wanted him to stay forever. Losing Roger forever was a big shock, and he was unable to piece his words together. He had never been this upset.

The sight of the sobbing brothers parting brought even more tears to the onlookers, and Liam's wife rushed over to try and comfort him. Roger, with the aid of his stick, slowly eased himself into the car and cast one final look at each sad face. Even Carlo was choking back tears as he revved to drive off. Despite his best efforts, Liam could not bring himself to say anything comprehensible. As the car drove off. All he could do was wave.

Roger could barely decipher the sights in front of him as he left his village for the last time. He knew he was a coward by instructing Carlo to drive past Carey's at speed, leaving a heartbroken Rosa behind without a proper goodbye. But Roger just could not face that. He was hoping the money and note he had left with Liam for her would go some way to make amends.

His tears dried up as the car zipped through the bog and woodlands along the narrow sandy road on the bright February morning. Roger gazed up at the dip in the mountains where Crafton Lake lay hidden from view, and thought about poor Willie and the death he must have had endured there. Maybe THAT is where he should have placed the cross. But he wanted it to be visible for miles, and Bunmore Hill suited that purpose more.

His final thoughts as he was leaving his parish were of his dead friends. He was now the last of the 'Boys of Ballycroy'. But it was an achievement that meant little to him. He would have much preferred having them all alive.

"This is one hell of a parish Carlo, isn't it?" he said to his driver. "It sure is!" came the reply. "A little piece of heaven. Scintillating scenery. Untamed inhabitants – but good wholesome people. You can actually FEEL the goodness from them ward off any threatening evil clouds that hover from the outside. Like wonderful wizards of the western waves and way of life".

"I could not put it better myself!" smiled Roger, "I better write that down!"

CHAPTER 50: MISTER TOTALLY UNNECESSARY

Five days later, a sickly Roger was a first class passenger on board the magnificent liner which was about a third of its way across the Atlantic. He ached for his own comfortable bed. He knew he was deteriorating.

Also sailing that week – but eastwards - were the Bourke family and Fr. Rea, *en route* to Germany for the military burial for Major Bartholomew Vandenburg. Some 16 years later, old Patrick Bourke would tell his fellow drinkers in Carey's Bar that he could swear that the man with the small moustache and slicked black hair who had just caused another world war had been present at his son's funeral – one Adolf Hitler!

In Bunmore, Liam was still trying to come to terms with what Roger and then Rosa had told him. He and his wife discussed the phenomena. They wondered if the deformed foetus had been the main reason for the childbirth death. They were aghast. Liam said he was considering selling some of the livestock to make the trip to America. He was refusing to believe that he had seen his larger-than-life brother for the last time. To him, Roger was immortal.

In Ballycroy Village, Rosa's hand shook as she penned a letter to Roger. She was still angry that he had not called to say goodbye, but she did not want this anger to manifest itself in the letter. Like Liam, she was actively considering a voyage to see Roger one last time.

In Newport, Toothy Lucey and Harry Heraty were making some progress in convincing the people there that they had been misguided in blaming the McDonnells for the Ownsworth murders. The two men, along with Fintan McDonnell, had led large search groups up into Skirdagh to check out the hundreds of lakes and bogholes there. Many Newport men joined in. Tensions between the communities evaporated. But the anchored bodies of the brothers were never found.

A policeman had noticed dark trails of congealed blood on the sandy road and informed his senior officers that it looked like a body had been dragged along the road up into the hills of Skirdagh. The police were also keeping an eye on old Alfred as they found blood in his yard and in his barn, as well as the teddy bear that Sylvester had been witnessed buying. Although he had not admitted anything about the brothers when interviewed, the police were convinced that old Alfred would eventually reveal more. And in time they were to be proven right.

As Roger continued his final transatlantic journey, Carlo was still in Mayo. It was hard for a six foot four inch giant of a man with olive skin and Latin good looks to remain unnoticed in Mayo, but he used his theatrical experience to keep himself disguised as he played out a dangerous real-life role. His boss had left him with a job to do, and as ever, the loyal servant would successfully carry out any task required of him.

On Carlo's final day in Mayo, the owner of the abattoir in Ballyhaunis was annoyed that the two Brophy brothers had again been late for work. As he cursed them and promised that they would be sacked when they next reported for duty, little did he know that they were lying in their tenement room side by side, with their throats slit. It would be almost a week before the stench from their rotting corpses would prompt the Gardai to find their garish remains. And it was almost a year later that the same Gardai revealed that a typewritten note signed by Billy Brophy had been found alongside his body, in which he admitted that he, his brother and Royston Carey had murdered the McDonnell brothers and the Ownsworth sisters. Ironically, the person in charge of the Ballyhaunis Garda Station was one Sergeant Scully – formerly of Ballyveeney RIC Barracks! So this was not his first time coming across the Brophy brothers, but it would be of course his last.

On Carlo's final night in Mayo, Royston Carey followed his usual routine of sorting out his wooden beer barrels in the yard right beside his new hotel that overlooked The Mall, the public green lawn in the centre of Castlebar town, near the courthouse. Unknown to him, as he carried out this chore for each of the previous three nights he had been monitored from a distance. This was to be his final night doing this for the week, before driving back to his wife and family in Ballycroy for his weekly break.

As he whistled beneath a hanging oil lantern after another profitable day and night, he heard footsteps approaching from the street. He left down a barrel and stopped moving. The footsteps had stopped. He knew there was someone there near the lamp but he was dazzled by the brightness when he peered to make out who it might be.

"Who's there?" he asked anxiously. "Identify yourself!" He heard another footstep being taken. Because of the glare from the lantern, he still could not see who it was.
"Who's there, I ask!" repeated Royston, his voice beginning to tremble. After several seconds, the silence was broken:
"It's me again! Mister Totally Unnecessary!" stated the American accent calmly. Then a shot went through Royston's heart and he stumbled back onto his barrels, which started to tumble down around him.
"Ah, ah no...ah no!" cried the Ballycroy man in pain. "Not now...not...no...please..."
The tall Italian American gunman stood over his wounded victim and calmly aimed his Luger handgun at Royston's head.
"This is for the McDonnells – from your old friend Roger!" he said before pulling the trigger a second time. Bang! Just a week before his 40th birthday, Royston Carey lay dead.

His assassin walked slowly away towards the waiting white van of Joey Jarvis. Then they drove in the direction of Ballinrobe, from where they would drive to Foynes in Limerick where a cargo ship would take Carlo back to the east coast of America.

As expected, the killing of the well known businessman was major news in Mayo, and Ballycroy again became a magnet for reporters and onlookers. The undertaker was in one of his own coffins very prematurely, and the sight of his mourning wife and sisters all dressed in black standing by his laid-out corpse could not fail to touch any heart. Alongside them, the upset youngsters Louis,

Charlotte, Royston Junior, Philip and Robert; who were all wondering how someone could be so cruel so as to take their father from them so early. It was a pitiful and distressing sight. Even though Royston had not been as popular as his father, everyone felt his loss and decried the waste of yet another young Ballycroy life.

*****

Back in upstate New York, Carlo got back to leafy Croton Falls safely and reported back to his boss that the assignment had been successfully completed. The two men hugged each other and sat down to catch up on recent events. Roger felt some guilt for the pain he had caused Rosa, but in many ways he knew that she would be better off without 'that tyrant' in her life. Roger was thinking more about Fintan and Claire McDonnell, and even though they were unaware of Royston's involvement in the disappearance of their sons, he felt that he had helped them gain some justice.

Roger's contentment with the revenge was not to last long though. A week later, Carlo handed his ailing boss a letter that just arrived from Ireland. The man from Ballycroy sat back in his chair and read the letter from Rosa. It quickly became obvious that it had been posted before her brother's death. Carlo studied Roger's face as he progressed through the pages. He noted the changing expressions. Then, all of a sudden, he noticed the reader go pale. Roger threw his head back onto his cushioned chair and groaned aloud.

"What is it, Roger?" cried Carlo.
"Oh no!" moaned Roger. "Oh no, what have I done? What have I done?!"
"What is it, PLEASE?" repeated the bodyguard.
"Oh no, Carlo. Young Louis. Rosa's Louis. He is MY son! He is mine!" came the reply.
"You jest!" was all that Carlo could muster to reply.
"Poor, poor Rosa. I left her pregnant, and so did that Scottish bastard!" cried Roger angrily.
"Joey?" asked the stunned Carlo.

"Yes. The bastard raped her. Impregnated her. You will have to take your Luger back to Mayo! The poor girl. But I am as bad as he is, leaving her to rear them boys all by herself!" said Roger sorrowfully, with his head still thrown back looking skywards and his right hand gripping the sheets of paper.
"What kind of man am I? I hate THAT man – the man who deserts his child!" cried Roger.
"But sure you were not to know Roger, what could you have done? It's not your fault. You cannot blame yourself!" stated Carlo, crouched by his boss.

The two men tried to make sense of it all. And now of course the shooting in Castlebar had changed the whole context of the letter. Many's the script that had altered their lives in the past decade, but the contents of this from Rosa's pen defied belief. Anger, disappointment, betrayal, loneliness, despair, secrecy, a son, a rape, humiliation, pain, hope, faith, love and regret – they were all in there.

"*Eli, Eli, laba sanactami*" shouted Roger to Carlo's bewilderment. Then he came out with a statement that stuck with the bodyguard forever:

"Mo bhrón. Mo bhrón. Haven't I gone and killed my son's father".

CHAPTER 51: BOB

On the morning after St. Patrick's Day, 1924, Roger lay in his Manhattan hospital bed, awaiting his surgery. He was calm. The previous few days had been frenetic. He had his accountants re-assess his worth. He had his lawyers re-draft his will. He had been in hourly contact with his studio over his latest creation.

As he lay staring at the ceiling, contemplating his fate, he hoped he would survive long enough to see the three who were somewhere in the Atlantic sailing towards Ellis Island. Rosa and her two sons, Louis and Robert, were on their way. Roger had arranged payment of their fare.

Behind them they had left a devastated Carey family. A family still immersed in grief. A family now ripped apart. Rosa had packed her meagre belongings and was bringing her two offspring across the ocean for a new life. Even though she might not even get to see her former lover on the other side, anything was better than remaining in her quarters over the family business. One would have thought that Royston's passing might have made her life easier, but it had not.

Benny Hughton Junior moved swiftly to assert his authority on the family business, and his wife Rebecca did not dissuade him. The new widow Antoinette was too weak to do anything about the manoeuvre, and Rosa quickly found that her ruthless stern proprietor had simply been replaced by a new version. Instead of moving up the pecking order and vying with her sister for joint ownership, it was made clear to Rosa that she was merely one of the staff. The whole family dynamic had changed, to the detriment of Rosa.

The relationship between Rosa and Antoinette became irrevocably damaged when Rosa moved to extract her two boys from what the parishioners had once thought was the perfect little family of four boys and one girl that Royston and his wife were rearing. Ballycroy looked on in shock and sadness as the esteemed Carey family disintegrated in front of them. Louis and Charlotte were no longer twins, and had to be physically pulled apart from each other's grip as the close couple were forcibly split. The two eldest children had just lost their father, and could not cope with the added distress of now losing each other. The two year old Robert was unaware of the surrounding trauma and heartbreak, and just as well. It was a tragic situation.

As the taxi carrying Rosa, her two boys and all of the belongings pulled away from the rain-washed cobblestones by Carey's Bar – a hysterical Antoinette tried to grab onto it. Just weeks after losing the cornerstone her life, she could not bear to be losing the two young boys who she had reared as her eldest and youngest. She collapsed on her bloodied knees as the taxi disappeared from view, wailing sorrowfully. All she was now left with was her daughter and other two sons. She was at the mercy of the Hughtons. The family of two dashing parents and five happy children had been reduced to one haggard mother and three distraught children. It was no wonder she pleaded aloud to be allowed join her husband in his grave.

*****

Back in Manhattan, Roger awoke from his surgery in great pain. But he was relieved to be still alive. All he wanted was to meet his son. As his son. When he had spoken playfully with Louis by the roaring Carey fireside weeks earlier, he had spoken to him as Rosa's nephew. Now it would all be so different. Just an hour with his boy would complete his life.

The surgeons who had travelled from Paris and London to watch their American counterpart carry out the rare operation were the first to speak with Roger. It had been a success, and the foetus was now removed. They had tried to patch up the damage done to his liver and kidneys. But the damage had been severe. They would leave it to the head surgeon to give the overall assessment. They bade farewell to their famous patient and wished him well in his recovery.

The next person by his bedside was his ever-loyal Carlo. He had positive news as he grabbed hold of the limp right hand of the patient.

"Pengilly has accepted the deal on Bob!" he whispered excitedly. "They're taking on the lot – the book, the screenplay and a movie. We get forty per cent!!"
"Good!" came the smiling reply from Roger.
"I've told Urs and the Sheldons already. They are redrafting everything!" added Carlo.
"Good!" repeated the weak Roger. "We will use our money more wisely this time".

The 'Bob' that was being referred to was the latest project that Roger had been working on. After a long battle, he and his people had eventually struck a deal with the studio to get it turned into a book and movie deal. This particular project had been closest to the creator's heart, as it was a long-running piece of work that stretched from his early days in America right up until now. He had been determined not to sell himself short on this, especially now that it would be his final project. The good news now was that the Pengilly group of publishers and producers had taken it on, and 'Bob' was going to reach Roger's public. It was the story he most wanted to tell. And now 40% of all profits would be going to his estate.

The reference in regard to using his money more wisely was to do with a severe burning he had received from an investment in the notorious Ponzi scheme. He had met Charles Ponzi in person – who was now in federal prison for fraud – a number of times and had fallen for his convincing promises. But he had fallen for a con, and Roger had ended up being swindled out of thousands of dollars. Almost all of his American-based money had been wiped out. It was only his income from Britain and Europe that was keeping him afloat.

Despite appearing affluent, in the immediate aftermath of the Ponzi collapse in 1921 things had looked very bleak. He had to offload most of his property portfolio. The disaster contributed to Roger's ill health, and he blamed the stress for the physical pains he suffered. Things had been so bad that Roger had agreed to accept an offer of ten thousand dollars from the American College of Medical Science, on condition that they were allowed use his remains for research. They wanted desperately to find out more about the *fetus-in-fetu*. Roger had little choice but to accept the macabre offer and had signed a contract giving them the permission to take possession of his corpse and what had been living inside of it. For Roger, it was simply fate taking its course. Although tempted to defy the curse of the 'White Cow', he resigned himself to the fact that he would not lie in an Irish grave. As he had once stated "If I book my coffin on a boat back to Erin, it will probably sink and bring hundreds of innocents with me. Let the White Cow have her worldly way".

Roger's surgeon came to his bedside the day following the surgery. Ominously, he had asked to meet his patient alone. Roger was sitting up but in a lot of discomfort. He welcomed the surgeon with another warm smile.
"How are you feeling Roger?" the grey haired man in his sixties asked.
"Not great to be honest with you", came the reply, "But sure I didn't expect to be out playing tennis today!"
"True, true" came the gentle reply. "You did very well". But then came a long silence as he looked down at the floor and out of the window gazing over the stores and factories of lower Manhattan.
"But the news isn't positive, Roger" he said. Roger took a deep breath that hurt his stomach greatly, but he tried to remain composed.
"Tell me, Doctor Baxter" he replied staring at the man who had operated on him, "I need to know".
"The damage was severe. The growth had attached itself to your kidney and liver. More so to the hepatic gland. It was like rust attacking a lead pipe; it has eaten your insides away. That is what was causing the severe pain. To be truthful, I do not know how you survived this long. You defy belief!" stated the doctor.
"I know all that" replied the patient, "But I need to know how long. My family are here in a week. Will I make it?"
Again, the doctor took a long pause. He was averting eye contact with the anxious man on the bed. After what seemed like an eternity he looked up at the sorrowful Irish eyes.
"You may make it, but you will probably wish you had not. Your body will be severely malfunctioning and I'm not sure there is enough morphine in America to ease your pain. I pray that you

do get to see your son, but you will not see the month of April, I fear".

Roger looked at the wall. He was refusing to crack. All he now wanted was for a strong wind to get behind the boat and carry his son to New York quicker than expected. His own father had passed away when he was on a sea journey, he did not want his son to endure the same. He thought of how sad it would be for the emigrants to arrive after a long arduous trip to find him dead. He thought of how upset Carlo would be. He thought of how sad Liam would be back in Bunmore. He took another deep painful breath and looked at Doctor Baxter.
"I'll see April the first, I swear I will. My insides may be dead but my mind is still alive. I WILL see my son, Doctor" he said calmly with determination.
"If anyone can defy me, it is you!" smiled Baxter, rising to leave the room. "We will get you back up to Croton Falls. With all of the green up there, you will feel like you're back in the old country again!"

On March 26th, Roger's dream came true. He met Louis. His eleven year old son. He wept as he studied the young boy's face. Now, he could see his father's jaw. He could see his brother's mouth. He could see his own smiling eyes. How come he had not noticed this when they first met?!

Rosa wept tears of joy at the sight of the father and son union, whilst Carlo held the sleeping Robert. And in the wooden hideaway on the edge of Lake Mahopac, Roger's heart leapt with happiness.
"I have more than just scripts and reels to leave the world" he exclaimed from his sitting position, "And I have wonderful you to thank for that!" he added, beckoning Rosa to come towards him for her hug.

They all had to be careful, as the least touch on his tortured torso caused immense agony. An overcome Rosa looked around at the homely furniture and the burning fire. It was so cosy, so warm, so calm. The boys tried to dash outside to the boat so that they could take to the placid lake water. But the doors were locked for their safety. The place was beautiful, but it was not the mansion that Toothy Lucey had vividly described.

"I know what you are thinking" whispered Roger, still in tears from his meeting his offspring. "I lost a lot of my properties to Ponzi. But I'm on the way back!"

"Who's Ponzi?" she asked.

"Better for now that you do not know" replied Roger as she sat by his bed.

"Roger, my God, you look like a ghost" she whispered. "You poor creature".

"I should be a ghost by now. I should be dead! In fact – maybe I AM a ghost!" and they both laughed.

"But I hung on for ye! Even the Grim Reaper himself could not stop me from meeting ye" he added. "He can wait a while longer..."

"Thanks so much for bringing us over. It's like escaping from hell. Thank God for you. My hero!" she said.

"No. Thank God for YOU, Rosa" came the weak reply. "YOU reared our boy. YOU carried the burden alone. But you should have told me".

"I wish I had. I only wish I had. But I could not. I wanted you to live your dream" she replied.

"I DID live my dream. But today is the best day of my life! It really is, Rosa. You will never know how proud I am of you both. And of little Robert there as well" stated Roger, as Rosa surveyed his withered neck and sunken eyes. She could scarcely believe that her big, beefy man had been reduced to skin and bones. But she wanted to remain strong. She did not want him to see her cry.

"And I was sorry to hear about your brother" said Roger, with total conviction.

"I know. I know" she quietly answered. "I just...I just cannot speak of that now. We are here now and I want to look forward".

"So do I!" smiled Roger. "I have only days left, but they are the crock of gold at the end of the rainbow. I will die the proudest man on earth. Not the happiest, as I wanted to spend more time with the boy. But the proudest, Rosa. And if I had my choice of all of the women in the world to mother my child, it would be you. Amn't I so lucky?"

It did not take long for the new arrivals to settle into their surroundings. They had expected tall buildings, fancy shops, fast cars, trains and crowded streets – but this was even quieter than Sheeaun! A wooden house by a picturesque lake, surrounded by beautiful evergreen trees.
"Are there bears in them woods?" asked Louis of his ailing father two days later.
"Loads of bears" Roger answered weakly. "Always bring a good stick with you. They're all afraid of the Irish blackthorns".
"Really?" replied the youngster.
"You ask loads of questions, don't you?" smiled Roger.
"And why wouldn't I?" replied Louis. The adoring father laughed.
"Where's Robert?" asked Roger, now lying flat on his bed, unable to sit up.
"Oh he's with Carlo, helping him for the men coming later" answered Louis. "Carlo called him Bobby, why does he call him Bobby?"
"Because, because it is short for Robert" whispered Roger.
"And is Bob short for Bobby?"
"It is."
"So who is the Bob you and Carlo keep talking about, is it Robert?"
"No, son" smiled Roger. "Bob is the name of the work project that Carlo and I are finishing. It's a pet name. Every project, Louis, we give it a pet name".
"So the men coming over later, didn't you say they are here about Bob?"
"I did indeed" replied Roger.
"So will I see Bob then?"
"No. You will see Bob in the cinema. When you are twelve or thirteen. And when you see him, think of me" whispered the sick man.
"I will. I will think of you and my real Dad. He was shot, you know. Did you know he was shot?"
"I did" replied the ailing voice, sadly.
"And Mammy says you will die too. Why do Daddies always die?" asked Louis innocently.
"I think God wants them – I mean us – all up there in heaven together."

"Why doesn't he just leave them down here with us, to play football with and go hunting with?"
"I must ask him that when I meet him. That's a good idea" said Roger as tears crept down his cheeks.
"Daddy, why are you crying?" asked the little boy.
"Because I am sad that I cannot kick ball or go hunting with you".
"Don't worry. Robert will be big soon and he will play with me. And maybe then Charlotte and Royston and Philip can come over too. Can they?" asked Louis excitedly.
"They can. They sure can" smiled the tiring man.

Later that evening, two teenage neighbours came over to the house to play with the Irish boys as the adults gathered by the bedside of the dying man. The Sheldon brothers were over to go through the revised will and get Roger to sign it. The lawyers went through the will line by line, as Rosa and Carlo sat with a handkerchief each. The will reaffirmed that all of Roger's properties, other than the one in Croton Falls, would be signed over to his loyal servant Carlo, along with the sum of twenty thousand dollars and 5% of future earnings. To Urs his agent, went another twenty thousand dollars plus 5% of future earnings. Twenty thousand dollars went to Liam O'Grady in Bunmore, plus a trust fund for his three children. Two thousand dollars went to Ballycroy church. Two thousand more towards the white cross memorial. One thousand dollars each to the families McDonnell, Bourke, Cooney, Dyra, White, McArthur, Lucey and Heraty. And one thousand dollars each to reverends Roland and Rea.

Finally, to Rosa and her two children, he bequeathed the rest of his estate. This included the Croton Falls property and all future profits from his work other than those assigned to Carlo and Urs.

"All I want is you" whispered Rosa into Roger's ear.
"You had me" he smiled. "And hadn't we fun?"
"We had", she smiled. "But why is God being so cruel to us? Why didn't he spare us some more time together?"
"*C'est la vie.* God works in mysterious ways" was the weak reply. "It would have been crueller if I had not lived to see ye reach here. Now I am happy. Ye are looked after. Ye will want for nothing now. Bob will look after ye".

The following day, March 30th, began with everyone in the house been awakened by the painful cries coming from Roger's room. The doctor was called but all he could do was administer some more morphine to the dying man and shake his head. "The surgeon was right, he will not see April. He won't even see this afternoon. You better prepare yourselves" said the doctor, before taking himself and his medicine bag away.

Roger was a pitiful sight as his gaunt face looked up from the crumpled pillow. His mouth was parched and a tearful Carlo fed him sips of water. He was breathing heavily. And rapidly. When he mustered the energy to speak, his voice was barely audible. "Thank God I finished Bob. Bob will look after ye" he panted. "Yes. Thank God for that" said Carlo. "Your life's work. I will be so proud of you when we see that on the screen. We will all be proud of you. You sure did save the best until last!"
"*Veni, vidi, vici*" came the faint reply.

"I don't know what I will do without you!" cried the bodyguard.
"Carlo" said the mournful eyes looking up. "Thanks for all you have done for me. You have been a great friend. A true friend..."
"You made me what I am, I owe you everything" cried the tall bodyguard, tears falling onto the sheets that wrapped the dying man in comfort, before he stood aside for Rosa who Roger had called for.
"Rosa. I'm sorry" he panted.
"Don't be silly!" she responded hoarsely, her throat raw from days of crying. "You are a man amongst men. You have nothing to be sorry for".
"I'm sorry for not being there, there when you...needed me Rosa" he whispered. "And you are so good. You are here now for me, when I need you".
"Of course I am!" she cried.
"I was thinking. None...none of the others...of the other 'Boys of Ballycroy'...none died like this, with their family around them. I, I am so lucky. Thank you my love, thank you Rosa for my boy. Thank you my love..."

"And here is your boy" sobbed Rosa, as Roger reached out to hold Louis' hand. The little lad was frightened. He did not know what was happening. It always upset him to see grown-ups cry.
"What's wrong?" he asked the man gasping for his final few breaths.
"I have to…I have to go now" came the low whisper. "You're a good boy…be good for your Mammy…be a good boy…make your Daddy proud".
"Where is he going Mammy?" asked Louis in tears, looking up at his mother.
"He's going to heaven" she replied.
"To Daddy?" he asked.
"To Royston and Granddad. They will all be your guardian angels, Louis" she sobbed.
"I have to go now…the pain…oh the pain…" gasped Roger.
"Say goodbye to your father, Louis" sobbed Rosa but the boy just clung onto her.
"I…I see the seagull…he's here for me…time to go now" whispered the dying man, his eyes going into a trance as he stared up at the wooden ceiling.
"Good bye my love" wept Rosa stroking his bony cheek. "Goodbye my dear Roger".
"Oh please no" choked Carlo.
"I have to go now. They are waiting for me….all of them…over there…and look – is that you Dad? And is that you Mother…is that really you…you're here for me…for your little boy…and…and you're just…you're just so beautiful…" Roger called out with his penultimate breath, as a final smile stretched across his pain-etched face.
"Off you go and join them my love" wept Rosa as she clasped his cold hands.
"They are all waiting for me…over there by The Sandyba…."

And they were the final words of Roland O'Grady a.k.a. Roger a.k.a. Jean Pierre Roland. The seventh and final Boy of Ballycroy was dead. Aged 33. In his Croton Falls bed, by beautiful Lake Mahopac. As he had often said "From 'Croy to Croton and from Mayo to Mahopac!"

It was typical of the man that in his dying moments, when in cruel pain from what nature had done to his insides, he remembered his six friends who had died in less fortunate circumstances. The seven were all now united in death. But what lives they had led! What action they had packed into their scarce years on earth!

And thanks to Roger, their lives would forever be remembered in his final piece of work. It took five years for that work to eventually appear on screen, but when it did, it won every possible award. Of course B.O.B. stood for the 'Boys of Ballycroy'. That was the full title of the novel. That was the full title of the movie. By 1930 the whole world knew who the 'Boys of Ballycroy' were, where they came from, and what they had achieved. Michaeleen, Batty, Roger, Sylvester, Terence, John Peter and Willie – all became immortal characters who the rest of mankind wished they had met. Their names and their parish became famous the world over. And although between them they had no headstone in Ireland, they lived forever in books and on film.

*****

On the fifth anniversary of Roger's death, the resilient people of Ballycroy gathered for a significant event. The massive cross memorial on top of Bunmore Hill was being unveiled.

The parishioners gave thanks for the cloudless day that allowed them to admire the breath-taking surrounding landscape from the crowded breezy summit. The view was glorious.

Father Tim conducted the ceremony. Toothy Lucey scribbled down quotes from the speeches. Parliamentarian Harry Heraty TD spoke of how one of his soldiers, Sylvester McDonnell, had been captured at the very spot where the cross now stood, but that he had managed to symbolically escape the clutches of his British captors.

The task of officially unveiling the giant monument to those who had lost their lives fighting for freedom fell to a sixteen year old tall handsome New Yorker – Louis O'Grady Valenti. He smiled down at the 'Guest of Honour' section to his right. There sat his proud mother Rosa, her hand being held by her Italian husband Carlo. His half-brother Robert Valenti sat there too. As did his uncle Liam O'Grady.

Also sitting in that section was Philip Carey – now revealed and acknowledged as Terence's son – who sat between his grandparents Fintan and Claire McDonnell. They also had another grandchild with them in that row of seats, the strapping Harrison Huckerby McDonnell, who was alongside his English mother Alice, back in Ireland from Surrey for the special occasion.

In front of Fintan and Claire McDonnell sat two more grandchildren - young Noel and Josephine McDonnell - with their Scottish mother Eleanor. And the pretty Agatha Vandenburg sat alongside her German mother Ruth and widower grandfather Patrick Bourke.

It was a day of reflection. A day of remembrance. A day of thanks. A day of pride.

The 'Boys of Ballycroy' had gone...but their legacy forever lives on.

ACKNOWLEDGEMENTS

To my late grandparents:
You instilled a love of storytelling, which lives long after you have sadly passed on.

To my parents John and Irene:
For your never-ending love and support; and for taking me from the city to raise me in beautiful Ballycroy.

To those REAL Mayo people - past and present – who were good to me and will always be my heroes:
The Gintys. The Rowlands. The Leneghans. The Walshs. The McManamons. The Carmichaels. The Sullivans. The Gaughans. The Rices. Kathleen O'Sullivan. Mary O'Dowd. Mary Rooney. Kevin Hegarty. Freda Kenny. Eddie Moran. Cecil McDonnell. PJ Collins. John Broderick. Brendan Carey. Sean Reilly. Michael Flannery. David O'Rourke. Charlie Healy. AJ Keane. Hughie Conway. John Corrigan. Martin Costello. Phelim Conway. Niall Conway. Liam Togher. Kieran Mongey. Eugene Connolly. Rosaleen Wallace. Anne Marie Tolan. Máire McNally. Maura Cawley-Doherty. Paidín Conway. Tony Tumbler. Philip Keane. Peter Paul Conway. John Cleary. Eamon Finn. Jerry Cowley. Fr Chris Ginnelly. Breege Grealis. The Dunleavys of Birmingham. Barry Regan.

To Sharon, Shelley, Blair and Diarmuid:
Thank you sincerely for your professional assistance.

To my delightful darling daughters Leah and Eva:
I hope Ballycroy remains a home to you after I have gone.

And above all to my wonderful wife Laura:
Thank you for EVERYTHING. Your inspiration knows no bounds. You constantly amaze me by fitting so much love into every single day. This book is dedicated to you.

(Dear Reader: Thank you for your valued time. If you enjoyed this book please 'like' 'The Boys of Ballycroy' on Facebook. Thank you!)